On a Stormy Primeval Shore

Canadian Historical Brides

Book 9 New Brunswick

By Diane Scott Lewis
and Nancy M. Bell

Amazon Print 9781772998559

A quality publisher of genre fiction.
Airdrie Alberta

Copyright 2018 by Diane Parkinson
Series Copyright 2018 BWL Publishing Inc.
Cover art by Michelle Lee

All rights reserved. Without limiting the rights under copyright reserved above, no part of this publication may be reproduced, stored in or introduced into a retrieval system, or transmitted, in any form, or by any means (electronic, mechanical, photocopying, recording, or otherwise) without the prior written permission of both the copyright owner and the publisher of this book.

D0791807

CALGARY PUBLIC LIBRARY

APR - - 2019

APR - 2019

Dedication

BWL Publishing Inc. ("**Books We Love**") dedicates the Canadian Historical Brides series to the immigrants, male and female, who left their homes and families, crossed oceans and endured unimaginable hardships in order to settle the Canadian wilderness and build new lives in a rough and untamed country.

Acknowledgement

Books We Love acknowledges the Government of Canada and the Canada Book Fund for its financial support in creating the Historical Brides of Canada series.

Funded by the Government of Canada | Canada

I also want to thank the helpful people at the **New Brunswick Museum** who provided information and rare documents
Jennifer Longon
Gary Hughes
Ruth Cox

Chapter One

Nova Scotia (New Brunswick) 1784

The British merchantman dropped anchor in a rattle of clanks and Amelia Latimer rushed to the rail, her breath held. From the ship's deck, she scrutinized the port of Parr Town in its jagged harbour off the Bay of Fundy. Father should be here to meet her.

A gust of wind swept loamy scents into her nose, masking the briny ocean and the stink of the mildewed cabin she'd lived in all these weeks. She gripped the teak with gloved hands. The voyage was over. Dread tinged with curiosity rippled through her at what awaited her on shore.

Sailors aloft continued to furl the sails. Their chatter echoed over the water.

Amelia' hair and clothing crackled with salt when she shifted for a better look. The town was a jumble of log buildings in front of steep, reddish-hued cliffs that jutted up along the craggy shore. Most of the one-storied structures appeared slapped together. This colony, once known as Acadia, comprised the western portion of Nova Scotia. It looked so primitive.

She bit down on her lip and prayed she hadn't made a huge mistake.

Waves slapped the ship's hull, then roiled against the slimy quay as men emerged from warehouses, calling to the people on-board. The ship rocked and creaked like an old carriage. Amelia widened her stance as she'd learned, while the sailors secured the lines.

The captain's wife, Mrs. Hubble, walked up beside her. "We've arrived, my dear. And all in one piece." The older woman, small and delicate, had served as Amelia's chaperone on the ship. "I hope you won't be disappointed by the remoteness of this colony."

"I'm certain I'll find plenty to like." Amanda's hopes floated around her, fragile as paper. Nerves twitched beneath her surface calm. She stretched up on tiptoe, but didn't see her father among the increasing people, the numerous soldiers, who gathered on the quay. Their voices rose and fell in various accents. "I don't mind new experiences."

An untamed land, where heathen tribes lurked, spread out before them in the tepid August air. Tall pines, among clusters of birch and maple, on the hills beyond, speared their tips into a grey sky. A pity her new domicile would be so far from her home in Plymouth, England—so far from her ailing mother. She fought a shiver.

"The hordes of refugees from the American war seem to have enlarged the town already." The woman gave her a fleeting smile as if relieved she wouldn't have to stay. She patted Amelia's arm. "This colony is still a dangerous wilderness. Your fortitude will be tested, in many ways."

"Indeed, I'm sure it will." Amelia tightened the ribbon under her chin to busy her fingers. Compared to the stone firmness of Plymouth, Parr Town was a ramshackle village that looked as if a strong wind might blow it away. Could she make a good life here, with a stranger?

The ship's gangway was lowered with a thud to the wharf.

She sighed and had to remain steadfast. At four and twenty, she was well down the road to spinsterhood. But her father had the cure for that malady. An officer, a widower with two children, anxious for a wife, housekeeper, and child-minder. Her uncertain destiny.

Amelia turned to her chaperone. She stood a head taller than Mrs. Hubble. Tall and skinny, like a willow switch as her brother had often teased. "I want to thank you for your kindness, Mrs. Hubble. You made the journey so much easier for me."

"The captain and I quite enjoyed your company." Mrs. Hubble looked up with a sympathetic expression. "I trust you'll find your 'arrangement' here satisfactory."

"At least one of mutual respect, I daresay." Amelia nodded, unable to form any more appropriate words on that subject. What could one say about being—steeped in a dollop of wry and desperate humour—the sacrificial lamb?

Additional people gathered on shore, shouting, crying out, excited about the supplies the ship carried, no doubt. Salt, wine, nails, shovels, and much more.

"We must unload quickly, long before the bay's unpredictable tide decides to turn," Mrs. Hubble said. "The water can drop forty feet out in the main bay when it goes out to the Atlantic. And this can be the foggiest of ports, even in summer. You should return below and make ready to disembark." She pressed Amelia's shoulder. "Good luck to you in everything, my dear."

Below decks, the tiny, canvas-draped cabin she re-entered reeked of mould and body odour. The wood-framed room had offered little privacy.

Amelia forced a smile on her maid, Louise. "Let's make haste and abandon this fetid dungeon." She'd be glad to see the last of their accommodation and hurried her maid along in packing. "I long for decent food without dead worms in it."

"What do the place look like? Is Captain Latimer waiting for us, Miss?" The girl folded and stuffed the clothing they'd washed in salt water the previous day into a trunk. Louise was only fifteen, and a little timid, but she was sweet and reliable. She'd been with Amelia for two years. They'd both suffered sea-sickness, and had depended on one another during the eight-week voyage.

"I didn't notice Father, but there are many soldiers on shore. I pray he hasn't forgotten me." Amelia spoke glibly, but she hadn't seen her father in years. What would their reunion be like? And might the lieutenant, her beau, be with him? No, too soon. She scratched at her prickly bodice. "The port isn't as established as Plymouth."

She stacked her books in quick movements in another trunk, on top of her clothing. Several herbal accounts were among them. What unique flora would she find here? She planned to cultivate medicinal plants. Would she have to hide her love of reading and other interests from her Intended? Smart women were seldom appreciated. However, if she was fortunate, he might be a man who encouraged learning, and perhaps they'd share lively discussions.

"Did you see any of them savages or Frenchies up top, Miss?" Louise asked, her hazel eyes wide with apprehension as she sat on the trunk lid to push down the contents.

"Not a one. Don't worry, the military will protect us." Amelia grinned, perhaps too broadly, at her maid. After all, the girl had been ripped from her family and country, too. "I'll keep you safe as well. Mayhap I might even learn to fire a flintlock pistol."

Amelia tamped down her qualms, which mostly concerned this groom her father had picked out for her. She longed to make her own choices, though women were rarely granted that privilege, and strained to suppress her aversion to this untenable position.

Lt. Harris was nearly forty. Was he handsome or ugly? Weathered from a life in the army, or pasty from sitting behind a desk. Would he like her? Would she like him?

She stifled a groan. She really didn't want to marry an unknown man, but her mother, so ill with consumption, had lamented her plain daughter's lack of suitors, her poor prospects. Also, her modest dowry deterred many. After much discussion, Mother had convinced her to undertake this long expedition. Amelia cared little for wedded bliss, but at last agreed to the match, just to see her parent's contented visage.

"I hope my mother continues to drink the Lungwort tea I cultured and prepared for her." A tea good for chest complaints—though it wouldn't delay the inevitable. Throat thick, Amelia latched her trunk and was certain she'd never see Mother again, so distant in this outpost. She swiped an errant tear from her eye.

Footsteps pounded overhead, and up the many ladders. The sailors prepared the ship.

"I'm sure she will, Miss." Louise dragged a trunk toward the canvas opening. Her curly blonde hair sprang out from her white cap. "You is good with your herbals. I know you do fret 'bout Mrs. Latimer."

"Very much, yet fretting solves little. We must look ahead, mustn't we?" Amelia buckled closed a valise. She couldn't allow her spirits to sag. In truth, she'd sought an adventure, a life away from the routine of England, where young women were 'expected' to behave in a stultifying fashion. If only her mother had been well enough to accompany her. Her parents might share a life again.

Shoulders stiffened, she called to two passing sailors to carry their trunks topside. She inhaled a slow breath. Off she went to meet her fate. Head high, she'd show herself as the best of bartered goods.

Out on deck, Amelia, with Louise, descended the gangway. A slap of wind whipped at her skirt as she searched the crowd. Her father, Captain George Latimer, emerged and approached them. He waved, his smile expectant. Her heart lifted to burst as she pushed through people to be swallowed into his embrace. The bergamot smell of his familiar cologne calmed her slightly. The medals on his scarlet tunic with buff lapels, cuffs and collar, scraped against her chest. He wasn't much taller than she, but he had towering brothers—a trait she'd unfortunately inherited.

No other officer was with him, to her relief.

Louise trailed behind, scanning the port town as if a hatchet-wielding aboriginal might jump out at any moment. Commotion from the many inhabitants and the stevedores preparing to offload the ship jostled around them, along with pungent sweat.

"My dear, my dear. I'm so glad you've arrived. But you look a little gaunt. Are you well?" Father held her at arm's length, glancing over her dull green sack dress. She was hardly the swan he might have wished for.

She almost replied she always looked gaunt. "I'm quite well, Father. It was an arduous voyage." In the nearly three years of their separation, he appeared thinner, more lines in a ruddy face, though his eyes were still bright blue. His lean, angular visage matched hers. "How are you?"

"Getting on, my dear, getting on, as we all must do. Very busy with all the changes here." Greying hair peeked out from under Father's trim white wig, topped by a cocked black uniform hat.

"We'll have infinite time to visit, and catch up." Amelia counted on not meeting her betrothed for a few days. She tucked a loose strand of the hair her mother bemoaned as mousy brown behind her ear, her straw hat ruffling in the breeze. She swayed slightly, her legs feeling as if she still manoeuvred the heaving ship. How gratifying to stand on an immobile surface.

Louise attended the trunks that were unloaded, her pixie face half-hidden in her lilac-coloured bonnet.

"Well, I'm happy you're with me and safe. Let's get you settled in." Father directed them toward a cart, where a driver, a young soldier, sat on the front bench. Porters loaded the trunks. "How is your dear mother? She tells me little of herself in her letters."

Amelia hesitated. She had blamed her father for leaving their mother for so long, but his army service must come first. He'd told his family to stay in Plymouth, the distance here too great. Regret pressed down on her. She doubted the captain would ever see his wife again, either.

"She's not in the best of health, and is very weak, but insists that you not worry." Mother had pleaded with Amelia not to tell him how sick she was; her facial skin stretched over bones- the blood in the handkerchiefs more frequent. Did her father, so caught up in his career, ever worry about those he'd left in England?

"Ah, that does sound like my stalwart Margaret. I'm sure she'll recover." Father flicked her a glance. Was there a hint of guilt in that look? Or did she only wish it to be so? "And William, he thrives, I trust? He doesn't write as much as I might wish." He helped her into the cart behind the driver.

"He is quite occupied and enjoying Oxford." More the camaraderie of his fellows than the studies, she didn't say. Her heart warmed thinking of her scamp of a brother, four years younger and dear to her, despite his teasing. On the hard bench, she arrayed her small panniers that pushed out her skirt.

People in rough clothing bustled about the town, men with scruffy beards, women in dull scarves. Several inhabitants were dressed finer, but looked out of place—like bone-china among wooden trenchers.

Many Negroes were among the population, their dark faces standing out against the pale.

A burly man rolled a hogshead by them, nearly crushing a child of about twelve, who cried out in anger. Two men argued, hands flailing in the air. A swarthy native strutted by wearing feathers and beads, a powder horn strung over his shoulder.

Amelia studied them all, wondering how she'd fit in here. Louise's eyes looked about to pop from her head as she hunkered with the luggage in the cart bed.

"The population has increased greatly since last year." Father sat beside Amelia. "Thousands of British citizens fleeing the American Revolution have poured in. Because of their loyalty to King George, their property was seized by the devil Patriots." He grunted, as if the humiliation of losing the lucrative American colonies, as stated in his letters, still plagued him.

"At home, we prayed our army and navy would crush the rebellion, but then…" Amelia squeezed his fingers. Their defeat had been a great shock for England.

"These Loyalists have succeeded in forming a government separate from Halifax, the capital further east. They're building many homes and businesses. Our settlement is growing quickly." Father raised a hand and instructed the driver to start forward. "But I won't bore you with the details."

Wood frames poked up all around them, logs dragged, and hammers pounding. Sawdust floated in the air.

"Oh, Father, you're aware I'm not an addle-brained female." Amelia rocked as the cart moved through the people along a pitted road. She already knew much of the background, thanks to Mrs. Hubble and her ship's captain husband, and what she'd garnered in Plymouth. The refugees wanted to form a British base in Nova Scotia.

"This colony will be a buttress against rebel expansion." Amelia used the kerchief around her throat to brush sawdust from her face. An iciness slid down her spine that Lt. Harris might be watching her from afar. "I—I heard this section will have a new name. What will it be called?"

"You have been keeping up with reports." Father sounded surprised. "We await the official word on the name. These newcomers, forced here under duress, insist on taking over this portion of land west of the Isthmus of Chignecto. No one trusts the bureaucrats in Halifax who once appeased the rebels." He pointed with his finger. "There is where we're headed."

Fort Howe stood on an exposed limestone knoll that loomed over the harbour and a river that flowed into the bay. The view of it on the majestic hill took Amelia's breath away. Would it be a prison or a haven?

15

"British soldiers built the fort seven years ago, to defend this port from American Privateers coming up to raid the hamlets along the Saint John River," Father said.

"Are we in danger now even with the war finished?" Amelia glanced about again. She recalled Mrs. Hubble's words, and decided she might need that pistol.

"Not at the moment, however, this is a frontier full of challenges." Father's smile wavered. The cart hit a bump in the road. "The King's American Dragoons, comprised of Loyalists, were sent here to build roads. You can see more work is needed. Many of the militia have been sent farther north to settle the land around the Pokiok River."

So many new places to learn about, Amelia mused.

Their cart, pulled by two dun-coloured horses, trundled up a slope past small, plain log houses. A child chased a scruffy dog down the incline, both with mud-encrusted feet. Then the cart began its ascent on a winding road that zigzagged precariously up the knoll and to the fort. Amelia grasped the cart bench, darting a gaze down the sheer cliff.

Louise had her eyes squeezed shut.

Three soldiers followed them on horseback. They glanced at Louise, their whispers suggestive and sly. They'd given Amelia the familiar dismissive air she was used to from men.

16

She tensed on the bench seat, vexed that women were only worth anything if they were pretty. She must rise above such idiotic prejudices. Soon she would have the protection of a husband. Fingers white on the bench, she wondered why that idea did not comfort her.

* * *

Gilbert Arsenault lowered his small telescope. Atop a cliff above Parr Town, blasts of salty wind off the harbour battered his face and whipped the black mane of his horse. A merchantman had docked below. Great Britain's manufactured goods would be traded for raw materials and foodstuffs in the colony. To sustain the English invaders with provisions in *his* land—the land of his ancestors.

He shifted on *Vaillant's* saddle. The buckskin stallion snorted and Gilbert patted the beast's golden neck. He jerked his hat low and stroked his thick beard. A disguise to keep him inconspicuous, skirting the fringe, apart from the British—unless he was conducting his business.

He scanned the construction around the harbour, where hammers and saws banged and ground, the buildings spreading out in the Lower Cove that pointed out into the bay. Last year, the Loyalists from America had created the towns of Parr Town and Carlton, which faced each other across the Saint John River.

"Our country is altering again, and it doesn't bode well for us, *mon ami*," he said to his horse, an animal who usually agreed with him. "So many English swarming up here. Thy are already demanding acreage, advantages."

He glanced toward the fort, then turned the horse around and galloped into the woods. The resin smell of the pines entered his nose. He smiled, enjoying the scent. A reminder of his youth, playing in the dense woods. Later, he found out from his *maman*—who warned him the English were devious people—that they were in hiding. He'd been so young he didn't remember the worst years. Most of the Acadian expulsion began before he was conceived, or still in his mother's belly. Ships had sailed in and hauled off his people to unknown fates.

The Roman Catholic Acadians believed everything was the mysterious plan of God, and they must accept it. But though he was raised Catholic, that perception gave him trouble, his piety never robust.

His hand tightened on the pommel as Vaillant moved beneath him. *Maman's* stories had kept him mesmerized and wary. His caution remained. He didn't trust the soldiers who spilled like drops of blood over the terrain. In the past, every time he'd spotted a scarlet tunic his gut clenched, remembering the tale of his mother's mistreatment, her disgrace.

Gilbert slowed his mount. Sadness draped over him for this nation he loved. The colony was always caught in the middle of battles fought elsewhere, a tug-of-war between France and England. In the previous century, the French had set up fishing and fur-trading enterprises, but the stations were never permanent. As a young boy Gilbert had learned well the skills of a trapper, then as a man he became a trader. He scoffed. The English and those new Americans to the south cherished their beaver hats.

He stopped his horse and inspected an empty trap, though he no longer dealt in this part of the fur trade. Bits of grey fur and gore, which resembled squirrel, clung to the ugly contraption's teeth.

Three Mountain Bluebirds flapped overhead, chasing insects. Gilbert watched their brilliant azure bodies skimming through the air. His mood lifted at the rustic simplicity of nature.

A loud crack of a twig. Gilbert whirled around, his hand on his pistol. A man in a long, red coat scowled at him, musket raised.

Chapter Two

The young soldier stood a few yards away, musket lowered now. "What are you doing, mister? I saw you spying on the port." He walked forward through the grass in his high black boots. Bland features stern, he wore a uniform minus the epaulets of an officer. He looked to be a mere private.

"I was observing the supply ship. I own a trading post." Gilbert stared at the soldier, masking his disgust. Of course, the man was far too young to have been part of the English who'd ravaged the Acadian settlements thirty years ago. He cursed himself for not noticing the enemy lurking so close.

"You're French." The private said it with scorn, fingers tightening on the musket.

"*Mais oui.*" While Gilbert's English was perfect, he knew he carried a strong accent, which he never bothered to tame. "I'm *Acadien*, a descendant of the original French immigrants." He sat taller in his saddle.

"I wouldn't boast of your useless heritage." The soldier snickered. "We destroyed your fleet, took over your forts. You have no business here."

"And you British had no right to ruin what we created." Gilbert's anger heated inside, but he made an effort to curb his temper. "Nor to slay innocent people."

"The victor always gets the spoils." The private grinned. "Soon this land will be full of more British settlements, more soldiers. And you'll be run out again."

Gilbert hated his fears being revealed. The young man was an ass, an animal useless to argue with, yet Gilbert couldn't resist a taunt. "Why are you so far from the fort, alone? Derelict in your duty, *non*?"

The soldier's face seared red. He raised his musket once more.

"*Vous arrêtez.*" Gilbert drew out his pistol. He should have resisted. "Young man, I'd advise you to put that down. Do you want to cause more commotion, in the midst of this chaos caused by your scarpering countrymen?" He aimed the gun. "And I seldom miss when I fire."

The soldier's mouth quivered. He finally lowered his weapon. "Get out of here, you frog-eater!"

Gilbert flicked a finger on his hat brim, aware the youth, practically a boy, was a coward. Bullies usually were. He kicked Vaillant into a gallop, hooves flinging dirt high in the air. His thigh muscles gripped the horse's sides.

"*Mon Dieu,*" Gilbert muttered to himself as he clung to his undulating horse. He wouldn't risk killing a soldier just for an insult, as satisfying as that might be.

Would the young man feel the same and not shoot him in the back?

Farther along, among a copse of birch trees, he slowed. He comforted himself with the idea that this encroachment of civilization would increase trade, with the additional people to feed and clothe. He vowed to grab whatever opportunities might come his way.

Something scrabbled in the trees. More soldiers? Cougars roamed these forests, limber cats that scaled and crawled along the tree-limbs. A low growl. He scanned the area, even more on alert, but saw nothing.

Gilbert urged Vaillant to a canter. The hard ride had soothed him. He often wondered if he was a man too caught up in yesteryear. His encounter with the private sharpened his acrimony, though *Maman* always said one must change with the situation—though she too harboured resentments. He still wasn't certain where his allegiance lay. His fingers twisted at the leather reins. He was sure of one thing. No foreign invaders from the south would destroy his home and livelihood.

* * *

"Lieutenant Harris looks forward to meeting you," Father said when their cart

22

entered the fort's palisade, a wall of wooden stakes made from tree trunks embedded in the ground and sharpened at the top. The guard saluted.

"I look forward to meeting him as well." A little lie. Amelia wouldn't mind delaying the introduction until she became accustomed to this new environment. She was curious about him, even with her stomach in knots at the prospect. Could she make this marriage work, cultivate a companion who would cherish her? A wife was expected to keep a happy, calm home for her husband and never criticize. Hands clamped together on her lap, she'd make certain her feelings mattered as well.

The cart was driven through an open expanse where soldiers and others busily went about the fort's duties. Each officer they passed might be Harris. She kept her eyes forward as much as possible.

She heard the clang of a blacksmith's hammer, and inhaled fragrant bread baking. A barracks and block house sat at the western end, and another blockhouse at the eastern. Her father pointed out that the coastal end of the Appalachian Mountains formed a part of the fortifications. They stopped in front of a simple, two-story wooden dwelling, among other buildings of similar size all shoved together. The soldiers carried the trunks inside. A woman in a white apron and cap met them at the door.

"This is Mrs. Fulton, my housekeeper," Father said.

Mrs. Fulton's old, weathered face smiled. She nodded to Amelia. "Very nice to make your acquaintance, Miss." Her thin form stepped aside for them to enter. The quarters smelled clean, like beeswax.

In a tiny upstairs room, Amelia and Louise arranged the trunks' contents. Their clothing into the clothes press, personal items in and onto a dresser. Louise would have to sleep on a truckle bed, as the house was too small for her to have her own space.

"Now that we're here, I'm extra nervous about my betrothal." Amelia placed a pair of slippers in a drawer of the press. Her heart twinged. "I suppose it didn't seem so real until now."

"I do pray this Lieutenant Harris be a good man for you." Louise dropped their dirty laundry in a pile, then shook out shifts and gowns before folding them again.

"Your desires are the same as mine." Amelia stared out the window's wavy pane, which overlooked the fort's parade ground and wondered how long she'd be in her father's home. "I think the lieutenant and I should take time to get to know one another before any wedding is planned."

"Aye, to be sure, Miss." Louise stopped her folding, her mouth in a frown. "This be a rocky land with strange folk."

"Rugged people, to be sure. And the town isn't much, but at least it's being improved." Amelia placed handkerchiefs in a dresser drawer. She caught her reflection in the mirror above it. Her thoughts returned to Lt. Harris. Had Father informed him his daughter was no beauty?

Her face was long and narrow, her mouth small and chin rather pointed. One of her brother's friends had called her a stork. Her skin prickled. Boys could be so cruel. What if she disillusioned the lieutenant, and he turned her away?

She'd stewed much over this alliance after her mother received the letter from Father, suggesting the marriage. This might be her last chance to have a family, Mother had cajoled. Would Amelia be a good, compliant wife, and a loving parent to children who'd already lost their own mother?

Could she be nurturing to this family? She'd learned not to bother with flirting and was known to be outspoken. She had little idea how to please a prospective husband.

A knock at the door. Louise opened it.

"Beg your pardon, Miss Latimer, but Lieutenant Harris is downstairs in the parlour," Mrs. Fulton said. Her eyes showed a hint of disapproval; whether for Amelia or the lieutenant, she wasn't certain. Then a flash of pity appeared. "Captain Latimer requests you attend them."

No time to change her traveling clothes, to clean up? Her face heated. This seemed rude and presumptuous. Already she was being treated as a commodity of little value. Or was Harris only an eager suitor?

"Tell my father I'll be down in a few minutes." Teeth clenched, she glanced at Louise. The girl quickly undid Amelia's bun, brushed her hair, pinned it back up, then brushed the dirt off her clothing. Amelia washed her hands and face in the ewer on the washstand. The cool water refreshed, but her pulse thumped.

Walking slowly down the stairs, she took a deep breath and entered the parlour. Her father stood near a fireplace with another man of medium build, also in uniform, his back to her.

"It's our tenuous luck that the provincial army settling up the Saint John River aided in inducing Halifax to make this a separate colony," Father was saying.

"I hope only quality people are settled here, no criminals." Lt. Harris had a dry voice.

Father turned. "Ah, here is my daughter. John, may I introduce Miss Amelia Latimer." Father reached out his arm. She felt presented like meat on a platter. "Amelia, this is Lieutenant John Harris."

Lt. Harris faced her. He nodded. No smile touched his thin-lipped mouth. His grey eyes were chilly in his square face. "I'm pleased to meet you, Miss Latimer." His tone sounded flat.

Any warmth was sucked from the room. Her heart sank. Was she to have a husband she had to unfreeze like well water in January?

"I'm pleased as well, sir." She made a slight curtsey.

Father rubbed his hands together, his smile tight. "I'm delighted to bring you two together for this auspicious meeting. I must attend to a few errands. I'm involved in settling the disbanded officers from the States. They're promised land but don't yet have it, a quagmire. I'll give you time to get acquainted. Mrs. Fulton will serve tea." He left the room.

Amelia tried not to glare after him. He should have stayed to ease her way.

Lt. Harris gestured toward a triple-back sofa. "Please be seated, Miss Latimer."

She did so, her back straight as a broomstick. She tried a smile on him, with no effect. He averted his gaze for a moment. The knot in her stomach doubled. This was going to be harder than she thought. Was he already disappointed by what he saw?

She fought a twinge of irritation, yet was determined to rise to the challenge. "I hope you and your family are well."

"We are." Harris sat in a chair in front of her. His red tunic was similar to her father's and smelled of pipe smoke. He too wore a small white wig. The face beneath had lines around the eyes, but he wasn't bad to look upon. "I like to get right to business. I'm certain your father has written to you that I've been a widower for the past two years. My mourning period is completed. I have two sons, eleven and fourteen years of age. They need a mother. I need

27

someone to keep my house in an orderly fashion."

Not exactly what she wished to hear in their initial conversation. "Yes, I do understand, and can't wait to meet your—"

"I like things in strict, military precision, no frivolous undertakings, the children kept in line, clean and devoted to their studies." He tapped his fingers like drumbeats on his grey trousers.

Uneasiness washed over Amelia. Her pulse quickened again. Perhaps his first wife had thrown herself out of a window.

"You are a man of discerning taste." She had to make this work, she'd promised her mother, and travelled so far. Despite that, Amelia's hands fidgeted in her lap.

"This is strictly a business arrangement for my convenience," he went on. "With the political changes about to take place, I will be sent on important missions which may last for a week or two."

No thoughts of her, no compassion or friendliness whatsoever. She strained to keep an open mind. "I'm certain we can find interests in common when we come to know one another better."

"I'm not good at idle chitchat. A simple yes to the marriage will do." He nodded again, waiting. "You're quite undernourished-looking, and I understand your prospects are minimal, so you should be honoured by my offer."

What a horrid man! Amelia stood, her blood curdling, cheeks hot. He had gone too far with those insults. She had to put him off, to gather her thoughts. "Thank you, sir. I will give you my answer in—three days."

Now he stood, his brows lowered. "But I'd assumed this was all decided. I have plans to make. I don't have time for tomfoolery or female giddiness."

She fisted her hands behind her back. "You will have my answer soon, as I said. I'm rather tired after my lengthy voyage. I give you good day, sir." Amelia turned to hide her scowl. Her brain a fog of confusion, she stalked out the parlour door, toward the stairs, almost knocking the tea tray from Mrs. Fulton's hands.

Chapter three

Gilbert's skirmish with the soldier bunched his muscles like twists in a rope as he galloped his horse over the low, moss and grass-covered hills and plateaus that were common to the colony's interior—so different from the ragged, stony coastline.

He approached a grist mill and a cluster of small houses that overlooked the Kennebecasis River. The river spilled into Grand Bay twelve miles south, directly to the west of Parr Town. The mill was located a mile north of the village of Quispamsis, which had become swollen with Loyalists the year before. They crept like a fungus up every bay and river, claiming land as their right. *Déjà vu!*

The private's words sliced back like sword jabs, "*...and you'll be run out again.*"

The splash from the turning mill wheel made a rhythmic sound. The pretty aspect of the area should have cheered him, with hemlock, beech and red oak trees, the sunny goldenrod, and black huckleberry bushes whose sweet berries his mother baked into muffins. Tall stalks of fireweed trimmed the field's edge with bright pink flowers. A grassy bank sloped to the flowing river.

His resolve intensified to protect it all. Thankful he could read English well, he devoured the journals and newssheets passed around to keep abreast of the changes looming.

He cantered Vaillant up to his mother's home. Her dwelling was simple, constructed of tree trunks resting on thick mortar. Smoke swirled from the clay chimney, drifting above the roof's cedar shingles. The British had torched most of the Acadians properties during the expulsion. This place was a replica. He dismounted, knocked then entered. The aroma of cooking chicken wafted over him. His stomach growled.

Marie-Cateline Arsenault, short and slender, bent over two pans in the smoke-stained hearth. She glanced over her shoulder. "So how is it, out in the world, *mon fils*?"

"What we feared, *Maman*. The Loyalists are demanding the best land and other privileges. England has even provided them funds and provisions for their forced exodus." He removed his hat. "Our part of the colony's break from Halifax is imminent. Different leaders will be in charge, and breathing down our necks."

She turned to stare at him. A faded scarf covered her shoulders, a white cap sat on her still-dark hair—the deep black he'd inherited. She adjusted the front laces on the black bodice that she wore over a white shirt. Even at forty-six she remained an attractive woman.

"More trouble for us, *oui*. The Loyalists run from their defeat, hunted like dogs by the Americans. Demoralized by their ousting? They'll have a taste of how we were treated."

The Acadians, after refusing to take an oath to Britain, had been murdered, starved, or died from disease when chased from their homes.

"Our family refused to leave, and were fortunate to hide out on Boishébert Island." She clomped in her wooden clogs, her sabots, to a wide table, picked up a large knife and began chopping onions. A well-stained apron covered her striped skirt. "Soon I was breeding with you."

"And we survived by fishing." Gilbert had heard her harrowing story many times over the years. The anguish evident in her voice when he was a child, before she'd risen above what had happened with a stoic hardness. Nine years after their exile—when he was nine himself—in 1764, small groups of Acadians were allowed to return to their demolished villages. Others settled in the often-flooded marshlands near Chignecto.

He walked over and leaned on the other side of the table, the pungent onions making him blink. "It's ironic that the English who stormed in and slaughtered our kin now worry about the Loyalist incursion. As you say, 'a taste'. Governor Parr has his hands full, but not for long. Though he protests the division of *his* colony." Parr, a huge blob of a man over in Halifax, was disliked by many, and deemed too incompetent to handle the long, spread-out colony.

"These *bouffon* newcomers want their own kingdom." She sounded partially amused as she swept the chopped onions to one side with the knife, then sliced the potatoes in smooth, even strokes. "Several are building grand manors along this coast instead of finding a way to support themselves."

Gilbert frowned. "Already these men have set up a trading post at St. Andrews on Passamaquoddy Bay, dealing illegally with the rebels they fled from." He shook his head. Near the colony of Maine, their country's western boundary, the Loyalists were 'trading the lines.' "They ignore the Navigation Acts that forbid the United States from trading with British ships enroute to the islands."

Nova Scotia was no longer America's halfway point. Only English vessels were permitted to deliver to the British West Indies. Trouble was brewing, which might disrupt his trade.

Maman waved the knife in the air. "St. Andrews is many leagues away. We must focus right here. Not one of these intruders better set foot on my land. I won't cower this time. I'm older and tougher." She resumed chopping, her words pragmatic. "We're supposed to believe it's God's will, but my blunderbuss will be oiled, loaded and ready."

"I'd never allow you to be evicted or harmed again." Gilbert gazed around the simple one-room house, always clean even with a hard-packed dirt floor. A cross hung on the wall over her bed. He'd acquired this acreage for her through his trading expertise. But land was being stolen or swapped back and forth with little care since last year.

He watched his mother once more. "We will have to be careful when the new governor arrives, to see what 'privileges' we'll be allowed to keep. You must behave like a good Christian woman, and not shoot any soldiers." He cocked his head, his smile an attempt at teasing.

She narrowed her eyes. "I used to fear *you* would be the one to fire on the army."

He smirked to hide his true feelings. Gut tight, he might reconsider that action after today, though she'd always warned him against thoughts of revenge to defend her long-lost honour. Defence, survival, now those were altogether different reasons.

"These English forget that we built the dykes to tame the high tides that irrigate the hayfields. We improved this colony. The past is past, but this time I will fight to keep the present." She removed the browned pieces of chicken from the pots, tossed in the onion chunks and sautéed them. She added flour and stirred. Then transferring the chicken and onion to a larger pot with the potatoes, water and carrots, she sprinkled in salt, pepper and fresh summer savoury. "Will you join in and feast on my Chicken *Fricot*?"

The delicious smells enticed him, even through the morass of his worries. Despite his willpower, everything could be snatched away. He gripped the rough-hewn table he'd built for her.

"As much as I would like to, I can't stay. I know you need to feed the mill workers." He straightened, keeping his expression calm to placate. His mother made her living providing food for the workers. She also created and mended clothing, and grew vegetables and hay to sell. He filled with tenderness. "I only came to check on you. I must go down to the post."

"If you were married, you'd have a wife waiting for you with a hot meal, *non*?" Lowering the huge iron pot on a hook nearer the flames, she gave him another quick glance over her shoulder. "You are almost thirty. Time to start a family. I want grandchildren."

Gilbert was surprised by the pinch in his chest. He thought he'd come to terms with his loss. Now her face swam before him. Monique, pretty as a porcelain doll. The girl he almost married three years ago. The remembered pain had kept him from courting anyone else, or it was a good excuse to remain focused on his business.

With a deep breath, he replaced his hat and bowed to his mother. "When I find someone to care about, I might do that. *Bonjour*, dearest

Maman." He kissed her cheek, walked to the door and opened it.

Outside, the warm air washed away the tantalizing scents of his mother's kitchen. The hayfield rippled in the breeze thirty feet away. He heard a heavy rustling in that grass, about to flower, soon to be harvested with the hamlet scything the crop. Gilbert walked closer. A man was bent over, creeping through the field, obviously trying to remain concealed.

"*Arrêt!* Who goes there?" Gilbert demanded.

The swish of footsteps hurried away. Gilbert plunged into the sweet smell of grass that brushed below his chest. Two sets of footfalls sounded as he pursued the other person, pushing stalks out of his way. He drew near and saw a native in an elk-skin tunic belted around his waist.

The Mi'kmaq stopped and faced him, his dark face in a grimace under the blackest of thick hair. "Why do you chase me?" He spoke in French, a bow and arrow gripped in his hands.

"Why are you sneaking about in my mother's crop?" Gilbert halted, the trampled grasses flattened under his feet. He slowed his breathing.

"I am *getanatl*—stalking prey. This grass is a good cover." The younger man lowered his bow with its moose antler nock. "I asked your mother not to mow it, but soon she insists she

36

will." The brave raised his chin, his eyes piercing.

"She must mow. She sells the hay to earn money." Gilbert spread his legs apart, arms crossed. "You should understand that. Your tribe has usually worked alongside we Acadians."

"We all must survive." He sliced one arm in an arc through the air. "Once this land belonged to everyone, to share among the 'People' until the French then English came and divided it up the way they wished."

"The French have always been your allies. We've worked closely with your tribe in fishing and farming." Gilbert brushed loose chaff from his clothes. "I agree, the British foreigners have damaged our way of life."

"Not so foreign for you." The native scrutinized him. "You claim to be Acadian, but some say you aren't pure. You are a half-breed. Half English."

Gilbert clenched his jaw, though he'd heard this insult throughout his life. The severe jolt it once caused had faded to a strong nudge over the years. He pressed his knuckles into the sides of his leather breeches and kept his words neutral. "I ask you to leave my mother's crops alone."

"You better be careful. A fine-clothed British man has asked about who owns your trading post, about the land it sits on. That's a warning for you." The young brave swished his way through the grass and headed into the forest.

"*Merde*." Gilbert swiped the grass aside and strode for his horse, his mind churning.

* * *

Amelia resisted slamming the bedroom door after her hustle up the stairs. Closing it, she leaned against the hard surface and moaned. She massaged a muscle on the side of her neck, the pain acute.

"Oh, my, what's amiss?" Louise left the clothes press and approached, her gaze full of concern.

"I...I cannot marry that man." Amelia's words came out raspy, stunned. Her entire purpose for being in the colony had crumbled to dust. "He's despicable."

Louise took her arm and led her to a chair. "Come and sit, Miss. You look about to faint."

Amelia dropped into the upholstered chair and wheezed in her breath. A headache started. "What will I tell Father? How could he have chosen such a man for me?"

"What did the lieutenant do?" Louise knelt before her, stroking Amelia's hand. The girl smelled like the lavender sachets, provided by Mrs. Fulton, she'd been putting among Amelia's clothing. "Shall I fetch a feather to burn, Miss?"

Amelia rubbed her temples. "No, I promise not to faint—I never faint. There's a possibility I might scream, though." Her eyes grew moist. "Lieutenant Harris is a cold, calculating martinet. I tried my best, but he has no kindness in him. I am nothing more than a 'business' arrangement, undeserving of even a shred of compassion. He could have at least pretended to be civil to me."

"La, Miss. How terrible. You deserve better, 'tis true." Louise stared up like a puppy, her large hazel eyes full of emotion, pale blonde hair curling out from her mobcap.

"We'll have to return to England. There's nothing for us here." The thought of another sea crossing made Amelia's throat constrict, yet she wouldn't mind re-joining her mother. Nevertheless, humiliation coiled through her. She'd failed to obtain a husband. Mother would be so disappointed.

"England? Oh, fie. That wretched voyage, the nausea…" Louise blanched, looking seasick already.

A quick rap rattled the door. Louise hopped up and opened it. Father stood there, his face flushed, eyes stern. He gestured for the maid to leave the room, then shut the door.

Amelia stood, squaring her shoulders for the onslaught.

"What happened, Amelia? John told me you would not give him an answer. That he must wait three days? He is not pleased."

Father's words were curt, anger simmering beneath them. "What is this nonsense?"

"The lieutenant won't have to wait three days," Amelia trembled with her own anger, "I refuse to marry him. He is a cruel man without a trace of human feeling."

"What? Have you lost your wits, my girl? He would give you a decent life, provide you with support." Father held out his hands, palms up, his mouth agape. "You'd have your own household to manage."

"And I'd be miserable under his tyranny. I cannot exist like that. I'm sorry, Father." She bowed her head for a second, more to avoid seeing her father's irate expression than from being ashamed. "I will return to England on the next available ship. Mother needs me."

Father's glare smouldering, he turned toward the window, fists on his hips. "You were always a wilful girl, allowed to run amok in my absences, but to travel all this way then reject a suitable proposal. I cannot fathom your actions."

"Do you care nothing for my happiness?" She struggled to keep her voice even. Her entire future was unravelling. The plans she thought she had, fashioning a nice home, raising the two Harris boys, and babies of her own, were trampled in the mud. "Don't you see what type of person he is? Why has he never been promoted beyond lieutenant at his age? I might as well marry a fence post shot through with spikes."

Father's shoulders slumped, his back still to her. He faced her once more. "Harris is a man of strict temperament, I admit. He might not be the perfect one for you, but I see few opportunities. Everyone has flaws. Will you give it more thought, in these 'three days'?" He put his hands on her upper arms, his eyes beseeching. "You need the security of a husband, my dear."

Amelia took a slow breath, chin raised. "Very well. Let me...ponder this situation." She wouldn't change her mind. Harris' personality, or lack thereof, was obvious. His flaws were as deep as the ocean, as cutting as a shark. She'd rather die a spinster.

"That's my sensible daughter. I'm certain you'll come to the correct decision. Don't fail me." Father stroked her cheek, then left her room.

She collapsed back in the chair with a groan. Louise entered, her gaze inquisitive.

"We might as well prepare our minds for the voyage back to England, Louise." Another eight or more weeks at sea? Amelia wrestled off her frustration. "The husband I'd hoped for never existed."

"I'm that sorry, Miss." Louise grimaced. Was she sorry for Amelia, or for having to endure the rough Atlantic passage? "I wouldn't mind seeing my family again."

"Nor would I." Amelia would nurse her mother, whom she knew couldn't have much time. Then what? What existence lay before her? The Latimer's did well, but weren't

41

wealthy. She could hire out as a governess, a companion to a higher-born lady, or be the spinster aunt dependent on the largesse of her brother when he married and had children. Perhaps this last would be the least objectionable, if whomever William married agreed, or even liked Amelia as a sister-in-law.

She must make the best of it, though trepidation sat like a stone inside her.

* * *

People shouted. Cracks of gunfire? Amelia sat up in the bed, groggy. Troubled dreams had given her a restless sleep. Her neck ached; her hopes were bruised. She stared up at the bed's canopy. Before she'd fallen asleep the previous night, she'd tormented herself with the idea she'd made a huge error in rejecting John Harris. Then her pride surged up and enveloped her, holding her perseverance firm. She wanted a man who would at least treat her with respect and not like his servant, or slave.

More shouts and the thud of boots. Was the uproar in her distressed head or from outside? She reached down and shook her maid's shoulder. "Louise, please go and see what that racket is."

Louise yawned, crawled from the truckle bed that had been pulled out from under the four-poster, and stumbled to the open window.

The girl's night shift flowed around her slender form. She rubbed her eyes. "The soldiers and others be celebratin', seems like, Miss."

Amelia left her warm blanket, pulled on a wrap and joined her maid at the window. She pushed it open and peered down. People below were crying out, some flapping newssheets in the air.

"It's official this day, August 16th, in the year of our Lord 1784," a man in uniform announced to the rougher dressed people who looked confused, obviously unable to read. "We're now the colony of New Brunswick, separate from Nova Scotia. A new government is forming."

Amelia pulled her wrap tighter though the air was mild. The excitement of a new beginning thrummed through her. However, this change would mean little. She'd experience no adventures in this far-flung land. Soon she'd be on a ship headed back to Plymouth. She pressed her forehead against the cool window pane and must steel herself for a final battle with her father.

Chapter four

The trapper, a grizzled old Frenchman, glared at Gilbert's every move as he sorted through the man's beaver and muskrat pelts. The trading post, built of stacked oak trunks, was situated on Grand Bay, four miles northwest of the burgeoning Parr Town. Trade had increased with the newcomers, something to be thankful for.

Gilbert and his partner had named the building Nákúset, the Mi'kmaq word for 'sun'—though there was no sun this day. Windblown rain slapped against the windows that faced the bay.

"*Eh bien*, are my furs good enough?" The trapper's voice held its familiar sarcasm. He dripped from the storm and stank like something that crawled from the river. His buckskin jacket was stained, ripped along one seam, and reeked of smoke and blood.

"Have patience. *Un moment*. You know I'm thorough." Gilbert was used to the man's gruff personality. He continued his inspection, the fur soft beneath his fingers. Unfortunately, the summer coats weren't as thick or desirable as the winter pelts. The trapper had skinned the animals quickly he could tell. The pelts weren't tainted nor the fur allowed to slip—no decay or loose hair.

A native woman holding a child's hand hurried in the front door and shook the rain from the ends of her long hair. The high-peaked cap she wore showed she was Malècite, or Maliseet. She paused before the displays of knives, tools, and kettles.

Gilbert appreciated the order of the post. Guns hung on one wall and colourful cloth lay folded on cabinet shelves. Furs of marten, squirrel, raccoon and mink were in locked chests behind him. The logged building with thick beams smelled of wood, leather, fur and damp.

Several more people milled about, inspecting the goods for sale. Gilbert's co-owner in this enterprise, Marcel Fougère, an Acadian wearing fifty-seven years in his leathery face, kept a watchful eye on them.

A tall, lanky, young stranger dressed in a fine wool frock coat and neat wig hovered in the background, making no move to sort among the items. Gilbert flicked him a wary glance. Was this the British man the brave had warned him about? Fougère had noticed him as well.

"These look fine, *mon ami*. Your pelts usually are." Gilbert turned back to the aging trapper, who for all his dishevelment always brought in a decent product.

"So what's this news? Why call the broken apart colony New Brunswick?" The old man

45

clamped his unlit pipe between yellow, half-rotten teeth.

"Named in honour of the English king, it's said. He's from the House of Brunswick, a German state." Gilbert shrugged, as if these changes mattered little, which wasn't true. He darted another look at the bewigged stranger who hadn't moved, then eyed the trapper. Perhaps he'd talk the man into trading the fur for a new jacket. "I have the finest buck—"

"A German, bah! Enough Germans here, and Dutch, not to mention English and Negroes." The old man had emigrated down from Québec—though he was born in this colony. "I want one of those boxes." The trapper pointed to a round box on a shelf behind Gilbert. "I have a lady friend."

Gilbert suppressed a raised brow, and retrieved the birch bark container, handing it to the man. These boxes were made by the Mi'kmaq who used moistened, dyed porcupine quills to decorate the lids, usually in an eight-pointed star configuration of reds and blues.

The natives traded their craftwork for iron pots and copper kettles, to replace their flimsier vessels made of clay, bark or skins.

"We're a mixture of many nations, each claiming the right to prosper. We all balance on the cliffs, praying not to fall over." Gilbert laid the fur out flat on the counter, his own qualms edging up. The fancy-dressed stranger had moved a few steps forward and appeared to be scrutinizing him and his partner.

"*Merde.* You speak the truth, Arsenault. My family was displaced by those New Englanders who came up, back in '63." The old man jerked his pipe from thin, cracked lips. "They grabbed land to set up trade with the heathen *First People*. Now those American scoundrels have taken over the settlement of Maugerville."

Another gust of rain splattered against the window's glass, which juddered under the force. Thunder boomed, joining the hum of conversation that rose and fell among the patrons.

"That displacement was long ago. As was mine." Gilbert thought of his mother's words to hold on to the present, yet she too brought up the past. "Why don't you try on a new buckskin jacket? The softest yet hardiest deerskin." He waved his hand in the direction of the coats. "You look like you could use one."

"And who'll be governor here?" The trapper ran his dirty, bony fingers over the box. He disparaged the heathens but admired their handiwork, Gilbert mused.

"A ship is probably on its way from London, with men who know nothing of our country and customs." Gilbert's shoulder muscles tightened. Such men might create laws to the Acadians' detriment—more restrictive than the current British government's. When would they find peace?

"I'll keep my jacket. Don't want no one to think me too above myself. But I'll look around for anything else I might need." The trapper laughed, his foul breath wafting over Gilbert.

"We have sweet-scented soap balls as well." Gilbert nodded toward a shelf of lilac and lavender soap wrapped in muslin, nestled in baskets. His woman would be better off if she lacked a sense of smell. "For your lady friend, *non*?"

The trapper winked and moved off toward the soap.

The man in the wig finally approached. "You run a good business here." He scanned about as if sizing the place up. "My name is Mr. Daniel Jarvis, recently of New York."

A Loyalist, of course. Gilbert inhaled deeply and pasted on a smile. "I am Monsieur Arsenault. What can I help you with, Mr. Jarvis?"

"I'm interested in your location, and the number of customers this post attracts." Jarvis stuck his thumbs in his silk waistcoat pockets, rocking back on his shiny buckled shoes. He appeared in his late twenties and had a long nose and slightly pocked, sharp-boned cheeks.

"We do a decent business, as you say." Gilbert bristled at the man's possessive attitude. "Is there anything you seek in particular?"

"An investment." Jarvis averted his gaze. "Or ownership, if necessary."

"*Mai non*. We need nothing like that in this post. St. Andrews might be the place for you." Gilbert started to fold up the furs in quick movements, anxious to discourage this interloper. "Why would you talk of 'ownership'? Have you experience in trade?"

"I might just covet the property; it's on the bay, near to town." The young man stared out the windows. "A good place for me."

"Have you been in touch with the landlord?" Gilbert tapped the counter, his irritation growing. The property the post sat on was—regrettably—owned by an Englishman, who still lived in England. A man who might side with his compatriot? "There's other land on this bay."

"I'm considering my options." Jarvis' eyes turned flinty. "My father fought in the Seven Years' War, which proved our supremacy. You're no longer New France, but in British territory. I might put my own people in the post. I've been forced up to this desolate colony, I should have choices."

"We all need choices, but not a history lesson. Have you no care for the people already here?" Gilbert fisted one of the furs, hair and hide in a twist, his jaw clenched. "Our business is successful, my partner and I adept."

"I need the income, the room. My home was confiscated by the Patriots. My family threatened. I *will* be in touch with the landlord. He's a family friend." Jarvis rapped the counter, his smile smug. He turned and sauntered from the building.

Gilbert burned with anger. His worst fears could become reality. "We will see, monsieur."

He'd fight to stay, to keep him and his mother solvent—protected.

Fougère came over, his salt and pepper hair shaggy around his lined, sun-burnished face. His head reached Gilbert's shoulder, his stature short and wiry. "I smell trouble. What did that malingering poof want, *mon ami*?"

Gilbert unclenched his jaw. "The arrogant prig was admiring our location. He intends to be bothersome, or he has a wish to be dunked in the river." He whispered the last part. Spiteful comments—words that could be used against him—were best kept to himself.

* * *

Tired of being cooped up in her father's house, festering with the decision she'd already made, Amelia left the fort's palisade with Louise. They passed an earthwork where eight large cannon pointed toward the harbour. From atop the fortress's knoll, she gazed out over Parr Town, which stretched to her left. The town straggled in different directions with varied levels of wooden buildings, the streets bumpy with rocks and even chasms. A lone church spire poked up in the distance.

At the waterfront, most of it directly below, ship's masts jutted into the sky—teeth in a comb. Wharves protruded finger-like below the river mouth and into the blue depths of the Bay of Fundy. An island sat at the entrance to the harbour. The barren isle of jagged rock had steep, towering cliffs that defied her imagination. Foamy waves broke against the precipice, leaving sudsy splashes.

Across a narrow gorge of the Saint John River squatted the village of Carleton. A ferry carried people between the towns.

"Such a view. It's magnificent." Amelia gulped in the brisk breeze. A storm had just passed and the air smelled damp yet fresh. The country began to fascinate her.

"'Tis rough-looking, but still somethin' beautiful, Miss," Louise said, her voice amazed.

"This land has a primeval beauty. The last of civilization at the end of the world." A world Amelia had hoped to be part of. Her shoulders drooped at her dashed expectations.

The wind whistled around her, snapping the fort's flags and making her skirt dance. When she looked down toward her feet, the limestone rock resembled streams of smooth marble glistening in the sun. She bent and touched the glassy surface.

A thirtyish, plump woman stepped up. "That's part of the Ashburn Formation; 'tis rock baked so hard under pressure, the top's turned to marble." She carried a basket containing a flour sack, sugar, and jars of jam. Red hair peeped out from her straw hat. She had a light sprinkling of freckles over her upturned nose and round face. "I'm Mrs. O'Brien. Everyone calls me Mary."

"A pleasure to meet you. I'm Miss Amelia Latimer." They both made a slight curtsey. Two days had passed since Amelia's confrontation with Lt. Harris and her father. Today she vowed to tell Father she definitely would not marry John Harris. She'd put her confession off to give the appearance she was giving the matter careful contemplation.

Amelia fought a sigh and strained for distraction. "You seem to know a lot about the land's history."

"Aye, I've been at the fort six years. My husband is the assistant purser. He likes history, too. He said the ancient glaciers caused this marbling." Mary's smile beamed as bright as gold. The wind ruffled her white, stained apron worn over a shabby beige gown. "I don't mind the colony, except for the long, freezing winters."

"What of the island there. What is it called?" Amelia asked, pointing. She wouldn't have to worry about the colony's bitter weather.

"That's Partridge Island." Mary stared off across the bay. "They're talking of putting a Pest House on it. For people that have smallpox or cholera. Dreadful thought, aye?"

"It is indeed." Amelia grimaced, then mused they should put John Harris in charge. She quickly reproached herself for her uncharitable notion—the man did have two children.

"A lighthouse might be built on the island, too. So much change," Mary said. "We're not even used to an actual town. Do you know when the Loyalists came, they camped out in hurricane houses, tents made from ship's sails. Then they erected their log cabins."

"Sounds rather desperate. Were there women and children?"

"Aye. A poor lot they were. 'Tis been so disorganized." Mary shook her head.

"I hope things gets better." Amelia meant it, her sympathy softening her own concerns. She turned to the right. "That large body of water, is it part of the river?"

"That's Grand Bay. There's a good trading post there run by two Acadians." Mary rocked her basket. "I'm glad to know you, Miss Latimer. If you need anything, please come to see me."

"I'm afraid I won't be staying." Amelia tugged at her kerchief. She regretted admitting her departure, since her father didn't yet know. "I'll be home in England soon."

"You don't say? I thought you were marrying Lt. Harris." Mary blushed, eyes lowered for a moment. "Sorry for being too personal, Miss Latimer, when we've just met." Though Mary, with her friendly personality, seemed a woman who thrived on being 'too personal'.

"Don't worry. I'm often overly straightforward myself." The entire fort probably gossiped about Amelia's business. "I've decided the lieutenant and I don't suit one another, but I haven't told my father, so please keep this to yourself." Spirits sagging briefly, she hoped she could trust this stranger.

"I will, dear, don't fret. Such a shame you came all this way and now must undergo that odious voyage back." Mary didn't sound shocked or censorious, only compassionate. "The next large supply ship should arrive in a month."

"A month?" Amelia hid her dismay. She'd have to stay with her father and withstand his disappointed expression for four weeks or more. He might continue his effort to talk her into marrying Harris. She could never let that happen. "Well, that gives me time to explore a little of this new country."

"Pardon me, Miss," Louise nodded at both women, her cap fluttering in the breeze, "but we might hunt for herbs, like we did outside of Plymouth."

"We could, certainly. I planned on working with herbals." Amelia turned to Mary. She had to remain busy, keep her mind off what others might perceive as her failure. The time she'd spend on-board, trapped again in a dank makeshift cabin, made her skin creep. "What sorts of healing herbs grow in...what is now New Brunswick?"

"I know several, and could show you. You'd do well to ask your cook, too. Mayhap you would decide to stay." The woman leaned close. "There are many unmarried soldiers, of caring dispositions." Mary emphasized the 'caring.' She must be aware of Lt. Harris' ill-temperament.

Amelia felt herself drawn to this honest-speaking woman, even in the midst of her turmoil.

"An interesting thought, but no thank you. I'd rather stay a spinster. And my mother needs me in England." She refused to be the passed down bride. Her scarred vanity had to be ignored, that sinking idea of insult. She'd grasp what dignity she could. "Excuse my directness, but you must be Irish, Mary?"

"Aye, but not Catholic, so no worries there. We attend the Anglican service here at the fort." Mary gestured with her chin. "Down on Queen Street, they just built a Presbyterian Church, but no Anglican one yet."

A group of soldiers shouldering muskets marched out of the fort and down the hill. The men made a perfect line of red and buff, with high-stepping black boots that thumped the ground in unison.

"Who's in charge of this fort?" Amelia asked, suddenly curious.

"That's a difficult question." Mary shrugged. "Major Studholme was in charge for many years. He and the Royal Fencible Americans built Fort Howe. They disbanded last year, and the major retired too. He still keeps an office in the fort, but his health's not so good." She shifted her basket from one hand to the other. "Sometimes we seem to be on our own, too far from Halifax for them to care. The different officers run their units for now. We'll see what happens when the new governor comes."

"You're in for a stimulating time. I'm sorry to miss it. I'll probably be before a warm fire in England, reading with my mother by then." Amelia clung to the one good side of her return.

Mary glanced back toward the palisade. "I best see what my children are up to, the scamps. I'll ask the fort's cook about the herbs he uses. Good day to you. I hope we'll talk again soon." The woman gave her another warm smile, then disappeared around the high wooden wall.

"And I must speak to Father and confess my decision. I'm certain it will not please him." Stomach knotted, Amelia urged Louise to follow and they re-entered the fort.

After dinner, Amelia stood in the parlour doorway, fingering the jamb. Father sat in this chamber he also used as an office, going over papers at his desk. The room was furnished with sturdy but plain furniture, devoid of a woman's touch. A painting of a hunting scene hung on the wall. One glass-fronted bookcase was crammed with books. She hadn't noticed much her last time in the room. The day she'd met Lt. Harris.

She stepped to the desk, her nerves in tangles.

Father looked up. "Ah, my dear. Are you here to tell me you have come to your senses and reconsidered the marriage?" He smiled, a bit anxiously, eyes crinkling at the corners.

56

"I've thought it over thoroughly," her breath nearly stuck in her throat, "and it's my judgement that my first impression is the correct one. I have no wish to marry Lt. Harris and will return to England as soon as a proper ship arrives."

Father grunted and pushed back in his chair. His eyes flashed with annoyance. "Amelia. That is *not* the answer I wanted to hear. Think of your future and—"

"I am thinking about my future. Lt. Harris hasn't a drop of kindness in him. I cannot be his wife. I will be a companion to Mother, then—someday—find myself a respectable position." A shopkeeper, or governess. Chin raised, she blinked back her emotions. "I don't know why you'd wish me to marry such a cold man."

Father stood, shoulders bunched. He came around the desk, spreading out his hands. "John is difficult to get to know, yes. But he'd be a good provider. It would be your duty as his wife to bring out his better qualities."

"I don't believe he has any," she blurted, then cringed at losing her composure. "I wonder if his first wife ever managed to bring them out."

"Lower your voice, please." Father glanced toward the parlour door. "You speak too boldly. Perhaps that was the cause of John's distemper."

"You would blame me?" Amelia stared, shock mixed with hurt. Her body quivered.

"I'm trying to guide you. That's my responsibility as your father." His ruddy face darkened. "You need a husband."

"Mercy, I thought you cared for me more than this-this arrangement. I see I was mistaken."

He stared toward the ceiling for a moment. "I do, my dear, I do." He grasped her upper arms, his forehead in deep furrows. "I only meant, that since you're…getting older, you might never have another chance. And I cannot increase your small dowry. Reconsider, please. The loss of his first wife might have made John act the way he does now."

She hadn't thought of that, but didn't wish to be persuaded. Harris's callousness seemed a part of who he was.

"I realize I'm a plain girl, but I will find my own way without a husband." She backed away from her father's hold, struggling to cage her resentment. The bergamot scent of his cologne no longer a comfort. "I will—"

He slapped his hand on his desk, rattling the quill pens in their leather holder. "Have a care, young lady. You shouldn't be so mulish!"

She flinched, surprised by his show of temper, then stiffened her spine. "Unless God decides to drop the perfect man in my lap, which is doubtful, my decision is final. I'm sorry." She whirled and headed for the stairs, a lump in her throat.

The next morning, Amelia sat half-awake at her toilette while Louise brushed out her hair. "Father's behaviour quite dismays me." She fought a yawn after another restless night. Dark circles had formed beneath her eyes. Thank goodness her mind remained adamant, no misgivings at turning down the lieutenant. "He's so set on this match, and I wonder why."

"Aye, Miss. 'Tis a befuddlement. Fathers can be a trial, very strict." Louise's fingers deftly rolled and pinned up Amelia's dull brown hair.

Amelia smiled wanly at the girl's reflection in the mirror. "I already resemble a prim old maid. I wish I had some of your blondeness, Louise."

"You've talked afore of an herbal tincture that lightens hair. We might find the proper herbs here." Louise patted down the bun she created then met Amelia's mirrored gaze. "Oh, Miss, I see how you suffer. 'Tisn't right."

"I'd suffer worse if I gave in." Amelia tugged on a loose strand. "We should seek amusement, if we must wait a month for another ship. Then all those uncomfortable weeks of travel." She rubbed her aching forehead. "So we'll look for those herbs to blonde my hair. I wonder if my *Culpeper's Complete Herbal* will be of help."

At a knock, Amelia tensed, praying for no more argument. However upset she was with her father—he seemed a different man—she didn't wish for any bad feelings to remain between them. She must at least soften their relationship before her departure.

"Amelia, I must speak with you." Her father's voice sounded sad through the door.

Louise let the captain in, though he hovered just over the threshold. He held a letter, his face scrunched in pain. "A fast schooner sailed in with the tide last night, bringing news from England." His voice dithered. "I've just opened this letter."

Amelia stood, alarmed by his shaky manner. "What has happened, Father?"

"My dear daughter, this missive is from my Man of Business in Plymouth." Father's eyes welled with tears. "I'm afraid my much beloved wife, your sainted mother, died about a week after you sailed from England."

Amelia felt her heart plummet. She gripped the back of the chair as dizziness swept through her. "I knew…I *knew* I should never have left her."

She staggered over and sat on the edge of her bed, then pushed two knuckles to her lips to smother her sobs.

Chapter Five

Gilbert stood near the open mill door. The water wheel scooped and emptied in continual splashes of river water; its actions turned the gears that moved the two fifteen-inch thick and four-foot-wide stones. He'd observed these activities as a child on their island of exile—a semi-relaxing interlude in the mire of his churning thoughts.

Into the hopper, the receptacle above the huge grinding stones, the millworker poured a bag of dried corn that rattled like grapeshot. The dusky Acadian then stirred with the 'damsel,' a vertical rod, to shake the corn into the 'shoe' and into the top millstone. The stones ground together to pulverize the corn. The scent of crushed corn mixed with the refreshing pine-scented breeze. Corn dust floated in the air, and the worker coughed.

"Do you think this Monsieur Jarvis will go through with his threat?" Maman leaned one arm against the splintery mill wall, her plump mouth drawn into a frown. "*Mon Dieu.* Can they just snatch away land and buildings like they did when I was a girl?"

"Our post has always been lucrative, and if enough money changes hands..." Gilbert strained to keep his words calm, yet worry coiled inside him. "The landlord, a family friend he says, might prefer to sell the acreage to a fellow Englishman. Jarvis seems unpredictable." Gilbert needed a scheme to protect what was his, but if the land was sold out from under him...

"*Peste* on these intruders." She scuffed her clog along the dirt. "I've been patient, mostly, with our circumstances. But now, *more* English. If only those loyal to their Crown had been shipped to England and not invited up here after the war."

"We'll stand firm in any way we can." Gilbert fisted his hands and prayed for strength. Had they a shred of power in the face of this huge migration? Or would the Acadians be forced into the interior, onto the least cultivatable rocky hills as before? Many of his expelled people had fled to France, or the southern American colonies, the territory of Louisiana. He'd die in confrontation before he'd be chased out.

Two horses with riders trotted up as if Gilbert's and *Maman's* words had conjured the trouble. A man in a long, expensive, buff-coloured frock coat dismounted and approached, as did his companion, a rough-looking fellow wearing old buckskin and a moth-eaten beaver hat.

Gilbert stiffened, but kept his gaze steady.

The first man's cocked, three-cornered hat covered a neat grey wig. Stocky in build, he appeared to be about forty. He tipped his hat to Marie-Cateline, then looked at Gilbert. "Good day. May I ask who owns this property?"

The stringy-haired man in the beaver hat hung back, scanning the scene like a raptor.

"I own the land where that house is. And the house, too." Gilbert indicated his mother's home. He grew even more leery. He considered the land hers, but a single woman was in a precarious position. "Why do you wish to know?"

"You possess the legal deed?" The man pursed his lips in his wide face.

"We have the deed," Marie snapped before Gilbert could reply, her glower penetrating. "All legal and above-board, *monsieur*. Who are you?"

"My name is Hiram Wilcox, a former merchant from Massachusetts." He gave a slight bow, raising one brow at her.

She scoffed, arms crossed. "Running from those new uniting of the states."

"*Maman*, please go into the house so Mr. Wilcox and I might speak." Gilbert gave her his most indulgent smile, glossing over his irritation with this Loyalist. They crept out of every corner like cockroaches.

She shot Gilbert a hard look, then Wilcox, but finally strode toward her home, probably to prime her blunderbuss.

"A fiery woman, your mother." Wilcox nodded as he half-smiled. "She should be careful."

"Is that a threat?" Gilbert scrutinized the man, his question arch.

"No, no, of course not." Wilcox turned away.

"My mother was part of the Acadian expulsion, and won't soon forget that as history might repeat itself. I'm Gilbert Arsenault." He emphasized the *zheel-BAIR* of his first name, and didn't offer the merchant his hand. "Now, why do you ask about my deed?"

"I was only curious. The Surveyor-General, George Sproule—appointed but not yet arrived—and his deputies will be overloaded with the difficulties of finding homes for us." Wilcox began to walk away from the noise of the mill. Gilbert followed. Beaver-hat trailed a few feet behind. "The land is abundant, but many of the titles are tied up in pre-Revolution grants. Too many absentee landlords own property but have never set foot here."

Gilbert nodded slowly. A similar situation as his landlord for the trading post.

"I'm certain the government can work out these issues without grabbing property already owned and inhabited." Gilbert put his hands behind his back and kept pace with Wilcox, his shoulders rigid. "I have no intention of selling."

"I understand. The disbanded troops who fought for the king were also promised land." Wilcox stopped several yards from the house.

The curtain at the window twitched— his mother spied on them.

"You've been given free parcels up the Saint John River, and money to spend," Gilbert said through stiff lips. "That's more than we were granted on our return."

The merchant, who stood of middling height, gazed around. He wasn't handsome, his face wide, cheeks and chin too round, but had an affable way about him. "Ah, but we aren't used to these backwoods after living in grand cities with civilized pursuits. No one wants to go that far from the towns."

"My place is over fifteen miles from Parr Town. And I hear London is quite grand with civilized pursuits. You might settle there, *non*." Gilbert fought a smirk, though his resentment simmered. "Just what is your reason for coming here today?"

"I'm not really interested in this property. I wished to make your acquaintance, sir." Wilcox faced him, his large green eyes serious. "I work as an agent for several clients from the 'uniting of states' as your mother so aptly put it. I must keep journals on land availability, difficulty of transportation, deed transactions, and much more.

"This push on both sides, the 'old-comers'—the English here before—and we Loyalists, makes us desperate men." He rocked on his feet. "You have a trading post down on Grand Bay; but the property itself belongs to a

65

man my one client's family is associated with in England."

"We are all desperate in such times. And we Acadians were here long before the English, *mon ami*." Gilbert's gut lurched. His worst nightmare, as he'd just discussed with Maman, seemed about to come true. He couldn't allow this merchant, or that *bouffon* Jarvis, to evict him from Nákúset. "I've been a reliable tenant at that post for a decade."

"We deserve this better territory, including this place," Beaver-hat finally spoke, his tone belligerent. "You French should clear out and move up to Québec."

"I was born here, as was my mother and her parents and so on." Gilbert turned to face the coarser Englishman who'd moved close. He stank of sweat and slaughtered animals. Who was this filthy rogue, a last-ditch bodyguard? "We won't be forced away again. This is our home."

"Calm down, Bent. We didn't come here to get anyone upset," Wilcox said.

Beaver-hat, or Bent, raised his fist, shaking his dirty knuckles near Gilbert's nose. "Or your lot should be sent off to Europe."

Gilbert didn't flinch. He brushed the man's hand aside like a pesky insect. "You need to leave my property, monsieur, if you intend to behave like this."

Wilcox backed away, his gaze surprised. "That's enough, Bent. You have no reason to act—"

"You want me elsewhere, as I want you to be." Gilbert's temper surged through him. After all his hard labour, he was damned tired of being challenged at every turn. "Don't you dare threaten me on my own land. We've worked like beasts for everything we have."

"Perhaps we should depart and talk another time, Mr. Arsenault." Wilcox's lips twitched. He glared at Bent. "Come along."

"Only decent folk should live here." Bent snickered, nostrils flared. "Not a Frenchie gal who couldn't resist playing Itch-Buttocks with the soldiers when she was young."

"You *morceau de merde!*" Gilbert raised his fist—he'd never heard the term, but it couldn't be good—and slammed it into Bent's big mouth, his skin catching on crooked teeth.

Out the house's open window slid the barrel of the blunderbuss.

* * *

In the first days of September, three weeks after the devastating letter reporting her mother's death, Amelia walked through the hills behind Fort Howe. Her heart still heavy and full of grief, she adjusted the black armband on her left sleeve. Normally, she'd have sewn black crepe trimming on her clothing, but the shops were out of such material due to shipment delays.

Searching for herbs, Amelia had learned much about the country's wild plants from Father's cook, Mrs. Stuart, and Mary O'Brien. Starting eight days ago her new friend had shown her the best places to look. Mary had expressed her sincerest sympathy for her loss and coaxed Amelia out of the house.

She bent to pluck asparagus fronds, and wild mustard now devoid of its sprinkles of yellow flowers, then dropped the tangy-scented plants into the basket Louise carried. She'd also found the weed, shepherd's purse, a plant in the mustard family, good for eating and medicinal purposes. Mrs. Stuart might appreciate the gesture.

Amelia stopped to inspect a patch of common burdock, with its large, heart-shaped leaves. "This will be good in soups. Since the plant is large, and browning, it's time to harvest its seeds. We don't want the smaller cocklebur, which looks similar but can be poisonous if not prepared properly."

"Let's hope we got the right one, Miss," Louise said.

Amelia smiled to reassure her. "Burdock's also useful in infusions for stomach ailments."

Her movements remained lethargic, and she wished she could shake off her melancholy. Father had not broached the subject of Lt. Harris since he received the tragic news of his wife. In fact, she and Father had spoken little these past weeks, as if his guilt over neglecting Mother, and Amelia's regret over leaving her, walled them off from one another.

"Your hair do shine prettily in the sunlight, Miss." Louise gave her an encouraging grin.

To cheer Amelia up and lighten her hair, with Louise and Mary's help, the three had gathered St. John's Wort, lily roots, and broom. Amelia had traded three silk handkerchiefs for a pinch of turmeric and saffron from the fort's kitchen. They'd purchased briony and yellow stechas from a merchant in town. Louise burned vine twig to ashes for alkaline salts, and she'd washed Amelia's plain brown tresses in the concoction a few times.

"You did a fine job. I see a different person in the mirror." Amelia straightened. The bun she wore was looser, and thick tendrils of hair brushed her cheeks. Until this morning, she'd taken little notice of her grooming in her haze of despair. And since she'd acquired no husband, her absence from Mother had been all for nothing.

A flock of birds with bright orange bellies soared above. Two small animals scurried through the grass.

Amelia glanced around at the wilderness, the elegant pines and mountains. The loamy smell of earth and the sweet fragrance of late-blooming wildflowers surrounded her. The fresh air curled like a caress around her body. Childhood moments of laughter and hugs embraced her with less sadness and more joy. The remembrance of her mother's soft voice soothed, as if her parent floated in the cottony clouds above.

The fog in Amelia's brain shifted. A strange idea came over her. An idea to stay here and not return to England. Her sadness would dissipate. After all, she'd known her mother was quite ill. Dwelling on her demise did no good. Why go back to a place—and perhaps manage the house for her brother and who knows what temperament of future wife—that would remind her of her loving parent in every aspect? Amelia needed to carve out her own future.

She closed her eyes and drew in air, deeply, and stretched all her muscles from her neck to her toes. She craved a new beginning, just like this colony. Although she didn't know what her purpose here would be. And what would Father say? He might be glad to send her away after her "mulish" behaviour. Or he'd parade half the regiment before her, displaying her as a brood mare, seeing which soldier took a liking. They might even inspect her gums and teeth.

She nearly laughed, then ruffled her feet in leather half-boots through the grasses, raising more scents that tickled her nose. She stooped to pick nettles, thankful for her gloves, the prickly plant useful for diarrhea.

"How would you like it if I decided to remain in New Brunswick, Louise?" Saying it out loud made the notion disturbing, yet exciting, as the words left her tongue.

The girl stared at her, holding the basket close. The woven fibres crackled. "Truly, Miss? You…changed your mind about the lieutenant?"

"No, never that." Amelia huffed, then laughed at the irony. "A woman can remain unmarried if she wishes." She'd face ugly gossip, but she struggled with scorn before. She stepped over a stone and mused further. "I could grow medicinal herbs close to the fort and cultivate them for the doctor to use on the soldiers. And eventually start my own herbal practice."

"You was always clever with that skill, helping out your mam…" Louise glanced away. "Oh."

"It's all right." Amelia stepped close again and slipped her arm around the girl. "We can speak of Mrs. Latimer. She was a brave woman, managing a house and every difficulty that came up, including my brother, while on her own most of the time." Amelia's umbrage toward her father niggled. How would they manage to live in the same house?

"Your mam was brave, Miss, for certain." Louise nodded. "She were a fine woman, God rest her soul."

"The best of women." Amelia smiled for the second time in these long days, as if given permission. "Look down there." She pointed toward a slope that descended to a stream. "I believe it's chicory. We can add it to coffee beans to stretch the amount. I heard they have many shortages here." She stepped toward the

71

beginning of the slope to the plant with spiky blue flowers.

A growl startled her. Turning, Amelia gasped. Out of the trees lumbered a large, snarling black bear. The animal's fluid grace belied the menace in his glare. Saliva dripped from the creature's mouth when it bared sharp teeth. Fear shot through her like arrows.

Louise froze, eyes bulging. Amelia instinctively stepped back. Her foot found no purchase. She slipped, tumbling down the short embankment, rocks poking into her flesh. Her gloves were ripped off as she groped. She landed with a thunk in the marshy soil next to the stream. She struggled to rise amid her tangle of skirt and petticoats. Hips and knees aching, her hands smarted, scraped and embedded with pebbles, but she scrambled to her feet to scuttle up the hill with muddy fingers to help Louise.

She wanted to call out to the girl, but that might attract the bear. Nearing the crest, dirt dislodged above her, sifting down on her face and scalp. Amelia blinked up, her pulse hammering. She heard movement, footsteps.

A large man with a black beard, wearing buckskin clothing and a leather hat, stood at the top of the slope. He aimed a musket in the direction of the bear. The animal growled louder.

"Don't move, either of you, *mes jeune femmes*," he commanded in a French accent.

Chapter Six

Gilbert's muscles taut, he pointed his musket at the bear. The beast aggressively swayed its huge head, popped out its jaws and snorted. Deep scars, devoid of hair, etched the creature's side—evidence of prior cruelty or attacks.

"Get out of here. *Sors d'ici!*" He spoke clearly, careful not to make eye contact. The bear swung its head again. Gilbert's fingers tightened on the trigger. He hated to have to shoot the animal. It would be cumbersome to haul away, and if left, a waste of fur and meat. This close to the fort, the gunfire would draw the soldiers as well.

A girl in a mobcap cowered close by, clutching a basket, breathing in gasps. Another young woman peered over the top of the slope to the stream.

Gilbert ordered the bear away again. The animal kept moving toward him, ears flattened, head lowered. Usually these animals ran from humans, unless harassed or protecting cubs. He jerked the musket barrel and smacked the bear on his snout. "*Sors d'ici!*"

The creature swiped at him, snarling. The stink of the animal scorched his nostrils.

"Stop him, please!" the mob-capped girl cried.

"Shhh! Louise," the young woman warned as she struggled up the slope.

Gilbert prepared to fire. The bear swiped again, knocking the musket from his hands. Claws scraped his right arm. He hissed at the scratching of his flesh, the pain radiating up to his shoulder. The animal snapped at him, teeth close.

Gilbert ducked, just missing a bite from those teeth, his face sprayed with saliva. He reached for the musket, his breath harsh.

The young woman crawled to her feet. She screamed like a lunatic, but it sounded more from anger than fear. The bear backed away.

Gilbert grabbed up his musket and thrust it forward into the bear's face, jabbing the beast's nose. Before he'd no choice but to pull the trigger, the animal whined, turned and loped off back into the woods.

The young woman who'd climbed the slope rushed to the girl in the mobcap and embraced her. The girl, who was probably a servant, started to weep.

"You took a great risk," Gilbert scolded the woman in her dirty gown and loose hair. He wiped the spit from his cheek. "You should have stayed where you were, Mademoiselle."

"Mercy, sir. I frightened the creature away." The woman placed her hand on her chest, her voice breathless. Her hair, the colour of dark honey, hung in waves over her shoulders. She was tall and thin, her cheeks rose-tinted from a flush. "Not that I don't appreciate your help. Thank you."

"I believe I frightened him, too." That sounded defensive. A red stain spread along Gilbert's shirt sleeve and jacket through the rip in the material. A coppery stench. The long scratches burned like fire.

"You're injured." The woman released the servant, picked up the basket and dug around in a heap of plants. "I have Shepherd's Purse, good for stopping blood." She massaged the plant between her hands, softening it, extracting the garlicky juice. She rushed over, pulled up his tattered sleeve and rubbed the juice on his arm. "This should help until you can see a doctor."

He grimaced at the sting, the pressure of her hand. "*Merci*. My name is Gilbert Arsenault."

"I'm Miss Amelia Latimer, and this is my maid, Louise." Miss Latimer tore the rest of his shredded shirt free and wrapped the material around his wound. "Excuse me for being so forward but you need care."

She wasn't beautiful, though she had a vibrant look about her, her bright blue eyes intense. She also smelled nice, flowery. A woman who screamed to frighten bears.

"Where do you live? You should return home. The bear might decide to come back." He gazed around. "You should not be out here alone, Mademoiselle Latimer."

"I made an error, but I'm new to the colony." She stepped back and wiped her hands on her grey gown. A breeze tousled her hair. Now looking embarrassed, she gathered the tresses together. She wore a black armband. Was she recently widowed?

"Please, let's return to the fort, Miss." The maid snatched up the basket of plants. Eyes lowered, she curtsied to Gilbert. "Thank you, sir."

Gilbert tipped his hat to them both. "New to the colony? Are you related to Captain Latimer of Fort Howe?" He tried to keep track of the officers at the fort.

Not that the one man he'd like to confront was associated with this fortress, or would ever return after these many years. He might even have died in the war for American Independence. A gruesome death, deservedly—this father by force.

"Yes, I'm Captain Latimer's daughter." Her mouth thinned as if the name tasted bitter.

"And you're in mourning, I'm sorry." He'd never heard of the captain's daughter residing at the fort. She must have come from England, but for what reason?

"My mother recently died." Sorrow clouded her eyes.

"My deepest sympathies. *Je suis désolé.*" He removed his hat and pressed it to his chest.

An animal snorted. The maid jumped. But instead of the bear, Vaillant walked across the meadow where Gilbert had sent his stallion when he'd spotted the bruin.

"That's only my horse." He took the reins. "I'll escort you two ladies back to the fort, *oui*?" Leading the horse, he walked with the women through the long grasses until they neared the steep road that twisted up the knoll. "I'll wait here and watch until you're safely inside." He changed his tone to teasing, to calm them. "I doubt you'll encounter another bear before that."

"Then I'll refrain from caterwauling." Miss Latimer gave him a slight smile. "Thank you. Good day to you, sir." She nodded, put her arm around the maid, and they started their ascent.

When the two figures, now small and distant, entered the fort, he mounted his horse and rode down the lane toward Parr Town. The woman impressed him with her spirit. He grinned.

His arm throbbed, shifting his thoughts. He should see an apothecary.

Almost twenty days had passed since he'd struck the man in the scruffy beaver hat. Gilbert's knuckle healed. The merchant, Mr. Wilcox, apologized for Bent's behaviour. He was a last minute hire as a guide, obviously not a newcomer, but an oldcomer. So why the complaints over territory? And why had they asked about his deed? Gilbert needed to consult his lawyer.

Gilbert rubbed again on his stinging flesh. Then the *coquin* Bent had wiggled his loose tooth and sworn revenge.

* * *

"You was brave, Miss, to yell at that bear." Louise shivered under Amelia's arm as they neared the top of the knoll.

"I had no idea what I was doing." Amelia suppressed her own shiver. Her heartbeat began to slow to normal. She'd acted out of some primal instinct. "I could have been mauled and made it worse for the rest of you, and obviously myself."

She didn't dare tell her maid that, now that it was over, the whole experience left Amelia rather invigorated. The fact no one was killed increased her sense of daring.

She paused at the fort's gate and watched the Frenchman ride away on his golden horse with black mane and tail. Then she studied the girl. "Are you all right, Louise?" Her own body ached from her fall.

"Aye, I be fine soon, promise, Miss." Louise observed the horseman, too. "That Frenchie were a handsome one, wasn't he? I liked the way he talked. And all his wavy black hair." She smiled furtively as a guard opened the gate and they entered the parade ground.

Passing the bustling soldiers and civilians, they neared the Latimer quarters.

"How could you perceive his visage with that thick beard?" Amelia opened the house door. She'd also liked his accent. He had intelligent, large mahogany-coloured eyes and even, white teeth. However, she had no interest in him as a man, only as a sample of the colony's inhabitants. She was still learning about the history of the French here.

Mary O'Brien hurried up behind them. "Oh, Miss Latimer, your lighter hair looks beautiful, but your gown is ruined. Did you fall?"

"I did fall, but—"

"Do you know society ladies dye their hair brown if it's red? Red hair isn't fashionable." Mary touched her own russet tresses with an impish smile. "But you must hurry and pin yours up before the men think you improper."

"I have an excuse as to my dishevelment. We had a frightening mishap." With a rush of amazement, Amelia explained about the bear and the Frenchman.

"Bears! You poor dears. And the man was an Acadian, no doubt. His name sounds familiar. Their ancestors settled this land, as I've told you." Mary glanced over her shoulder. "They were treated terrible when the English came in, sorry to say. Whole communities burned and people killed."

Amelia felt a prick of shame for her own nation. She'd already heard some of the awful details. "That explains why he didn't ride up here to the fort with us."

"You best be careful, bears and strange men can both be dangerous." Mary wiggled a finger. "You must have walked further out than where I took you. Maybe a soldier could be spared to accompany you on herb searches."

"I'd rather go with just my maid." Amelia didn't care for anyone to follow her about, perhaps reporting back to her father.

Mary entered the kitchen with them. The kitchen had a large hearth charred by use, and a well-trod stone floor. A few copper pots hung on the chimney piece. A cupboard against the wall held dishes. "My husband just informed me that Mr. William Hazen says he's had word that a large merchantman could be here in the next week or so."

Mr. Hazen was a well-known trader in furs, fish and even ship's masts Mary had said previously. He owned a good deal of property in town and elsewhere, was once Commissary for the fort, and held great influence in Parr Town. He also had sixteen children!

Amelia's thoughts returned to the impending ship, a return to England. She blew out a breath. She'd have to speak to her father about her desire to stay in the colony before telling Mary. Washing her muddy hands redolent of garlic in a basin on the work table, she winced as her flesh stung from rock-cuts. Mrs. Stuart, a quiet woman of nondescript features whose mouth held a perpetual sulk, looked on with a scowl of displeasure.

"I hope you weren't too injured in your fall. I best be off, dear." Mary hugged her and departed.

Amelia and Louise spread out the pungent herbs on the kitchen table. Mrs. Stuart stirred a pot of fishy-smelling stew over the hearth fire. She added the burdock Amelia chopped into the mixture.

Father poked in his head. "Is my dinner ready? Mrs. Fulton has gone to market, and I have duties to finish up. The New York Agency should have sent qualified surveyors ahead of these fleets of evacuees."

Father had informed her the New York Agency was comprised of Loyalists after they'd fled to British occupied New York, and were coordinating the re-settlement. And apparently they weren't doing a very good job of it.

"May I have a word first, Father?" Amelia approached him.

"Of course, my dear." He blinked in surprise, given their recent estrangement. They entered his parlour. "What happened to you? Your dress is torn and filthy. And your hair is different somehow, and very untidy."

Amelia again described the run-in with the bear. And the Frenchman's intervention. "We were fortunate he came along."

"Why were you out there by yourself? You could have been killed. This is not like England." His frown increased the lines on both sides of his mouth. "There are numerous vicious animals and savages. But *like* England, a woman of good character does not wander about in the woods without a male escort. If you'd accepted the marriage..." He sighed, leaned both hands on his desk and shook his head. "Then you interact with French strangers? Rumours will abound if you continue in this manner."

Amelia bit down on her lip, but decided to let that go. She should have kept the incident to herself. If she could face down a bear, her father should be easier. "What I need to speak to you about is—I've decided I want to remain here. Now that mother is gone..." She gulped down the sadness of that truth. "There's no reason for me to return to England."

"I see." He straightened, his brows arched. "This is unexpected. In what capacity would you remain? Since you refuse to become Lt. Harris' wife."

She fought her own frown. "There's much I can do. I'd like to grow a garden of medicinal and edible herbs for use here at the fort. I'll prepare teas and tinctures. I can assist Mrs. Stuart and Mrs. Fulton." She prayed those two women would tolerate her assistance. She threw in the next for appeasement. "I can look after you."

His expression did not soften. He tapped his fingers on his desk's leather inlay. "Amelia. I don't have time to oversee your hoydenish actions, should they continue. I thought you'd outgrown such behaviour."

"I'm not a child, despite the way men think of, and treat, an unmarried woman." She breathed evenly to keep her tone reasonable and not waspish. "I don't wish to undertake that hazardous voyage. And my maid is terrified to board another ship. I will attempt to conduct myself in a more respectable manner." She didn't know if she could, as her newfound freedom and the unusual experiences sparked like flames in her blood. What had first disappointed her as a backwater now enthralled her. She'd try a little feminine wiles, though never her forte, and gave what she hoped was a pleading look. "Please, Father, give me a chance."

"Dinner's served, sir," Mrs. Stuart called from the small dining room next to the parlour.

"Allow me to think on it, my dear. Just as you should ponder your obduracy." He left the chamber, not even inviting her to join him at his meal.

Amelia summoned Louise, and they headed upstairs. Each step made her body ache worse. "We're staying. I just have to devise the best way to manoeuver around my father."

"You must let me attend your scratches from your fall down the slope, Miss." Louise stared in dismay at Amelia's ruined gown.

"I will." Amelia resisted rubbing her sore hip. Her panniers were twisted. "I believe I'll not wait for Saturday night, and take a long, hot bath." She should have cleaned herself up before speaking to her parent, but had been caught unawares.

The Man of Business in Plymouth had stated that Amelia had a small inheritance coming from her mother, so she planned not to be a financial burden to anyone. Perhaps, if she intended to explore in the wilds, plus encounter bears and interesting Frenchmen, *a bizarre notion*, she needed to obtain and learn to fire a pistol. Without Father's knowledge of course.

Chapter Seven

Gilbert's arm burning, the feel of claws ripping again, he directed his mount across Union Street, which ran east to west and formed the northern boundary of Parr Town. The numerous buildings clustered together on this patch of land faced the Lower Cove, the area over rougher terrain that surrounded the waterfront. Previously, a beach at low tide connected the two sections.

Wagons, drays, carts, crowds of people, along with the pungent sweat and piles of horse manure left steaming on the streets pushed around him. Dust and construction noise choked the air. He much preferred the country, the forests, the sweet scents of plants and earth.

He thought with a twinge of sadness of all the spruce and cedar trees that had been chopped down to clear the way for the new inhabitants two years before when the place was known as Upper Cove and Lower Cove.

Too much humanity caused problems. Just that past June a terrible fire had destroyed eleven homes in the town, with discharged soldiers of the 42nd Regiment being the principal victims. Not that Gilbert had much pity for soldiers, yet women and children suffered, too.

He tied his horse in front of the solicitor's office on King Street and entered dark-panelled rooms that smelled of linseed oil. The clerk glanced in curiosity at his hastily bandaged arm and shredded sleeve, then announced Gilbert to Mr. Johnson.

"Good gracious, man. You look like you've been attacked," Mr. Johnson said. A white wig hid his bald head. Eyes that had seen at least fifty years squinted in his chubby face. "Should I call a surgeon?"

"I'm fine, Monsieur. I'll tend to it later." After being invited, Gilbert sat and held his painful arm close. He stifled a groan. "Did you find all the paperwork concerning the ownership of my property on the Kennebecasis River?"

"Yes, yes, I have it here. My father left me much to reorganize." Johnson rifled through a high stack of papers that looked about to collapse onto his wide desk. The entire room resembled the aftermath of a hurricane. "I do have vital information. Our new governor, it appears, will be Colonel Thomas Carleton."

"He's who, the brother of Sir Guy Carleton?" Gilbert hid his displeasure. The governor would be a military man—a stickler for rules, a champion of all things British. But what did he expect? Sir Guy had been Governor General of British North America.

"His younger brother, yes. Colonel Thomas made his name during the Revolutionary War.

However, he's been in England the past couple of years." Johnson continued to dig through the precarious mountain of paperwork he'd told Gilbert he retrieved from Halifax after his father's death. "Sir Guy was offered the position, but he turned it down."

"Will Parr Town be the colony's capital?" Gilbert shifted with a spasm and flexed the fingers of his right hand. He'd go to see an apothecary he knew who could properly treat his wound. Then he thought again of the Englishwoman he just met. Her vigorous manner, and those defiant blue eyes.

"I don't believe so. The rumour is that Carleton might put the provincial capital at Ste. Anne's Point." Johnson pulled two sheets of paper out. The lines around his eyes creased in obvious exhaustion. "It's farther up-river, so not as open to any attacks by sea. And the location is a more central position in the colony."

"That is true." Gilbert grunted. He knew the history of Ste. Anne's Point. Fort Nashwaak had been built there a hundred years ago by the former Governor of Acadia, Joseph de Villebon. The fort had long since been abandoned.

"You are aware you'll have to re-register the land deed now that we're a different colony from Nova Scotia?" Johnson flipped to the second page of the papers he held. "It's required of everyone when the colonel takes his office."

"That should not be a problem." Gilbert pressed on his shoulder to redirect the pain. He was proud to be able to read and write in both

French and English. This skill helped in his business dealings.

"Umm...there seems to be a discrepancy." Johnson scrutinized the bottom of the paper. He sighed and finally met Gilbert's eyes. "I was afraid of this. The proper signatures to validate the sale aren't all here. There's no Halifax registrar."

"*C'est impossible.*" Gilbert lurched to his feet. "Your father had promised me that everything was in order."

"I must confess that my father mishandled a few legal matters and documents for nearly ten years before he retired. His mind wasn't what it should have been, and I was foolish not to notice. In my defence, I was practicing in Halifax for a good portion of that time." Johnson's mouth drooped. The senior Johnson had died only a month ago. "I'm truly sorry for any inconvenience."

"Inconvenience? This is so much more than that, Monsieur. So what do we do to clear up this discrepancy?" Gilbert gripped the elbow of his throbbing limb to keep from shouting. His mother might be evicted from her home by men who coveted the land's fertility. Not if he had any say. *Affreux!*

* * *

Captain Latimer stood beside Amelia near the streams of marble that cut through the knoll's surface in front of the fort. A three-masted barque rocked at the wharf below, anchored among smaller craft. The vessel arrived yesterday, eleven days after she'd told Father she decided to remain.

"That ship can take you back to England, if you wish," Father said as if it was neither here nor there, but she interpreted his undertone of dismissal. They'd kept up a polite coolness since her declaration against Harris. "I want you to be certain. This place has many hardships when winter comes."

"I am certain, Father. I want to be part of the colony's birth." Her hair whipped into her face, torn loose by a gust. As someone who'd grown up in a quayside town, she was used to strong wind along with the odour of fish and brine.

She refused to return to her home in Plymouth—a house for William's usage when he finished university—and roam the same rooms where her mother had laughed, smiled, coughed and grown weaker. She winced as she pictured it—no physician could save Mother.

For some odd reason, Amelia wondered if the Frenchman had sought medical attention for his wound. If not, it might become infected. She brushed her hair, and that concern, aside. "This new governor who's on his way, Colonel Carleton, the town across the river isn't named for him, is it?"

89

"No, the town's named after his older brother, Sir Guy Carleton. He was governor of Québec, Governor-General of this entire region, and commanded our troops during the American War." Father spoke proudly, even though they'd lost that war. He held onto his cocked hat in another blast of wind. "Sir Guy didn't wish to be governor of New Brunswick." He turned back to her. "If you really intend to live here, you'll forego any luxuries. Face many shortages. We'll see how you fare over these coming months."

"I realize I must consider all the possibilities in this unknown country. But let me experience it first." Amelia didn't wish to waver, yet was she hardy enough for this life? She'd have to have dealt with it if she'd married Harris. She gazed out across the bay, pewter-coloured under a cloudy sky. A harbour of opportunities, or deep turbulence as the tides?

Loud honking came from the sky. A flock of geese, with brown bodies and long black necks—in their elegant V formation—were flying south. Even they deserted the colony.

Amelia watched them. How she'd hate to return home to stagnate as the pitied aunt, or berated as a governess, chasing spoiled children whose parents were too important to raise them.

"But you definitely won't reconsider Lt. Harris?"

"Father, I'm not that desperate. It's so obvious the man would not make a suitable husband for me." Her annoyance flared. "Why are you so set on this particular connection?" When she faced him, he quickly glanced away. His neck flushed a shade of red. He didn't answer.

Back inside the house, Amelia removed her shawl. She had so many thoughts racing through her mind. Her father seemed to be hiding something pertaining to the lieutenant.

Mrs. Fulton came forward. "Miss Latimer, I wanted to say that I admire your new hair colour. So brightening. And daring." The housekeeper smiled, her wrinkles crinkling even more. "I do hope you're feeling better after your recent misery over your dear mother. God bless her."

"Thank you. I am better. And I've decided to live in the colony, but Father believes I won't survive the winter." Amelia pushed out a laugh. Mrs. Fulton had been very sweet to her since the news of her mother's death. "I'd like to be of whatever help to you I can."

"How kind of you to offer. The snows and cold here are a burden. Last winter was brutal, so many people died." The old woman tilted her head. "But I see you're a wise and courageous girl, Miss. You'll do fine."

"Why do you think me courageous?" Amelia folded her shawl, trying to ignore the idea of people perhaps freezing to death. "Have you heard the bear story?"

"Bear? Nay, for turning down the lieutenant." The housekeeper dropped her voice to a whisper, glancing about. "Forgive me if I

91

speak out of turn. I knew that man's first wife's housekeeper. Mrs. Harris wasn't a happy woman."

Amelia now felt sympathy for his sons. "I'm sorry to hear that."

"It's good you'll remain here. Lord knows the captain needs a decent influence, what with his doings with that—" The old woman's hand flew to her mouth "Fie, I've said too much. Excuse me, Miss." Mrs. Fulton picked up her skirts and disappeared into the kitchen.

Amelia slowly ascended the stairs. A *decent* influence? And 'doings' with someone, or some thing? A disturbing idea popped into her head. Did Father have a paramour, and that was why he didn't encourage Amelia to stay? Unless she married Lt. Harris, of course. Why? Her head started to ache. He had been alone without his wife for a long time. Was this the connection she needed to ferret out?

* * *

The next day Amelia searched for Mary to no avail. The Irishwoman might know the truth about her father. Instead, on another quest, she knocked then entered Major Studholme's small office, located directly off the parade ground. They'd been introduced previously by her father. The former commander of Fort Howe stood and bowed his bewigged head to her. He still wore his uniform, a shiny-from-wear red coat with faded gold-fringed epaulets. Only in his mid-forties, she was informed, he looked older with his thin cheeks in a weathered face. "What may I do for you, Miss Latimer?"

She gave a quick curtsey. "I'd like a carpenter to help me build a large, low box for soil so I can plant medicinal herbs, sir. And herbs for use in cooking."

"A good plan. This hard limestone isn't conducive to planting a garden." He gestured for her to sit in a chair near his desk. He sat as well. His office was full of books and papers neatly arranged. "Of course, you couldn't plant until the spring, but preparing the soil now is smart. Why do you seek me out to help in your project?"

"Since the new governor won't be here for a few weeks, I thought you'd be the best man to ask to make changes." She smiled, though not as an artifice—which had never worked for her. But a submissive politeness was expected from women.

He nodded slowly and leaned back in his chair. "I'm retired, you know. Not much use anymore." His weary eyes stared off over her shoulder. "I never married, too busy with the wars. I came over from Ireland. Built this fort up here on the knoll, for better security. I helped bring the natives under control. I also managed the communications between Halifax and Québec."

"My father says you helped in settling the first group of Loyalists last year."

He nodded again. "Not an easy task, as the captain can attest to."

Amelia listened to him speak of his career. He'd led an adventurous life with the 24th Foot, the Loyal Nova Scotia Volunteers, and as a captain in the Royal Fencible Americans. Men enjoyed such freedoms, which women were denied. She reined in her envy. "The colony owes you a lot, Major."

"I have performed my duties, my dear. That's what my country expected of me. And I might know just the man to build your box." He smiled, obviously happy to have someone to talk to about his experiences. "I'll find him and introduce you."

"Thank you, sir."

Once again on the parade ground, Amelia saw Mary drawing water from the large barrel the soldiers filled from a well near the town. She walked over, determined to get answers, no matter the consequences.

"Mary, you seem to know everything that happens here at the fort."

The woman rested her wooden bucket on the barrel's edge. "Aye, I like to think so. We're, or we *were*, a small outpost."

Amelia breathed through her nose, rehashing the immensity of her question. "Do you know...do you know if my father... This is so difficult. If my father is involved with—

another woman?" She said it softly, darting her gaze over Mary's freckled face.

Mary stilled, glanced away, fingered the bucket's rope handle, then looked back. "Now, Miss Latimer, that is not the sort of question you should ask."

Amelia suddenly wished she hadn't asked. Her heart flinched. "I suppose it isn't. But please tell me if you have *no* idea." She hoped for such a reply.

Mary said nothing, her eyes full of commiseration.

Amelia's frustration seeped in. "Is he having a…a dalliance? Do you know who it is?"

"You'll not appreciate me telling you." Mary lowered the filled bucket to her side. The water sloshed.

"I'd still like to know, please." Hands clenched, Amelia waited. She'd gone too far to retreat now. Her pulse echoed in her ears. The truth could injure her emotionally, and forever change her relationship with Father.

Two officers walked by. The blacksmith's boy came to scoop water and hurried off. Men shouted commands, soldiers drilled. The fort went about its everyday business.

"Oh, it's bad to say such things aloud." Mary stared toward the ground, then lifted her chin. She gripped the bucket's handle with both hands. The water sloshed again. "Your father, the captain, he has a woman he's…friendly with in town."

Amelia swayed on her feet, then stiffened. "Who *is* she?"

Mary swooshed out a long breath. "Her name is Dorothea Sutton. She's—Lt. John Harris' widowed sister."

Chapter Eight

Gilbert stepped off the log-strapped ferry, his boots soaked and squishing after the wave-battered voyage across the Bay of Fundy. He accompanied other men on their mission to retrieve any papers needed to re-register in the new colony. His deed just needed that important 'official' signature.

They entered the town of Conway on the north coast of Nova Scotia. The village was recently stripped of its name and renamed Digby, after a Royal Navy admiral. The growing community bustled, more buildings, more chimney's spewing smoke, as numerous people took the shortcut across the water instead of following the long road to the east and along the Isthmus of Chignecto.

He glared in that direction as if he could see the isthmus, the place his mother and her family had been chased from when she was a girl. The French had traded there, their gateway to Québec, until the British army besieged Fort Beauséjour for control of that narrow strip of land during the French and Indian Wars. Troops had pursued the fleeing Acadians, and his maman...

A conflicted regret shot up his spine. Without the incident, he wouldn't exist. He shook it off, bought bread, apples, dried moose meat and cheese to sustain him, and stuffed the food inside a leather sack that hung over his shoulder.

"There are no boats sailing around the coast because a storm is over the sea, the water too rough on the Atlantic," one of his traveling companions grumbled after checking. "We could wait for days."

"Then we wait, or we must go the more difficult way, over the terrain, *mes amis*," Gilbert said, shrugging off his concern about a bumpy, prolonged trek.

Nova Scotia hung like an anchor below the isthmus, the western prong with an extensive coastline. Yet with the right current it wasn't a bad voyage.

No one wanted to wait. Together the men pitched in to rent a cart and driver. The group still had over a hundred miles to travel before reaching Halifax. Since New Brunswick didn't yet have its capital set up, most official documents, registration of deeds, and grants remained in the former capital.

Scents of tobacco smoke, body odour and old leather clung to the passengers crammed into the rickety cart. Gilbert tried to avoid the arms that poked him as the vehicle jerked through scrub spruce, along rutted tracks pimpled with granite. No one had built the sturdy roads the government promised. He struggled to keep positive—this journey was important.

The wind blew strong and cool and he fought a shiver. Dark clouds blanketed the sky.

Nova Scotia's many hills and low mountain ranges were lush with grass, moss and forests. Several trees were starting to turn, their leaves in muted shades of crimson, russet and yellow.

"That Colonel Carleton won't arrive until winter, I heard," the sawmill owner said. "He was in these colonies before, Québec mostly, so he shouldn't be shocked by our temperatures. They have much to do up at Ste. Anne's Point if that's where the government's going."

"Maybe he'll reconsider Parr Town," a merchant said before he spat over the side. He was an old-comer from Maugerville. "She's got an established wharf system."

"The Point should do. A pretty place at the bend of the river. And much safer from ocean marauders." Gilbert didn't want the governor close to him. He touched his pocket where his papers were tucked away. He had to believe it would only be a formality to get the proper registration.

His arm, though covered in ointment and bandaged by the apothecary, continued to smart, especially when the cart's wheels bounced into a deep rut. The woman who had rubbed his wounds with the herb came to mind, and he almost smiled.

Five days later, after camping in rough tents rented in Digby, eating spare on provisions, they reached Nova Scotia's capital on the southern coast. The men crawled from the cart with sighs of relief. Gilbert stretched his back, shrugged off weariness, and stared around.

Halifax, founded by the British less than forty years before, sat in a shallow valley. The vast Atlantic Ocean crashed against the town's huge natural port. The Sambro Island lighthouse, a pillar of white and red, guarded the harbour entrance. On the waterfront the Royal Naval Dockyard served the large British naval presence.

During the 'expulsion' many Acadians, including a few of his relatives, had been imprisoned on an island in this harbour. He sighed and looked away.

Up on Citadel Hill above the town sat grim Fort George. The Mi'kmaq and Acadians raided this area numerous times during the various wars. English settlers were massacred, scalped by the natives, but the British prevailed.

Gilbert fisted his hand. He didn't condone murdering innocent people, but these constant wars brought out the ugliness in everyone.

He and his cart companions—Englishmen who'd treated him with civility if not friendliness—rambled down the town's narrow, hilly lanes to Barrington Street, one of the main cobbled thoroughfares. Stone buildings and ramparts, along with wooden structures, made up Halifax.

Gilbert coughed. The usual stifling scents of close-living humanity repelled him—sewage, overcooked food, dirty bodies.

St. Paul's, an Anglican church, loomed in the distance. He was raised Catholic, but hadn't practiced as he should have in his adult years. Would a merciful God have allowed the butchery of his people, or the English settlers for that matter?

Their group reached the Registrars of Deeds office. Inside the building, the place smelled musty. And though full of anxious men, lonely somehow—or at least that's how Gilbert suddenly felt.

"This isn't right, to make us battle to keep the land we've already developed!" A swarthy man slammed his fist against the wall. He looked Acadian. They exchanged a few words in French. This other man was being pushed out, his land enviable, flat and fertile.

Dread enveloped Gilbert. He'd failed his mother in not making certain the land deed was secured a decade ago. He couldn't leave her without a home after what she'd experienced as a wanderer in exile, and he a wide-eyed boy eventually beside her, confused by his circumstances.

* * *

Amelia barged into her room and tossed her hat onto the bed. The shock gushed through her in a torrent. Her father having an affair with Lt. Harris' sister? Whilst Mother withered away in England?

"Oh, no, Miss. A hat on the bed be bad luck." Louise snatched it up and placed the straw hat on the chest of drawers. "Your face, 'tis red as blood. What's happened?"

Amelia dropped into the upholstered chair near the window. She pressed her hands to her cheeks as if to shove down a cry. "I don't even know how to… I cannot comprehend the truth."

"What is it? Oh, la, what is it, Miss?" The girl kneeled at the chair arm, her eyes huge and searching.

"Give me a moment." Amelia tried to calm herself with deep, slow breaths. She gripped the chair arms. "Now I know why Father wants me to marry Lt. Harris. Such a betrayal."

"Who be betrayed?" Louise asked.

"My mother, *and* me. Even if many wives and families ignore such actions." Amelia hunched forward. How could she stay here with him—her father? Her stomach roiled with bile. Her respect for him had fallen into a cesspit.

"Tell me, please, Miss." Louise touched Amelia's back, her fingers gentle. They'd become close, more like friends.

Amelia straightened, fists on her thighs. She informed her maid of what she'd learned, her voice rising. "Reprehensible."

"Oh, criminy." Louise's hand flew to her mouth. She gasped. "I'm that sorry, Miss. I truly am. But men, they do such things."

"What should I do? I must think." Amelia massaged her temples, eyes closed. "Should I return to England, though I don't want to? Or would I be a coward to leave?"

"Maybe it be a false rumour. Or just an acquaintance, nothing more." Louise gave a tremulous, hopeful smile.

"I think Mary would know the difference. Or she *is* mistaken." Could that be true? Amelia quaked with doubts, plus a desperate wish to exonerate her father.

"Do you need a vinegar rub on your forehead, Miss?"

"No, I must speak with Father. But not while I'm so upset. I suppose he wanted me to marry the lieutenant not only to give me a husband, but so I wouldn't disapprove of his scandalous activities." Amelia rose and paced the room quickly, releasing some of her tension. She might need to race around the fort's perimeter. How did one approach one's parent over such a heart-wrenching breach of trust?

Father had intended to push her into the arms of a callous man—what kind of parent would do that?—just so he could enjoy his mistress. He hadn't known Mother was on the verge of dying, and still he strayed. Another stab of hurt sliced through her.

She plopped on the bed's edge, stretching her knotted neck, her head tilted back. "I refuse to be a ninny. Nevertheless, if I can't live here with him, where would I go?" Could she move out on her own with no 'protector' as was expected? She'd be shunned. She hardly cared at this point, but eventually she would need to make her way here. Few would purchase herbals from a brazen single woman.

"Wait until tomorrow to talk to the captain, Miss. It might be easier," Louise suggested in a soothing voice.

"You're right. I must keep in charge of my emotions." She huffed and pushed away the image of her mother, a woman who'd never said a word against Father. A loving wife, told to remain home, deserted and deceived. Amelia jerked to her feet. "I'm too restless to remain here. Come, let's walk into town."

After the long hike into Parr Town, Amelia hustled through a grocer's, dry goods store, a millinery shop, drapers' shop, picking up bags of sugar, hats, cloth, then setting them back down, unable to focus.

"I'm impressed the Loyalists built and stocked their shops so quickly. But they must be desperate to replace the lives taken from them in America," Amelia said as they bustled through.

Louise offered items to look at, although Amelia barely saw them, only intent on filling her mind with other sights, sounds, touches— anything but the disturbing thoughts and images that bounced around in her head. Had her father always been untrue to her mother, or had the ocean separated them in more ways than one?

Later when the sun dipped lower in the sky, Amelia thought of something else to distract her. "I've heard so much about this tide on the Bay of Fundy, that it drops and rises over forty feet. I've been curious to see the phenomenon."

"'Tis getting dark soon, Miss. Do you think we be safe down by the waterfront?" Louise watched the people around them. The shoppers had thinned out, and shabbily-dressed men entered the taverns. Loud laughter and voices drifted from these establishments. "What be a fenominan?"

"Something remarkable, supposedly." Amelia wrapped her cape tight about her. She knew she was behaving recklessly, but felt overcome with a compulsion to delay her return to the fort. She hurried her maid toward the quay. "Look, there are some army officers over there. We'll stand close enough to be safe."

They huddled together, ten feet from two red-coated soldiers with epaulets who were smoking pipes and conversing.

The tide was low, with bobbing boats that strained at their moorings. Craggy rocks were revealed as a salty, colder wind swept around the women. No larger ships were present.

The water, about five feet below, slurped against the quay as it washed in from the Atlantic, leaving a foamy line on the rocks. Streaks of orange light from the setting sun stretched like bursts of fire into the sky.

After what seemed an hour, the bay had risen another two feet. Riddled with embarrassment, Amelia realized this was folly. They'd have to wait here for hours during morning tide to watch the bay drop to the seabed, which was the view she sought.

A mist rose up, swirling over the water, dampening the air.

A young sailor, rank with alcohol, strode from the left and bumped into Louise. "Lookin' for company, me sweet lass?"

"Leave us alone, we're going home," Amelia ordered as Louise pressed against her. Amelia shivered with unease. This outing was a blunder.

"Oiy, that's not nice." The man swaggered in front of her, poking his face forward. He grabbed her arm. "You're a good enough piece, yourself."

"How dare you, you blackguard!" Amelia gasped and lurched away, dragging Louise with her. The sailor stumbled.

The seaman regained his balance. The women turned to hurry up the road. He followed, gripped Louise's shoulder and yanked her around. His lips puckered, he hovered near the girl's mouth. The maid shrieked. Amelia slapped his hands away.

The sailor pushed the maid aside, snatched Amelia's cape and jerked her against him. His bristly chin in a bony face scratched her cheek. His breath stank of rotten fish. Heart clogging her throat, she struggled, pounding a fist on his shoulder, and his neck. "Let me go!"

The two officers approached. "Enough!" One confronted the drunk. "Off with you, Jacktar, before I have you arrested. These women aren't interested."

The man backed away, weaved, sneering, then shrugged and shambled down the quay into the shadows.

"Ladies, why are you out here?" the other officer asked in his tobacco-smoke haze. "You don't look like trollops."

"You speak boldly, sir. We came to watch the tide." Amelia heaved in a breath, her body shaking. She knew she was careless to have suggested it. She pulled Louise close, shivering with her. "And we're decent women from the fort." She almost said she was Captain Latimer's daughter, but now that idea shamed her. Others must know about her father's peccadillos.

"You two do look familiar." The man chuckled. "You'll be here close to midnight to see the tide come completely in. I don't recommend that."

The officers escorted Amelia and Louise back to the fort, mostly silent on the twisting ascent, advising them like errant children to not be out after dark without male companions.

At the front door to her home, where a lit lantern hung, Amelia hesitated, her breath still sharp. "Louise, I'm so sorry I put us in danger, and that filthy man touched you."

107

The maid nodded, her cheeks bright pink. "I know, Miss. I was afeared when he grabbed you."

"You tried to warn me of the risk. Oh, my, I cannot face Father yet. I pray he's asleep, or in town with his...his doxy." Amelia's disappointment with him resurfaced, compounded by what had just taken place.

They skulked into the warmth of the house. Sneaking upstairs, Amelia shut her bedroom door. "I cannot believe what I have to discuss with Father tomorrow." She groaned, then grasped her maid's hand. "But I keep forgetting to thank you for putting up with my whims, and for being my friend as well as helper. I value you. Forgive me for what happened."

Louise smiled, though her gaze remained startled. She removed Amelia's cape, unfastened the back of her gown, pulled it over her head then removed her panniers and unlaced the whalebone stays. "Thank you, Miss. I'm much fond of you, too. I do forgive you. And I must say, you be certainly not boring."

Amelia nearly laughed. She needed the release. "We must form our strategies, and be more careful, if we're to have a life here."

* * *

The registrar, a stout man in a large wig that resembled a cauliflower, glared up from his desk. "Your deed is not recorded. Can you prove ownership? Since the original solicitor is dead, you must find the person who transferred the property to you and get his written proof, with a government official to witness that he did so."

Gilbert felt struck in the gut, his trepidations coming true. "But the owner signed this paper. And there are two witness signatures. That should mean something." He pointed to the scribbled names.

"We have too many people claiming land that isn't theirs." The registrar rattled the paper he held. Powder from his wig sprinkled his husky shoulders. "How much did you pay for the parcel?"

"I traded for it with furs that I caught, skinned and prepared myself." Gilbert recalled how proud he was that day, as a young man of nineteen, to purchase property on the river. Land where he'd build a house for his mother. "This was ten years ago. Land was cheaper then."

"Find this previous owner, uh..." the registrar glanced down at the paper, "Franklyn Oram. And one of the witnesses if possible."

"You cannot just sign this for me, *monsieur*? It would take but a second," Gilbert insisted, his frustration rising. "Why must I go to all this trouble?"

"That's not legal, sir." Cauliflower-head practically shoved the papers into Gilbert's chest. "Get that done, then take your problem to the new colony's Governor Carleton."

Gilbert tamped down his anger and returned outside. He didn't even know if Mr. Oram was still alive. Oram had been a man of sporadic habits and irresponsible disposition. How would Gilbert ever find him?

The other men poured from the building, all smiles and happy chatter. They'd accomplished what they came for. Gilbert kept a sullen silence, only speaking occasionally, on the long cart ride back to Digby. Had he been treated differently because of his nationality?

On the ferry, Gilbert watched the shifting waves of the bay. A water so turbulent it dropped to the seabed twice a day, revealing treacherous fingers of rock. A bizarre natural occurrence as shifting and traitorous as life. A Mi'kmaq once told him that they used to act as pilots, guiding ships in and out of the harbour to keep them from running aground, or being trapped in the rip currents.

He observed a pilot boat now guiding a large ship out of the bay, since it was slack tide, probably to safer environs or anchorage after the vessel must have unloaded its cargo. He gripped the ferry's rail. Who would guide him?

Once again in New Brunswick—difficult to get used to that name—Gilbert retrieved his horse and rode north past Grand Bay and up the Kennebecasis coast, toward the small log cabin where he dwelt about four miles south from his mother. Mr. Johnson had checked the deed for

110

that tiny property Gilbert had lived in for the last several years, and it *was* registered. He'd make certain to re-register it in New Brunswick. Johnson had that vital deed in his office.

Gilbert tightened his fingers on the leather reins. Could he force Mr. Johnson to help pay for hired men to search for Oram? After all, Johnson Senior had made the mistake, sick though he was.

It was a sickness hidden deep in the old man's brain, devoid of noticeable symptoms to start, unlike the Cholera epidemic that had swept the peninsula a few years back. Cantering on the road that wound through the woods, among dapples of light between the trees, and loamy smells, he thought of that other malady he'd carried for too long.

A wedding had been planned, but his chosen bride perished along with too many others in the pandemic. Monique, whom he'd known since they were children, had left a rip in his heart. He could never bring her back. He groaned, though his sadness was mending. Maybe he needed to return to church, just long enough to light a candle for her soul as well as his own.

Maman was right. He did need to turn a page on his personal life, start a family, find someone to love again.

As soon as he straightened out his business problems.

Birds squawked and thrashed from the branches overhead. Leaves scattered. Something rustled in the trees off to his right. Vaillant snorted, tossing his head. Gilbert stared into the forest to see if a large animal, a moose, or a bear, lurked.

A shot exploded and a musket ball whizzed by his cheek.

Chapter Nine

The salmon, sprinkled with tarragon and sagewort in a cream sauce, seemed to jeer at Amelia through one dead eye as her supper grew cold on her plate. Even the slight fishy aroma turned her stomach. She could hardly look at her father, though the need for the truth seethed inside her.

"Have you no appetite this evening?" Father asked. He forked fish and potatoes into his mouth, his meal already half eaten. They sat at the small table in the cramped dining room, her father at the head, she to his right. A branch of flickering candles sat on a sideboard, giving off a burned beeswax scent.

Sometimes they had guests, other officers and their wives. Amelia was glad they dined alone tonight. Rain splattered on the window behind Father. Thunder boomed.

She cut off a piece of fish, but left it to congeal on the plate. "I have many issues on my mind."

"Are you re-thinking your decisions of late?" He sounded a little hopeful. He sliced his last carrot into pieces, put one in his mouth and chewed.

"Not exactly." She took a large sip of her sweet wine to dampen her throat, dry with apprehension. She observed Father, the man who'd tossed her in the air as a child, placed her on her first pony, and brought gifts from faraway places. This officer in his scarlet uniform had once seemed heroic to her, but he was all too human.

"I have something I need to ask you." She'd stewed over how to approach this subject the entire day.

"Very well." He made an effort to smile, or so it appeared. He laid down his fork.

"There's no easy way to inquire about this." She pressed her fingers on the table edge. How she wished she didn't have to—but she needed to know. "However, I will be blunt. Do you have a-a woman that you're very close to here in New Brunswick?"

"Amelia. Good heavens." He reared back in his chair, his eyes sharp, stunned. Then he stared toward a corner as if to find the answer there. His throat tinged red. "You have no business asking such things or even to broach this topic with me."

With no outright denial, she feared she had her answer. Distress streamed through her, though she'd anticipated the worst. "If you do have a friend like this, is her name Dorothea Sutton?"

Father bunched his napkin in his hand. He continued to avoid looking at her. "This still isn't your concern, or a proper discourse between us." He paused then sighed, finally meeting her eyes. "If you must know, Mrs. Sutton is an…acquaintance of mine."

Amelia pushed a greasy potato around on her plate. "She's Lt. Harris' sister, isn't she?"

"Where did you get your information? From that gossipy Mrs. O'Brien?" Derision hardened his voice. His brow furrowed in anger. "She is not the sort of person you should associate with."

"Mary has been a wonderful friend and is always honest with me. But let's not change the subject, please." Amelia stiffened in the chair. She dreaded her next question. A question no daughter should even contemplate. "I know you'll think this rude, but—have you been untrue to Mother?"

A minute ticked by in her brain. His neck grew redder, like a crimson scarf. "I'm your father, young lady, and you should never speak to me in this way. I won't be insulted by my own daughter." He snatched up his fork again, but held it in his fist, eating nothing. "I loved your mother."

"I once thought you loved Mother, however… Is Mrs. Sutton the reason you want me to marry Lt. Harris?" Amelia held her breath, biting her lower lip. Then her upset took over. Tears pricked behind her eyes. "A man who would treat me like chattel, and it didn't matter to you?"

Father groaned then grimaced. "Of course you matter."

Mrs. Fulton hurried to the dining room entrance, casting a quick, worried glance at them, then left just as swiftly.

Amelia leaned forward, her voice lower so the servants wouldn't hear. "If I did, you'd never have tried to betroth—"

"That's quite enough!" Father stood and tossed down his fork and napkin. His black armband, worn to honour her mother, now appeared a mockery. "I told you before that everyone is flawed. No one is perfect. You must learn to accept these things. I've worked with John and he seemed a decent fellow. Perhaps you should make alternate plans and return to England." He strode from the room.

"And yet you admit nothing," Amelia said to his empty chair. She wanted to slide off her chair and under the table in a heap. Still, she held fast, refusing to slip into female hysterics. The pain of her father's betrayal—the fact he had a mistress; but more so, that she was Lt. Harris' sister, a woman who'd probably encouraged Amelia's match to her cold-hearted brother—must be dealt with in a rational manner. Covering her face with her hands to hold in her muddle, she just didn't know what that manner would be.

* * *

Gilbert hunkered down on his stallion's back, his heart jolting. He touched his scalp. He'd almost been shot in the head! Who the hell would do that? He jerked the reins and urged Vaillant into the woods on the left side of the road. Dismounting behind a large bush, he pulled out his pistol and listened carefully.

Footsteps ran off in the other direction, as if the assailant had only brought one ball. Gilbert cursed, frantic with confusion, remounted and dug his heels into his horse's sides. The animal bolted back across the road, into the forest on other side. Ahead bushes swayed and birds flapped from the trees into the sky. More footfalls reverberated through the brush.

"Halt!" Gilbert kicked his horse and galloped after the runner. Why would anyone try to kill him? His breath hitched. Branches and prickly bushes snapped against his shoulders, almost knocking off his hat. He scrunched his hat down tighter and leaned low, his thighs gripping the saddle's sides.

"Stop, you coward. *Vous arrêter lâche*," he called out.

Vaillant's hooves thumped along the ground, the horse's muscled body charging through the foliage, the green scent of plants strong in the damage.

They came to a deep ravine, a dangerous gouge in the earth. Gilbert pulled up his horse, both of them breathing heavily. The wind hissed through the grass. A few insects droned. He pushed his hat back from his forehead now

117

damp with sweat. No other sounds, yet Gilbert sensed he was not alone.

The person could be reloading and Gilbert was too exposed. He wheeled Vaillant about and rode behind a large outcropping of rocks. Dismounting again, he peered to one side of his stony rampart as he aimed his flintlock. "Who are you? What do you want, besides my death?"

Brush rustled several yards away. Another shot cracked through the air. Gilbert ducked. The ball hit the rock, sending chips over his head. He rose and fired back. The acrid smell of gunpowder and burst of smoke filled his nostrils.

A yelp and curse. The footsteps ran off again to the south, in a limping rhythm. The man was English, or at least his curse was. And Gilbert must have hit him!

He grabbed his powder horn, measured and poured powder into the barrel. *Peste*, who was this foul person? He jerked a piece of cloth over the muzzle, pushing down the ball with his thumb. Then he rammed it in, half-cocked his pistol, pressed a flint flat upwards and clear of the hammer. He checked the cock and primed the pan.

He left his horse and dashed after the sounds of footsteps. Birds scattered from the tall grasses. Many paths crossed here. The man could have gone anywhere, or be hiding in the brush.

"Come out and face me, you coward," he called. His legs swished through the grass.

Olive-grey sandstone rocks poked up here and there, and this person could be lurking behind them.

He slowed to listen. His skin prickled. Any moment another musket ball might explode and find its mark. Heaving a furious breath, he ran through his mind all the people he might have angered lately.

He stepped a little further, his rage overriding fear. A black-capped chickadee made its two-note whistle, a vestige of breeze ruffled the grass, then silence.

The bastard must have been scared off after being wounded. Gilbert explored three more paths. He saw no fresh footprints, no trampled foliage. Many minutes went by. Sweat gathered at his collar.

Sprinting back to Vaillant, he mounted, gripped his horse's reins, and turned the beast. He rode north to head for home. He had a suspicion about who his assailant was. He'd find him later, and identify him by his injury.

* * *

After a long gallop to clear his head, Gilbert slowed his horse. He wiped perspiration from his forehead and throat with a kerchief and inhaled several deep breaths. The birch and beech trees' leaves rustled. Their limbs cast crooked patterns along the road. Birds tweeted, but no sound of anyone pursuing him. Mouth dry, he uncorked his moose-skin pouch and took a swig of tepid water.

Vaillant could use a drink. He directed the stallion toward a pond he knew was nearby. As they drew close, the bright sound of a child's laughter surprised him. He rode on, where the trees cleared out revealing the pond lined with sedge. Two boys were digging muck and mud from the water's edge. A red-haired woman stood over them, supervising. One soldier, holding a musket, stood close, beside a cart with horse.

Gilbert halted his horse, wary of the soldier. The wounded runner hadn't worn red, but could still have been military—if he wasn't the man he initially suspected.

Miss Latimer, the bear-screamer, and her maid were there, too. Miss Latimer turned. A green ribbon on her hat fluttered in the breeze. He nodded to her. She stared at him, nodded as well, then gave a small wave.

Tipping his hat, he knew he had no business speaking to her, nevertheless his heart warmed at her acknowledgment and wave, almost calming him after the altercation. The soldier cast him a glare of disapproval.

Gilbert scanned the vicinity for any danger, then urged his horse past the pond. At least the women had protection if his shooter had followed. He should warn the soldier, but the words, the idea of conversing with any English military, stuck in his craw.

At a brook north of the pond, near an alder shrub swamp, Vaillant drank his fill of water.

Deep in the hills, four miles south of the village where his mother lived, Gilbert cut through dense pines, the sticky scent of resin like a welcome. A burbling creek announced his closeness to home, as it always did. In a narrow clearing sat the small log cabin he'd built. Sturdy, fashioned of red oak logs with neat shuttered windows, the place was well kept. He liked order, especially after the disorder of his childhood.

With a glance about, Gilbert dismounted. He'd made sure no one had followed him. He quartered his horse in the small stable beside the cabin, rubbed Vaillant down then gave the animal hay and water he hauled up from the creek.

Removing the large iron key that hung from his belt, he unlocked his front door. Most people didn't bother, but he liked to feel secure. Inside, the cabin consisted of a stone fireplace, a table, two chairs, a bed in one corner and a rag rug, made by *Maman,* on the pinewood floor. No dirt-packed floors for him, though his mother was adamant on tradition and insisted that hers would be kept earthen.

Abruptly, loneliness flooded through him, where before he'd always felt comforted in his home. He leaned on the rough-hewn wood mantel. He had searches to make, not only for Mr. Oram, but the man he believed—though the reason eluded him—wanted him dead.

Chapter Ten

In the long, narrow, two-foot high wooden box outside the Latimer's kitchen that faced the parade ground, Amelia mixed rich soil gathered from the riverbank. She added silt from a pond with chopped bark, sand and ground limestone. Nose wrinkled, Louise dumped in old horse manure, which was preferred, to enrich the soil. With a spade, Amelia worked the manure into the soil, glad to bury any stink beneath the fresher, earthy fragrances.

Father had detailed one of the soldiers to chaperone herself, Louise, Mary, and Mary's two sons, to gather ingredients. Nevertheless, he and Amelia had said nothing to one another except a polite 'good day to you,' in passing after the disastrous supper. His forcing her to leave the colony was not discussed. She cringed every time she passed him, hoping for some type of reconciliation, understanding.

She and her maid dragged a soldier's canvas tent over the box. "Mary told me to plant the herbs once spring arrives, but the night temperatures can still become frigid." Amelia straightened and brushed off her gloved hands.

"We'll mix in more soil and manure then. And attach cold frames to keep in heat."

Louise swept dirt from her apron and wiped her nose on her sleeve. "Where do we get the cold frames, Miss?"

"Well, the box is part of it. But we'll have to search in town for old windows to make the cover. The glass lets in the sun and keeps out the wind. The windows need to be hinged to the box so they can be easily opened." Amelia put her hands on her hips, smiling at her progress—anxious to achieve progress somewhere.

"Your physic garden is comin' about nicely." Mary stepped up to them. Her two sons trailed behind. The boys, Fergus age nine and Timothy eleven, argued over a feathered shuttlecock. They both waved battledore rackets. She turned to her sons. "Hush now, lads. Go find your sister, who should be watching you, and wash yourselves up for dinner."

The boys scurried off, dodging a soldier.

Seeing Mary always reminded Amelia of their uncomfortable conversation about the enigmatic Mrs. Sutton. Yet the boys brought back that day at the pond, when the Frenchman—the one who'd intervened with the bear—rode by and tipped his hat to her. Her mouth went dry at her foolish thoughts.

A cold gust of wind blew across the parade ground. Amelia shivered in her light linen caraco jacket.

"If you're cold in October, wait until you experience January." Mary laughed, her smile indulgent. "You have that lovely maroon cape, but you'll need to line it with fur. And I know the best place to purchase some. At that trading post a short way out of town, on Grand Bay."

"I'll have to wait until my inheritance arrives. I'd hate to request any money from my father." Amelia's cheeks burned over her discord with Father, and the reason she had her mother's inheritance in the first place. "I asked him about Mrs. Sutton."

"Oh? Begorra. You mentioned Dorothea Sutton to the captain?" Mary hissed. "I should never have told you. Many men have mistresses, and a daughter doesn't question her father over—"

"I'm sure I'd have found out eventually. I realize such relationships are tolerated, but it's not the sort of behaviour a daughter wishes for." Especially if it meant the woman might have influenced an intolerable betrothal. Amelia fought a sigh and ignored the deeper hurt. Could she ever bring up the subject with Father again? She had the need to get away from the fort. "Do you think this post might carry old windows? Do they take credit?"

"Aye, for some customers they do take credit. You're of respectable stock and should expect that courtesy." Mary tapped her chin. "My cousin has a cart. If he's not busy, we can travel out there in a day or two and see about furs and windows."

124

Amelia began to doubt her respectability thanks to her father, but was intrigued to go.

Three days later, Mary's cousin, Seamus, a retired soldier who grumbled about everything, when he spoke at all, drove the cart along the rugged road north of Parr Town and west of the fort. Amelia breathed in the fresh air and piny scents as she crammed on the bench seat with Mary and her cousin. Louise sat in the cart bed.

They travelled through red spruce and balsam fir, past bogs with springy sphagnum moss. A squirrel 'chucked' at them from a branch. Two white-tailed deer leapt off the road into the deeper forest. The shimmering body of Grand Bay spread out to their left.

"Here is where the land widens, after the St. John River meets the Kennebecasis, then the bay narrows to the south at the river gorge before the Bay of Fundy," Mary said.

Soon they approached a string of buildings. One large log dwelling had the words 'Nákúset Trading Post' carved into a long sign that hung over the front door. People gathered outside, wearing fringed buckskin jackets and beaver hats. The men smoked, talked, and two were having an amiable-sounding argument. Whites intermingled with Negroes and the aboriginals who wore colourful leather clothing, their hair pitch-black and expressions sombre.

"That's a Mi'kmaq. They decorate clothes and crafts with dyed porcupine quills," Mary whispered. "Now, over there is a Maliseet. He's wearing a birch bark raincoat and fox skin shoes. They're the two main tribes in the colony. They settled here long before the French."

"Quite pretty and inventive, their clothing," Amelia said, interested in the native people. How had they been treated when the Europeans arrived?

"Damned savages," her cousin growled as if in answer to her thoughts.

"Are they friendly?" Louise asked, hands gripped together.

"Don't worry, you'll be safe, lass." Mary climbed down. "Will you stay with the cart, Seamus?"

"Won't set foot in no Frenchie post," he mumbled.

"Then guard the horse well." Mary rolled her eyes at the women.

Amelia and Louise followed her onto the porch. Amelia smoothed down her plain navy blue dress, the black armband giving her an even more severe look. She studied the decorative quills, reds, greens, blues, woven into animal skin in various patterns on the natives' tunics as the women passed, then they entered the post.

Inside, the smell of new leather, and lavender-perfumed soap, made her smile. Customers milled about, inspecting pots, cloth, guns and tools.

"Mr. Fougère," Mary called to an older man with shaggy, greying hair. "What furs do you have to sell? And give me your best prices. I have a captain's daughter with me."

"Mademoiselle Latimer?" a familiar voice said.

Amelia turned. The younger Frenchman with the black beard stood behind a long table with shelves beneath. Her heart fluttered—an odd reaction.

Louise tugged on her sleeve. "That be him," she whispered.

"How do you do again? Do you work here, sir?" Amelia couldn't remember his last name, since she'd met him in the midst of chaos. She approached the table.

"I own half the place, Mademoiselle." He gave her a slight nod, his brown eyes sparkling.

His handsomeness and direct smile unsettled her. "Do you sell windows? I'm making a cold frame for my physic garden."

He arched a brow. "You don't require a cage for bears, *non*?"

She laughed. Men seldom teased with her, and Amelia liked it, though she should curtail her amusement for propriety's sake. "I hope to never encounter another bear." She glanced at the wall behind him. She needed protection. "May I see one of your flintlock pistols?"

"From windows, which we do not sell, to pistols?" He turned and removed the gun from its display. He faced her again, holding the piece flat in his hands. "Have you ever fired a pistol?"

"No, but I can learn." She raised her chin. "In this country, I believe I should have one."

127

"A smaller weapon might be better for you." He held out the gun. "Feel the weight."

Amelia was surprised he didn't deter her from buying *any* weapon. She took the pistol, cold and heavy, a smooth wooden stock and brass barrel. It would be awkward to wield. "You may be right. Do you have anything smaller?"

He leaned down, picked up a wooden box and placed it on the table. Opening the box, he pulled out a tinier pistol, about five inches long, also with a wooden grip and brass barrel. "This is usually called a Muff Pistol. Ladies carry them concealed in their muffs. Who do you plan to shoot?"

"Anyone who annoys me, I assure you." She'd try a tease. She took the pistol, which was much lighter and shorter, and balanced it in her hands. The Frenchman's scrutiny of her, an interest she'd never experienced before, put her on an edge both uncomfortable and interesting. He had strong, yet clean hands. His mien exhibited a quiet authority—and he owned half this post? She smiled. "What is the gun's price?"

* * *

Gilbert appreciated the mademoiselle's candid manner and humour. She was an unusual woman. "This gun has a removable barrel and can be hazardous to load if you don't know what you're doing."

"I'll find an experienced person to teach me." She traced her long fingers over the pistol.

His chest tightened. For some ridiculous reason he wanted to be that person, but kept that to himself. Her thick hair looked even blonder today, or was it a trick of the light inside the post?

Behind her the young maid glanced about. A native walked past her and she skipped aside. People babbled and shuffled around each other, picking up wares to inspect.

"I thought we were here for fur." A round-faced, red-haired female moved up beside Mademoiselle Latimer. "Why are you holding a gun, my dear?"

Gilbert had seen this woman in here before. She'd also been at the pond with the children. Loud, though friendly, she had a husband who worked at the fort.

"When I hunt for herbs, the pistol will protect me, Mary." Mademoiselle Latimer waved her free hand toward Gilbert. "This is the man who helped me chase away the bear." She looked at him. "And this is Mrs. O'Brien."

"Gilbert Arsenault, at your service." He wondered if Mademoiselle Latimer had forgotten his name. That bothered him, but shouldn't. He also wished Madame O'Brien hadn't interrupted them. "Do you wish to look at furs, too?"

"Mr. Fougère showed me the mink he has, but that's too expensive." Madame O'Brien eyed him shrewdly. "Do you have any rabbit or squirrel?"

"*Mais oui*." Gilbert unlocked the chest behind him and dragged out the rabbit and squirrel pelts. He looked at both women. "What do you plan to do with these?"

"Line my cape. I hear your winters are bone-chilling." Mademoiselle Latimer set down the Muff Pistol, gently, like it was an egg. "And I'll barely survive it. Woe is me."

He chuckled. "Then you'll need several pieces." He spread out the fur, caressing the softness. "I have snowshoe hare, with the summer rusty-brown coat, and red squirrel."

"She'll take the red squirrel," Madame O'Brien said.

"Mary! I'm capable of choosing. Can I put the fur and gun on credit, Mr. Arsenault?" Mademoiselle Latimer's lively blue eyes showed she wasn't as sure of herself now. "I'll be receiving money, soon, I daresay."

"*Bien sûr*. And I'll give you information on where to find cheap windows." Gilbert wanted to bring back her smile, though he was a fool to flirt with an English officer's daughter. He shoved the Muff Pistol back into its box. He hadn't flirted with anyone in years, and this woman was far out of his range.

* * *

130

Amelia swept the broom over the kitchen's stone floor. Mrs. Stuart had cut her finger slicing lamb for the Sunday meal, now to be served after the household had attended the Anglican service at the fort. Amelia advised her to see the fort's surgeon, the cut deep. She'd placed the meat, bread and cheese on the dining room table and then decided to clean up in the cook's absence.

It was the 21st of November, the air during the nights blowing cold. A dusting of snow had fallen.

Amelia had sewn her red squirrel fur into her cape, thinking of Mr. Arsenault as she stitched. He was probably the type of man who showered his charm on every woman he met, especially his post customers to encourage them to buy. She shouldn't make anything out of his attention towards her. Why would a handsome Frenchman be interested in a plain Englishwoman?

She pushed the broom harder, sweeping crumbs and other debris into a pile. Why would a well brought up Englishwoman even consider the attentions of such a man? No matter how few her choices had been so far.

She stepped in front of the low-burning hearth fire and felt the warmth slide up her back. A ship had arrived a week ago and aboard was the money she'd inherited from her mother. She winced again at her loss. However, now she could pay what she owed for the furs, the Muff Pistol, and the windows purchased in town for

131

her cold frame. The money was more than she'd expected.

The house was strangely quiet. Mrs. Fulton had Sundays off, and her father was in his office. They still had exchanged few words.

The kitchen door opened and Mrs. Stuart bustled in, her injured finger bandaged.

"There's a great clamour down in the town. Cries of 'huzzah'. I glanced out the gate and spotted a sloop coming into the harbour. I think our new governor is here."

Amelia stared in wonder. The cook had never spoken this much to her before. A loud boom shook the house. Amelia jumped and set aside the broom. She left the kitchen, grabbed her cape near the front door, and hurried out onto the parade ground. Soldiers were gathering at the gate. The cannon fired again. Smoke drifted on the breeze. She joined the throng. The cannon fired a third time.

Father also left their quarters and the men parted to let him by and through the gate. Other officers followed. He stood on the edge of the knoll and raised a telescope. Amelia rushed to stand beside him.

The fort's cannon kept firing, and she put her hands over her ears, coughing in the acrid gunpowder smoke. Out in the harbour a ship sailed towards them, skimming over the grey water.

"It's the *Ranger*. Governor Carleton should be aboard. He's been in Halifax, talking to

Parr." Father lowered the telescope, then handed it to her like a peace offering.

Amelia almost smiled. She put the instrument to her eye, the sloop coming into clear focus. Two masts with billowing sails guided by a pilot boat. Cannon continued to fire. The knoll seemed to vibrate.

The cannon finally stopped after seventeen shots. People below were shouting. "Long live the King and the Governor!"

"Leonard House, the corner of Dock and Union Streets, is readied for the governor. He'll live in fine style." Father retrieved his telescope, but didn't look at her. "Still, Carleton will have to deal with a dire situation. There are reports of starvation in the outlying settlements."

"How will they feed—"

"Carleton may rearrange everything here at the fort. I pray I'm not transferred once the disbanded officers are settled." He turned and walked back through the gate.

"Transferred?" Amelia would have to go with him. Alarm slithered through her. She wrapped her cape close, the fur pressed snug against her body, and stayed where she was. She watched the sloop prepare to dock. Notions of mistresses and a dark-eyed Frenchman filtered about in her head along with this new worry. The wind slapped tendrils of hair into her face.

Chapter Eleven

Gilbert locked up the post and turned to Fougère. They hesitated on the porch in the chilling air. He blew out his breath. "Did you hear that Englishman? They're still arguing over the separation of this colony in Halifax. Sending complaints to London to change the boundaries again."

"I'm not surprised. With the split, many lost lucrative land and cattle that's included on our side." Fougère slipped out a native-made pipe from inside his coat and stuffed the stone bowl with tobacco from a pouch.

"I'm not certain we Acadians have a side, *mon ami*. The British government is also confiscating neglected or uninhabited territory." Gilbert rubbed the back of his stiffening neck. He wanted to feel safe, but with his deed still unregistered, he didn't. He had one year to register his claim in New Brunswick—but would the new government consider it legal?

He'd asked around about Franklyn Oram, but no one knew, or were unsure, who he was, except the man standing before him. "You're positive you have no idea where Oram went?"

"I remember him coming to the post, many times, years ago. He seemed, I don't know, scattered in his thoughts. Who can say what happened to such a peculiar man?" Fougère pulled out a pocket tinder box, struck steel to flint, sparked a char cloth, and lit his pipe. "I'll ask a few old timers like me if they know anything."

"That's what worries me. Even I thought Oram was foggy in the head." Gilbert tugged at his beard. "The authorities might use that as another excuse to repossess my property. The seller wasn't in sound mind."

"I won't say a word about the man's bizarre character." Fougère puffed and blew smoke out his nostrils. "Have you located the witnesses?"

"One is dead, sad to say." Gilbert sniffed the sweet scent of sizzling tobacco—though smoking was a habit he'd avoided. His frustration dug deep. "The other, a man named Sterling, moved up to Lower Canada I was told." That territory comprised a long strip of land far to their north.

"Sorry to hear it. Life is a steep mountain for us. We must keep climbing." Fougère sucked on the wooden stem. More smoke swirled up like a smouldering ribbon. "What will you do?"

"I might have to ride up there to find him." Gilbert gritted his teeth. He'd fight this no matter the consequences. Steep mountain was true. Hands fisted, he'd learned perseverance at an early age.

135

"Stop at Ste. Anne's Point to see what they plan. The new governor is definitely developing his capital there. They're calling it Osnaburg, in honour of George III's second son, the Bishop of Osnaburg, an English merchant said." Fougère scoffed. "Are we ruled by the British or the Germans?"

The sun dropped low, the night encroaching. The landscape blurred, draped in shades of browns and greys.

"We shouldn't be ruled by anyone but ourselves. The English won't do much at Ste. Anne's until spring." Thankful for his thick leather coat, Gilbert watched his breath mist as the cold increased. He should head for home, but didn't feel like being alone. "That area is full of half-pay troops. I guess Carleton will feel protected with them around him."

He suddenly wondered if Mademoiselle Latimer had found an expert to teach her how to fire the little pistol. Or if she traipsed into the woods with only that gun for defence, unaware how to use it. He shook his head over something that should be none of his concern.

"At least the English sent food from the Royal stores to feed people after the poor crops this year." Fougère shrugged and puffed more on his pipe.

"That proves no one is all bad, I suppose. There must be decent Englishmen." Gilbert admitted that grudgingly. "Will different nations ever live together here without rancour?"

"Someone always wants to be, how you say, the dog in lead, *non*? Let's just hope our landlord, or whoever takes over the deed, keeps fair." Fougère nudged Gilbert's arm. "On another subject, who was that tall blondish-haired woman you were speaking with days ago?" He grinned slyly. "I haven't seen you smile like that in a long time."

Heat rose in Gilbert's chest. "A British captain's daughter. She's an interesting woman." He stepped to the end of the porch. "But she's out of my league, *mon ami*." Regret over that weighed him down—and that response surprised him.

"I understand." Fougère hunched in his coat. "More snow is coming. A long winter. My bones never lie. I'm off to bed." Fougère lived with his Mi'kmaq wife in one of the small cottages close by. The English frowned on their union, but the old Acadian hardly cared.

Wishing he had a warm body to go home to, Gilbert dashed away thoughts of Mademoiselle Latimer, said good night and mounted his horse. Should he find himself a native mistress, or wife? The idea did not appeal. Still, he needed to open himself up to the possibility—he'd been alone too long.

He rode away through the lengthening shadows. Not far from the post, into the thick foliage, he heard the chirps and mournful night calls of animals.

Dry leaves crunched, heavily. A horse's steps? Slow and deliberate. A chill crept up his back. Was someone following him? The scoundrel who shot at him before? He gripped one hand on his pistol. He reined in Vaillant, who snorted then sucked air into his large nostrils as if sniffing the air like a dog.

Another crunch off to his right. He stiffened in the saddle. It could be a cougar, stalking them, but they usually crawled through the trees.

"Is anyone there?" Gilbert asked in a stern voice. The sunlight faded, the forest gloom pressing around him. A barred owl made an eerie hoot. He nudged his horse forward. No similar sounds followed.

"Ah, perhaps it was only a forest beast," he whispered, hurrying Vaillant through the woods before they'd be enveloped in darkness.

* * *

While Mary and Louise picked through items in cupboards at the post, Amelia approached the long counter where Mr. Arsenault stood setting out baskets. Outside, a light snow started to fall. Flakes sprinkled and glistened like crystal on the windows.

"Mr. Arsenault, I've come to pay my bill as I promised I would." She reached through her skirt slit, into the pockets tied around her waist. Pulling out several coins, she laid them on the counter with a click.

"*Bon jour*, Mademoiselle Latimer." His eyes lit up, but it must have been for the money. "I'm pleased to see you. You brighten my post. Have you learned to fire the Muff Pistol?"

He was charming, nevertheless she grew irritated. The off-balanced feeling unnerved her. "Not yet, but I'll find someone to teach me, soon." She didn't know who to ask other than her father, which discouraged her. Father would disapprove and refuse anyway. She touched the tight weave of one of the light-coloured baskets. "These are beautiful."

"The Malècite, or in their own language *Wolastoqiyik,* make them from birch bark. They add accents of sweet-grass and spruce root. This one has brown ash." He indicated the darker design low on the basket, almost like a checkerboard pattern. "These native people once flourished at the river mouth here on the bay."

"They're lovely, so intricate. Such talent." She touched the dark squares, very aware of every motion she made. His telling her of the local history intrigued her. The information was obvious—the English had overtaken the tribe's territory. "How is your arm? Healed, I hope."

"Much healed, thank you for asking." He rubbed his arm slowly, glanced away then gazed back. "Would you like me to teach you to fire the pistol?"

Her stomach twinged in disbelief mixed with curiosity. "I...how would you make the time?" She needed an excuse, though his offer drew her more than she should allow. "Why would you feel the need to be so—helpful?"

"I don't wish to see you shoot your hand off." His smile looked sincere. "Since I sold the gun to you…"

"You feel responsible, I see." That at least made sense to her. She had the sudden urge to encourage him. "If you aren't too busy, some day, perhaps."

He cocked his head, his grin now mischievous. "How about tomorrow? In the hills behind the fort, not too far out, around three of the clock?"

Staggered by the quickness, Amelia faltered. Her pulse jumped. Hopefully he didn't consider her a woman of loose character since she was picking herbs that day without proper supervision. "With my maid by my side, of course." The words came out of their own accord. She still sought adventure, but must not act overly reckless again. She did need to learn how to handle the gun even if his presence unsettled her. "I suppose I might be available for a serious lesson."

"Mr. Arsenault." A tall, thin young man in a prissy wig walked up to the counter. His cheeks were scarred with pox, his nose long and pointy. He was dressed in fine wool, a dark brown cape and frock coat and nankeen breeches. "I'm Mr. Jarvis, if you recall."

Mr. Arsenault stiffened, his mouth tight. He obviously disliked this man. "What may I do for you, *Monsieur* Jarvis?" he asked in a cold tone.

140

Normally, Amelia would have excused herself and left them to talk. Instead she slid about two feet to the side, speculating on what this dandy was up to. Why she cared, she couldn't say. She dragged over a basket and pretended to inspect it.

Jarvis gave her a surly look, then he turned to the Frenchman. "I've heard from the man who owns this property. He will sell it to me, if I wish."

"Then you will own land with a fine trading post that has done decent business for many years." Mr. Arsenault smiled, though now it looked forced.

Amelia turned the basket to inspect the other side. People milled about the post in scents of perfume, old leather and sweat. They conversed in different languages, some haggling for price with the older partner. Louise and Mary examined a swatch of cloth.

"I may raise the rent on this land. It is valuable, being here on the bay, close to Parr Town." Jarvis smirked, hands on his skinny hips.

Amelia bristled at his swaggering attitude.

"Are you in touch with Monsieur Wilcox?" Mr. Arsenault crossed his arms, his eyes narrowed. "Are you his client who is interested in this property?"

"Yes. Wilcox is my agent." Jarvis gave a slick smile. "I know he's spoken to you, at my behest."

"Why raise the rent and cut into the profit of folk who aren't rich?" Amelia couldn't help but ask, her annoyance growing. She couldn't stand people who were arrogant braggarts, but should she involve herself? "You look like you don't need the money, Mr. Jarvis."

Jarvis' mouth gaped, his pointy nose stabbing forward. "Who are you to address me in such a way, Madam? We have not been introduced. Besides, women should never meddle in men's business."

Amelia swallowed her affronted retort. If she had been a pretty woman she was certain she'd have received a more gallant response. Then again, in this man's case, perhaps not.

Mr. Arsenault seemed to fight a smile, before he gave Jarvis an assessing stare. "Monsieur Jarvis, when you can show me the deed for this land my post sits on, then we can discuss the rent, along with my partner, Monsieur Fougère."

"The transaction will take time due to the landlord being in England. I await his legal consent. I wanted you to be aware of my intentions." Jarvis glared at them both in turn, then he spun about on his patent leather shoes and departed the post like an offended child.

"There's a disagreeable man." Amelia stroked the basket. "I guess I should have stayed quiet." She wouldn't be presumptuous enough to ask if the Frenchman could afford a raised rent.

"You're not afraid to speak your mind. I wish we could converse further, but I must get back to work." He pulled out two more baskets and set them on the counter top. "I will see you tomorrow at three, Mademoiselle. Watch the surroundings carefully, though the bears should be in hibernation."

"Very well." Amelia nodded, wishing she wasn't looking forward to their meeting quite so much. She shouldn't let this man, a simple trader, affect her. "By the by, I'll purchase this basket."

* * *

Gilbert nudged Vaillant forward past the looming fort, the fortress's shadow cutting a dark swath across the land.

Why had he offered his services and set up this meeting? Nothing good could come of it. He shouldn't encourage a friendship with the captain's daughter, it would only compromise her.

The wind rustled through the pines in the crisp, cold air. He perused the area, ever vigilant for the man who'd recently threatened him and, he was certain, tried to kill him.

Mademoiselle Latimer and her maid waited in the once tall grass, now matted down by frost. Both of them were wrapped in capes, their hoods pulled up. The girl held the wooden box the pistol came in.

Gilbert dismounted and approached them. "*Bonjour*, ladies." He tipped his hat.

"Good day to you, Mr. Arsenault." Mademoiselle Latimer smiled and pulled the pistol from her muff. "I thought I'd put the Muff Pistol to its original purpose."

He chuckled, happy to be in her company, though disturbed that she had this tug on him. He took and examined the small gun, then got right to business. "First, let me show you the trigger mechanism. This lever is called the sear and the trigger lowers from here. Engage the sear to keep the trigger in half-cock. That will keep the pistol from going off unexpectedly." He caught her eager face, then stared at the weapon again. "When you're ready to shoot, you pull to full cock and the hammer forces the trigger down. The sear and trigger are locked together, and pulling the trigger releases the sear. Now the pistol will fire." He fingered the metal pieces gently as he glanced up. "No one has loaded this, have they?" At her head shake, he pointed the barrel at the woods and pulled the trigger. The gun clicked. He handed the pistol to her. "You try it, and always treat the pistol with caution."

She didn't hesitate, which impressed him. Arm extended, she pulled the trigger.

"*Bon*. Now we'll load it. Observe closely." Gilbert went to the maid, and took the box, which contained balls, flints, a powder flask and cleaning rod. The girl smiled, as if relieved to be rid of her burden.

Setting the box on the ground, he crouched, unscrewed the pistol barrel, and inserted only seven grains of the acrid powder into a chamber behind the threads. He placed a ball over the powder. "Now I *very* gently re-screw the barrel. If any powder residue is left on the threads, the stuff could ignite and the gun may explode. So clean these threads with a cloth after each use."

"Oh, my, that does sound dangerous. But pistols aren't toys, are they?" Mademoiselle Latimer rubbed her gloved hands together. The cold pinked her cheeks attractively. "I don't know how many people or beasts I'll have the need to shoot, yet."

"Be aware, this little gun won't stop a large animal, though the noise might." Gilbert hid his amusement, half-cocked the weapon and stood. "Please make certain you clean this pistol, care for it diligently, so you don't get hurt." This time instead of handing her the gun, he stepped behind her, put his arms around her and pressed her finger on the trigger. She felt warm against his body. Her hair smelled flowery. "Use both hands and be prepared for a slight kick-back."

She quivered under his touch. "All right. I'm ready." Her voice trembled, then she straightened her arms and pulled the trigger. Smoke puffed out and the bang echoed around them.

The maid had crushed her hands over her ears. Mademoiselle Latimer gasped and slipped back, deeper into his arms. Gilbert released her as a heated thrill wriggled through him. He shouldn't have held her, but he'd meant it for support—hadn't he?

* * *

Amelia hissed in her breath. When the gun kicked-back, she'd pressed against Mr. Arsenault. In the pungent smoke and gunpowder smell drifting around her, her pulse spiked and she'd experienced the strangest sensation. A spark that had nothing to do with the pistol, now hot in her hand.

Gun lowered, she turned to face him. His eyes were shining on hers. Were they attracted to one another? Impossible!

"You did quite well, Mademoiselle Latimer." His voice sounded strained. He retrieved the pistol, crouched, unscrewed the barrel, and wiped a cloth over the threads. He replaced the gun in the box. "Every time you use the weapon, don't forget to clean the threads."

"I won't, I promise." His officious words disappointed her. Had she only imagined his interest? She knew it was wrong to even long for this man's attention.

He stood and handed the box back to Louise, now not meeting Amelia's gaze.

"Good firin', Miss. La, it were loud."
Louise held the box away from her body as if it
might explode. Brow knitted, her eyes switched
from the Frenchman to Amelia, and back.

"I'll walk you to the knoll's road."
Arsenault grabbed his horse's reins, and they
moved in that direction. The buckskin stallion
snorted, mist rising from its flared nostrils.

At the foot of the knoll, Arsenault turned to
Amelia. "Why have you travelled all the way to
our remote colony, if I may ask?"

Taken aback by his question, she paused.
The excitement of shooting was overcome by
the odd titillation of being near him. He
appeared as uncomfortable as she was. "I came
at the request of my father who…desired a
marriage between one of his lieutenants and me.
I didn't care for the man, so turned him down."

He raised a brow. "But you've decided to
stay, *est-ce vrai*?"

"Since I learned of my mother's death, I
saw no reason to return to England." Unless her
father was transferred. How could she refuse to
accompany him? Where would they end up? Ice
formed on her spine at the possibility of leaving
New Brunswick; she stared at the man before
her. She'd been honest, now she yearned for
information from Mr. Arsenault, or perchance to
detain him. "I'm certain you'll think me rude,
and I have been lately, but why are you not
married, or are you?"

"You sound like my mother, as bold as she
is." He half-smiled. Then his expression

147

darkened. "My fiancée died over three years ago, from cholera." He tipped his hat. "I'll bid you *adieu*. Be safe with the gun."

That sounded final. Her stomach dipped. "I'm sorry about your fiancée. Thank you for your instruction. Mayhap…I'll see you at the post."

His eyes softened. "If God wills it, Mademoiselle." He nodded, and waited, his gaze traveling up the knoll.

"Come, Louise." Amelia put her hand on the girl's shoulder. They walked up the incline. Amelia resisted looking back. He was right to discourage any over-friendliness. They were too different, in religion—she assumed he was Catholic—nationality, and position. Or she just wasn't beautiful enough for him.

Halfway up the road, Louise whispered, "That Frenchie be smitten with you, Miss."

"Oh, hush now." Amelia felt a rush of pleasure, then shoved it down. "I'm sure you're mistaken."

With a quick glance to observe Mr. Arsenault riding away, Amelia greeted the guard and they entered the fort. Sadness seeped into her. Her limbs felt heavy. The two of them skirted the fort's activity, including a farrier shoeing horses, and headed for the Latimer quarters.

Amelia's heart jolted. Lt. Harris stood in front of Father's home, observing her, closely, brow deeply creased. Had he seen her with the Frenchman?

148

Chapter Twelve

Gilbert sighed and stoked up the fire in his cabin's hearth, the scent of ash wood smoke like a tonic. Still, his childhood memories around campfires—when the Acadians gathered together and swore to remain strong and united—couldn't dilute his worries.

He grimaced. First, he had to forget *her*, that outspoken, remarkable Englishwoman—the clever, blue-eyed lady who made him smile. There was no place for her in his life, but more so, no place for him in hers.

Miss Latimer liked him, he saw it in her face. However, such an attraction would do neither of them any good. She'd turned down an officer, but no doubt would find another one of rank to marry.

Pouring himself a glass of whisky, he took a gulp to coat his sorrow, his sense of being too alone. The oaky-flavoured liquid burned his throat. Just his luck, the second woman to pull at his heart was far out of his reach, lost in the English's strict sense of propriety.

He'd vowed to open up his heart after Maman's urging, but any female would be a distraction in the midst of his current problems.

Women. He'd taken comfort now and then from native women who were happy to be paid for their compliance. Most were fatherless, or husbandless, after the war, and in dire straits. At the time, and most especially now, those actions shamed him.

He sat in the chair by the hearth, the flames soon toasting his knees. Head rested against the chair's hard back, he held the smooth glass on his thigh. The green calico curtains, sewn by Maman, were closed, but he knew darkness pressed around him. A wolf howled not too far off—sounding lonely, too.

Gilbert took another sip. He still needed to locate Franklyn Oram. He'd ride to Parr Town in the morning and consult with Mr. Johnson. The lawyer might assist him in this search. Johnson had been away in Halifax when Gilbert returned from Nova Scotia after the Registrar rejected his petition. They must have just missed each other.

The single candle on a table near his elbow flickered. The hearth fire warmed his face. He finished the whisky, set the glass on the table and closed his eyes.

Almost dozed off, he jerked upright at a noise. In the narrow stable attached to the outside wall of his cabin, his horse thumped his hooves against his stall. Vaillant neighed, thumping again, in obvious distress.

Gilbert hopped up, pulled on his jacket and grabbed his musket. He crept to the wall. Loud shuffling noises came from the stable. He retreated to the back door, opened it slowly, and slipped outside into the pitch-black darkness.

His breath misted in the cold as he felt his way around the splintery wood at the rear of the log stable.

Grunts and snickers came from the cabin's front. Sounds he'd never heard his horse—or any horse—make. Gilbert clenched his teeth, raised the musket and stole along the side wall. When he reached the corner, he peered around and yelled out, "Who is there? *Vous arrêtez!*"

In the shadows, a man backed out of the open stable door. He weaved, slightly discernible in the glow from the candle and hearth fire inside the cabin that filtered through the curtain. Clouds parted and the moon shed more light. The intruder wore a beaver hat and smelled as if he'd bathed in rum.

"I warn you, I have a loaded gun, so don't try anything you'll regret." Gilbert clutched the stock. "What are you doing in my stable with my horse?"

The man laughed in a drunken bray. "I was but teasin' this fine beast. I'd do well with such an animal as mine. I should take him."

His voice sounded familiar—and that ratty beaver hat.

"Don't ever touch my stallion. You're Bent, aren't you?" Gilbert gripped the musket tighter, his anger rising. He'd suspected this so-called guide of Mr. Wilcox of trying to kill him out on the road. "What do you want with me, Monsieur?"

"I intend to have your parcel on the river," Bent slurred, guffawing.

Gilbert's hackles rose higher. He stared down his musket barrel. "Why do you think you're entitled to it?"

"I'm British. All this land should belong to us." Bent thrust his arms up and waved them—a shadowed parody of a lunatic bird.

"You are drunk, *stupidement*. You better not have harmed my horse." Gilbert stepped closer, shoulders stiff as granite. "And if you dare try to shoot at me again, I'll kill you." If he wasn't murdered himself. Why was this rogue so set on the land on the river? He doubted he'd get a coherent answer with Bent in this condition, but he tried. "Explain to me why that piece of land is so important to you."

"It's because my fam… None of your bloody business." Bent swung a fist toward Gilbert, but he appeared to carry no weapon. The rascal was inebriated beyond sense. Was he in league with Wilcox, trying to intimidate him?

Gilbert lowered the musket. "What did you plan to do by coming here? Go home and sober up, then we'll speak again."

Bent raised both fists. "Too cowardly to fight with me, Frenchie?" The man lunged around the musket. His knuckles clipped Gilbert's jaw.

The pain was light, a sting, and Gilbert refused to shoot an unarmed man. He shifted the musket and punched Bent on the chin with his fist. The man staggered, swung back and caught

Gilbert on the bone to the right of his eye socket.

A jar of pain shot through his sinuses. Gilbert shoved the fool to the ground. He poked the musket barrel into Bent's skinny neck. His finger tugged on the cold trigger. "I'll blow off your head if you set foot near my cabin again, or the land on the river, and I won't ask questions. Now leave my property, *sur l'heure!*"

Bent scooted back in the dirt. Then he stumbled to his feet. "Beware, Frenchman, I'll get what I want, what's mine, by any means." He jabbed a finger, spun around, and almost fell again.

"Did you shoot at me in the woods earlier?"

"Eh? Was you skeered?" he mumbled as he staggered through the clearing. "I *am* in my rights, you'll find out." It was impossible to tell if he limped from Gilbert's previous shot.

Gilbert hurried to check the welfare of his horse. The stallion acted skittish, but after he checked the animal's head and body, calmed with a few words, the horse appeared fine. Confusion, wrath, and fear for his mother coursed through him. He massaged his throbbing eye—he must warn her.

* * *

"Good afternoon, Miss Latimer." Lt. Harris bowed his head as Amelia approached her

153

father's quarters off the parade ground, Louise behind her with the gun box.

"Lt. Harris." She wrapped her cape close around her. She hadn't seen him in three months, except for a glimpse now and then around the fort. "I apologize for not telling you personally that I can't accept your proposal."

"That's what I wish to discuss with you." His gaze remained cool, his words stilted. "Could we speak in private?"

Amelia bristled at being ambushed. He could have sent a note. "I don't see what we need to discuss," she said as politely as possible, though anxious to leave his company.

"I realize I wasn't...fair to you the first time we met." He sounded rehearsed, still inflexible.

"You insulted me, sir." Her affront resurfaced, which she wished to have concealed. "I'd come all this way, and you treated me heartlessly."

Louise hovered beside her, her gaze wary on the lieutenant as if he were a growling bear.

"I'm aware of that. My rudeness." There was still no benevolence in his grey eyes.

A unit of soldiers marched by. Drill commands shouted by an officer echoed off the buildings and palisade.

"If this is your apology, I'll accept it. Now, please excuse us." Amelia moved to step past him, wanting nothing more to do with him.

"Miss Latimer, I'd like you to give me a second chance. If you would be so generous."

154

He touched a finger to his hat and still sounded stiff, like a bad actor in a cheap play.

Stunned, Amelia gathered her wits. How could he think she'd reconsider? That was the last thing she wanted.

Louise gulped loudly, and the box rattled in her hands.

"I'm sorry. I haven't changed my mind." Her experience with Gilbert, the warmth she'd felt, was not at all present when near this man. Harris gave her the chills. "We do not suit, sir."

A young soldier skulked by them. He saluted Harris, but kept his head low. He knocked on her father's door, handed something to the housekeeper when she opened it, then scurried off.

Amelia stared after the lad in curiosity.

Harris grimaced and cleared his throat. "May we take tea some afternoon, to talk further, Miss Latimer?"

Even if she couldn't have Gilbert—and when had she thought of him in such intimate terms?—she *didn't* want John Harris. But she felt trapped into accommodating him, to a tiny degree. "Very well. Some afternoon we'll have tea." A discourse to prove they were incompatible. She took a step to slip by him. "Now, I really must go."

"Is tomorrow afternoon satisfactory?" He appeared to attempt a smile.

She stifled a groan. "Not really. That's quite inconvenient. Day after tomorrow is better. Around four. Good day, sir."

Entering the house with Louise, Amelia blew out her breath. "I cannot believe this. Father must have put him up to it. Why has he waited all this time?"

"Oh, Miss, what will you do about the lieutenant?" Louise held the box in front of her as if desperate for Amelia to take it.

"Turn him down, of course. But Father will be even angrier." Another trial. Throat tightening, she remained uncomfortable with her father—and wanted his admission of an entanglement with Harris' sister. Regardless, they still needed to heal their relationship.

She moved to the stairs. Hand gripped on the newel post, she closed her eyes and relived Gilbert's touch when he'd held her. His name was pronounced *zheel-BAIR,* as she'd heard at the post. The sound was poetic.

More heat and bewilderment trickled through her body. Society was too narrow-minded. But for a woman unused to the feeling of 'attraction' she might be confusing the signs.

"Amelia!" Father's sharp voice cut through the air from the parlour.

She turned to her maid and whispered, "Quickly, hide the box upstairs."

"Aye, Miss." Louise tromped up the steps, skirt swishing. The box bumped on her knees.

Amelia calmed her breathing, patted down her gown, and entered the parlour with an impassive expression. "Yes, Father? Did you need me for something?"

The captain stood behind his desk, his face in a thunderous scowl. "I've just received a disturbing report." He waved a folded piece of paper. "You were seen in the hills with a man, who by his manner of dress is either a woodsman or a Frenchman. What have you to say about that?"

The young soldier! Father had someone spying on her. Fury tumbled through her. She had to be honest to keep from erring. "He's a trader, a merchant, and was showing me how to fire the pistol I bought from him."

"Without a proper escort? And what are you doing owning and learning to fire a gun?" Father stepped around his desk, his hands fisted. "This is beyond unseemly behaviour."

"Everything was proper. You don't need to have people watching me." Amelia wanted to say her father had some nerve mentioning 'unseemly behaviour', though men were given more latitude in their actions. She huffed her annoyance. "I'm still decent, and Louise was beside me. About the gun—"

"You won't be perceived as such. Reputation matters. I warned you about hoydenish conduct. You are far too old to act like this. In the spring I might have to send you home." He scrutinized her, the lines around his eyes deeper. "And what have you done to your hair?"

Amelia's fingers went to her head, touching the soft, loose tendrils. He'd only just noticed? She bit back her ire at being spoken to like a child. And he was *not* sending her home. "I used a special hair wash."

"Are you trying to look *fast*, my dear? It won't do at all." He shook his head, his neck reddening like a rash.

Amelia gulped back a retort- *fast, like your mistress?*

Father pointed a finger close to her nose. "From now on you will not leave the fort without a proper male escort, approved by me. I forbid it."

Chapter Thirteen

Gilbert paced his mother's kitchen where afternoon light spilled through the front windows. He pressed his fingers on the back of his neck. "I will find out who this scoundrel Bent is." He touched the sore welt beside his eye and winced. "He won't get away with threatening me, abusing me and my horse. He's a quarrelsome, drunk of a man."

Marie-Cateline sat before the sizzling fire. "I hope you gave him worse than your black and purple eye, *mon fils*. I'm relieved he had no weapon." She sewed the seams on a shirt, her needle diving in and out of the fabric with expertise. "Why does he think he has any right to my, to *our* property?"

Gilbert scratched near his injured eye. To calm himself, he inhaled the scent of *Il fait des yeux,* the buckwheat flatbread she'd cooked up in her greased iron skillet. "I'm riding to Parr Town after I leave here, to locate Mr. Wilcox. I'm hoping he knows something of the guide he hired." He tore off a piece of the bubbled bread, savouring the crisp, bitter-grain edge. "Unless he sent the fool to menace me in the first place."

"Anything wicked the English do would not surprise me." Her hands stilled. "What are you doing to clear up the mistake of the deed?" She stared up, her study of his bruised face sympathetic.

"I'm also stopping in to ask Mr. Johnson for advice in finding Mr. Oram." He frowned. What if Oram were out of the country or even dead? He couldn't allow his mother to be kicked off her land—a repeat of the past. "Now watch out for strange activity, as I said. Keep your blunderbuss loaded, listen for suspicious sounds. I don't trust Bent not to sneak around here as he did my cabin."

"I will enjoy shooting him, since he could have done terrible harm to you." She returned to her sewing. "Don't worry, I'm always wary of my surroundings. You should know better than anyone that I've lived most of my life that way."

And living unprotected these later years, he didn't say. He wondered, not for the first time, why his attractive mother with her ebony hair and kittenish face never married. Did the other Acadians shun her for what had happened with the soldier? The brutal rape was not her fault. She'd barely been fifteen years old. Of course, the soldier had never been punished. Gilbert ripped off another piece of flatbread, though now it tasted like bland paper.

"I'm off now. Take care, stay alert, as you claim you do, *Maman*." He might insist on sleeping here at night until he'd located Bent—though his mother would refuse the offer.

"You keep safe, too. I never wish to lose you." She nodded, eyes sharp, then lowered her head over her work, needle flying. He kissed her cheek and left.

Two schooners sailed up the river. Gilbert glanced north and thought of the new village of Kingston, which had formed near the portage between the Kennebecasis and Saint John Rivers, about twelve miles away. A place, it was reported, that could become a main stopping point between the Bay of Fundy and the new capital. He prayed having so many British Loyalists passing by his mother's cabin wouldn't cause more problems.

In Parr Town, at the corner of Market Square and King Street, the main road through town, Gilbert tied his horse to a hitching post. A two-storey, long, wooden building, newly built by Loyalists, loomed before him. Named The Coffee House, the newcomers gathered here for comradery and to conduct their sordid business.

If Wilcox wasn't here, someone might know his whereabouts. Then he'd walk over to see Mr. Johnson.

A shop occupied the ground floor. Gilbert climbed an outside flight of stairs to the first floor, where the aroma of coffee drifted out, along with men's chatter. He entered the spacious coffee room. Smoke drifted around the pipe puffers who sat at tables, discussing events, or reading newspapers. Bewigged patrons nodded and gestured, sipping from their mugs.

Two men sneered at Gilbert as if he didn't belong—which he didn't. The room was packed with the English, most influential merchants and others of lofty status, forced to flee America. They looked like a disgruntled group with their frowns and sharp tones. Who would bother to help him?

His jaw tightened. He wore his finest clothing today, no buckskins, but a plain brown frock coat and unstained black breeches. However, his boots were old, scuffed, a new pair too expensive. His beard also picked him out as a woodsman.

Gilbert took a measured breath and passed the bubbling coffee cauldron that sat on a counter, where a short, fat fellow ladled the brew into tall, porcelain cans.

A huge fire burned in an expansive hearth on the back wall, adding to the smokiness. These Loyalists complained about their predicament, yet they'd built this grand establishment, which included bed chambers and an assembly room.

He spotted Wilcox in the right-hand corner conversing with another man.

Gilbert approached their table. He had to secure this man's cooperation. "Good afternoon, Monsieur Wilcox. I would like to speak with you."

The agent stood, his gaze surprised, and a little uneasy. His maroon frock coat was finely cut over his stocky form. Yellowish coloured breeches of cotton nankeen hugged his bulky

162

thighs. "Mr. Arsenault." He signalled to his friend, who left them without a word. "Have a seat. What may I do for you? What happened to your eye?"

Gilbert hadn't been introduced to the other man, which reinforced his idea of low status. He sucked back his offence and sat across the table from Wilcox. "My eye? An accident. What I want is to know more about this man Bent you hired as a scout. Are you still in touch with him?"

"Thank goodness, no. He was a bounder, and too fond of the sauce." Wilcox took a sip from his coffee can. "Would you care for a mug?" The black brew looked gritty and thick, smelling almost of soot.

"No, *merci*, I can't stay long." Gilbert placed his arms on the table, hands gripped. "How did you meet him?"

"He approached me. By the way, how is your mother?" A slight smile curved Wilcox's lips. "Still poking guns out of windows?"

"She is well, and armed, as you know." Gilbert shifted on the hard bench. "Are you, or rather Mr. Jarvis, interested in my land on the river, or the property on the bay where my post is?" Either loss would put him in a precarious position. He *must* find Oram.

"The trading post property is what I'm involved in. Mr. Jarvis has been in correspondence with the absentee landlord in London. A transfer could be forthcoming." Wilcox sounded evasive. He glanced around the

163

room, as if looking for rescue. "The young pup is fortunate he has funds, when many Loyalists have come here without a shilling."

"I know well the struggle for money. Back to the man called Bent." Gilbert squeezed his hands tighter. He had to talk loudly to be heard above the other discussions. "Did you send him to harass me at my cabin?"

Wilcox's brows jerked high. "You wound me, sir. I'm sorry I ever dealt with the jackanapes in the first place. He harassed you?"

"Threatened me." Gilbert, for some reason, wanted to believe this agent. "Do you know Bent's full name? Did someone recommend him to you, Monsieur?"

"Like I said, he contacted me after I'd asked around for a guide to show me up the peninsula." Wilcox leaned back. "I thought he looked...rather sinister, untrustworthy, and I never learned his full name. But he said he had ties to that property where your mother lives."

Gilbert's nape prickled. "Did he say what sort of ties?"

Wilcox flicked a finger on the side of his grey wig. "Only something about his family owning the land first."

Gilbert stood, to contain the astonishment that sliced through him. "*Ma foi*, do you know how I might find him?"

* * *

164

Amelia struck her fist on the mattress as she sat on the edge of the bed, her bottom lip between her teeth. She bit down hard then released her flesh at the sting. Forbidden to leave the fort without an 'approved' escort?

"Father accuses me of looking 'fast.' I'm curious to see what this Mrs. Sutton looks like. I wish he'd be honest with me concerning her."

"What if they are but friends?" Louise asked.

"If only that was the extent of it." Could she still hope? Amelia kicked off her half-boots before Louise helped her to remove them. "He can't stop me from leaving the fort, I am of age. But since I live in his house he could make my life even more difficult. And he's right, unfortunately. For unmarried women especially, reputation does matter."

Louise retrieved the boots from across the room. "Captain Latimer really threatened to send you home when spring comes?"

"He did. I loathe dishonesty, but I need to sneak around Father." Amelia rubbed her temples, her thoughts skipping in and out of frantic places. "I must act obedient while I think of what to do."

"And Lt. Harris be comin' for tea tomorrow." Louise placed the boots beside the clothes press, shaking her head.

"Oh, don't remind me." Amelia dragged her fingers through her hair, pulling it free from the pins. The flicks of pain redirected her remorse at inviting him. Men's demands crowded in on her! "I must have a plan to be rid of Harris. Without being rude, of course, since I'm a well-bred young lady." She said the last flippantly. "I wish women weren't expected to marry, and there weren't so many rules to follow."

"Aye, Miss. Even the likes of me have rules." Louise half-smiled. She picked up Amelia's brush. "In our large family, nine children, we had to behave so's not to overrun the cottage, nor waste the food. Everyone had to work since they was mites, to help out our mam and father."

"Of course you did. And you had to be of good character, or you couldn't be a lady's maid." Amelia waved the brush aside and patted the place beside her. Louise hesitated, then sat. She smelled slightly of gunpowder, as did Amelia. "If I ever treat you less than kindly, please let me know. Such as my flinging clothes or shoes around like a spoiled child."

Louise laughed. "You have a strong mind, Miss. Are you certain you couldn't tame Lt. Harris into bein' a good husband?"

"I'm afraid he's too sour and fermented beyond my talents." Amelia sighed and plucked at her counterpane. "If I married him, he'd be stricter than Father. He'd probably wrest control over my inheritance. Not to mention we'd have to be…intimate. I just don't care for him." She quivered and hunched forward. Gil—Mr. Arsenault's face again entered her thoughts. Father would never consider an Acadian as a

166

husband, and, of course, why would the man ask her? Why was she so drawn to him?

After glancing at the Maliseet basket on her chest of drawers, she turned quickly to Louise to change the direction of her musings. "Do you miss your family? Would you rather return to England?"

"I did when we first came here, but I'll stay where you are, Miss." The girl's words sounded honest, her hazel eyes shining. "When younger, 'tis true I be homesick all the time, but not now."

"And we're so much farther from home." Amelia squeezed her maid's hand. "Now let's think of a way to 'entertain' Lt. Harris tomorrow that's acceptable, but won't be at all to his liking."

* * *

Two afternoons later, Mrs. Fulton cast Amelia a pitying look, then arranged fragrant current scones, a teapot, sugar bowl, milk jug and cups on a tray in the kitchen. Father smiled at Amelia from the hall as she stood in the kitchen grinding Blue Vervain root in a crockery bowl.

She pretended not to notice his triumphant manner.

"I'm relieved you've come to your senses, my dear. To give the man another chance." Father rubbed his hands together, though he didn't sound as sure of himself this time.

167

"Perhaps you will enjoy my hospitality longer. Until a wedding might take place?"

"It's only tea, Father. I'm being polite, that's all. Don't expect anything more." She kept her tone airy to soften her annoyance, and wouldn't give him false hope. She quickly broached something else that worried her. She pictured an even more desolate outpost, while New Brunswick brimmed with energy. "Are you still concerned the governor will transfer you?"

"I don't think so. It appears that he needs me here. The land grants are a muddle, the assessments inadequate or lacking." Father sounded convinced, if weary. "The Provincial officers are grumbling over having to wait to establish their homes."

"I'm glad you'll remain here to take care of them." Hopefully her father would need her, too, but not because of Harris. She swiped her hands on her apron. The herb left only a slight grassy smell. "I'm making a tincture for calming the blood."

"Well, leave that for now. You have company." He gestured down the short hall.

With a deep inhale to steady her nerves, she removed the apron, left the kitchen and entered the parlour where Lt. Harris waited.

Louise had pulled Amelia's hair back in the tightest of buns, and she wore her plainest gown, dark grey, closed robe, with the black armband in full view as always. A large white cap hid most of her hair.

The lieutenant approached, with what must pass for a smile on his face. She felt no flutter or warmth as she did when near Mr. Arsenault. Instead, she had to stifle the urge to tell him this tea was a mistake.

Father entered behind her. "Good afternoon, John." He shook hands with Harris. "It's good to see you again." Her father's hopefulness radiated off him like sunshine, increasing her discomfort.

Mrs. Fulton brought in the tray and set it on the low table before the sofa. Amelia indicated the housekeeper could pour.

"Good afternoon, Miss Latimer." Harris made a stiff bow. His grey eyes dissected her again with that coolness that made her skin crawl. A snake sizing up a mouse.

"Lt. Harris. I hope you're well. We're all well." Amelia gave a swift curtsey, whilst she wished she could scuttle up the stairs.

Father joined them this time, as if knowing he had to *keep* her from fleeing the room. They all three sat on the sofa and Mrs. Fulton passed around the white porcelain cups of tea, and then, after permission, departed.

Amelia breathed in the aromatic tea. The scones smelled delicious, yet the idea of food knotted her stomach. Silence closed in on them. She wanted her father to leave so she could begin her scheme of discouragement and dig for information about Harris' sister.

Harris cleared his throat, and finally spoke. "I heard that Governor Carleton is dividing the colony into seven counties, sir, with parishes in the more populated areas."

"That's true. The governor is anxious to build up his capital as well," Father replied. "Ste. Anne's is a decent choice, as it's the highest point on the river and large ships can still navigate."

Amelia gripped her teacup, took a sip, and said, "Aren't the Loyalists demanding the combining of the towns of Carleton and Parr Town, and then wish to rename it? Presumptuous, isn't it?"

Both men nodded slightly, brows arched, no doubt without an ounce of respect for her astuteness.

"Governor Carleton is directing that incorporation. The Tories formed those two towns to start with, my dear," Father said. "This area was a primitive and swampy settlement, mostly military, before that."

"I'd wondered. You hear so many rumours around a fort. You don't know which is true and which is not." She picked up the plate on the tray. "Scone, Father?"

"Thank you, my dear." Father's reply crisp, he averted his gaze. He took one, nibbled three bites, and dabbed his mouth with a napkin. Then he slapped his thighs. "Well, I'll withdraw now, and leave you two to talk." He rose and with a nod to them, left the parlour.

Face impassive, Harris turned to her on the sofa. "Have you thought over what we discussed?" He wasn't wasting any time!

She cringed, and thrust the plate in his direction. "Scone?"

"No, thank you." He tapped his fingers on his knee. "I'd like to—"

"Don't you have a sister who lives in Parr Town?" She returned the scones to the tray, aware she couldn't eat a bite. She wouldn't waste time, either.

"I...uh, yes. Her name is Mrs. Sutton." Impatience flashed on his face for a second. "Miss Latimer—"

"I'd like to meet her." Amelia stretched a smile across her lips at this lie. "She's a widow, isn't that so?"

He grimaced. "Her husband was killed four years ago, in the war with the American rebels."

"I am sorry to hear that." Her pulse thumped. She took another sip of tea. Now for the sensitive—and her seeking to embarrass the man—subject. "She and my father are great friends, aren't they?"

Harris' face stained ruddy. "We don't need to speak of that. I'd like to know what you think of my renewed proposal. We could be married by spring. My sons need a woman's influence."

She suppressed a shudder at the mention of a wedding—although she pitied the sons. "I heard my father and Mrs. Sutton are closer than mere friends, much closer. Isn't that true? Father must be lonely so far from England." She acted like the lieutenant hadn't spoken, and intended to keep up her attack. She grinned like a naïve girl.

"Miss Latimer. Decent young women do not ask such questions." He reared back, mouth open slightly. "Those...sort of matters are private."

"I realize that, but I am curious." She forced herself to scrutinize him, to keep him on edge. The gossip about her father was true, as she'd feared. He wasn't infallible, only an ordinary man. Her skin goose-fleshed. "What I really want to know is, did your sister suggest to my father that you marry me?"

A minute of silence passed. "There might have been such a recommendation. But I will hear nothing further about it." Harris turned from her, his hand fisted on his knee. "I can see you are a woman of few boundaries. You need to learn discretion."

"I'm merely trying to understand. I want the best for my father, and I've always been inquisitive." Amelia pouted, or what she hoped was a pout. Inside, her muscles twisted in worse knots. Harris' sister *was* involved with this disaster of a near-betrothal. "And you're criticizing me again, sir."

"I have no patience with a loose-tongued woman." He glared at her. His words dropped like chips of ice. "If you cannot change—"

"Can you change, sir?" She raised a brow as she clutched the cushion beneath her. "Become sweeter in temperament, perhaps?"

He stood, his glower deep. "You were right, Miss Latimer, we will never suit. I could not entrust my children to you."

172

"Yes, that seems to be true. Such a shame." She rose, half relieved, half vexed that her father *had* served her up like a leg of mutton, and for his paramour.

Harris snatched up his hat. "I'd advise you to curb your curiosity and tongue, young lady. You will never find a husband with your disposition."

"My disposition? Perhaps you could use a Blue Vervain tea to cool your blood." Her tone touched on sarcasm.

"I think not. Good day to you." With a quick bow, he strode from the room and out the front door.

"Good day forever, sir." She scoffed, yet felt deflated after her performance, and almost collapsed back down on the sofa cushion. Instead, she sat slowly and closed her eyes. "I'm rid of him, thank God." And now, with no chance of wedding prospects, would Father insist on sending her back to England? She'd never see Gilbert again. Her heart clenched with confusion. Of course, she'd still refuse to go. But what could she do about Mr. Arsenault, and would he even notice?

Chapter Fourteen

Lt. Harris stormed from their home, slamming the front door. Dishes rattled in a cupboard. Amelia jumped to her feet when Father entered the parlour.

"What happened, Amelia?" Beneath his wig, the captain's brow was deeply furrowed in consternation. "Why-what exactly did you say to the man?"

"Please calm down, Father." She breathed slowly to calm herself. "I want us to be candid with one another. I still don't care for Lt. Harris. He's very rude to me. I refuse to marry him."

"Perhaps if you'd tried more acceptance."

"No. *No* more trying. I believe his sister, Mrs. Sutton, suggested that you bring him and me together." She strained to keep bitterness from her tone. "Did she hope to bind you closer to her, whilst providing her brother with a child minder?"

Father groaned and sat on the sofa. "Amelia, you are much too bold and opinionated. I'm beginning to think you will forever remain a spinster. I'd hoped to solve two issues. A protector for you, and yes, John does need help with his family."

"Have you no care about my feelings?" Her hurt trembled inside, coated with the same feeling of betrayal. "I once thought you loved me."

"I do." Father pressed on his thighs, head lowered. "All right. I admit…I can see now that he's not the man I thought he was."

"Truly?" She started. That last statement validated her, a bit. "What's changed your mind?"

"I eavesdropped just now, if you'll pardon me." He thrust up his hands. A reluctant surrender? "I finally see the overbearing person John is. He showed you little respect, though your questions were inflaming."

"I did rattle him, but he has no respect or kindness at all." She held her breath and sank onto the cushion beside him. "And what of Mrs. Sutton? Do you have a close relationship?"

"I didn't wish to injure your sensitive female nature, but now I see you haven't, or don't care to, perfect one." He said it gently, as if a sad disappointment and not a reproach. Then he shook his head, eyes averted. "Very well, I have been calling on Mrs. Sutton. It wasn't fair to your mother, I agree."

She found herself numb, ice in her veins, knowing this truth was coming. Poor, dear Mother. Amelia had to reconcile herself that her father wasn't the white knight of her childhood. Yet she must adapt if she was to stay in New Brunswick without a battle. Her heart fisted in her chest. "Thank you, for finally being

175

forthright. I cannot help but think how Mother would have felt if she'd known."

"I was selfish, there's little doubt. Forgive my weaknesses. However, this subject isn't something a man discusses with his daughter." He slumped and sounded defeated. "I will apologize for trying to force your marriage. I relied on Dor—Mrs. Sutton's endorsement. I'd just hoped…" He raised his chin. "Can we come to a truce of some sort?"

Amelia smoothed her skirt over her knees. "That is my wish as well." To remain steady, she put no emotion in her reply. Father was admitting to everything, but it would be difficult to forgive him for using her as a pawn. She still wanted to understand his reasons for straying. Was he simply a lonely man in a faraway station? He'd professed love for Mother, but cheating was a poor way to show it. Could Amelia forgive him? Despite that, the ice inside her melted around the edges. "Will I ever meet her, your Mrs. Sutton?"

She really didn't want to, but hoped this would heal their relationship, plus solidify her place here. Could she trust herself to be civil toward his mistress?

Father's eyes widened, then narrowed. "Let me—think on that, my dear. We'll speak more later." He stood, shoulders squared again. "I have troops to inspect and a letter to write to our new governor about the state of the fort and forward the many grievances from the refugee officers crammed like cattle in Parr Town. The field officers alone were promised over one thousand acres each. If you'll excuse me?" He left the parlour, looking perturbed.

Amelia sagged against the sofa back and rubbed her cheeks, pushing her problems with her father to the side. What would she do next to keep occupied, with a long winter to face and deprived of the ability to start most of her herbal industry until spring?

A French voice entered her thoughts. She quivered with that odd warmth, and yearned to speak to Mr. Arsenault. He was the first man she'd ever felt an interest in—and he'd seemed attracted to her—and that prodded her onto a crumbling ledge.

She hopped up and gathered all the tea things onto the tray with clatters and clinks. Why couldn't she be friends with the handsome trader? Regardless of the many hurdles. The idea enticed her, and she would not be a coward.

* * *

Gilbert left Mr. Johnson's office. The lawyer promised to aid him in locating Mr. Oram. A slight relief, but it could still take many weeks. Out on King Street, Gilbert took a slow breath and pulled his coat close in the cold late afternoon air.

Before he'd visited his lawyer, the agent Wilcox had told him where Bent might be living. Deep in the woods, in a run-down settlement on the Black River east of Parr Town. He grunted.

Spotting the grocers, he walked down the street and entered the small shop. His mother and he were out of sugar, and he wondered if the last supply ship had brought any from the West Indies. Before the merchants traded on the quay, or in posts such as his, now the Loyalists had built their stores.

The old man who ran it shook his head. "Sorry, Mister. We're probably out until March."

Deprivations were already amassing before winter's unforgiving blast.

Next, Gilbert went into the dry goods store to purchase the red thread *Maman* had also requested. He half-laughed—still her errand boy after all these years, but Marie-Cateline hated to come near the harbour. She might actually encounter an English person.

A woman in a burgundy velvet gown and fancy flowered hat spoke at the shop's counter with Mrs. Pengilly, the proprietress. The elaborately dressed female picked through lace-trimmed handkerchiefs. Her strong perfume, perhaps jasmine, overpowered the space.

"…just turned down my brother for a second time, George told me," the burgundy woman said. Her dark eyes flashed in an attractive oval face framed by lush brunette hair. She frowned. "Unfortunate for John. He needs

178

someone to keep his house and be a mother to my nephews."

"Oh, my. Such a shame." Mrs. Pengilly slowly stacked bolts of fabric on shelves behind her. "I have seen the young lady here in town, in my shop. She's not overly pretty, but she has lovely eyes and is comely enough when she smiles. She came all this way, too. Do you know why she refused?"

Gilbert searched among the skeins of thread twisted on their bone winders. His ears pricked up, though embarrassment stung him at listening to women's gossip.

"Well, I have to be honest, John isn't the easiest man to know." Burgundy lady sighed. "He is abrupt and no-nonsense. I insisted he try again with Miss Latimer and act like a gallant gentleman. George's daughter must be too stubborn."

Gilbert suspected, but now knew who they spoke about. He gripped the winder in annoyance. These women were casually discussing Miss Latimer's personal business. He suddenly wanted to find her and—and what, hold her close? A capricious notion.

"Will the young miss return to England?" Mrs. Pengilly asked while she arranged a display of needles and thimbles.

"George hasn't decided, or at least that's how he felt before John's second try." The woman shrugged as she held up a handkerchief to the window light. "Miss Latimer wants to stay in the colony, he says. But I liked things the

179

way they were. Now with his wife dead, and if his daughter is sent back across the sea, I hope for a marriage proposal."

Gilbert headed for the counter. "I will take this red thread, Madame Pengilly, *if* I may interrupt." His words clipped and cold—the proprietress' eyes widened—he paid and opened the shop door, one foot out.

"These French can be so rude," Burgundy lady said, loud enough for him to hear.

I should have been rude with more finesse, he almost retorted, then decided not to lower himself. Closing the door, he returned to his horse left in the front of the law firm. He stuffed the thread in his saddlebag, untied Vaillant, and rode east out of Parr Town.

So Miss Latimer turned down the officer a second time. And who was this arrogant woman in burgundy velvet who gossiped about the captain's daughter? *Mon Dieu*! She might be the captain's mistress, and now expected to be his wife.

Miss Latimer had recently lost her mother, and her father has had a female companion. Not unusual, but did the young lady know? His sympathy rose as the chill increased in the pine trees' thickening shadows.

Gilbert leaned close to the warm smell of his stallion's neck and urged Vaillant into a gallop—to redirect his energies, his jostling thoughts.

There was no doubt now. He wanted to know Miss Latimer better. To what degree exactly, he'd contemplate later. His belly and chest warmed at the prospect, a feeling of happiness he hadn't experienced in years. He'd skirt the social order, but only if she didn't mind. She seemed caught in an unfair situation, yet she had the most to lose if he dared to interfere.

* * *

The Black River, which flowed southwest into the Bay of Fundy, burbled past as a light snow began to fall. Gilbert rode along the windy crest until the scattering of rough log homes and sheds that hugged the bank, came into view. Strange Englishmen from the dregs of society lived here. Men who preferred to remain remote and undisturbed.

Smoke poured from a few jagged-stone chimneys. A goat bleated. Then a donkey brayed from a lean-to. The area stank of manure.

Gilbert slowed his horse, the snowflakes sprinkling his cheeks in sparks of ice. He needed to find Bent, have a sober conversation. Could this rogue be related to Oram since he'd told Wilcox his family had once owned the property?

A man in frayed buckskins tromped from the nearest cabin, a musket in his hands. His unkempt beard hung down his chest. "Who are you? What do you want, eh?"

Gilbert stiffened at this unpromising reception, but had expected it. "I am searching for a man, a guide, known as Bent. Does he live here?"

"And who's askin'?" the man growled, stepping closer. His beaver hat was soon frosted like a hairy cake. The grass around them started to glisten with a light dusting.

"I'm Gilbert Arsenault. I own a trading post above Parr Town." He shifted in the saddle as Vaillant snorted. He kept a sharp eye on the musket. "Is Monsieur Bent here?"

"I ken who you are." The man laughed, though more a snicker from his bony face. The donkey brayed again. "Bent told me you cheated a fuddled man out of his river property."

"Who? Monsieur Oram? Does Bent know him? Do you?" Gilbert leaned forward in the saddle, his jaw rigid. He touched the pistol he always carried in his saddle holster. "I cheated no one, but I must speak with Bent."

"I'll tell him you came by." The man fingered his musket, then raised it slightly. A breeze swirled the falling snow around them. "He's away now, scoutin'."

"Inform Monsieur Bent he needs to meet me clear-headed. No more tantrums. He can find me at the Nákúset Post." Gilbert wheeled his horse around.

He hurried his mount through the thickening snowfall, sifting schemes through his mind. Bent must know the whereabouts of Oram, and could be a relation. A drunken, volatile relative, he'd be tough to deal with, as he'd already shown.

Gilbert frowned and rode up over the crest. His nape prickled. At any moment a musket or pistol ball could be fired and rip into his back.

* * *

Amelia, too restless not to stay busy, planted her burdock seeds in a crockery bowl. This plant was useful for burns and gout. She checked the feverfew, helpful in fevers, and the buttercup, good for the heart. Neither had started to grow. Mrs. Stuart had agreed to her using a shelf in the kitchen, near a window for light. At night and on gloomy days she'd put the plants near the hearth for heat.

She hoped the seeds would sprout, survive the winter, and she could transfer them to her box outside in the spring thaw. She planned on many more herbs. Her attempts to speak to the fort's doctor about making tinctures and syrups for him had so far ended with, "I'll let you know if I need you."

Men!

She chopped up dried burdock roots and added them to the grain-alcohol Mary's husband had gotten from a Loyalist who'd started a whisky still. Stirring, she poured the liquid into a narrow glass bottle. This tincture was good for indigestion.

One of the officer's wives who'd learned about her healing bought herbal remedies from her. Other women had soon followed.

Three days had passed since her second rejection of Lt. Harris and she and Father had spoken in general, polite terms. She lamented the closeness they should have shared. He was absent much of the time, either on fort business, dealing with his Provincial officers, or visiting Mrs. Sutton. She'd almost stopped cringing at that last notion.

If Amelia ever met this woman she vowed to be courteous. Mrs. Sutton could make life uncomfortable—and insist Father send Amelia home, especially after she'd twice rebuffed her brother.

She placed the bowl on the shelf as she deliberated on ways to sneak from the fort, out from under her father's scrutiny—and still be considered in the realm of 'respectable'.

A knock on the kitchen door. Amelia opened it to Mary, who rushed in, her cheeks rosy from the cold. She warmed her hands by the low fire in the grate. "Is anyone about?" she asked quietly. "I saw Mrs. Stuart head across the parade ground for the baker's."

Amelia peeked into the dining room. "Not at the moment, why?"

"I wouldn't ordinarily do such a thing, but...and I almost didn't." Mary straightened, mouth pinched. "And I promise I didn't read it, aye."

"What are you talking about?" Amelia brushed gritty soil from her fingernails.

Mary pushed aside her cape, dug through her skirt slit into a pocket, and pulled out a piece of paper. "'Tis not the thing to be doing. But I was in town, and he asked so politely, then scribbled the note."

"Who? Is that for me?" She prayed it wasn't anything from Lt. Harris. Her fingers curled. She'd toss it into the smoky fire.

"You ken, the man who saved you from the bear, and works the trading post. Mr. Arsenault." Mary held the paper close as if reluctant to part with it.

"He sent me a note?" Amelia's heart swelled, then dipped in nervousness. She reached out her hand. "Give it to me, please."

"A man like him shouldn't write to a woman of your position. But I've always found him kind enough." Mary darted her gaze around, then handed the paper to Amelia. "It will be our secret. Still, you best be careful."

The paper crackled in Amelia's hand. She slowly unfolded it, her throat compressing.

Mademoiselle Latimer, forgive my presumption. I wish to speak with you. If you feel the same, meet me at The Sweet Corner pastry shop, in town tomorrow at 3p.m. Ask for Madame Bouchard.

G. Arsenault

Chapter Fifteen

The pastry shop was located at the end of a building that faced Market Square in Parr Town. Amelia, heart in a jumpy flutter, stared up at the sign over the shop window, *The Sweet Corner*. She steadied herself and entered with Mary and Louise, her entourage. A bell over the door tinkled. What did Mr. Arsenault want? She'd mulled it over most of the previous night.

She'd convinced Father to allow her to shop in town without a male escort. Perhaps his guilt over Lt. Harris—and Mrs. Sutton—made him more lenient towards her. She glanced over her shoulder. Of course, his young spy of a soldier could still be trailing them.

The enticing aroma of baked goods wafted over her and almost calmed her racing pulse, her feeling of a stumble into the unknown—her secret meeting with a man.

"This place always smells like heaven." Mary sniffed and surveyed the pastries on display under a glass case. Little cakes, fruit pies, and decorated biscuits. "I've purchased desserts here many times since it was established last year."

A door behind the display case opened. *"Bienvenue,* welcome." A dark-haired woman with a triangular face and wide smile greeted them. "We have French delicacies, and the Acadian *pet-de-soeur.* It's made with pie dough, brown sugar, a little butter. Also *Poutines à trou,* with apple filling. *Très* delicious." Thirtyish in visage, she wore a bronze-coloured gown under a linen apron. She looked over the three women, then toward the front window, and back again. "Is there a Miss Latimer among you?"

Amelia stepped forward, her mouth dry. "I am she. Are you Mrs. Bouchard?"

"Mais oui. Please, will you follow me to the kitchen storage area?" Mrs. Bouchard indicated a curtain on the right side of the shop.

Amelia took a jittery breath. She gestured for Louise to come with her.

"I'll stay right here, filling my nose with these delightful smells." Mary moved to the window and positioned herself like a hound on the watch.

When Mrs. Bouchard parted the curtain, Amelia's pulse thumped in her ears. What did she expect from this meeting? Would Mr. Arsenault think her too forward for coming? Nevertheless, he wouldn't have written if he didn't care.

In the dim room, shelves with baking pans, sacks of flour, one sugar sack half empty, and crocks of butter lined one wall.

The trader stepped from the shadows, his hat in his hands. His dark gaze looked as uncertain as her spinning emotions.

Mrs. Bouchard eyed them both then returned to the shop. Louise hung back near the curtain that had swept closed with a whisper of air.

A hearth in the back held a low fire. A sweet aroma emitted from a large covered pot, a Dutch Oven, on the hearth's floor. A girl of around fourteen attended the ovens.

"I am honoured you came, Mademoiselle Latimer." He bowed.

His deep voice fringed with that French accent quivered through her.

"I'm glad you sent me the note, Mr. Arsenault." She pulled her cape close, though the room was warm. "I decided it would be all right...to meet you."

He smiled. A smile as sweet as the pastry smells. "I am presumptuous, *non*?"

"A little." Amelia's fingers clenched on her cape edge. Why couldn't she think of something witty to say? "Has-has your arm healed?"

"It has, *merci*. You must excuse me from listening to gossip, but I heard you've turned down the lieutenant's proposal a second time." He bunched the brim of his leather hat in his large hands. "Are there any other officers you are considering?"

Amelia's heart near burst from her chest. He *was* interested in her. This was so wrong, so outside of society's dictates, but she didn't want to care. "Not a one. I find that I—that my attentions lie elsewhere." A silly grin broke out on her face. She immediately pulled it back.

He smiled again, slowly. "I have a definite attentiveness in a particular place, too, if you'll pardon me. I've always admired women who scream at bears."

She laughed, which eased her tension. "I'm pleased I impressed you." She darted a look over her shoulder again. "We might... Many will frown on—"

"I know, Mademoiselle. I don't wish to compromise you." He took a step toward her, his gaze growing intense. "This may not be appropriate, but if you agree, we should see where this leads?"

"We can be friends. Get to know one another, and then," her head swam with the problems and possibilities, "see where it leads, yes."

"This is a wild land with many prejudices. I'm having property difficulties, and I don't want to drag you into them, if..." He regarded her steadily. "Just to make you aware."

"I wouldn't mind. Perhaps I can help." She half-feared losing herself in his chocolate-brown eyes. His mention of property difficulties gave her a firmer subject. "I know Major Studholme, a man of influence. I'm not afraid to take chances, to a point."

"No soldiers, please." He held up a hand, visage stern for an instant. "I didn't think you were afraid to take chances." He then stroked his beard, his eyes enveloping hers. "You appear to be a woman of great courage."

"With the bear? I might have been more hasty than courageous," she said after too many seconds passed. Behind her, Louise shuffled her feet. The girl in the kitchen clanged lids.

"And Monsieur Jarvis, at the post." His lip thinned in brief disdain. "You had your say with him as well."

"I am often too bold." Was she stepping in the wrong direction now? "Have you heard from him again?" She didn't wish to talk of Jarvis, but grappled to keep the conversation going.

People had entered the shop. Voices sifted through the curtain. They both stared at one another as if caught with their hands in the till.

"I'm certain I will see Jarvis. He is part of my difficulty." Mr. Arsenault lowered his voice and put on his hat. "We must meet again, soon. Here, if possible."

Amelia pressed her elbow on a shelf to keep from swaying. The air seemed to sizzle between them. Must he leave her so quickly? However, she wouldn't beg. "Yes soon, here will be fine." She saw they were both too overcome to make enough sense at the moment.

"Come to visit this shop, where I will leave word. I shouldn't have involved your friend." He bowed, then reached over and took her gloved hand. Bringing it to his lips, he kissed her lightly on her covered knuckles.

If she'd been a swooner, she'd have swooned. The warmth of his lips tingled even through kid leather. Her entire body trembled. Words wouldn't come. She nodded.

"*Bon jour*, until another day, Mademoiselle. Very soon." He nodded as well, turned and walked toward the hearth. A rear door opened and closed.

Amelia sighed, then pressed the heel of her palm on her forehead. She'd have to defy all she'd known for this friendship to proceed. Her life would be tumbled upside down, and Father might dispatch her back to England if he learned of her brazen behaviour.

She felt lost in a dream. "I'm giddy, acting like a flibbertigibbet of a girl, not as a woman. I probably shouldn't have allowed him to kiss my hand." She laughed, fingers curled. "But he is a Frenchman."

"Oh, Miss. This be so exciting, an' risky, too." Louise clutched her hands to her plump cheeks, her smile tremulous. "I thought I wouldn't like no Frenchie, but I do like him."

"That's good. And *I* don't know how to behave around him. My mind is in a jumble." Amelia laughed a second time to rearrange the foreign emotions that thrummed through her. Then her father's face shot in front of her. The clashes that lay ahead. Her amusement faded. "I'm certain I can count on your discretion, Louise."

"Of course, Miss." Louise nodded vigorously, her mobcap lappets flapping. "But please be careful."

"I must becalm myself. I never thought this would happen to me. And with such a rugged man." Amelia fought a moan of pleasure, then prayed Mr. Arsenault's intentions were honourable, no matter the inappropriateness of their liaison.

* * *

In a brisk walk along King Street, Gilbert bumped into a pedestrian in his distraction. He knew he'd lost his wits. He was letting his heart rule and not his head. But he was tired of being lonely and Mademoiselle Latimer intrigued him, began to fill that empty place in his core. She was a brave, spirited woman with a beautiful smile. His affection grew each time he was near her. Could he love again? There'd be repercussions for his courting an English captain's daughter, but he still grinned.

Someone disappeared around a corner in a flash of red coat. Suspicious, Gilbert turned down the alley flanked by log buildings. A very young, stick of a soldier stood there, glowering down at his boots.

"Out for a quick, furtive stroll, young man?" Gilbert asked casually, though inside he tensed. He had no business questioning a soldier, but had an instinct this one was following him, or Miss Latimer.

192

"I saw you…leave that shop, where Captain Latimer's daughter went. I've seen you before with her." The young man lifted his gaze, his pale brows knitted.

"Mademoiselle Latimer is of age, and is allowed to have friends, *non*?" Gilbert shrugged, pretending nonchalance.

"The captain is concerned for her reputation." His attention went again to his boots. His brow stained pink. "She must be protected."

"She's hardly a child. I will tell her of your tracking. I'm sure she'll disapprove." Gilbert hovered close, his large shadow covering the soldier. The troubles had begun, but he wouldn't back down. "These are not the duties you would expect a proud soldier of King George to be carrying out."

The young man sighed, proving his embarrassment. "I must report to the captain."

"I was in my cousin's pastry shop, Madame Lisette Bouchard. What is there to report?" Gilbert put his hand on the young man's shoulder, resisting a stronger grip. The boy twitched. "I know you have your orders, but *espie*—spying on Mademoiselle Latimer is a sorry occupation."

The soldier jerked aside. His cocked hat almost fell off. He slapped one hand on his sword hilt. "I am an upright soldier of His Majesty, the King. And you should take heed, and stay away from Miss Latimer. My superior says you're not good enough for her."

Gilbert was damned tired of the English stealing so much from him, ordering every aspect of his life. He thrust his fist against the wooden wall on his left, bruising his knuckles. "No one, not even your captain, has reason to judge. I will make my friends where I please."

The soldier screwed up his features. He tugged on his sword hilt. "Captain Latimer will feel differently."

Gilbert's fingers dug deep on the youth's shoulder. "Keep your weapon where it is. You are too young for us to fight over an attachment." Pulling aside his jacket, he revealed his pistol. He'd flatten the whelp against the wall, but arrest would be imminent in the midst of Parr Town.

"Release me," the boy snarled, though he sounded a little afraid, like a cornered puppy. The sour odour of sweat proved his agitation. "I must hurry to Fort Howe."

"Then do your distasteful duty. Be cruel and inform on an innocent young woman." Gilbert raised his hand, forced another shrug and continued down the alley, jamming down his disgust. *Mon Dieu*!

He immediately regretted accosting the private, but his brain was overturned by his rendezvous with the Mademoiselle. He'd meant to intimidate the *espie*, yet he'd no doubt made the situation worse.

The captain could have him arrested for interfering with a soldier, or even on a false charge to keep him from Amelia. He shook off

194

the ramifications and strode to his lawyer's office. Perhaps Johnson had located Mr. Oram.

Mr. Johnson splayed his blunt fingers on his desk. The tower of papers looked a third of the way diminished, the office more organized and not as musty-smelling.

"What is the news, if any, monsieur?" Gilbert took in the man's sympathetic frown and braced himself. He was already on edge, too agitated to sit, after the quarrel with the soldier intermixed with his hopes for Mademoiselle Latimer. Had he caused irrevocable problems for her? He needed to keep his temper in check.

"It wasn't easy, but...I'm afraid the news isn't good." The chubby lawyer adjusted his wig. The circles were deep under his eyes. "I found a death recording for a Mr. Franklyn Oram. He died six months ago. The age seems correct." Johnson ruffled through papers on his leather inlay—a delaying tactic? "As far as I can tell, he had no children. But his now deceased brother had a son. A man named Bennet Oram."

A chill sliced through Gilbert. Bennet— Bent? Was he the nephew? He'd never get that explosive scout to assist him in recording his deed properly. The rascal wanted his land. Gilbert slapped on his hat. He might have to speak to Governor Carleton himself.

Chapter Sixteen

Amelia entered her father's house, full of delightful thoughts after her discussion with Mr. Arsenault. His whispered words still tickled in her ear—the scant warmth of his kiss lingered on her gloved hand.

Father waited in the front hall, his scowl thunderous. Her enchanted musings whipped away. She didn't wish to face more of his disapproval.

"What is it, Father?" She removed her cape and handed it to Louise, though the girl already had her hands full with a basket of biscuits and bread from the pastry shop.

"Come into my office, if you will, Amelia." He turned and stalked into the parlour.

"Oh, dear, what rule could I possibly have broken now," she hissed to Louise in sarcasm. She grabbed the cape from her maid before it fell to the floor and hung the garment on the newel post. "Take the basket into the kitchen, whilst I attend my flogging."

"Pray not, Miss." Louise gripped the basket and rushed toward the kitchen.

Amelia followed him into the parlour, struggling to keep her face impassive. She clasped her hands in front of her and resented the dampening of her mood. "Yes, Father?"

He cleared his throat as he stood behind his desk. "I realise I'd promised not to send anyone to watch over you today, however—"

"You *did* send someone?" She stiffened, wedged between his betrayal and the fact she'd been caught out. Now, she could hardly insist that Father should trust her. "I visited a pastry shop. Delicious biscuits and bread await in the kitchen."

"And so, it appears, this visit included the Frenchman from whom you purchased the pistol." Father grimaced, but his eyes were strangely sad. "What did I tell you about your reputation?"

She took a long breath. "I wish you wouldn't send people to spy on me. I'm four and twenty, not sixteen. I could say that Mr. Arsenault and I met by accident in the shop, but I won't." Her fingers twisted together. "He and I are friends and enjoy each other's company. We plan to meet again."

"He's an Acadian and below you in station." Father's glare turned cold, like blue ice. "Any association will *not* be perceived in your favour."

"That's unfortunate." She knew if she and Gilbert went forward in their relationship, she'd have to throw her reputation into the wind. Discard everything she'd been taught to believe in or expect—a cook, housekeeper, a decent status, and issues beyond her ken. She'd be

197

tainted in the eyes of polite society. Her will surged up and masked her shiver. "This colony is full of many different people who must learn to cohabitate. England's rules and restrictions are far away. I have warm feelings for Mr. Arsenault."

"I forbid such a... Warm feelings?" Father's mouth gaped. "You're choosing the wrong sort of man. This Frenchman threatened the private who was protecting you."

"I cannot believe it. In what way threatened?" Amelia pressed a hand to her chest. She dearly hoped there hadn't been a scuffle and Mr. Arsenault wasn't arrested. "What happened?"

"Never mind that. Is this why you turned John Harris down the second time?" He huffed, shaking his head. "Not that it... You need to understand that your actions affect me as well."

"I meant no disrespect, Father. Why can't I seek my own happiness?"

He pointed a finger at her, his face flushed. "I see once and for all that it will be better for you if you return to England in the spring. You can help look after your brother, who is under the care of your uncle while at college."

"William doesn't need me. I'm sorry, but I'm staying. I'll find work at a shop in town if I must, and rent a room." Her frustration boiled at being treated like a possession that could be dispersed anywhere without a say—and she refused to be sent away when she was on the verge of discovering herself and, possibly, finding love. "I'm determined to make my life here in New Brunswick."

"Rent a room? Have you lost all sense of propriety?" He flung up a hand, his words strident. "I worry about you. As my unmarried daughter you are under my supervision. I'm responsible for your behaviour."

"I don't wish to embarrass you, though I apparently am. I'm creating a new life for myself. Not the one you expected, nor did I, though one I pray will make me content. I know people will disparage me but I would think that deep down you'd want me to be happy." She hesitated and met his eyes. "You, yourself, sought—inappropriate pleasure here." She turned and walked to the parlour door, her cheeks on fire. "Perhaps Mrs. Sutton has a room to rent."

"Amelia!" He covered his face with one hand. "You've gone too far."

"Excuse me." She'd said the last to poke at his facade, then wished she'd said nothing. Glibness wouldn't help her case. Rushing up the stairs, breathless, Amelia congratulated herself on not lying to Father, but now what would her thwarted parent do? Her unstable future could crash down around her.

* * *

December snow fell heavily, coating Gilbert as he rode Valliant through the stark, white landscape. He steered his mount, hooves crunching into several inches of hardpack, toward a 'snow bridge'. Young men shovelled snow onto the covered bridge's floor. A sleigh carrying a man and woman now glided easily over the boards pulled by one horse.

People trudged toward the bridge in their unwieldy snowshoes made of ash timber frames webbed together by untanned moose hide. The long shoes left strange prints in the snow, as if beasts from legend roamed the countryside.

Gilbert hunched for warmth in his buckskin jacket lined with sheep's wool. A beaver hat, plus the woollen cap favoured by his people, protected his ears from the frigid air. He still hadn't been able to find Bent, and Bent hadn't approached him. Maybe the guide hibernated over the winter, stewed in alcohol.

Days before, Gilbert had tried to see the new governor, but was told the man was too busy and he'd have to make an appointment. He gushed out a frosty breath. The appointment was in January, the most freezing month, when the storms would make it even more treacherous to travel.

Down the slope into Parr Town, Gilbert brightened at the idea of seeing Mademoiselle Latimer this afternoon. It had been nearly two weeks before this meeting could be arranged, with his cousin Lisette as the intermediary.

Outside the pastry shop, he brushed snow from his shoulders. Thankful to enter the comfortable, sweet and savoury-smelling space, he removed his heavy gloves. "*Bonjour.*"

"She has not arrived, yet." Lisette rounded the counter. "Come, you can warm up near the hearth. I'll prepare you tea or a glass of fir water."

"Heated fir water, I hope." He followed her into the kitchen, where two Dutch ovens sat in the hearth, smouldering wood piled up their sides. A delicious aroma tickled his nostrils. A brick oven to the right of the hearth emitted the fragrant fruity scent of pies baking.

"*Mais oui*, if you wish it heated." Lisette went to a small barrel where he knew she stored the boiled fir branch water, with added yeast and molasses. He enjoyed this fermented drink, a popular beer among the Acadians.

"I pray Miss Latimer didn't encounter any problems that might prevent her coming." He sat in a chair and reached his hands toward the fire.

Lisette's daughter, Irènée, a girl of thirteen years, who assisted in the kitchen, kneaded dough on a table. "*Ma filles*, go out front and mind the shop," Lisette told her. The girl hurried off.

"Far be it for me to tell you what to do, but are you certain you want to pursue this young English lady?" Lisette ladled some of the brew into a pewter mug and placed the mug on the

201

hearth floor. She heated a poker, then stuck it into the liquid, which sizzled.

"Many will warn me away, but…the heart wants what it wants, and mine has been dormant too long, *ma cherie*. This woman has begun to open it." He rested his elbows on his thighs. Was he behaving too rashly? Miss Latimer would be shunned by her own society.

"So, do you love her?" Lisette handed him the heated mug. She was one of many cousins whose connections had been tangled with time and migration. Her husband Henri was a pig breeder, who made a good living, his expansive farm on the Kingston Peninsula north of Parr Town. Gilbert knew him well—a good man.

"Love? I'm not certain I know the true meaning of that word anymore." He warmed his hands on the mug, then took a sip. The beer's yeasty sweetness was a treat on his tongue. "But I care for her, very much. She makes me want to smooth my rough edges."

"You will stir up the English, the army. You couldn't find a woman to court among our own people?" She rearranged the wood around the Dutch ovens with the poker, releasing the smoky wood smell. "I realize…after Monique—"

"That is in the past." His words were abrupt, but the pain was so faded, it barely registered. Just a pleasant, while it had lasted, and now sad memory to be left behind.

The bell tinkled out front and he shoved to his feet, his breath sharp with anticipation.

202

Lisette scurried out through the curtain. Soon, Miss Latimer and her maid entered. Gilbert grinned and had to stop himself from embracing her.

"*Bienvenue,* Mademoiselle Latimer." He removed his beaver hat along with the cap and bowed. "Did you have any trouble?"

"Please, call me Amelia. If I may call you Gilbert?" She sounded winded, her cheeks red as raspberries from the cold. "Yes, I did have difficulty as a matter of fact."

* * *

Amelia removed her cape, watching Gilbert's face. His brown eyes glistened on hers. A heat pulsated through her, yet she trembled. She smoothed down her mussed hair. "I-I had to sneak out of the fort. My father is extremely perturbed…and I heard you had a run in with the soldier he promised *not* to send after me the last time we met."

"*Pardon,* I should never have confronted that young man. I was frustrated because he was there." He reached out and cupped her elbow. "Sit by the fire, please. Tell me what happened with your father."

His touch caused sensations that weakened her knees. "Of course." She settled in a chair close to his, her cape in her lap. She turned to

Louise. "You sit, too. We had quite the escapade."

"Aye, Miss." Louise sat on a stool, huddled in her cloak, a few feet from them near the balmy brick oven.

"Oh, this cold is beyond anything we've ever experienced, but I can't say I wasn't warned." Amelia inhaled the aroma of cake and pie that hung tantalizingly in the air. Although the rugged scent of his leather and musk excited her more. She glanced over at Louise who shivered. "Is there any hot tea?" she asked Gilbert.

Gilbert stood and went to a cupboard, where he pulled out a wooden box of tea leaves. He filled a kettle with water and put it on a trivet in the hearth. "I just arrived, or I'd have thought to ask my cousin to have this ready."

"That's quite all right." Amelia strained to gather her rushing thoughts, her hands fidgeting in the soft folds of her cape. "I told my father the truth, about meeting with you. He wanted to betroth me to an officer, as you're aware, so…"

"Your papa hardly desires an Acadian Frenchman, a simple trader, to pay you attention." Gilbert sat and leaned toward her, his expression earnest. "How is this for you, these problems?"

"Don't worry, I'll manage." She had to manage, *had* to be in this man's company. She studied his large, capable hands, the black hair that curled slightly around his ears and collar, the short, neatly-trimmed beard, the kindness in

204

his eyes. "Today, I told him I was visiting my friend Mary. I'm sure the entire battalion watched me enter her home. Then Mary's husband, who has a strong dislike of Lt. Harris, my almost-betrothed, snuck us down the hill in a wagon. We hid under a blanket in the cart bed."

"*Ma foi*, you cannot suffer such burdens every time." Gilbert touched her knee. After several more minutes, he checked the cast-iron kettle. He put tea leaves in an earthenware pot and poured in hot water.

"I don't mind, really." She sighed and smiled—though the constant animosity with Father was exhausting. "My brother and I were allowed to run wild with Father gone so much, and my mother so gentle and indulgent." A twinge of sadness. "Thus, I'm rather a hoyden, as my father accuses me."

"I admit, that's one of the many traits I like about you." His gaze tugged at her, his smile inviting. "I hate to cause you so much distress, *cherie*, but I'm pleased you're here."

"So am I." She leaned forward, intent on drawing him closer whilst his scrutiny unnerved her. "I want to know more about you. Did you have a hazardous childhood in the back country?"

"Much of the vilest of acts happened when I was too young to understand. We Acadians have endured the worst of mankind, but we persevere." His expression grew sombre, gaze

205

distant. "My maman was strong, and kept us safe."

Now she rippled with guilt for asking. "I'm sorry you suffered. What does 'Acadian' mean. I've always wondered."

He clasped his buckskinned knees. "I was told by a wise old man that the first explorer in this area called it Arcadia, an 'idyllic place' in Greek. Later, the 'r' was dropped. Our home has been far from peaceful. An irony, *non*?"

"Is there any peaceful place on earth..."

She longed to discuss where this might lead—whether there was a future for them—but they seemed to skirt around the subject. Maybe it was too soon.

After the tea steeped, she rose and served the drink to Louise and herself. He declined a cup. The hot liquid slid down her throat and soothed her. "I see now that because of this oppressive winter weather, it will be hard for us to meet."

"We are in a challenging position, on many levels." He scraped a finger on the pewter tankard he held.

"What shall we do about it?" She said this softly, aware it was a bold question. Would he dismiss her as too much effort? She swallowed hard. Was her animosity with her father for nothing?

He straightened in his chair, flicked a glance at Louise, then met her gaze again. "Mademoiselle-Amelia, I wish to be honest with you. I do live a rough life, in a log cabin in the

206

woods. At the moment I'm fighting with a man over the land where my mother lives. It was never properly recorded." He frowned. "This man, whom I suspect is the nephew of the person I bought the property from, has already shot at me."

"Oh, no." Her heart jumped. She almost caressed his thigh. "Are you all right?"

"I'm fine, *ma cherie*. But I want you to realize the dangerous life I have." He paused and scrutinized her. "There's no fancy parties, no tea with the aristocrats."

"I'm a soldier's daughter. None of those elaborate things appeal to me." She turned the smooth teacup in her hand. "I'm brave enough, as you must know." He could be trying to gently discourage her, to push her away. She bit on her lip and hated to sound like a clinging female.

They talked for several minutes, mostly about New Brunswick, the history and wars. At her urging, his life as a trapper and trader.

He leaned close again, his hand hovering over hers. "Amelia, what I want is—"

Madame Bouchard pushed through the curtain, her expression vexed. "Shhh." She bustled up to their chairs. "Captain Latimer is in the shop."

Amelia stood, hands fisted in anger. How dare her father track her down. She felt like a runaway dog. "Is he asking for me?"

"He is, Mademoiselle." The woman shook her dark head. "I told him I'm teaching you baking techniques. I don't think he believes me."

Gilbert stood, his eyes flashing in affront. "Do you wish me to speak to him, Mademoiselle? To tell him of our…friendship?"

"I doubt that would appease him." Amelia wasn't sure what to do. Was Gilbert going to ask Father if he might court her? It couldn't be just a casual attachment. Her head spun. "Let me think."

Louise scuttled over to the curtain, as if to block anyone's entrance with her small form.

"You should go, Gilbert. *Sur l'heure*." Madame Bouchard thrust her hands on her hips. "I want no trouble from the captain."

"She's right, you should go." Amelia's throat thickened. Dratted Father for ruining her grasp at happiness!

Louise peeked through the curtain to the front of the shop.

"I will only leave for your protection from your father's ire." Gilbert pressed Amelia's upper arms. "We can meet again, when the weather is better. I don't want you hiding in carts."

Months from now? She tried to hide her disappointment. "Yes, I suppose it might be—"

"Go, go, *mon cousin*." Madame Bouchard tapped on his arm, mouth puckered. "I cannot afford to alienate the officers. They are my customers."

Gilbert tugged Amelia to the rear door with him. "I'm sorry for this interruption. There is much to talk over." He pulled her close, his lips on hers in a quick kiss. "Pardon my brazenness. *A bientot.*"

Amelia staggered back as he slipped out the door into an alley. She touched her mouth where his warm lips had caressed, her pulse pounding like a blacksmith's hammer in her throat. Then she turned and stared at the curtain, bracing herself to face her father's accusations.

* * *

Back at the Latimer quarters, after she endured another lecture from Father on her reputation, and undignified actions such as sneaking away in a wagon—in addition to her daring to defy his order of a proper chaperone, Amelia scrabbled to fathom his rancour.

"Father, let us try to understand one another. Could you explain this English scorn for the Acadians?" Amelia fought her frustration and massaged the resulting stiffness in her shoulders.

"Do you admit to these ongoing clandestine meetings with your trader friend after I forbade it?" He removed his hat and slapped it on a peg by the door.

"Might we have a civil discussion in the parlour?" Her body tense with upset, she was determined to manage his paternal anger.

"Amelia, I believe we've said enough on your defiance for today…"

"No, no. I want to ask you about the reason behind the English hatred for the Acadians." She needed to settle herself and perhaps ease their hostility with one another. "I'm curious about a British soldier's opinion on the colony's inhabitants."

"Are you serious?" He sighed, hesitated, then nodded. First, he asked Mrs. Fulton to serve them tea. "I'd say hatred might be too strong of a word."

"It doesn't seem an overstatement to me." Seated on the sofa, the tea soon before them, Amelia poured in milk and two cups of the steaming liquid. "All right, I'm ready to hear your view."

"Ah, I have such a headache." He rubbed the side of his head, then removed his wig. His sparse hair, brown streaked with grey, stuck out at odd angles. "So much paperwork on land grants, I don't really—"

"Please. I've heard bits and pieces of the history." Would Father's version match Gilbert's? "There was a treaty with France?"

"The Treaty of Utrecht, around 1713. This region known as Acadia was ceded to us, to England." He cocked his head, the lines around his eyes deep. "Do you really want all this information?"

"You know I'm not a flighty woman who cares only for clothing and parties." Amelia sipped the hot tea, savouring the rich, almost flowery taste. The beverage warmed her insides, if not her emotions. "And the Acadians objected?"

"Indeed, they did. The people living here thought themselves no longer French, but independent, separate. They refused to recognize our rule. They insisted on their Catholic religion, and refused to bear arms with us if another war started." Father massaged his knuckles over his trousers, his movements restless. "This was accepted by our government, at first."

She understood about wanting independence, and thought again of Gilbert's sweet kiss. Would she ever have another? "But that changed?"

"In 1749, if my memory serves, England desired a permanent settlement in Nova Scotia. We built the city of Halifax and wanted the cooperation of the Acadians for supplies and such." He sighed. "But with all the British soldiers deployed, the Acadians grew agitated and many left the area."

"I couldn't blame them for feeling overwhelmed with English dominance, and so much military." She tried to keep her responses even, perceptive.

"There were complications." He took a slow drink of his tea and stared away from her. "When the new governor, Charles Lawrence, arrived, he mistrusted these 'French'. He threatened deportation to France if they didn't swear allegiance to the British Crown. Most rejected that, and Lawrence had the Acadians arrested and they were deported."

"They were here before us English. I suppose that prompted their feelings of being unfairly treated." Amelia smirked at the irony, before putting her serious face on again. "And the Acadians, from what I've heard, worked well with the natives who already lived here. How shattering to be deported from the only home you know."

Father frowned. "You must understand, we feared that their friendliness with the savages might one day be aimed against us. Unfortunately, many Acadians perished on the long voyage during deportation. And the ones who hid in the wilds died of starvation."

"What about the burning of their villages, the slaughter of the people?" She cringed even imagining such acts. She thought of Gilbert's family.

"Is your Acadian friend telling you these gruesome tales?" Father huffed, one brow arched.

"His name is Mr. Arsenault. And I do have some education all my own." She breathed harsh in indignity, though Mary and now Gilbert had told her much of the history. "These tales are true."

"Yes, sadly, those travesties happened, the soldiers overzealous. However, the Acadians did take up arms with the natives against us during the French and Indian War. English settlers were also murdered." He shifted on the sofa, picked up his wig. "At least the Acadians were allowed to return twenty years or so ago."

"Overzealous is a tame word for such atrocities." Amelia started to lose her composure. "The Acadians still had to swear allegiance. And 'Planters' from New England had stolen most of their land."

"The strongest survive. It's the way of the world, my dear." Father groaned and stood. "Now about—"

"Why should you be prejudiced against a people who wanted to preserve their home and traditions?" Her aggravation threatened to spill over.

"You have a reasonable to some argument, but... I'm the Crown's soldier first and foremost, we don't need dissenters among us. And as your father I have a duty to see to your future. Don't make excuses as to your actions." His glare pricked over her. "I pray nothing improper has happened."

"Father, you belittle me to imagine I would!"

After he left the room, she set down her cup with a loud click. So much for a friendly father and daughter discussion. She refused to be restricted from seeing Gilbert, and vowed to be in charge of her own fate.

Chapter Seventeen

Days later, determined to help her friend Mary, Amelia left her father's house hauling her heavy burden. She crossed a parade ground already covered in white. The wind swirled about her, driving thick snowflakes that stung her face. At the O'Brien's front door, she shook snow from her shoulders and stomped more from her boots.

She knocked, very unladylike, with her knee. "Mary, it's me, Amelia Latimer!"

Mary yelled for her to enter. Amelia nudged up the latch with an elbow and stepped inside the cramped quarters, thankful to duck out of the weather. Mary called her back to a kitchen that smelled of cabbage and onions.

"Good afternoon. Or at least it's afternoon. I made it here." Amelia slipped the venison haunch wrapped in oilskin linen from beneath her cape. The meat had been like toting a bulky baby. "Here, please take this."

Mary stared. "Nay, I couldna accept something so generous." Despite her protest, her round face glowed. She swiped her hands on her apron.

"I had little idea how bad food shortages were here. But a soldier brought my father an entire deer, cleaned and cut. I insist, we can spare it. You have children to feed. It's close to Christmas, think of it as my gift." Amelia removed her fur-lined cape. "I also brought the feverfew to make tea for your daughter."

"You're too kind. I was out of the herb to prepare it myself. And with the big storm arrivin', I won't be able to go to town." Mary accepted and cradled the haunch in her arms. "Thank you so very much, m'dear."

"You're most welcome. The wind has gotten strong." Amelia tried to reorder her hair under her cap. As if on cue, the gale whipped against the building. The windows rattled and walls creaked. She laid the herb in its pocket of muslin on Mary's kitchen table. "Fresh is better, but this dried herb will have to do."

The two women busied themselves with a kettle, a teapot, and brewed the tea in Mary's smoke-blackened hearth. Soon Mary, with Amelia following, entered an alcove where Maureen lay in a narrow bed.

The girl smiled up at her mother. At thirteen, she was small for her age, and Mary's oldest child. Her red hair was damp around her face, her skin flushed.

"Drink this, love. 'Tis bitter, an' we have no sugar. But will soothe your fever." Mary helped her daughter sit up. The girl sipped the steaming tea, and frowned, then she stuck out her tongue.

Amelia felt the child's forehead. Thank God, she wasn't burning up.

After much cajoling, Maureen finished the cup and huddled back under her covers. The women returned to the kitchen where the warmth was welcomed.

"You best hurry home, afore the storm gets too bad." Mary gave a tired smile.

"The snow was only a few inches deep when I came across." Amelia wasn't anxious to return under her father's scrutiny.

"You've not seen these snowstorms." Mary laughed. "They come in with a furious blast and last for days. This is called a nor'easter. A twisting mass of wind that blows all before it."

"Father keeps warning me about the storms and how long the winters are. He was talking about terrible food shortages out in the countryside. Starvation seems to be normal here." Amelia frowned and shook her head. Had she the fortitude to withstand the privations in this wild land? She thought of Gilbert, and his handsome smile. Her body grew heavy. How was he managing in his remote cabin? That kiss he gave her on the lips had to mean something.

"Aye. The people further from the harbour suffer much. The bay doesn't freeze, not with those tides. Though few ships can battle the surf to get in with supplies." Mary stirred a pot that smelled of pungent herbs and fish over the fire. "But we have the town, and the royal stores. Mr. William Hecht, who handles supplies for this fort, gets food from the former supplier, Mr.

Hazen. He has huge farms that produce much, but 'tis never enough."

"Father said people cut holes in the ice so they can still fish." Amelia had a difficult time picturing that. "I trust this new governor will find ways to improve the colony."

"To God's ears. We hoard what we can in winter, and hibernate like the bears." Mary stirred some more, then glanced over. "How are you and your father gettin' along?"

Amelia hesitated. "He conveyed again his disapproval about my...closeness to an Acadian man. He wants me kept on a tether. Why can't I, at my age, make my own choices?"

More wind howled against the closed shutters. The walls and roof groaned.

"He's tryin' to protect you, in the only way he knows how. You still need to be careful with Mr. Arsenault and your expected place here." Mary smiled in sympathy. "You don't know what it's like in the backcountry."

"Of course I have much to learn." She glanced around Mary's tiny yet cosy kitchen, intent on changing the subject. "How did you obtain quarters here at the fort? I've heard most families live in town, or earlier in tents, and the soldiers in the barracks."

"Aye, 'tis true. When we came with our three bairns, I asked, nicely mind, if a single high ranking officer might give up these quarters for us. He was kind enough to do so." Mary winked. "We'd arrived from Ireland, that rough crossing, and I wanted it convenient for

217

my husband to have his wife and children near. This country be wilder than my home."

Amelia smiled. "You're a resourceful woman I plan to emulate."

"Remember, we woman must be subtle when we want to gain our way. As abrupt as I can be, I admit." Mary laughed, then nodded toward the door. "You'd best return home afore we're snowbound."

"I suppose I better. You've convinced me, to depart, but I'm not certain about being more subtle." Amelia laughed, wrapped on her cape and pulled up the hood. Mary must believe her a fragile petal, and too outspoken at the same time. Both of them were women of contrasts, that's why Amelia appreciated the Irishwoman. "Let me know if you need anything more, and I pray Maureen is recovered soon."

Amelia opened the door. Icy snow sprayed her face. Jerking the door closed against the wind, she watched her boots disappear in the fallen snow. The sky was pewter grey, yet flurries surrounded her in a white cascade. She lifted her feet and slogged her way through the blizzard, leaning against the wind. Her cape flapped around her, the hood blew back. She trembled in the frigid temperature. In seconds her cheeks felt frozen.

Was she taking on more than she was prepared for, her Father's warnings true?

Everything turned white, like she was enclosed in cotton. Her heart raced and she almost turned back to Mary's. Then she slipped and fell onto her hands and knees. The cold shot through her and she cried out.

For a moment she panicked that she'd be found frozen to death the next day. "Help! Anyone!"

Someone grabbed her arm and pulled her up. A young guard white as a snowman. "You should have snowshoes on, Miss. Although it's best to stay inside in these storms."

He assisted her across the parade ground, her skirt and cape soon stiff with ice, to the captain's door. This is what she had to look forward to, every winter, if she stayed. A gloomy idea filtered through her. Perhaps Gilbert would forget about her.

* * *

The blizzard pushed against Gilbert as he moved the heavy stone, unlatched and lifted the cover to the pit he'd dug deep in the ground when he built his cabin. The wind tried its best to bang the hatch onto his head. He elbowed his way down into the dark space and retrieved the gooseberries and other dried fruits, plus the onions and potatoes he stored every winter to get him by—food beyond salted meat, needed to prevent scurvy. These he stuffed in a hemp sack.

The dried and salted salmon and cod were stacked like wood against the earthen wall he'd lined with stones. He grabbed two slabs, inched his way up from the pit and let the hatch slam shut. He fumbled with gloved fingers to re-latch

219

it, and pushed back the stone with his boot. Signs of claw scratches on the cover proved that wolves had been here, trying to get to the food to prevent their own starvation.

The wind howled like a living thing as it hurtled snow into his face. His beard and eyelashes felt brittle as ice. Half-blind, he shivered with cold and trudged through the increasing mush back the ten feet to the cabin's rear door.

Gusts of wind rattled a loose shingle. He prayed his roof remained intact. Snow banked against the cabin's walls, but that helped to shelter and hold in the heat from his fire, along with the spruce boughs he'd piled up as buffers against the biting chill.

He opened the door, while the wind attempted to snatch it from his hand, and piled into the house, along with the chunks of snow stuck to his boots. He kicked out the snow and shoved the door shut with his shoulder. He dropped the food on the table, then jerked off his beaver hat, and the now-frozen woollen cap.

These winters were fierce, but they were all he'd ever known. How would Amelia endure in such weather she'd never experienced? Would she be frightened back to England?

With the shutters secured to protect the windows, the cabin was dim. He'd shoved moss into the kinks between the log walls where mortar had crumbled. Two candles flickered in his sitting area. The fire in the hearth spat and sputtered as a blast of wind and snow found its way down the chimney. The shadowed corners were still frigid. Gilbert coughed in a room thick with smoke. Could he bring—if he could be so fortunate—a wife here to live?

A spark ignited in his chest. He needed that saucy miss, more and more. She filled up the hole he hadn't realized remained inside him. Yet due to his situation, that sounded selfish.

As he settled more wood onto the fire, wood he'd chopped and stacked beside the fireplace in the autumn, he listened while the wind flapped his shingles. One ripped off and tumbled loudly over his head, like a trotting fawn.

The entire cabin groaned as if squeezed by angry, giant hands. Poor Vaillant probably shivered in the stable. He might bring the stallion inside, near the fire. He'd tie a sack under his horse's tail in case of accidents. A wife might object to sharing a room with his horse.

He dragged out an earthenware bowl, poured in water, and laid in a stiff slab of cod to soak. A shutter pulled loose with a snap and banged against the outside wall. His shoulders twitched. If Amelia accepted him and came here, she'd have no servants to stoke a roaring fire, no abundance of delicate food. He couldn't afford luxuries. Was it wrong of him to expect a proper Englishwoman to exist as isolated and discomfited as this? He might be making a huge mistake.

Chapter Eighteen

His day of reckoning, Gilbert approached the governor's residence for his afternoon appointment. Leonard House sat on the corner of Union and Dock Streets. Dock was once a footpath where you had to hold onto bushes to keep from falling to the rocky beach below. Widened, the street now ran crookedly along the shoreline of Parr Town's quay.

He stepped onto the handsome terrace, his gut in knots. The expansive dwelling sat back from the street fronted by a now frozen, snow-covered lawn. Icicles hung like crystal daggers from the edge of the roof.

Gilbert hesitated, though the glacial air of January, usually the coldest month, pinched the skin on his face. He stared at the carved front door. How would Governor Carleton treat him?

To please his Maman, he'd spent Christmas with her and attended the midnight mass. With no church or priest in residence—the English frowned on their Catholic religion—it was held at an elder's home. They'd eaten the *réveillon*, a long meal, splurging on oysters and lobster. Another gathering of Acadians was held on January sixth, the feast of the Kings. His people held tightly to their traditions. Yet his mother's contentment could be ripped asunder today.

Gilbert shook snow from his coat and beaver hat when he was admitted inside Leonard House by a clerk. Other men milled about in the hallway, anxiously conversing while they waited. He spoke with the people he knew. Most were as uneasy as he was about their property rights.

"When they first laid out the town you could purchase a lot for a jug of rum," one man said with a derisive chuckle. "Now we're scrambling to claim our territory."

A half hour later, the clerk bade Gilbert to enter a room set up as an office. Governor Carleton stood from behind a large mahogany desk. He waved Gilbert to a leather chair that faced the desk.

The well-appointed room held dark shelves with numerous books. A tall walnut case- clock ticked beside the shelves. A fire crackled in a fancy white marble hearth, emitting the fragrant smell of apple wood. This Englishman was warm and safe as he enjoyed his elaborate accoutrements.

"Mr. Arsenault." Carleton, a man of fifty years with a sleepy expression, held up a paper. "You petition for ownership of land on the Kennebecasis River, approximately twelve miles north of here. The parcel is ten acres."

"That is correct, monsieur." Gilbert sat on the chair's edge, his teeth on edge as well. "I paid the late owner, Franklyn Oram, for the

223

property with the finest mink that I trapped myself. My family has lived there for over ten years."

"But the deed wasn't properly registered." Carleton rubbed his long, cleft chin.

"It was not." Gilbert rolled the furry hat in his hands. "My lawyer at the time, Mr. Johnson the Senior, was having memory problems, and neglected to follow through, but no one knew of his illness then."

Carleton set down the paper. "I understand there's a nephew of the original owner involved?"

"If he's the man I believe he is, I've been trying to locate him. I left a message at the village where he lives," Gilbert replied. "This man has problems with drinking too much and quite the temper. He's never spoken to me with a clear idea of what he expects."

Carleton settled in his chair. "However, he's disputing your claim?"

"He has threatened me, but never with proof or word he is a relation." Gilbert bunched the hat, then smoothed it. "We, my mother and I, have made all the improvements to the land. I built a house. She farms a hayfield and grows other produce. Mr. Oram had left the place undeveloped."

Carleton leaned back in his chair, hands folded under his ribcage. "Obviously, you're aware of the pandemonium over land settlement that started in '83. I need to find homes for thousands of refugees from the rebellion in

America. Loyalists who consider New Brunswick and the Canadas a bleak wilderness."

"You can be assured my property is well taken care of, monsieur. I paid for it fairly. My family has been in this land for more than a century, and my mother and I are decent, hardworking people." Gilbert slowly inhaled. He must make his case the best he could, so much was at stake. "I also run a successful Trading Post north of here."

"So I've heard." Carleton nodded, staring off into space. "This, for me, is a temporary post. I hope to be governor of Québec. And soon I'll move to St Anne's Point, which we've renamed Frederick's Town rather than Osnaburg. A better location geographically from which to govern the colony." The governor seemed to be speaking to himself.

"There's a fine trading post near that point, run by the merchants Simonds, Hazen & White," Gilbert said, straining to be friendly, accommodating. Still, the English came in, took everything, renamed everything—and *much* worse—as though the Acadians had never existed.

Carleton sat forward again in his finely-cut green frock coat, elbows on his desk, fingers under his chin. "I don't wish to cause any unnecessary hardship for people already settled who *have* improved their land. An Executive Council and Land Committee will inspect any enhancements. We take into consideration the poverty of the local people, and may waive fees.

Other inhabitants have had no clear titles, and we've assisted them."

Gilbert prickled at being considered poor, but hoped it didn't show on his face. "I welcome the inspection. We are able to pay any reasonable fees."

"There's one issue." Carleton met his eyes, his steady and serious. "If the land falls into the areas reserved for the Loyalists, you will be paid for your improvements and given first choice of land that's available elsewhere."

Merde! Gilbert's fury spiked through him. He hadn't counted on this travesty—pushed out again to make way for the English. "It would be a definite hardship for my mother to move." His words barely held onto civility. "There's a grist mill that she serves near her property. She is an honest woman who deserves—"

Carleton put up a hand. "I'm not saying this will happen. Nevertheless, first you must deal with the nephew, if he is such, of Mr. Oram. He'd have to come forward and also petition. The news of your claim will be put into the local papers, such as *The Saint John Gazette.* The information will be published for three months. If the nephew doesn't show himself to prove ownership, and you're not in the Loyalist Reserves, you will be given final title to the land."

Gilbert stood, his jaw so rigid he thought his teeth might crack and splinter on the man's elegant rug. "I thank you for your time, sir. How will I know if my land is in this reserve?" What effrontery! Hadn't enough been done to them?

Carleton rose, his gaze weary. "The Executive Council, which will be run by my registrar and provincial secretary, Jonathan Odell, will decide that. The Surveyor-general, Ward Chipman, is also poring over the land deeds and grants. Both men are gathering the old documents and creating new ones. An onerous task. I give you good day, Mr. Arsenault."

Gilbert headed for the chamber's door, throwing a quick "*Bonjour*" over his shoulder.

"Oh, Mr. Arsenault." Carleton's voice made him pause. "If you don't agree with the council's decision, you can always present your case in court."

Outside, Gilbert pulled on his hat as he blinked in the blast of cold wind. An English court would hardly side with an Acadian, especially one not a member of the elite. He'd no longer search for Bent. Let the fool lose out and miss his three-month chance to petition. The drunken *coquin* would only ruin the property.

Gilbert jerked on his gloves. Loyalist Reserves? He'd be damned if the English stole his land, though Carleton seemed a decent enough man under a huge burden.

Tramping through the crunchy snow, Gilbert wished he had Amelia to talk with. A kind voice and tender smile. He longed for her in his solitary nights, though maybe he shouldn't have kissed her. If she remained

227

steadfast during their winter separation, he'd be more confident she was a woman resilient enough to be with him.

* * *

A sleigh brought Amelia and her father down the fort's twisty knoll road, an exhilarating ride that took her breath away. She huddled in the furs, the bone-chilling cold like nothing she thought existed—a frozen land where everyone slid, shovelled and shivered. She brushed snowflakes from her eyelashes and tugged her squirrel-lined hood further over her forehead. As she leaned into Father's warmth, her thoughts went to the man who'd occupied it during these snowy days and nights.

What was Gilbert doing, she wondered? It was impossible for them to meet in such inclement weather—she'd have to steal a sleigh— especially if you had soldiers sniffing down your neck. She must prove to him she wouldn't be a burden.

"You might think twice about staying in the colony after this winter." Father patted her gloved hand. Too bad he sounded so hopeful.

The sleigh, pulled by two horses and driven by a private, bumped at the bottom of the hill and soon entered Parr Town, the vehicle's runners cutting with a grind through the snow.

"I'm certain I'll become used to the weather," she replied in an arch voice. She tried to put that day she fell in the blizzard from her mind. The severe cold had shocked her, but she wouldn't give in. "I'll line more of my clothing with fur."

Father harrumphed. "And what of your Acadian friend?"

She heard the overt sarcasm and hunched deeper into the furs to mask her pique. "Mr. Arsenault? I still have deep feelings for him.

He gave her a sharp look. "My dear—"

"You wouldn't wish me to lie to you, would you?"

"We are a small community, and word will..." He drifted off, as if realizing he had little room to talk of improprieties.

Her relief that he hadn't asked more about Gilbert dangled by a thread. Did he have deep-enough feelings for her?

On a side street off Union, the private halted the conveyance before a row of unconnected—to discourage the spread of fire she'd learned—narrow wooden homes two stories high.

Amelia swallowed slowly as Father helped her from the sleigh. She was to meet Mrs. Sutton for the first time. How should she act? Arrogant, cold, politely courteous? Could she rely on this one meeting only, then go on with her plans without completely alienating her father?

"I know you disapprove, my dear. However, I find it hard to explain, especially to my own daughter." Father sighed. "I never meant my…activities as a slight to your mother."

Amelia refrained from answering. The slight was obvious. Were men so carnal they couldn't be celibate when stationed away from their wives?

Admitted inside a confining hall with flowered wallpaper, an older woman in apron and mobcap took their coats.

Amelia wore a simple closed robe gown of darkest brown, her black armband in full display out of respect for her mother, and a reminder to the mistress. Only since she'd met Gilbert had she wished for the mourning period to be over so she could wear brighter colours—but tonight solemnity was appropriate.

From a doorway at the opposite end of the hall, an attractive brunette-haired woman walked toward them with a huge smile. Medium in height, she wore a violet-coloured gown over her curvy figure, the front of the skirt open to reveal a yellow silk petticoat. A white kerchief was tucked in her bodice, a white lace cap perched on her head. Everything too overly neat and in perfect place.

"George, uh, Mr. and Miss Latimer, I'm so delighted you could come." Her voice was clear and pleasant.

"Mrs. Sutton, this is my daughter, Amelia." Father's smile twitched.

The two women curtsied quickly as if anxious to get that over with.

"How...I'm pleased to meet you," Amelia replied, to say something, though 'pleased' wasn't what she felt—but polite courtesy seemed the best approach.

"As am I. Let's sit in the parlour." Mrs. Sutton gestured to a room on the right. It was small, but cheery, with a fire roaring in the grate and the faint scent of linseed oil in the air. Cabinets held various knickknacks, china horses, shepherdesses and couples holding hands. A portrait of a handsome blond officer hung near the fireplace. Was this the dead husband?

Amelia sat on a red-striped silk settee, a maroon Turkey rug beneath her feet, and wondered if her father had paid for any of these things. Then she chided herself for that uncharitable thought. She *must* learn to accept this liaison to strengthen her own position.

Father sat on the other side of the fire in a leather chair, looking as if he'd lingered there many times before. They all studied one another, like weasels circling a campfire.

"I hear you delve into herbal healing and have set up a box garden." Mrs. Sutton perched on another chair between Father and Amelia. The fire illuminated her features, her nose a little too turned up at the end. She didn't resemble Lt. Harris at all.

Compared to her mother, this woman had a livelier expression, and was even prettier,

Amelia had to admit. Although she didn't appear to possess Mother's quiet grace.

"Yes, I hope to work with the fort's doctor." Amelia hadn't told anyone she'd offered her help to the fort's surgeon again and he'd finally dismissed her out of hand. Insufferable man. She'd set up her own business if she could. Share a shop in town? "I also aspire to have remedies available for any physician or surgeon in the vicinity. Or the incoming housewives from the rebel States." She'd prepared more bottles of herbal medicine in Father's kitchen.

"Very good, Miss Latimer. Though it would be easier with a man to assist you in any business venture." Mrs. Sutton's smile was too broad. She clasped and unclasped her hands in her lap. She seemed as ill at ease as Amelia. "So you plan to remain in New Brunswick?"

The servant woman came in with three delicate glasses on a tray.

"Apéritif? Dry sherry, before dinner?" Mrs. Sutton passed out the small crystal glasses.

"I do plan to live in the colony." Amelia sipped the pale wine, tangy and nutty in taste, and strove to relax the knots in her stomach. She'd ignore the 'man to assist' remark. "It's said the new capital will be called Frederick's Town, after the King's second son. The place is a good sixty miles from here. I heard there was once a French fort there."

Father crossed, then uncrossed his legs. "Hmmm, true, long ago. Amelia does want to stay, Mrs. Sutton, but she is getting an example of the horrid winters and other limitations we suffer." His tone was cool, yet his glance warmed on the widow. "She needs to decide what is best for her."

"Adversity should make us better people. I have my future in mind." Amelia had to sound positive, though the details were blurry, uncertain. She darted her gaze around, hoping the lieutenant didn't lurk in a corner. She'd turn the tables. "How did you meet my father, Mrs. Sutton? Were you formally introduced?"

"Amelia, please." Father's words were a soft warning. He drank from his glass.

"We..." The woman's eyes widened a fraction. "It's all right, George." She turned to Amelia. "I understand, dear, that this isn't a comfortable arrangement for you."

Amelia touched her black armband then dropped her hand. Mother was gone, no longer able to be hurt. "Sometimes we find ourselves in situations we hadn't expected." She finished the sherry, and looked at Father. "But I suppose we should try hard to accept the changes."

Father grimaced. He obviously knew she spoke of Gilbert as well as his liaison with this woman. He nodded at Mrs. Sutton, then stood. "If you'll excuse me, ladies. I won't be long." He walked out and down the tiny hallway toward the rear of the house.

Amelia knew instantly that this was deliberate, to leave the women alone. She turned her attention warily from Father's departure to her hostess.

In a rustle of skirts, Mrs. Sutton left her chair and sat beside Amelia on the settee. Her jasmine-scented perfume drifted around her. "I hope we can become friends, Amelia. No matter how awkward the circumstances."

Amelia pressed her palms on the slick silk cushion. She kept her tone as steady as possible. "You'll find I'm a plain spoken woman. If there is still a scheme to convince me to marry your brother, I'm afraid I have an attachment for someone else."

Mrs. Sutton tilted her head. "Your father tells me you're interested in an Acadian man. He's concerned that, perhaps... Or, rather, he prays that no liberties have been taken."

Amelia bristled, although the woman's forwardness shouldn't have surprised her. They did have that in common.

She remembered that quick kiss at the pastry shop. Her lips seemed to burn. "Liberties? He did mention that to me, briefly. You may inform my father that I'm still 'pure'."

"You do appreciate that to marry beneath you will shut you out from any decent society here, sparse though it is." Mrs. Sutton's voice was growing stern—and she showed little shame considering her relationship. "Or *is* there marriage in the plans?"

"Of course, there's always a possibility of marriage." Amelia stared into the flickering fire. Gilbert hadn't asked, it was too soon. They needed more time to know one another. Was she simply too eager to slip away from her father? She turned again to her hostess. "I do have morals."

"Indeed?" Mrs. Sutton raised a plucked eyebrow. "You have no idea of the prejudice you'll encounter if you continue with this Frenchman. You'll live a hardscrabble life, one you are unprepared for. Don't be naïve." Now the woman sounded on the verge of annoyance. "My brother would have been the better—"

"*Never*. I hate to be rude, but your brother needs lessons in compassion and deportment. He was insulting to me more than once. Even Father realizes that now." Amelia fought a jab of anger. How dare he instruct his mistress to lecture her. "Tell my father to respect my wishes. I know what I'm doing." She wanted freedom, her own life, a man who could love her on more equal terms.

"I think you're too stubborn for your own good, and too particular. Or befuddled over your choices." Mrs. Sutton stood, her expression now haughty. *That* resembled Lt. Harris.

"And I won't be vulgar enough to say you haven't made the most 'decent' decisions in life. Oh, I just did. Excuse me." Amelia turned again toward the fire to hide her frown, her pinch of embarrassment. She'd let her anger get the best of her. Orange and yellow flames licked over the wood, devouring it to ashes. Skirts swished as Mrs. Sutton swept from the parlour.

Amelia hunched forward, lip between her teeth. If she and Gilbert found their relationship untenable, and her father demanded she leave in the spring for England...

He couldn't force her onto a ship, but he could leave her with no place to live. She refused to return to England to be a maiden aunt to her brother's future family. Here were more possibilities. She'd have to devise a way to start an herbal shop with her inheritance, find a home if she didn't marry—and thrive in this harsh colony.

Chapter Nineteen

Behind his mother's house, Gilbert dug in the shovel with a loud crunch, the blade slicing into the snow. Shoulders and arms straining with the effort, he cleared a path from the rear door to the well. Then from the door to the privy. He needed to keep the property well-tended, for his maman and the new government. Land inspectors could be watching.

Shaking off the shovel, he entered the home's warmth, and leaned the implement against the inside log wall.

Marie-Cateline stood at her work table, but her hands were still. She regarded him with a measured stare. "You will find nothing but sadness and disappointment if you continue."

He removed his gloves and thawed out his fingers at the fire. He'd told his mother about Amelia before he'd gone out to clear the paths. "There will be difficulties, but even you cannot foretell the future." He grinned into her sour expression.

"An Englishwoman, *peste*. You have lost your senses." She shook her head. "And an army captain's daughter. How much worse could you choose?" Maman began to jerk the splinter-like bones from the soaked and simmered codfish laid out on the table. "Perhaps the new governor has a daughter for you to woo."

"Maman. I understand your disapproval." He pulled off his coat and heated his lower back close to the flames. He'd known this would be very hard for his mother to accept. "But you're the one who told me we must change with the times if we could. Don't decide—"

"I didn't mean for you to *romance* yourself into the changes." She cracked an egg, separated the yolk and slid the yellow moon into a bowl, added milk, and viciously beat the ingredients with a fork. "I'm worried no good will come of it. This English miss will hate the way you live and go home to papa. She will turn her nose up at me."

Gilbert stifled a chuckle. "She is not conceited like that." The idea of Amelia in his life, and having her contend with his mother, verged on a pleasing adventure. A cherished balminess filled his soul. "I'll bring Mademoiselle Latimer here to meet you as soon as I can. You'll like her. *Je te promets.*" At least that's what he prayed for.

"I want you to think this through carefully." His mother added flour to the egg mixture. "I don't want any army captain in my home as a guest—if her father doesn't disown her." With a wooden spoon, she mixed the ingredients into a paste and added pungent chopped onions. She pointed the sticky spoon at the cod. "Pick that apart for me."

Gilbert shredded the damp cod between his fingertips, the fishy scent mild. If he thought too much about the obstacles, he'd become a recluse from courtships again. "She's a strong woman, just like you." He sprinkled the fish into her mixture. "Give her a chance."

"If you go so far as to marry, does she even know how to cook?" Maman beat the ingredients together, adding salt and pepper, then dropped a small portion into an already sizzling pan of bear grease set over the hearth fire. She browned each piece of her salt cod beignets.

He washed his hands in a bowl of water. The fishes' fried smell made his stomach growl and reminded him of his childhood.

"I—don't know if she cooks. But she can learn." He hadn't thought too far beyond the courting. Was he as ready as he assumed to take on a wife? He realised he had much to learn about Amelia, but he intended to savour the exploration. Maman could *not* discourage him.

"Aha, see. She'll be lost, out of her element, this English 'lady'." Maman placed browned fish on a plate. "Will she convert to Catholicism, return to the true faith?"

"You're rushing things. That is something she and I will discuss." He didn't care one way or the other, yet said this to mollify his mother. Religion had held her firm, but had always seemed full of mysteries he'd little time for. He

239

felt closer to the natives' idea of worshiping nature.

"Make certain you do." She browned more hunks of batter mixture. "I'm impatient about the land, that we must wait three months to see if the nephew protests."

"The man's intemperate habits, hopefully, will keep him from ever seeing the announcement in the newspapers." Gilbert slapped his hand against his thigh. He'd know by April or May whether the property he'd vigorously developed and thought was his, would legally *be* his.

"Is she pretty, your Englishwoman?" Maman asked as she continued to arrange the beignets. "Is that why you're so infatuated?"

"To me she is beautiful." He forced a shrug then smiled. "It's only who she is inside that matters. A courageous spirit with a loving heart."

His mother swiped her hands on a cloth, then stepped close to him. "I only want your serenity, *mon fils*, you know that." She touched his cheek, her black eyes clouded. Chin up, her head barely came to his shoulder. "There are so many differences between us and the English. Since the arrival of these crowds of Loyalists, the idea of being chased into the woods again, I haven't been in the best of moods."

Gilbert clasped the small, sturdy hand that had guided him through the sharp ridges and deep valleys and swamps of their lives. He'd mulled over the complications he'd face with an

Englishwoman—but he didn't want to wallow. "Mademoiselle Latimer and I have a close friendship for now."

Someone knocked on the door. Maman went and peered around the window's curtain. "*Mon Dieu*, it looks like that man, Monsieur Wilcox. I mention Loyalists, and one arrives." She glanced over at her blunderbuss, balanced on two pegs on the wall.

Gilbert gripped his pistol handle, then flexed his fingers. He hoped the agent hadn't found Bent. "Return to your cooking, *s'il vous plaît*. And no weapons. I'll see what he wants. Perhaps news of Jarvis." He opened the door to a blast of chilly air, and fast realized he had to invite the man in, or they'd both suffer from the cold.

"Monsieur Wilcox, come in," he said.

The agent entered and tipped his cocked hat to Marie-Cateline. "Good day to you, Madam. Hiram Wilcox at your service. What a heavenly smell, but I won't impose on your hospitality."

More like 'hostility' Gilbert mused, watching his mother's suspicious expression as she said, *bonjour*, with little emphasis on the 'bon'. She turned her back on them, her striped skirt swinging.

"What can we do for you, Monsieur Wilcox?" he asked in an officious voice.

"I wanted to speak to you about the plans of Mr. Jarvis." The agent surveyed the one room house, then sniffed at the beignets Maman was cooking.

241

"Please sit. Would you care for a cup of tea or cider?" Gilbert forced his courtesy though Wilcox had usually been respectful toward him.

"Cider would do well." Wilcox sat in a plank-seat chair to the right of the hearth and elbowed back his heavy cape.

Gilbert served the drink and sat across from him, his chest tightening. "Now, what about Monsieur Jarvis?"

"Of course it's too soon to have heard back from the landlord on the property purchase on Grand Bay." Wilcox sipped the cider in its pewter cup. "But I'm certain my client will prevail. Unfortunately, he is already talking of raising the rent on the parcel where your trading post sits."

"I am not surprised. He said as much." Gilbert grasped his thighs in his buckskin breeches. Such greediness from an intruder.

"This man Jarvis wishes to shove us out, *non*?" Maman said in a remarkably even tone. "If we were English, he'd leave a prosperous business as it is."

Gilbert gave her a wary glance. A pan of hot grease might fly in Wilcox's direction at any moment.

"I think he'd still raise the rent. He's a rather—stubborn young man. And upset over his lost estate in New Jersey. Many men loyal to the king were beaten near death or hanged there. I'm still trying to talk him into being fair." Wilcox smiled at her.

242

"I'm familiar with brutal treatment." Maman swiped a cloth along the table.

"I am grateful for your efforts, Monsieur, but will you succeed?" Gilbert wanted to ask about Bent, but not draw any undue importance to the man—or his own concerns. Certainly the agent hadn't travelled all this way to inform them that Jarvis would raise the rent. And how would he and Fougère manage if it was raised too high? He rubbed on a muscle in his upper arm. Too many problems pushed down on him like boulders. "We must wait and see how bad it is, *n'est-ce pas?*"

"Have a taste of my cod. It's very good." Maman placed a plate of beignet on each of their laps. Gilbert almost fell out of his chair in shock. His stoic maman was playing at being persuasive.

"You are too kind, Madam. I am most honoured." Wilcox grinned, his eyes contemplating Marie-Cateline in appreciation. Was the man attracted to her, and that's why he'd come?

Another reason to fall out of a chair. Gilbert scratched through his beard.

"Have you seen your guide, Bent he was called? He was so rude on his one time here," Maman asked as she handed them both forks, her gaze sly on Wilcox. "I pray you never bring him back to my home after the cruel things he said, *mon ami.*"

243

Amelia enjoyed the children's laughter as their sleigh glided through runner marks made by previous sleds. Such ruts crisscrossed the roads, until the next heavy snow would obliterate them in winter's fury. Mary and her two sons, Fergus and Timothy, and daughter Maureen huddled with Amelia under lap furs. Thank goodness the girl had completely recovered from her fever.

Two soldiers sat on the driver's bench, one handling the two horses that pulled the sleigh. The other was her father's 'spy' who she now knew as Private Roberts.

Ice kicked up by the horses' hooves sprinkled her cheeks, the tip of her nose growing numb. Her nostrils even stuck together and she had to rub them. The group were on their way to a frost fair at a lake on this late January day. Father had given permission for her to go as long as Roberts went with her. A small price, she supposed, though a tinge of resentment remained.

Her parent was still annoyed by her words to Mrs. Sutton over a fortnight ago. Amelia bit back a sigh. She had to be true to herself. Today she wished for pure pleasure.

"You've been to these fairs before?" she asked the children.

"Aye. There'll be roasted apples and hickory nuts," Fergus, the younger boy, declared. "I'm hungry."

"The Mi'kmaq roast seal meat. It's good and tastes like veal," Timothy said with the authority of a brother two years older.

"I hate to eat the pretty seals." Maureen wiped ice-spray from her pale, freckled face. "I'm going to skate on the pond. And listen to the fiddle players."

"Settle down, we'll all have time to have some food and fun, me dears," Mary said. "Lord knows we need it."

Amelia breathed in the crisp air that chilled her lungs. "I wish I had ice skates, though I've never skated before. It rarely froze anywhere in Plymouth." She was relieved to be out of the confines of the fort. She longed for spring, a chance to see Gilbert, and to ascertain his interest in her. Her throat constricted.

The sleigh hit a patch of thick ice and skidded to one side. Amelia held on as they all swayed. The sky had darkened to a steel grey even though midday. The daylight was short here, with the sun rising late and setting early.

"Looks like a snow storm up ahead," the soldier driving the sleigh said.

Amelia gripped the vehicle's sides, the man travelling too fast in her opinion.

Mary leaned close. "I know 'tis not proper to speak of money, but will you have enough to open an herb shop in town?"

245

"I'll need a partner, there's little doubt. Perhaps one of the shopkeepers, a woman, would allow me to share their space." Amelia pulled her cape snug. In winter, even in England, people had to rely on dried herbs. Here the growing season would be shorter. The bottles of simple syrup mixed with herbs and her tinctures would also keep her business solvent, she hoped. "If you know anyone who might be so generous, please tell me."

"I'll ask about," Mary replied. "But the majority of shops are run by men. You might try Mrs. Pengilly at the dry goods. Her husband is in Halifax most of the time."

"I will, thank you." She'd contact the woman as soon as possible.

The sleigh bumped over rougher, rutted areas. The children hunkered down in their fur-lined capes like a litter of kittens. The sky grew even darker and a cold flake landed between Amelia's eyes. The sleigh bounced, skidded again, then swooped to the right. The driver jerked on the long reins to steady the horses. The vehicle's right runner sliced up and hit the frozen snow bank, tipping everyone to the left.

"Slow down, please!" Amelia gripped the side again and held onto Maureen, the child nearest, to keep her secure. Fear coursed through her.

"Begorra, me lads!" Mary cried as she grappled for her other two children. "Control those beasts."

The sleigh continued to tip, then wood cracked as if the shaft broke. Suddenly the vehicle lurched over, dumping them. Amelia's butt hit the road, the ice like a stone wall, her breath knocked from her body. Her hips, knees and elbows burned with pain, fur landed on her head, blinding her.

Skates clattered onto the ice with their sharp blades. She dug out of the furs. "Is everyone all right, anyone hurt?"

The children whimpered. She groped for them. Something stabbed into her side. Her whalebone panniers had cracked, twisted, bunching up her skirt.

Maureen popped up from the furs, fingers in her copper hair. "I think I'm not hurt, aye. Oh, but me bum smarts."

"My leg, my leg!" Fergus wailed. He was sprawled on his stomach.

"Mary! Your son is injured." Amelia crept in the dimness, toward the child's crying, wincing at each move. His leg was caught under the sleigh's higher sides. The child was pinned. He cried louder. She cringed and stared about. The bottom of the sleigh, now a ceiling, seemed to press down on her head. "Mary, hurry. Are you all right?"

"I'm fine, fine, but my knees feel smashed." Mary crawled toward her boy. "Fergus! I'm coming. Where's Timothy?"

"I'm here. I'll get help." The eleven-year-old flattened himself and slid out like a snake where the side was lower. "Help, please, for my brother!"

Mary reached Fergus and stuffed fur under his head. She gripped his hand. "Oh, my poor love. Hang on, lad."

Gloved hands wrapped around the sleigh's sides and heaved on it.

Maureen shivered, and Amelia coddled her in more fur. She hugged the girl, and placed a comforting hand on Fergus' shoulder. "The soldiers will help us, don't worry."

Men grunted, the vehicle creaked, the sleigh slowly lifted. Amelia and Maureen helped Mary move Fergus out into the open. The child yelped. Strangers were there, trying to help.

"Are you hurt, Miss?" Private Roberts limped over. "I'm afraid the driver has busted his arm and injured his head. With the sled flipping, the pole broke in half."

"Your driver was careless. I believe I'm only bruised. But this child needs a surgeon's immediate attention." She brushed back her loosened hair and pulled up her hood. She rearranged the panniers as discreetly as possible and swept her cape close.

Men on horseback, and another sleigh, had joined their group. The sky darkened to dusky pewter and the snowfall increased. Fergus's cries had lowered to moaning. A woman from the smaller sleigh waved Mary over. Roberts picked up Fergus and carried him. There was just enough room for Mary and her three children to squeeze in.

"Go on, hurry," Amelia said. The man turned his vehicle around to head back to town. She spun to Roberts. "You need to get your reckless friend the aid of a doctor, too."

The squall hit like a blast of white and Amelia ducked her head. She could barely see a few feet in front of her. She hunched in her cloak, blinking flakes from her eyes. Her elbows and knees ached. Her hips felt like she'd been beaten with a cricket bat.

Roberts helped the staggering driver over to a man on horseback. Amelia glanced about. Everyone seemed taken care of, on their way to medical aid.

She checked on the horses. Miraculously, they hadn't been dragged down, the shaft breaking just in time. The harnesses had snapped. The animals rolled their eyes. Their harnesses had dug deep, leaving pink gouges in their flesh. She stroked the horses' muzzles, cold even through her glove. Roberts unharnessed them.

She stepped away and the falling snow wiped out their forms, the other people, from her view. She felt caught in an avalanche, but as if in a dream, the snow fell in slow motion.

From behind, a hand came down on Amelia's shoulder. She jumped.

Chapter Twenty

"Amelia, stay quiet, please," a familiar, French-accented voice whispered. Gilbert asked, "Are you injured? Will you come with me? We need to talk."

"I think I'm all right." She hummed with the thrill and tangle of nerves caused by the sleigh accident—then to leave with *him*. "Yes, I'll come."

Strong arms lifted her to sit sideways onto a saddle on a golden-haired horse. Amelia's heart seemed to leap into her throat. Gilbert mounted behind her, held her with one arm, and they rode off through the thick snow.

"Where are we going?" she asked, resisting a nestle into his chest.

"To my cabin. You'll be safe."

In a clearing, through a dense forest of stark trees which turned to pines with snow heavy on their boughs, a small log cabin appeared. Amelia shivered in her ice-crusted cape, her face numb and stiff, her feelings jumbled.

At the cabin, Gilbert dismounted and helped her down. He unlocked the door and urged her inside. "Warm yourself up. I will put Vaillant in his stall."

She stepped into a plain but uncluttered chamber, then limped to a low-smouldering fire. Adding more logs, she stirred the ashes with a poker, encouraging the wood to spark. The smoky scent, the increasing warmth, soothed her trembling body.

Gilbert entered the cabin behind her. Now she quivered in excitement, off-balanced by his presence.

She smiled. "You came out of nowhere and kidnapped me." Confusion at what to do next kept her rigid and in place. "What are we to talk about?" She'd give him the opening.

"I heard the commotion and rode down. When I saw you, I wanted to bring you to safety as quickly as possible." He smiled shyly, and removed his buckskin jacket. His white shirt and leather waistcoat stretched across his broad chest. "But I think you came willingly."

"You're a rogue of the first order." She laughed to relax her nerves. "What will poor Private Roberts think when he sees I've vanished?" She turned and stirred the flames higher, the heat thawing the length of her. Gilbert must still be interested, or he wouldn't have brought her here to talk.

He came up behind her and she heated even more, with that strange, heavy desire she longed for. They were alone in his cabin—anything could happen.

"The militia will be searching for you." His fingers brushed her upper arms. "Are you certain you weren't hurt, Amelia?"

"Just bruises, it seems." She sucked in her breath, her arms tingling. Perhaps she wasn't safe, and should have stayed at the accident scene. "I do hope Mary O'Brien's son will be all right after the sled crash."

"Let us pray he is."

She fingered her kerchief, anxious for occupation. "Can I—make us tea, or coffee?"

"*Excusez-moi*, forgive my lack of being a fine host. I should have offered you a hot drink." He stepped away, to her disappointment and relief.

While he prepared tea she took stock of his cabin. Only one large room with simple wooden furniture he might have made himself. A table with two plank-seat chairs, an attractive raised panel-fronted cupboard, a settee, or more of a bench, with beige cushions, the wood painted red. A more comfortable chair was situated near the stone fireplace. The wide-planked pine floor appeared well swept. He was a man who obviously liked order.

A bed with a beige and white quilt was in the back left corner. She flushed, walked over and sat at the table, her back to the bed. Her bruised hips protested. This was wrong, her being here.

"The pot was a gift from my mother." He set a cream-coloured crockery teapot on the table, the steeping tea releasing a fragrant steam. "This isn't the finest blend."

"I'm sure your tea is fine. I could have prepared it for us." Amelia had the urge to show her capability, to distract the unspoken tension. She furtively met his eyes.

"My mother worries that you might not know how to cook." He smirked and placed two teacups on the table. "I'm out of sugar. I do have a little molasses."

"This is all right. I can concoct a few items for meals, but your mother may have reason to worry." Amelia laughed again, nerves thrumming. He appeared to be thinking of a future together—he'd mentioned her to his mother. She removed her cape and gloves and draped them over the back of her chair. "If we ever... I'll need her expertise, I suppose. To teach me Acadian dishes."

"My mother is a force of nature, sometimes worse than the bears." He grinned, then raised an eyebrow, uncertainty now in his gaze. "I'm sure you know that our being here, just the two of us, has compromised you. I wasn't think—"

"I'm very aware. I'm probably doomed and beyond help." She tried to tease. Her stomach tightened, and she massaged her aching knees under the table. Was he going to offer her something more permanent? Was she ready? Were either of them?

"Amelia." His voice softened. He reached out his hand to touch hers. "I've warned you of the dangers of sharing my life. I wanted you to see how simple it is here. There is nothing but the barest of bones."

She gripped the teacup. The liquid rippled. "So did you bring me here to discourage me, or take advantage?" Had she misread him after all? Anxiety stung through her. She would be ruined, but she refused to be trampled. Forcing a smile, she said, "How terrible of you."

"*Mais non*." He stroked her hand. His mahogany eyes held hers. "As much as you may regret it later, because your family and your society will renounce you, will you consider a serious courtship with me?"

Lightness filled her, though worries lingered. A long breath. "Of course, I will. Even if I might regret it, which I don't think I will. However, you might." Her words tumbled out. "I realize a woman is supposed to be commanded by the man, but I'm not very biddable."

He chuckled. "I am aware of your nature, and I admire you for it."

"It won't be easy, but I'm determined enough to face what comes." She also knew talk was brave, but action, living the cruder life, would be her true test. Her pulse skittered. "We need to learn more of one another."

All the difficulties crowded up in the background, but for the moment she basked in happiness and the glow of a growing connection. His wavy black hair and liquid dark eyes captured her. She almost reached over to caress his cheek. She wished he'd shave his beard so she could see more of him! It was all happening so quickly. She must be mad!

* * *

Her smile curled around him like a soft blanket. Gilbert ached to hug her against him, but he needed to move slowly. He held her long-fingered hand, delicate in his calloused one. "I believe you, *ma cherie*. We do need time to know one another. But you must tell me if ...if you require more discussion, to help with any decisions."

The wind groaned and pushed against the cabin, the walls creaking in protest. Gilbert rose and went to a front window. Snow fell in sheets, splattering against the glass. Frost had formed at the inside of the window's edges.

"The weather's a blizzard now. I won't be able to return you to the fort yet. If I had a sleigh, I might attempt to take you to my mother's." But he wanted her here, close to him. There was no going back now, and he didn't mind.

Amelia joined him at the window. "That would be the proper thing to do, though it does look too hazardous." She sounded concerned, but not panicked. "How far away does your mother live?"

"About four miles north, up along the river. An uncomfortable trip through any blizzard."

"Someone might have seen us leave together. Rumours will fly, but I...I made the choice. If we can't get out, hopefully nobody can search for us." She touched the windowsill, the curtains.

"Your father will be worried. The soldiers will be ordered to search." He fished for

255

conversation to divert them both from their raw emotions. The clean scent of her skin tempted him. He moved away, toward the kitchen. "I'll find us something to eat. I have half a Rappie Pie, if you would share that with me. I prepared it yesterday."

"A man who cooks. Well, I guess you must have to, all the way out here in the woods." She left the window and approached him. "What are the ingredients?"

"I layered rabbit meat and potatoes, though most prefer clams or scallops, but they are not in season."

She looked impressed by his skill, and that endeared her to him even more. He'd watched her from a distance at the crash—no hysterics, no weeping. She'd insisted on help for the wounded. A fine, resilient woman. He removed the pie from the cupboard and placed the dish in the hearth near the fire to warm it up.

"Can I help? Where do you keep your plates?"

He indicated the cupboard's top shelf. "I don't get much company out here."

She removed the two crockery plates and set them on the table.

"What do you think of my cabin? A bit small, *non*?" Gilbert turned the dish, the smell of rich, meaty rabbit enticing his nose. "I always thought I'd build a bedroom onto the back, but haven't gotten around to it. We Acadians live simple lives, as I said."

"I like your home. A separate bedroom sounds…practical." Her cheeks tinged pink as she arranged forks on the table after he'd told her where to look.

Soon, they were seated with a slice of pie and the remainder of the tea. Her thick hair was loose, messy, with soft golden tendrils trailing about her face and neck. It gave her an allure he found appealing. He wanted to protect her, keep her safe.

"How do you manage your trading post when the weather is this bad?"

"We don't get as many customers in the fierce snows." He took a bite of meat and grated potato flavoured with onion, savoury on his tongue. "My partner, Fougère, lives a few yards away from the business and he takes care of the ones who do come."

She tasted the pie. "Ummm, delicious. A hearty meal. I must learn the recipe." She took more bites, then sipped the tea. Her blue eyes met his again. "So, please tell me more about your family."

He watched her genuine pleasure in eating, and pictured her here, every evening. His wife. With a quiet sigh, Gilbert wished he could weave a fairy-tale about his origins, but that would be dishonest. "I told you the basic history our last time in the shop, *n'est–ce pas*?"

She nodded, frowning. "The raids sounded horrific."

"Much of the killings happened before my birth or when I was very young. My mother

257

suffered cruelly at the hands of the English." He clicked his fork on his plate, his portion mostly eaten. "I'm half English, though I rarely admit it to anyone. I never knew my father. He…forced Maman. She was only fifteen, escaping from the British attack on Fort Beauséjour on the Isthmus of Chignecto, which now divides New Brunswick and Nova Scotia. That was in 1755, in what the English call The Seven Years' War." He repelled the heavy sadness that tried to settle over him for his mother and his country. Courage, and a way to forge on, was what mattered. "That war was the end of New France and the beginning of British occupation."

Amelia put her hands to her mouth. Her eyes glistened with tears. "I'm devastated to hear that happened to your mother."

"My people, the ones not caught, fled to Miramichi to the north, where we hid out and struggled to survive. I was born there. More troubles came later."

"I regret your mother was attacked, but..." Amelia lowered her hands and tilted her head. "I'm glad you're here, even with the circumstances."

"*Merci*. But I'm a bastard." He gave her a wry smile. She didn't appear shocked, he appreciated that. His heart swelled, he grew even closer to her. "Something else to add to my repertoire of improperness for a captain's daughter."

Amelia laughed lightly. Mirth brightened her long face, her smile enchanting. Then she seemed to wrestle with a frown. "My esteemed father has a mistress in Parr Town. A relationship that started before my mother's death. So he's hardly a saint."

"Not uncommon for men far from their families, though I'm certain not agreeable to you. I am sorry, *ma cherie*." He finished his pie. She'd eaten most of hers, but had laid down her fork. He took their plates and put them in a bucket. He thought of the lady in burgundy velvet who spoke of marrying the captain. "Come, let's sit by the fire."

He offered her the leather chair, his one sacrifice to comfort. A place he'd spent many solitary evenings.

"No, I'll sit here on the bench. You enjoy your chair." She arranged her skirts after doing so, pushing her booted feet towards the fire.

"Would you mind living out here, remote, in the woods?" He sat in the leather chair and leaned forward, elbows on his knees. The fire warmed his legs and toes. The storm continued to moan outside.

"I don't think I would mind, though these heavy snowfalls must make life difficult." She laced her fingers together in her lap.

"You might get lonely with no neighbours close by." He wanted her to realize all the challenges. She appeared to have the fortitude to be a backcountry wife.

The wood in the hearth crackled and spit.

"Are you trying to deter me, again?" She smiled in expectation. The firelight danced warm light and shadows across her face.

He reached across and clasped her right hand, rubbing his thumb along her soft palm. "I want us to be honest with one another."

"I want that, too." She leaned towards him, her other hand touching tentatively, then she caressed his wrist. "No secrets that could come back to haunt us."

"We're well-matched in that regard, plain-spoken." Desire seeped through him. He swallowed slowly and fought the urge to join her on the bench. To squelch the impulse, he told her about his childhood, the good parts, their settlement on Boishébert Island, making a new home in exile. Then being allowed to return, no more hiding. And she spoke of hers, her early mischief with her brother, her love of her mother, and her father's long absences in the army. A separation she said that might have added to their strained relationship now.

Her life in a bustling city called Plymouth, plus her interests in the medicinal properties of herbs. An easy comradery settled around them.

An explosion. Glass shattered. A musket ball shot through the window and with a slam embedded itself in the far wall, leaving the stink of smoke and gunpowder in its wake.

Amelia's mouth gaped as if she'd scream. He jumped over and dragged her to the floor.

Chapter Twenty-one

Amelia dove, covered by Gilbert's heavy warmth, to the hard pine floor in a shower of glass shards, a gasp in her throat.

"Could that be the soldiers?" she asked between heaving breaths. "Private Roberts?"

"Why would they shoot and risk hurting you? *Mon Dieu*." His voice furious, he helped her toward a corner. "Are you cut? Stay here, away from the windows."

"I don't think I'm too injured." Amelia scooted to the cabin wall, brushing glass from her hands. Tiny spots of blood popped up on her skin, along with the prick of multiple stings. Her knees smarted once more. She gulped down a groan. "What will you do?"

"Grab my musket and see who's out there. Stay still so you're safe." He stooped low, hurried past the hearth, and snatched up a musket that leaned against the wall. He quickly loaded it, then came back around the other side of the room and peered out the shattered window. The icy wind swept in, spraying snow on the cabin floor.

"I thought I saw another gun. I can probably fire it." Amelia pressed a hand over her galloping heart. She hated cowering in a corner. She didn't have her muff pistol, but that tiny weapon would do her little good.

Gilbert put a finger to his lips. He whispered, "This may be the man I'm having land issues with, not soldiers. His name is Bent and he's unpredictable."

"Please be careful." She stared up at him, suddenly terrified he'd be killed. This man did lead a dangerous life, but she was more angry than scared. Her first thought was to join in, to protect one another.

"Who are you, and what do you want?" Gilbert shouted out the window as he slid the barrel of his musket over the frame in a tinkle of glass. "Show yourself! Be aware, I'm fully armed."

An eerie silence followed. Minutes crawled by. Amelia bit on her lip, keeping as still as possible. Gilbert flapped the curtain shut.

"I'm going out to confront this person." He jerked on his jacket and headed for the back door, musket raised. "You remain here, *ma cherie*."

Amelia stood. A chill shot up her spine, and she almost pleaded with him not to leave, but she refused to be that sort of woman. She'd seen a pistol in the cupboard when she retrieved the plates. When Gilbert slipped out, she rushed, ducking under the line of sight from the windows to the cupboard, and dragged out the flintlock pistol. Was it loaded?

Wrapping her still-damp cape around her, she pulled on her gloves, and opened the rear door. If she was to live a wilderness life, she had to manage any peril. Her hands shook on the unwieldy gun.

Footsteps sounded in the crunchy snow. She inched along the cabin wall. The snowfall had thinned, the sky still a dark grey. As she poked her head around the corner, the wind cut into her flesh, slapping off her hood.

Boot prints in the snow led into the woods to her right. She lengthened her stride and stepped into the prints, cradling the gun. Men's voices came from deeper in the woods.

She moved as quietly as possible, cringing at each crunch her feet made. Her skirt hem grew heavy with ice. She bumped into a low tree limb and snow sprinkled over her.

Nearing the sound of arguing men, she stared through the thick pines. Gilbert stood with his musket pointed at three soldiers, an officer with his musket raised, flanked by two enlisted men. Swatches of crimson flashed stark against the white landscape.

"The window was an error; the private swears his gun misfired. But where is Miss Latimer?" The unmistakable voice of Lt. Harris sent another chill up her back. "Are you holding her against her will?"

"*Mais non.* How dare you try to maim us! You frightened Mademoiselle Latimer. And you will pay for the damage to my cabin," Gilbert responded.

Amelia crept closer. A fourth soldier was sneaking from the left toward the group. He had a pistol aimed at Gilbert.

"Please, don't shoot anyone!" she called to the newcomer. She gripped the gun and pointed her weapon in case he didn't take her seriously.

The young man swung about, eyes wide, and fired. The crack of gunfire rent the air. Amelia flung herself on the freezing ground. She'd almost felt the passage of that lead ball in her hair. She shuddered.

"*Mon Dieu*! That *is* Mademoiselle Latimer, you fools." Gilbert hurried toward her and kneeled down. "Amelia, are you hit? What are you doing out here?"

Amelia groaned, the cold snow, and almost getting shot, quaked throughout her body. Her injuries from the sleigh accident pounded in pain. "Mercy, it missed me."

"Private Morrison! I'll have you court-martialled for your actions. Hold all fire!" Lt. Harris shouted. Then the man stomped toward them.

Gilbert helped her up and hugged her against him. "You could have been killed," he growled in her ear.

She clung to him, his warmth and secure hold a comfort. Her racing heart matched his. "That other soldier was about to shoot you. I'm sorry."

"Miss Latimer, are you all right?" Harris demanded. "What has this Frenchman done to you?"

Amelia gathered her wits. "He's protected me. Your soldier tried to murder me."

"I apologize, sir. And, Miss. It happened so fast." Morrison stood at stiff attention in his red coat and black cocked hat sprinkled in white.

"You've been reprimanded before for ill-handling weapons." Harris glared at the soldier. He turned to Amelia. "We'll return you to the fort at once. Your father is in a frenzy over your disappearance." Harris reached for her arm.

"Mademoiselle Latimer has been well cared for," Gilbert disputed, still clasping her against his chest. "Your men have caused the problems."

"Don't ever interfere with my soldiers, Frenchman." Harris glowered, brows low, his hand white-knuckled on his pistol.

Amelia caught her breath. "There's no need—"

"This is *my* property. You have no business here, monsieur. Miss Latimer is protected with me." Gilbert thrust out his jaw, squishing her against him harder now. Harris looked about to step closer, raise his gun.

"Stop. I'll come with you, Lieutenant; to speak to my father, to appease him," Amelia insisted, afraid the two men would come to blows, or blow one another's head off. "Give us some privacy, please, Lt. Harris."

The man grumbled, but finally moved away.

"Was that your betrothed?" Gilbert glared after Harris, then turned to her.

"Unfortunately, a nearly-betrothed," she whispered, reluctant to admit it.

"I should scold you for your actions, Amelia. Never do something so rash again." He gripped one of her shoulders, his eyes full of concern.

She wouldn't admit she agreed her behaviour was a little rash, though she'd probably saved his life. She touched a gloved finger to his cheek. "I'm a hopeless hoyden, remember. And you do lead a precarious life. But I... I can handle myself." Inside, she still trembled.

"I see that now. You are *tres* amazing. When can we meet again?" He bent lower, as if he wanted to kiss her. "To make firmer plans for us before more trouble starts."

"Soon, at the pastry shop. I'll warn my father not to follow me and upset your cousin." She smiled, her breath in huffs. "How about next Tuesday, if we're not in a blizzard?"

"Until then, *mon amour*. Good luck with your father. And mind yourself well." He kissed her on the forehead then turned to the hovering soldiers. "Try not to shoot any innocent women and windows when you deliver Mademoiselle Latimer safely home."

Amelia squeezed his arm then walked toward the soldiers. "I trust the fort's purser will pay to replace the glass. Oh, Lt. Harris, this is my fiancé, Gilbert Arsenault."

* * *

Gilbert swept up the glass and nailed a piece of birch bark over the broken window to stop the wind. What idiots those soldiers were. Nearly killing Amelia, twice! Happiness so close, only to be snatched away. But he'd blundered to have brought her here, risking such danger.

He slammed in the last nail. Then he wondered how the English knew of his cabin. He thought he was sheltered here, free from their scrutiny. Yet Bent had found him that one night. The guide's snarling face usurped his thoughts of Amelia.

Wilcox had told his mother, as he subtly flirted with her, that he'd heard Bent had gone to Québec. Hopefully the drunk would stay there. By spring, with no interference, the land on the river would be rightfully Gilbert's.

He snickered, thinking of the agent trying to woo Maman. An impossible task. Then he warmed, musing on Amelia again, his gun-toting fiancée. She'd proven herself to him. He grinned. She'd make the perfect wife, and had even announced their solidified relationship to the soldiers. How soothing that notion was.

At the back of the cabin he measured in his mind where he'd build the new bedroom on the ground behind it. As soon as the spring thaw, he'd get started on that project. And someday, another bedroom for children, or he'd construct a loft in the main cabin. More smiles.

As long as Jarvis didn't raise the rent too high, or displace them, he and his partner wouldn't struggle. He had to lean on Wilcox, and perhaps his mother's charm, to prevent that from happening.

Gilbert went to the hearth, and threw on another log. Would he be expected to 'charm' Amelia's father? From what he'd heard of the man, that would be another impossible task. The captain could make both their lives intolerable, such as sending a soldier to shoot him dead some evening here in the woods.

"Ah, my life has never been easy," he said aloud—though only a statement and devoid of self-pity—to the emptiness of the room, even more empty without Amelia there, "why should things change now?"

* * *

Father shook his head as he draped a blanket over Amelia's shoulders. "Well, I'm at a loss, my dear. You nearly scared me to death. I had to send men out in that storm. Thank God you're safe. Why didn't you stay with the group after the accident?"

"I apologize for slipping off, Father. And endangering anyone else, though the soldiers were overzealous when they found me." Amelia was still happy she had left. She huddled before the blazing parlour fire. Louise placed a wrapped hot brick under her stocking-clad feet, the heat so welcoming. The housekeeper rushed in and handed Amelia a steaming cup of tea.

Outside, drums sounded, boom, boom and on—the Beating of Retreat ceremony that summoned the night guard at sunset, something Amelia had grown used to.

"That soldier who shot at you will be reprimanded. Nevertheless, you were with that Acadian, alone in his cabin. What *were* you thinking?" Father came around in front of her and leaned on the mantel, his expression vexed, weary. "Your good character will be, sadly, no more."

"And I'm certain the soldiers will talk of the incident." She was beyond worrying over her reputation. She sipped the tea, warming her insides. The soles of her feet thawed on the brick. Louise stayed by the fire, perched on the hearth, staring up at her in curiosity.

Father sighed. "Lt. Harris said you called this man your fiancé. Is that true?"

Amelia smiled, remembering her and Gilbert's intimate conversation at the cabin. "His name is Mr. Arsenault, Father. And, yes, it's true. I'd like you to meet him, if that's imaginable for you."

Her father straightened and looked away, face and neck flushed. "You actually intend to marry this man?"

"I do." For the first time she felt certain this was her destiny. Life could be snuffed out so fast. "And I know I'll face deprivations as well as censure from English society, but I'm willing to risk it for my happiness." She swirled the tea left in her cup. The memory of Gilbert's French accent over tender words, his intense brown-eyed gaze, trilled up her spine.

Another idea came. She could run an herb shop at his trading post, an easier solution than at the fort or a shop in town.

Her parent rapped his knuckles on the mantel. "My warnings and guidance have meant nothing to you?"

"It's not that. But I'll strike a bargain." She finished the tea, her stomach in a slight knot. "I'll form a 'friendship' with Mrs. Sutton..." At least she'd try. "If you promise not to oppose my marriage, and not cause us any difficulty. I realize you cannot stop me, but please make it easier by not objecting."

Father sighed again. He was obviously reluctant to capitulate. "What can this Frenchman offer you? He is half owner in a trading post."

So Father *had* checked up on Gilbert. Amelia pulled the blanket tighter around her. "I know the situation isn't what you'd choose for me. But he is the man I wish to spend my life with." She looked up. "And I'd like for you and I to have a closer rapport."

"I'd prefer that as well, if possible." He moved away from the fire. "You're determined

to have your way, no matter the consequences."
He put a hand on her shoulder "I—might agree
to meet this man, but let's not rush anything.
You're correct, I don't approve." Shoulders
drooped, he left the parlour.

"Oh, Miss, I were so afeared for you."
Louise put her hand on Amelia's, her eyes huge.
"Tell me what happened. You was all alone
with Mr. Arsenault? Will you really marry
him?"

"I will, when he asks. I'm sure he intends
to." Amelia couldn't mistake the tender emotion
in his eyes. "And don't worry, you'll come with
me." She would pay her from her inheritance
now that Father would surely cut off her
allowance. She clasped her maid's little hand,
rehashing the obstacles. Then she told the girl
everything, her mind whirling with the new and
exciting options and twists her life had taken.
The hazards were always there, darkening the
edges. She must re-form herself into a frontier
woman.

Chapter Twenty-two

Gilbert rode out of Miramichi, a village on the Miramichi Bay in northern New Brunswick. His disgust at another failure poked like pinpricks along his flesh. A cold early March wind blew in off the water, matching his bleak thoughts.

He glared at the weather-beaten houses he passed. An Acadian village had existed here for about sixty years early in the century, so his maman had informed him after she'd escaped with family to this region. Then British forces burned it to the ground to further the eviction of his people. He was four years old by that time, living a covert life.

Scottish settlers had moved in later and built their own village. Now Loyalists vied for acreage along the bay. Who would prevail in these evolving changes of supremacy? *Mon Dieu!*

Gilbert returned his thoughts to the present. He'd discovered the remaining witness to his land purchase, a Monsieur William Sterling, hadn't gone to Lower Canada, but lived here in Miramichi with a Maliseet woman. One of

Fougère's long-time friends had given him that information.

Gilbert cursed that he'd found Sterling, but the aging man said he recalled nothing of the land sale.

"I don't know any Franklyn Oram, or if I did, I've forgotten him. You've come all this way for nothing." The elderly man's eyes had darted about like black flies, his wrinkled lips scornful.

"You must remember him. You signed an important document as his witness," Gilbert had insisted, his frustration bunching his shoulder muscles.

"I'm old, leave me be, Frenchie." Sterling had slammed the door in Gilbert's face.

He suspected the curmudgeon lied, but now had to count on Bent never seeing the newssheets with the announcement.

"*Merde*," he grumbled into the chilly air. A long way for nothing, *c'était vrai.*

He hurried his mount on as he pressed a palm against his aching back. The ground had thawed in places; mud formed, mixed with ice chips, to churn up and coat Vaillant's hooves and lower legs in layers of brown sludge. Gilbert glanced about at the thickly forested hills and rolling plains, attempting to redirect his anger.

The area still looked familiar. He'd lived on the refugee island of Boishébert on the Miramichi River as a boy. Established by a French officer, Charles Deschamps de

273

Boishébert during the Acadian Expulsion, the Acadians set up camp there in the dense forest and fished to endure. He sighed. That island was where he was born, existing hand to mouth, stomach always growling.

"The British soldiers chased us like animals through the bushes and trees. My mother, your wise old Mémère, she was almost caught," Maman had told him through her tears when he was young. Tears he'd seldom seen since. "Many of the captured were killed, or shipped away to other colonies. I had many beloved cousins who disappeared. The elders preach God's will, but why would God want us slaughtered?"

The invaders coveted the fertile land, and the lucrative salmon fishing, and no one would stand in their way

He slowed his horse and stared across the water at his once-island home still thick with pines. Sadness and happiness both threaded through him in an always snaking conflict. His people had starved, but also grown close in their struggles. He'd clambered over the sandstone rocks that popped up along the riverbank and picked butternuts from the trees with their foot-long leaves, while he wondered why he didn't have a father—even a dead one—like the other children.

Maman warned him not to feed on hatred, but aspire to overcome. Gilbert smiled slowly. He and his teenaged mother had been an indomitable team.

Riding on, his hips sore, he had nearly one hundred miles to travel south to the capital, now called Fredericton instead of Frederick's Town. Would the English ever decide on a name? Then he had about fifty miles from there to back home.

He patted Vaillant's neck. "We must be hardy, like my people, *mon cheval*."

For four days Gilbert camped in his crude tent, where he shivered as the wind seemed to saturate his body. He lived off dried moose meat, mixed with chokeberries, the natives called pemmican, and the occasional rabbit he could kill. On the fifth day, he rode past Fredericton.

Fort Nashwaak once stood here, the capital of Acadia, the elders said. The fort had been demolished in favour of a new fort further away, all this long before his birth. He tightened his lips. More of his heritage wiped away before he'd even entered the world.

Bitterness he couldn't afford clawed through him. Acadian farmers had once tilled the rich soil here and raised their families. Of course, the Maliseet had been chased from this point as well. They'd once formed a coalition with the Mi'kmaq and French to stop the English invasion, which failed. Each group stormed in and stole from the other.

Loyalists had been settled at the point two years past, in '83; but with few buildings, they'd frozen and starved to death in tents that first harsh winter. Many of his people had prayed this experience would have frightened the intruders to leave the colony and emigrate to Europe.

Still, he had grieved when he'd heard that during the frigid nights the English heated boards by the fire and laid them on their children to prevent them from freezing to death in their sleep.

The then tiny settlement had only three houses, and a trading post. After the spring thaw, the Loyalists had to rush to build log homes for shelter.

His heart clenched at the possibility he could lose his beloved post, along with his maman's home and land. If Jarvis balked, he might need to make alternate arrangements. He thought of his cousin-in-law, Henri, who owned all that land on the peninsula.

Construction was evident on the point now, setting up for Governor Carleton's reign. The St. John River bisected what would be the town, building beginning on both sides. The thud of hammers and scrape of saws seared through his brain.

Gilbert rode on, contemplating what all this change—the possible confiscating of property, *again*—would mean for him and his plans with Amelia. He must make arrangements in case they had to start over someplace else.

* * *

Weeks later, seated in the mouth-watering aroma of the pastry shop's kitchen, Gilbert held Amelia's hands in his. "We must find another place to meet, or I'll be as fat as an ox."

"I feel the same. I'm also ready for spring and my nurturing of fresh herbs." She laughed, squeezing his fingers. "Most of the plants I tried to cultivate in my father's kitchen didn't survive, but I managed to grind a few leaves for use in teas. And I've sold cough syrup, fever tinctures and stomach-ache powder at the fort, under the haughty nose of the army doctor."

"*Bon*. You're doing well. You can count on mid-May, usually, to grow plants." He glowed inside at the sound of her laughter. He massaged her silky wrist. "I should have my land title before that, if Bent never shows himself." He could only pray for that outcome. He'd explained in detail his property ills on a previous visit.

Since the shooting at his cabin, and his trip to Miramichi, they'd met here every week, sometimes twice a week. Their closeness entwined around them as they'd talked of their wishes, interests, worries and ideas for the future. They'd even enjoyed a few furtive kisses.

Now he was ready for something even more pleasant. His heart twitched. He cupped her elbow. "We need to discuss the most important matter. A wedding, *non*?"

Amelia smiled. So did her maid, Louise, who sat a few feet away. The girl curled like a cat near the shop's hot brick oven.

"Yes, of course. I shall be proud to be your wife. But who will marry us?" Amelia's sparkling eyes met his, her skin rosy with excitement. "You said you're Catholic. And I'm an Anglican."

"We do have many Common Law couples here, due to the lack of priests. In one island colony, I've heard a high-level merchant performs the ceremony until a priest might arrive." He tightened his hold. "But I want ours to be blessed by a church. A Protestant minister would probably marry us. I haven't been a very good Catholic."

Irénée rushed in, removed a pie from the oven, and put it to cool on a high table. A delicious aroma filled the kitchen. She left as quickly.

"We'd have to wait three Sundays for the banns to be called." She chewed on her lip, her gaze growing shy. "We should look for a vicar soon. Doesn't one of us have to reside in the parish where the church is?"

"Rituals, particulars like that, are more flexible here. The end of Lent, March 27th, Easter, is only two days from now. We can have the banns called after that, if it's required." He reached up and cupped her soft cheek. "Amelia, here is my pledge to you. I take this woman who screams at bears and attempts to shoot soldiers, for better or worse." He filled with happiness, yearning, fears, and hoped her father didn't have him hauled off to be tortured. "Your papa still refuses to meet me?"

"He's resistant, and I haven't pushed. At least he's given up on trying to control me." She cocked her head. "I think I should visit with your mother soon."

"The tracks are more passable for a cart. How about we travel there tomorrow?" He fought off the dire prospect of his mother's reaction, though she was aware of these meetings and his intentions. She continued to lecture him on his folly in involving himself with an English army officer's daughter and non-Catholic. But he needed to let this woman, who'd mended practically every crack of his being with her nearness, fully into his heart and seal their bond.

"Tomorrow?" Amelia slipped in a breath, brows raised. Their hands clasped together once more. "I'll bring your mother a gift. Nothing frivolous."

He kissed her knuckles. "I'll warn Maman you're coming." And he hadn't given his mother much time to refuse.

* * *

Amelia smoothed her hair with nervous fingers as Gilbert escorted her and Louise in a cart to a hamlet of houses and a gristmill. The

279

Kennebecasis River was mostly frozen, a gleaming ribbon in the weak sunlight. The mill wheel was stilled in the ice. They approached a cedar-shingled, log home where smoke drifted from the chimney.

The ground started to quake, and a great cracking sound rent the air.

"Mercy, what is that?" Amelia asked, pulse skipping. She fidgeted to retain balance. Louise hunched close, staring at her feet as if they might fly out from under her.

"Only the ice breaking up in the mountains." Gilbert chuckled, laying a warm hand on her shoulder. "It happens every spring, and is late this year."

"Then I must get used to it." Amelia laughed to disguise her amazement.

He opened the door and she was anxious to leave the wind and any cracking ice, though cautious of what lay ahead. A small woman stood inside, wearing a white shirt, black laced vest and striped skirt. A white cap sat atop her raven hair. She was attractive, despite her frown, and her evaluating dark eyes.

"Maman, may I present to you Miss Amelia Latimer," Gilbert said with a sweep of his hand, as if introducing her to a queen.

"I'm pleased to make your acquaintance, Madame Arsenault." Amelia made a quick bow of her head, stretching the tension at her nape. She straightened. This house was neat, also one-roomed, but dirt-floored. A bed occupied the far left corner, with a crucifix on the wall above.

"*Bonjour*, Mademoiselle." His mother did not bow. She crossed her arms.

"I brought you a gift, Madame. I hope you find it useful." Amelia held out the plain wooden sewing box she'd rushed into town to buy.

His mother slowly took it and opened the lid. Inside were thread, needles and a pewter thimble. "Hmm. Useful. *Merci*." She almost smiled.

Amelia nearly sighed with relief. They sat in front of the hearth fire with cups of tea his mother poured.

"What does your father, the captain, think of your...wished-for arrangement?" his mother asked, chin raised.

"To be honest, he isn't happy about it. However, it's my life and my decision." Amelia smiled at Gilbert, though she steeled herself for an uncomfortable interrogation.

"Do you know the difficulties of living in the *région sauvage,* this backcountry?" Madame's eye bored into Amelia's. "Shortages, damage from storms, the long winters. Wild animal attacks."

His mother had a melodious though firm voice with her exotic French accent.

"I'm very aware of the problems that might arise, Madame." Amelia nodded and sipped the weak tea. "And I realize I still have much to learn. But I've faced a bear, and an attack by soldiers. Even a nor'easter."

"Maman, I told you she isn't afraid to use a pistol." Gilbert clasped Amelia's hand. She took strength from his heated grip.

"Her people will treat her badly." His mother shrugged, staring at Gilbert. "That may be worse than the deprivations of this land, *non*?"

"I don't care about that. I think my father will reconcile himself, eventually." Amelia wasn't certain, but if Father couldn't support her desires, she'd have to go on without him, despite the sadness that brought.

"We'll see, Mademoiselle. You seem a smart young woman, and from what I've heard, brave." His mother rubbed her chin. "Only time will tell how you may cope. Will you convert to our religion?"

"That will require instruction from a priest," Amelia replied, vague on purpose. She swished her tea and had no plans to convert to popery. Gilbert had agreed with that decision.

"In good time, Maman. We all must go where our hearts lead us." Gilbert grinned at Amelia, then he studied his mother. "Speaking of such, has Monsieur Wilcox been by to call on you?" He winked.

"I should throw my tea at you, *mon fils*." Her lips quirked as if she fought a smile. She drank from her cup. "He wouldn't dare, unless he brings me good news."

"It's time you weren't alone anymore." Gilbert continued to tease, but there was an underlying hopefulness. "You're still a beautiful woman."

"Hah!" His mother's cheeks flushed. She opened the sewing box and picked around at the items, avoiding his gaze. "You only want me to soften up Monsieur Wilcox, so he is relentless with Monsieur Jarvis about not raising your rent. I might do that if needed, for your sake." She then met her son's eyes. "But don't ever ask me to have an affair or marry anyone, especially an Englishman."

"The English were barbarous to you. I can only apologize for my countrymen," Amelia said softly, guilt and defence wrestling inside her. "But most of us are good people."

"And I would never expect such a sacrifice from you for anyone's sake, Maman." Gilbert shook his head. "Just don't judge a man by his nationality, only by his actions. Is there a nice Acadian you'd consider?"

"I consider no one. Yet you may have a point in there somewhere." His mother stood with a swish of her skirt. "Now, Mademoiselle Latimer, let me show you how to prepare *pâté à la râpure.* You can chop the onions."

"I'd be happy to, Madame." Amelia rose from her seat. "I look forward to learning your recipes." She'd try hard to be the amenable bride-to-be—to gain this woman's trust.

"In the later spring, if you're still here, I'll show you how to skin a pig for our fatty pork ingredient." The woman cast a sly gaze and plopped two onions before her. "For now, we use salted pork."

Amelia suppressed a wince at the idea of skinning any animal, but this was one of many skills she needed to acquire. His mother tested her. Would she be able to manage the privations? She must form herself into a different person than the one she once thought she'd be. This excited and frightened her. "I'm more than ready to listen to your good advice, Madame."

After eating, they sat before the fire with earthenware mugs of fermented fir water. Amelia took tiny sips of the overly sweet beverage. Louise mended a piece of clothing Madame had in a basket, after asking permission.

"You want advice. Let me tell you about your countrymen, and what happened to me, so you understand my side of this invasion. *Les Acadiens'* side." Madame kicked off her sabots and wriggled her toes in woollen stockings toward the fire. "I don't normally dwell on such things. Anger only drags you down, *comprenez vous?*"

"I will leave you women to talk while I repair the chinks in your logs." Gilbert excused himself.

Amelia hunched forward, with Louise, becoming absorbed in the tale as if she'd been there alongside Mrs. Arsenault.

The fort on the neck of land called the Isthmus of Chignecto fascinated Marie-Cateline. She recalled when the French had built the huge edifice three years before, when she was twelve. The fortress had five pointy wings and resembled a star—a castle.

Her family had once lived across the Missaguash River, in the village of Beaubassin, situated on an upland near a saltwater marsh. She grew up smelling the sea, hearing the gulls and sanderlings. Wildflowers and brown, fuzzy cattails on long stalks nodded in the breeze during good weather. Her Papa raised cattle on the surrounding grasslands. Others raised hogs, or tended apple orchards.

Her brothers told tales of trading with the New Englanders by way of the Bay of Fundy, and up north with Québec. But there was always turmoil between her people, the Acadians of New France, and the British who controlled the colonies to the south.

Treaties were formed and broken. Skirmishes and wars fought. Soldiers came in 1750 to seize the important isthmus, and the Acadians burned the village to prevent the enemy from using it. Her beloved home was reduced to ashes. She'd wept with her maman over the loss.

Her people took refuge on Point Beauséjour. But the British wanted the trade, the land. Her papa explained that a war raged overseas between France and England and other countries that determined the colonies' fate. The

British built fortresses throughout Nova Scotia. The French gathered more troops, and erected Fort Beauséjour.

The British had the affront to build Fort Lawrence over their demolished village.

At fifteen, Marie-Cateline understood the ramifications, her family's struggle to hold on to what they'd cultivated, the possibility of their deaths. Her nerves remained on edge. The Acadians had refused to pledge fealty to the English king named George, and they refused to assimilate with the British.

She'd learn later the English decided these French abandoned by their own King Louis must be eliminated.

In June of 1755 warships arrived on the river. The Acadians ran to take cover in the fort. Her brothers were safe, trading in Québec. A bomb went off against the fort's casement, rumbling the walls, killing people she knew. She'd never forget the stink of gunpowder, the coppery stench of blood. The heart-breaking death of loved ones.

"We were devastated, *ma demoiselle*. And worse was to come," his mother said, lips pursed, eyes glistening with unshed tears. She talked on:

The soldiers in their red coats flooded the fort, chasing the Acadians out. Her papa was shot when he tried to fight back. *Dear Papa!* Her most shocking loss.

Marie-Cateline fled with her mother, but she'd tripped. A soldier grabbed her, wrestling her into the bushes. Her mother's screams and her striking his back didn't stop him. He flipped Marie-Cateline on her back, his florid, sweaty face hovering over her. Terror, helplessness, consumed her. He ripped her clothes and the unthinkable happened.

The soldier had left her there, her dress in tatters, body bruised, weeping, until her mother hurried her away. Thus began the long trek to the north, to hide on Boishébert Island, and await the birth of her son.

Amelia sniffed, tears clouding her eyes when Madame finished her story. Louise hung her head. Gilbert left his stuffing moss between logs and hugged his mother.

The woman stood, her expression enigmatic again. "*Vraiment*, I lost my dear papa, but gained my excellent son." She straightened her skirt. "You English took over our fort and renamed it Fort Cumberland. They burned everything we'd built."

"I'm so sorry. I'm glad my father wasn't in this colony then—he'd have been as young as you. I could never have forgiven him." Amelia fisted her hands. She could not blame Gilbert's mother for her hatred of the English. She must find a way into this woman's affection.

Chapter Twenty-three

Wariness snaked through Amelia at opening the package sent over by Mrs. Sutton. But she'd promised her father she'd 'befriend' or at least not disparage his mistress. With Louise watching, she laid out the enclosed rose-coloured satin on her bed. The material shimmered in the light from her window. "I suppose this is a peace offering. Exquisite, I must admit."

"'Tis beautiful, Miss." Louise ran her fingers over the cloth. "So smooth."

"The fabric looks expensive. She also sent a pattern to follow for a new gown." Amelia scrutinized the pattern. "A *Robe a l'Anglaise*. Open front, fitted back, a short train, and three-quarter sleeves. The dress requires a matching petticoat. It seems very fancy for this outpost."

"Pleated down the middle of the back, is it?" Louise studied the picture.

"Should I use satin? People will think I'm putting on airs." Not that this really mattered to Amelia. She knew she was equivocating. "Do you think we can fashion this?"

"'Twon't be easy, but I'm certain sure we can." Louise gave an encouraging smile. "Me mam were a seamstress, and I learned much from her afore I went into service."

"And I'll learn more about making my own clothes if I'm to live in the woods." Amelia's feelings of inadequacy emerged at that task, and others to come. She vowed to improve her skills beyond embroidery and piece work. "You'll be of much help to me."

"Aye, Miss. And you'll be lovely for your wedding."

"I'm relieved to wear something bright. I suppose it's time to give up my mourning." Amelia hesitated, then tugged off the black armband. She closed her eyes and said a prayer for her mother in heaven. "It's time to enjoy life once more."

"Again, I'm that sorry for losing Mrs. Latimer." Louise continued to stroke the satin. "She were the best of women."

"She was." And here Amelia was about to design a dress from cloth given her by her father's kept woman. The pinch of betrayal didn't hurt as much anymore. "I think we'll have enough satin to make you some pretty ribbons for your dress."

Louise gave a faint squeal. "Oh, thank you, Miss."

Drumbeats sounded outside on the parade ground.

Amelia sighed. "I can't get out of my head that terrible incident Gilbert's mother told us about. It makes me look at the soldiers differently."

"Her fate were the worst." Louise nodded, then a shy smile appeared. "But Mr. Arsenault would never have been here…"

Amelia warmed, her thoughts tranquil again. "That proves that sometimes good can come from evil."

Downstairs, at the dining room table, they cut out the satin according to the pattern. They pinned then sewed the skirt and bodice, and fashioned the pleats. Louise added laces to secure the bodice. Amelia could sew well enough, but she admired Louise's neat stiches and French seams. Her maid had learned much from her seamstress mother. Nearly a week of fervent work went by.

Amelia, after putting it off, laboured over how to sound neither overly appreciative nor aloof, sent a polite note of thanks to Mrs. Sutton. Her father expressed his pleasure.

"I won't try to discourage your plans, my dear," Father said over sherry in the parlour the following evening. "But don't be upset by the reception you'll receive from the British, especially the ladies."

"I'm well aware, Father. I know the pitfalls. I'll seek no friendships there if none are offered." She kissed his cheek, taking in his spicy scent of bergamot, in an effort to continue their armistice. "I only wish a friendship, a return of affection, with you."

He nodded slowly with a defeated smile. "I wish for that, too. Despite the debacle over Lt.

Harris, I only want the best for you." He sipped from his glass and patted her hand. "I'll confess my judgement was impaired when it came to him, and again I apologize."

"Thank you. I still wish you'd attend my wedding ceremony." She smiled, hoping to persuade him.

"You know that I cannot." He sighed and glanced away. "I can't risk any further taint on my character, since Governor Carleton relies on my efforts with settling the Provincials."

Amelia nearly bit into her tongue. Mistresses were acceptable, but marrying a lower status as well as Catholic man wasn't. She understood that religion separated people more than it brought them together. Any retort would have been shaded in disappointment.

The next day, she slipped the dress over her shift and stays. The sleek satin felt cool against her arms. "It's lovely."

Louise pinned the bodice and clapped. "'Tis perfect." The girl adjusted the pleats in back. "With a pretty white fichu, you will charm your Frenchman. La, I mean, Mr. Arsenault."

"We did exceptional work." Amelia twirled before a mirror, watching the folds of the skirt swirl like fairy wings, the matching petticoat revealed. "Gilbert and I spoke with the vicar at the Presbyterian Church. He's posted our Intent to Marry, for twenty days, sort of like banns." The vicar had looked down his nose at her, even so. "My nerves are showing." Amelia laughed, stroking the satin. "Of course, you already know this."

She and Louise now attended the services there on Queen Street in Parr Town, eschewing the Anglican service at the fort. Gilbert would never enter Fort Howe—not even for his wedding. Besides, he'd be ordered to denounce his faith by the strict Church of England, which wrangled to keep these settlers on the true path.

Amelia thought she'd die from the anxiety that kept her on edge as she waited. Soon she would be a wife, with all the mystery and responsibility that entailed.

* * *

On Easter morning, Gilbert rode to his Maman's. She held up a glass of the *l'eau de Pâques*, the holy Easter water taken from the river. The water could not be from a well or any still lake. It had to be a moving stream, and dipped just before sunrise.

Gilbert drank from the water, which was supposed to have magical properties, yet it tasted the same. But this year his spirits were high, his life was changing in exciting ways, soon he'd have a wife—perhaps that was the magic.

More people and relatives joined them from the local community and beyond. An elder said mass. Gilbert prayed for everyone's health and a good, fruitful marriage.

Maman served the traditional boiled eggs to break their fast. The aroma of a ham simmering in a pot over the hearth fire filled the house. "Relish my cooking while you can, *mon fils*."

"You will be Amelia's teacher of cuisine, *n'est–ce pas*?" He laughed and bowed.

His cousin Jean swaggered up and elbowed him in the side. A stocky man, he wore a plain white shirt under the brown woolen vest the Acadians preferred. "Romancing a captain's daughter, you *coquin*. And English, too. Have you decided to start another war?" He snickered.

"No more wars, *mon ami*. We all should stand together. My Amelia and I only want peace." Gilbert chuckled, wishing it so. He grabbed his mother's hand, to her surprise, as he heard the fiddlers tune up.

"I don't have time for this," she protested, flapping her apron.

The fiddlers played and the Acadians sang and danced. Gilbert dragged Maman into the group. Feet tapped, red or red-striped skirts swirled, bows sliced over strings as the walls vibrated with joy. They sang hymns from the day of their expulsion and ones that showed their faith: "*Vive Jésus, Vive Jésus; Avec la croix cher portage*." Sweet sweat permeated the air.

Maman laughed, her face bright with happiness, as she joined in the dance steps.

He hugged his mother once the dance ended. "A wonderful celebration, as always."

"*Merci*. Will your soon-to-be wife honour our traditions?" She gave him a sly look, her hand pressed to her chest from her exertion, cheeks flushed.

An elderly grandmother told the story "The Bell that Cries" to the children present. Their bright eyes turned up to her as they sat cross-legged on the dirt floor.

Gilbert smiled at his memories of these holidays as a child. His Mémère had told him and his cousins that story about two thieves who try to steal a sacred bell, but end up drowned. "You should never take what isn't yours," she'd admonished.

"Amelia will honour us, do not worry." He grinned. He could rely on Amelia to give her best effort.

* * *

In mid-April, Gilbert hired two men to assist him in framing out the bedroom off the rear of his cabin. He revelled in the progress, the changes in his life. They turned a window into a door, and would put two small windows in the bedroom, large enough to let in light yet discourage the cold. Of course, they couldn't yet dig in the footers because the ground was still frozen deeper down. But plans were made, drawings prepared, wood gathered. They cut timber for the floors and stacked them inside the cabin to acclimatise the wood.

He shot a bear he caught roaming just out of hibernation, and skinned off the huge pelt to make a fur for his—his and Amelia's—bed. Then he gave fresh meat to his maman, cooked himself a meal, and preserved the remaining meat by smoking or brining the flesh in salt and water, with a drop of molasses to replace the sugar he didn't have. He extracted oil from the fat for cooking. The meaty and metal stink of flesh and blood, the entire process, reminded him of his years as a trapper. At thirty years of age, he wasn't sorry to have left that roaming life behind.

He rubbed gritty salt over the hide and left it overnight. The next day he scraped the salt and flesh from the hide and hung it to dry. He'd tan and stretch it later.

The fur would do nicely for his new wife. Besides, he'd keep her warm at night. His chest heated at the thought. He shouldered a huge responsibility, and must protect her without incurring the wrath of her father, or the scrutiny of soldiers. The fact he'd take her from a life of relative luxury weighed heavily on him.

He turned the bear meat in the crock jars full of brine, the smell pungent. He'd wait for the time when Amelia joined him to show her how to kill and prepare fowl and small animals. Cougar meat was also tasty, but those big cats were risky to chase down.

Gilbert had also started to build her a chest of drawers and a matching clothes press, something a proper Englishwoman would appreciate.

"Gilbert." Jean, his cousin who was helping, approached. "A filthy, ragged lad handed this to me outside. He said it's for you, then he ran off."

Gilbert took the note on soiled paper and unfolded it. *You is warned. Trubles coming for you.*

He recoiled, half tearing the paper. No signature, the writing was amateurish at best. Was it the vile Bent, back in the vicinity? Or someone who opposed his upcoming marriage?

* * *

Amelia held her breath and entered the small church on Queen Street on the twenty-fifth of April. Louise and Mrs. Fulton were at her side and not her father. Her stomach twitched when she didn't see him inside the chapel—she prayed he'd have second thoughts, even after he'd told her again that he couldn't attend.

Gilbert's mother also wasn't present. She'd decried the sacrilege of his marrying outside of the Catholic faith. Hopefully that wouldn't sadden him too much.

To her relief, no one had objected to her and Gilbert's marriage throughout the twenty days, though many whispered and muttered about an English captain's daughter marrying an Acadian trader.

Gilbert awaited her at the pulpit, wearing a dark frock coat and breeches. Her heart lightened to see his welcoming smile. He'd trimmed his beard close, but hadn't shaved it off. His cousin Jean stood as groomsman beside him.

Most of the congregation stayed absent. Two young officers' wives who had been friendly with Amelia when she'd arrived in the colony, and invited her for card parties, dared to attend. One or two people in the pews observed the couple with stony silence. Amelia's annoyance flared over exposing Gilbert to this negative perusal.

Mary was there with her daughter Maureen, and they both nodded in encouragement, their round faces beaming.

At Mary's insistence, Seamus, her grumbling cousin who'd first driven them to Gilbert's post, stepped forward and escorted Amelia down the aisle.

"Last chance to change your mind and run, lass," he whispered, his expression disgruntled as usual. She smirked at him to hide her dismay at her lack of paternal escort. He snorted and deposited her in her shimmering gown beside Gilbert. Body odour, perfume and mustiness mingled in the air.

Louise and Mrs. Fulton stood in as witnesses.

Amelia quivered with anticipation as they said their vows. She blinked back moistness in her eyes. She was marrying a frontier man in an untamed country, and she'd have to be stronger than she'd ever imagined.

Gilbert's gaze on her, the deep affection she saw there melted the majority of her qualms. His vows said in his French accent delighted her. Amelia's heart soared and breath hitched.

In her new rose gown, worn over the repaired panniers that pushed out the sides, a soft muslin kerchief swathed about her neck, and pink silk flowers—a gift from Father—in her hair, she felt like a princess. Albeit a princess on the precipice of becoming a peasant. Her hand tightened on Gilbert's to hold him close. His appreciative perusal gave her confidence.

Once the rings, plain gold bands, were exchanged, the cool metal on her finger, the vicar said, "I now pronounce you man and wife."

The vicar, a doughy-faced young Scotsman, turned toward the scrutinizing spectators. Few looked very pleased, and some downright disapproving—except Louise in her best dress and rose-coloured ribbons, Mrs. Fulton, and their other guests, including Mr. Fougère and his native wife, Sesip.

Their warm smiles lit the dim chapel and glossed over the sad fact that Father remained absent. Amelia saw him again for the weak man he was, but had to forgive him with her own dignity, since he was her father.

Gilbert kept glancing out the windows, his brows knitted, as if he expected someone he didn't like, but his hand held hers firm.

"I present to you Mr. and Mrs. Arsenault," the vicar announced, his words echoing off the vaulted ceiling.

Gilbert bowed, turned to Amelia and gently kissed her, his eyes full of love. She revelled in their soft lips so sweet together. She was now his wife, and she was cherished. For the first time she felt beautiful. Elated tears blurred her eyes as her knees wobbled.

"It's an abomination." A portly woman stood, a white feather on her straw hat waving. "I'm the half-sister of Mr. Gabriel Ludlow, from the Governor's Council, and he'll probably be mayor of this town. I came to see if this would actually happen. Stuff and nonsense. It's bad enough that Frenchman," she stabbed a finger at the Fougères, "brought his native concubine." She glared back at Amelia.

"She's Mr. Fougère's wife, not a concubine," Amelia protested, watching Sesip's impassive face, a woman she barely knew but planned to befriend.

"Miss Latimer, you should be ashamed," the woman continued. "If your father couldn't, the officers of Fort Howe should have prevented this."

"Miss, I mean *Mrs.* Arsenault's married for love, to a good man." Mary jutted out her chin, eyes blazing. She'd finally approved of Amelia's attachment. "And this be a church, so show some respect."

The woman made a loud harrumph and waddled out from her pew to the aisle.

Amelia glanced at Gilbert, her stomach now in tangles. "I'm sorry for this rude embarrassment."

"Do not lament for me, *mon amour*," he whispered and kissed her knuckles. "I worry for you."

"Oh, dear. Lord, they know not what they say." The vicar pressed his fingertips to his mouth, said a quick blessing of forgiveness, then vanished through a rear door. He had expressed his reluctance to marry them more than once.

Gilbert stepped toward the large woman and bowed again. "Madame, I applaud you for having the courage to attend. We welcome you on our special day."

The woman started, as if taken aback by his courteous words. Her feather jerked in affront. "Well, I never…"

"We should *never* fall victim to prejudice, Madam. I'm proud to be the wife of this honest, upstanding man." Amelia joined them, encircled Gilbert's arm and smiled broadly over her upset. Here was a taste of the ugliness that could greet her among the populace. Her head reeled, but she'd find a way to persevere.

When they left the church, out into the warming air, Amelia glimpsed a couple hustling off in a step of polished black boots, red coat, and the swish of a yellow skirt. The man in uniform and a woman in an elegant gown. Her father and Mrs. Sutton? Father *did* care.

Amelia smiled and clutched her new husband's large hand, so strong on hers. Gilbert smiled down on her, reinforcing her decision to spend her life with this woodsman.

If only her father hadn't run off as if ashamed of her.

Chapter Twenty-four

Seated in The Coffee House, Gilbert surveyed the room, anxious to keep his livelihood intact in this sea of Englishmen who bartered for acreage. He accepted a cup of the sooty-smelling coffee from a waiter. The strong aroma of the beverage and wreaths of tobacco smoke hung in the air.

Mr. Wilcox sat across from him. "Jarvis should join us soon. He was not of a mind to do so, but I insisted." The agent held up his can then took a large gulp. "I understand congratulations are in order, Mr. Arsenault?"

Men's voices hummed like insects around them, making it difficult to hear.

"*Merci*. My cabin isn't yet ready for my wife, but she will move in tomorrow with her young maid." Gilbert smiled to mask his agitation. He wasn't sure where Louise would sleep but they'd arrange something. Most frontier women didn't have maids, but he hoped this would ease Amelia into her new life.

He remained on the alert after that badly written, cryptic note he'd received at his cabin. Again, the only person that came to mind was

Bent. Why hadn't the idiot come forward to protest the land sale?

"You've married into the military, so to speak." Wilcox studied him, one brow raised.

Gilbert sizzled inside. "I will have little to do with them, and only for Amelia's sake. I wed the woman of my affections." He was impatient to have her with him after their marriage the day before. She'd gone back to her father's house the same day to pack up her belongings, stay the night and say goodbye; ingratiate herself with her papa, she'd said. Would the captain treat her well? "You never know where attraction will lead."

"Ah, so true." The agent smiled slowly, then nodded his broad head. "I understand your animosity toward the soldiers. The Acadians suffered mightily. But we must all forgive."

"*Mais oui*. I pray such conduct stays in the past." With a glare toward the door, Gilbert tapped his fingers on his thigh. He needed to reach an agreement with Mr. Jarvis, so his trade remained safe. He had a family to support. He couldn't allow Amelia to fall into poverty.

A loud discussion broke out at a table nearby.

"We Loyalists are restless, to put it mildly," Wilcox said. "Elias Hardy, the common clerk who represents us, is leading protests over the favouritism of land grants. These delayed settlements, the corruption uncovered, are causing despair and idleness."

303

"Loyalists are applying for land cultivated by others who have lesser standing. That shouldn't be legal." Gilbert gritted his teeth. Anyone who wished could claim property, if enough money exchanged hands.

"Previous surveys were careless. I know this affects you with your land on the river."

"*Vraiment*. But favouritism should not be used to push the Acadians off their property," Gilbert replied. "The incompetence of this settlement process is rife. The English have shipped in brass-handled locks, bronze hinges, and those tiny brad nails to my trading post, among others. Not very useful in this remote country."

"So I heard. A bit elaborate, true. A shame the people in London aren't more attuned to our particular situation." Wilcox glanced toward the front door, then back on Gilbert. "How is your mother, by the way?" He smiled again, his eyes glinting. "I trust she's well."

Should Gilbert encourage this man in 'courting' his maman? He'd be a good resource, beneficial to have on their side, but would she be happy or cunning with him in manipulation? Or might Wilcox, though shocking it would be, bruise her heart?

"She's a fiery woman, as you once said. Tread carefully if you have any interest. Just remember, she's not fond of the English, and she's under my protection." As if Maman needed anyone's protection. "You seem a man of good repute, but are you?"

"Indeed, sir!" The agent frowned then seemed to correct himself. "I must admit that I've always tried to be an honest and decent man, and so far have been successful—even in the face of this current disaster. To tell the truth, we were shocked the Patriots *wanted* independence. Then our own government in England with their peace terms deserted those loyal to the king."

"Like France deserted my people, giving the country away to England." Could any government be trusted? Everyone seemed self-serving.

A shadow fell over them. Gilbert looked up to see the pointy-nosed, pock-faced Jarvis, a fop in his extravagant clothes and powdered wig.

"Mr. Jarvis, please sit with us." Wilcox stood. "Shall I order you a coffee?"

"I've had a letter from England." Jarvis coiled his thin body onto the bench next to Wilcox's stocky form, and smoothed his blue velvet frock coat. His flinty gaze scraped over Gilbert. "The landlord has given me the deed to the property on the bay."

Under the table Gilbert gripped his knee.

Wilcox beckoned to an aproned young man and ordered a coffee.

"Our post has always been profitable, and we've paid our rent on time, Monsieur." Gilbert sipped his coffee, the flavour bitter. He took a slow breath. "We're good, reliable tenants."

"And good tenants should be kept content." Wilcox's expansive smile pushed out his wide cheeks even more.

"I need money to build my manor house." Jarvis knitted his faint brows. "I've been forced on this shore against my will. A man of my status deserves proper accommodations."

"We've all faced privations, *mon ami*. But for your house, you might require the brass-handled locks and bronze hinges I have for sale. Quite fancy." Gilbert swallowed his irritation with this 'entitled' dandy. "What are your terms?"

The waiter placed the porcelain can of coffee in front of Jarvis. The man dipped his beak like a curious bird, his nostrils wrinkling. "A twenty percent raise of rent isn't out of the question."

Gilbert's gut tightened. This man was a buffoon. Gilbert and his partner couldn't afford such an increase. "I believe that is too high, Monsieur. We'd like to remain at that location."

"Twenty percent, that's a bit harsh," Wilcox said, his tone conciliatory. "How about ten percent? A much more reasonable amount."

"That's almost not worth the effort," Jarvis retorted like a spoiled child. He was obviously an inexperienced businessman with no sense of negotiation.

"I will agree to ten percent," Gilbert said through clenched teeth. "And you will retain tenants who don't cheat or take advantage."

"I could take over the post completely." Jarvis tipped up his nose. "Or start another business there, with a British proprietor."

"Ask around, Monsieur. Many businesses fail. Ours is of long standing." Gilbert's blood curdled—another British attack. "I'm an expert with furs, and—" He almost said his post was one of the most profitable enterprises in the colony, but that might encourage Jarvis to raise the rent higher. "I'm the best man to manage it, and in that location. I spent years as a trapper."

"Is that so? I will do as I please for what I need in order to live the life I once had." Jarvis stood, having never touched his coffee. "I doubt ten percent is feasible." He pressed a fist on the table, leaned over, his nose poking like a sword at Gilbert.

Gilbert clutched the table edge. He resisted a swat to the end of that nose. "There's no need for such rudeness, Monsieur Jarvis. You will find this wilderness requires experienced people."

"Damn this wilderness." Jarvis straightened, his mouth in a twist. "No one understands my losses. My estate confiscated, stolen by those treacherous Patriots."

Gilbert reeled in his ire at the man's haughty disposition, even if his people had experienced a similar theft of property.

"I'm certain you'll come to the wisest decision, Mr. Jarvis." Wilcox raised his brows at the cocky rooster. "And leave the post as it is, with only a small rent increase."

"I give no promises. Good day." Jarvis stalked off.

"I'll handle this. I'm sure I can get him to agree to ten percent." Wilcox didn't sound so sure now, his smile wavering.

"The man could use a good whipping." Gilbert made an effort to relax. "He might have suffered, but hostility is not the answer. I'm learning that lesson myself."

He snatched out his kerchief and swiped sweat from his nape. He'd speak with Henri again on his way home about renting part of his land, and building a new post if he could afford it. No more worries about prickly landlords.

Shouting came from outside and steadily grew louder. Men moved in the direction of the front door.

"Jarvis is young and impetuous." Wilcox held up his hand as if to stave off Gilbert chasing after the rascal. "He's grasping hard to his pride. I myself lost much when the rebels won the war."

"We all bury our pride when necessary." Gilbert stared toward the commotion. He was still surprised that Wilcox seemed sympathetic to him. Did the agent have an ulterior motive? "Is Jarvis an English aristocrat?"

"A baronet's younger son, so just barely." Wilcox winked and chuckled. "I'll finalize the amount with Jarvis, then come by to let you know."

"Should we meet here, or at my mother's?" Gilbert would have made it a taunt, but he was too vexed by the confrontation. "Her home would be better." He tossed out the bait. Maman said she'd charm the agent if needed. Then he cringed with guilt over using her. He rubbed his temples, a headache starting.

Further shouting. More people left the room. He and Wilcox rose and followed the exodus.

Outside, a crowd had gathered on the narrow street with its jumble of buildings. Fists were raised as well as voices. "The fisheries will be ruined. We'll starve. Trade with the United States must resume!"

"Traders from Massachusetts, where I used to live, are usurping Parr Town's harbour," Wilcox said to Gilbert. "Everyone wants to bypass the Navigation Acts." He scratched under his grey wig. "Unfortunately, these northern colonies depend on American foodstuffs."

Gilbert knew much of this, as a trader who assumed he'd received some of his goods illegally—but he didn't ask questions.

Men pushed past them, elbows jabbing. The smell of unwashed bodies and the briny bay filled the air. Dark clouds swirled overhead, threatening rain.

"Governor Parr in Halifax is dealing openly with the United States, why can't we?" one man yelled.

Soldiers rode up, along with Governor Carleton, stiff on a white horse. Gilbert eyed the man he'd once spoken to. Rumour said Carleton struggled to set up a provincial militia, initiated a few years before, that would call every young, able-bodied man to arms when needed. Would that include Acadians?

Gilbert scoffed. He wasn't even allowed to vote or join any government body because he was Catholic. The hell with joining a militia.

"Please, everyone, calm down. We'll come to some sort of agreement, I promise," Carleton cried above the grumbling crowd.

One roughly-dressed man stalked up to the governor's horse, causing the beast to toss its head. The soldiers raised their muskets.

"I don't trust you, sir!" he raised his fist. "We're being replaced, we old-comers! Just to make room for these refugees. And now without America, our fish trade is compromised."

A soldier dismounted and faced the angry man. He pushed the old-comer back. The man stumbled then thrust up both fists.

"No shooting, if it can be avoided," Carleton warned, standing in his stirrups.

The old-comer jabbed out his knuckles and caught the soldier on the chin. The soldier struck him back, then hit him with his musket barrel on the side of the head. A second soldier dismounted. He grabbed the man and jerked his arms behind his back. The two soldiers hauled him off, through the protesting crowd.

Another group of men began to fight and punch one another, yelling obscenities. Feet scuffled in the dirt, and blood dripped from noses. A soldier fired his musket into the air.

Gilbert recoiled; he elbowed off the heaving bodies, loathe to involve himself in a skirmish among Englishmen if he could avoid it. Even if the outcome would affect him as well.

Another shot fired. A few of the agitators dispersed as they threw insults over their shoulders.

"You English now battle among yourselves," Gilbert said with irony. Yet he was disturbed by what further anarchy this might produce.

"We do, on all sides. The men from America without status—unlike myself—fear people of position and influence will take the best land, and force them to be tenants." Wilcox nodded with a shrug of dismay. "No one is happy."

"Men of influence, like Jarvis. Everyone wants to be the pack's head dog," Gilbert muttered.

He and the agent wriggled through the grumbling crowd down to the port, now in disarray from the recent construction of additional wharves and warehouses. Many ships and boats crammed into the harbour. Merchants swarmed along the jetty, shouting prices as they flashed their merchandises. Gulls cried and cut like scissors through the overcast sky.

With honks and bellows, a flock of geese flew overhead, back from their winter migration.

"Carleton gave out licenses to trade, for certain British ships to bring American goods.

But unlawful activity is everywhere," Wilcox said with a shake of his large head. "People fear this harbour area might be seized by the United States if the leaders here aren't careful."

"*De rigueur.* This country always exists in turmoil. The American trade is needed. We Acadians used to trade our salmon for barrels of salt, a vital commodity. Your government was unwise to cut it off just because those rebels wanted freedom from the British." A sentiment he understood. Gilbert tugged his hat low in the wind. A fat raindrop dampened his shoulder. The fog already rolled in at the outer fringes of the bay.

"You may be right, sir." Wilcox swung his arm to encompass the port and buildings. "Soon this ramshackle town, along with Carleton across the river, will be incorporated in a city to be called Saint John. The first city in the colony."

The drizzle increased. Gilbert pulled his coat close.

"So you Loyalists have your way again, *non*?" He had heard the gossip for weeks. Still, more people drawn by a larger town—many of the crude homes now had shingles or clapboards—could mean increased trade for him. "I'll wait for a message from you concerning rent, then we'll meet at my maman's, the vivacious Marie-Cateline." He left the agent, and pushed back through the quarrelling citizens. He must arrange for a cart

312

for tomorrow, to move his wife into the cabin. His major good cheer.

Untying his horse, who whinnied and crabbed sideways at the commotion of the men who lingered, arguing, Gilbert couldn't let Amelia ever regret marrying him.

* * *

Amelia's trunks crowded the one-room cabin. She swallowed a sigh at the lack of space, made smaller by her possessions. Glancing through a door in the back wall, she observed the half-framed-in room that would be their bedroom.

"I'll construct you a greenhouse for your herbs." Gilbert came up and put his arm around her.

"I'd like that. I'll take the windows off my planter box at the fort, they weren't cheap, to set up cold frames in the greenhouse." She leaned into him, feeling his warmth, though her nerves jittered when she thought of the unknown night to come. "Double protection from the weather."

Louise opened the first trunk. "Where will I put your clothes, Miss?"

"I've built a clothes press for you." He pointed to a narrow cabinet in the kitchen corner. "I just need to finish a few details on the drawers. A chest of drawers is nearly done. I'll make us another kitchen cupboard as well."

Amelia walked over to the press and admired the polished finish on the cedar-lined oak. The woodsy smell of the piece made her smile. "It's lovely. Thank you." She turned to the man she still had trouble thinking of as her husband. His smile tingled in her stomach.

The two women unpacked and sorted the clothing and gifts from her mother that she'd brought from England: fine linen sheets, delicate china and expensive silver. Would she ever use such items in this rustic setting?

Gilbert worked on the clothes press. He finished the drawers, sanding, and sawing a few pieces then fitting them into the bottom of the press. He put in shelves, screwed on hinges and, as Amelia held the door steady, fastened it to the cabinet. Amelia wiped out the sawdust, then he dragged the press over and placed it beside the bed.

A small, simple chest there held his clothes. She stared at the bed, her body tensing. What would the night bring? They'd have no privacy. Where would Louise sleep?

Gilbert pulled her into his arms as if he'd read her mind. He kissed her slowly, his lips soft and moist, his beard tickling. Her body smouldered with love and she hugged her arms around his neck, even as she trembled.

They pulled apart and Gilbert returned to his wood-working, now on her chest of drawers. Amelia busied herself unpacking again, fingers moving quickly. Her mother had only told her to 'obey' her husband, with no details of the

314

marriage bed. Almost dropping a china gravy boat, she watched out a window as the sun dipped lower.

Amelia stood on Fort Howe's parade ground six days later. The familiar sounds of soldiers drilled around her. The smell of horses and smoke from the smithy replaced the clean scent of the forest. She'd had tea with her father, a friendly visit, until a disbanded officer showed up complaining that his assigned property didn't have enough riverfront. Since the roads were primitive, or non-existent, people depended on the rivers for travel.

Private Roberts now unscrewed the window hinges, and placed the windows beside the planter box before leaving her with a quick bow.

"So, my dear, how is it with your trader?" Mary bustled up and hugged her. "You look all a glowin'. Did you enjoy your…if I may be so forward, wedding night?"

Amelia's cheeks burned, even as her heart soared at seeing her friend. The act of love surprised her, and had seemed so invasive. Now she looked forward to her closeness, the sweet caresses and passionate kisses, with her husband. "Our intimacy is furtive, since there's only one room." She glanced around. "Gilbert has men at the cabin now, putting up the walls for our bedroom since the ground has thawed. I felt sorry for Louise. We put her near the stove, her preference, on a pallet. Gilbert hung curtains around our bed."

315

"Many people in Ireland sleep in the same bed as their bairns, and other family, so no privacy there either." Mary snickered and rubbed Amelia's back. "And we still manage to have more bairns."

Amelia laughed. How long did it take to start breeding? "Oh, how I've missed you. I wish I didn't live so far away." It wasn't the distance so much as the terrible roads. She held Mary by both arms. "You may have the planter box for any use you can find."

"Aye? I'll plant violets and some crimson Robusta. That'll pretty up this men's domain. And herbs for cooking, too, of course." Mary stared across the grounds. "Oh, no. I see Lt. Harris heading our way."

Amelia turned and saw him too. She chewed on her lower lip. "Will I ever be free of this man?" she whispered. "You'd better go. I'll speak to him alone."

"If you're sure? Come by to visit me before you leave." Mary pressed her arm, nodded to Harris, swept up skirts, and strode towards her quarters.

Lt. Harris halted in front of Amelia, his face in its customary scowl. "Miss Latimer. Oh, I'm sorry, you're now a missus, though I can't remember your French name."

She'd expected his icy reception. "Mrs. *Arsenault*. Good day, sir."

"I've sent my sons away, back to England for school." He said this with no emotion.

"I hope they'll do well there, and be happy." She forced a smile, but felt a hollow of sadness for the two boys who might have been her step-sons. They were probably better off sent away, free from this martinet of a father. "I wish them all the best."

"Do you?" It sounded like an accusation, though she might have heard a hint of regret. "You wasted little time marrying someone else."

"I married for love, sir." She strained to keep the irritation from her voice.

"A man beneath you in status." He arched a brow on his square face.

"That shouldn't matter." She lifted her chin, fighting a prick of anger. "He's a good, kind man. Society is too restrictive, too judgemental."

"I see I'm better off without a woman who flouts convention." He looked her up and down in rude appraisal, yet his eyes flickered with an emotion that unsteadied her. He *did* have feelings.

"You hide much about yourself. I...wish you the best in the fu—"

"Don't patronize me." He'd turned to stone once more. "A woman should marry as is deemed correct, then follow her husband's direction."

"*If* the husband directs nicely. No one appreciates a tyrant. Excuse me." She spun about to enter her father's home. Peering over her rigid shoulder, she added, "If you wish to find a wife, you'd do well in learning to be respectful and kind. And to instruct your sister that she should not have flouted convention with a man who *was* married."

Harris' jaw dropped. He advanced. "There is no end to your witchy ways. I will inform your father about your behaviour."

A number of soldiers had paused and stared over, whispering.

Her fury burned like hot coals. She curled her fingers and wished she could slap Harris' face, but that would only belittle herself. "I'm married, and no longer under my father's control. Mind your own tongue, sir. We have *no* more to say to one another." She swept into the house.

Chapter Twenty-five

Amelia stared down at the dead mallard duck flopped on the chopping block in the cabin's rear yard.

Gilbert had killed and hung the bird for twenty-four hours to tenderize the meat. She'd insisted he leave while she, with Louise, tried to remember his mother's instructions on how to prepare the fowl for cooking.

"Very well, here we begin." She reached for a feather on the breast, and tugged, but the feather didn't pull out.

"I can do it, Miss," Louise said. Her fingers inched toward the duck.

"No, I must learn myself." Amelia plucked harder, making certain the skin didn't break by pulling in the direction the feathers grew. The smell of raw flesh made her nose wrinkle. She held her breath, plucked the breast, turned the bird and plucked away from her as she'd been told. The naked pink skin looked unappetising. Her stomach churned. The knife grabbed up, she fumbled about with no success as she cringed, then finally located, and cut through the wing and leg joints to remove them. She blinked. It looked like a massacre.

"I heard 'tis easier, the plucking, if you boil the bird first," Louise said, nodding her mob-capped head, eyes averted. "Not that I know much about cookery."

"We'll try that next time." Amelia girded herself for the most difficult part. With a wince, she hesitated, the knife shook in her hand, then she sawed but failed to cut off the fowl's pretty green head.

Recalling Madame Arsenault's demonstration, she asked Louise for a mallet, and after several deep breaths, pounded on the knife handle to break through the bird's spine. The crack rattled through her. Congealed blood seeped onto the block already stained in red. She swallowed slowly, poised the knife twice, then sliced the bird open in a seam of blood. How could anyone do this day after day?

She plunged on, slicing through lungs, veins, sinew, trying not to think about it as she scooped out the duck's innards. Her fingers slimy, they stank of pungent liver and worse. Nausea rose in her throat. "Oh, dear. That was not pleasant. I have much more respect for cooks, I daresay."

Louise stepped back, her face in a grimace, but she came forward again.

Gilbert had prepared any meat or fowl before this, but she was resolute to become the backcountry wife she needed to be. She carried the bird inside to the kitchen table, where she wiped the cavity dry and sprinkled in salt. "We'll marinate this in wine for roasting, and save the legs for stewing." Amelia nudged a hair tendril back with her wrist, her fingers greasy with offal.

"Very good, Miss. Next you might shoot your own bird, aye?" Louise looked up at her, her smile a nervous tease.

Amelia shoved her hands in a bowl of water, trying to scrub them clean with a sliver of soap. "I should learn that, too. Each duty, for survival, in its own time."

She glanced around the cramped cabin. The bedroom was completed, swept clean of sawdust by Louise today, and soon they'd have more space. Gilbert had gone to fetch a friend to help him carry in the heaviest furniture.

He'd built a small bedframe for Louise and tonight she'd move into the curtained corner on a straw mattress the two women stuffed that morning.

Almost a fortnight in residence, Amelia had spent most of her time organizing the place and learning how to fit into her husband's life, and not grow discouraged by the limitations. Their nights of sweet lovemaking made up for most of her struggles.

The rear door opened. Gilbert came in with another man, who tipped his hat to the women. Amelia bid him welcome.

Her heart swelled at seeing her husband, so handsome in his buckskins. His masculine presence filled the room.

"Observe, I've completed my task, sir." She dried her hands on a cloth before pointing to the gutted duck.

"*Bon, ma cherie.* Since you're doing so well, I'll bring in a squirrel next." Gilbert winked. "Or perhaps a bear."

"I'll need a much bigger knife, or a saw." She turned from him with a frown, and couldn't imagine ever tackling the dismemberment of a bear. She rubbed at her blistered hands and chipped nails. Her skin stung and she'd need to slather it with the lavender essential oil she and Louise prepared.

Gilbert and the other man began to move the larger bed, clothes press, and chest of drawers into the new bedroom.

Amelia watched them for a moment, satisfied at the progress. She longed to collapse in a chair, but she turned to Louise. "We need to return outside to check the pot of mutton fat over the fire."

"I'll fetch the wicks." Louise went to a corner. If the fat was hot enough, they would dip wicks in to make tallow candles. No more the extravagance of beeswax.

"I had no idea how hard servants work," Amelia whispered to the girl as they headed out the rear door. "I'm grateful to have you with me."

Would Louise want to leave her one day, start a life of her own with a husband? The maid barely sixteen, Amelia pushed that idea away for now.

"Thank you, Miss." Louise smiled in reassurance. "This be quite a change for me too; so different from pinning up hair and tightening stays."

The air was losing its chill now in mid-May, the trees budding with leaves. Most of the snow had melted, except for the tips of the mountains in the distance.

"I feel so grimy all the time. We need to purchase a proper bathtub. But I must convince my husband. When we bathe in that rough wooden tub, even on the sheet it's occasional splinters; as you know." Outside, Amelia approached the bubbling cauldron of fat. She picked up the paddle and stirred the thick concoction. The meaty-scented vapour moistened her face.

A low growl surprised her. The sound came from above. She stared up. A cougar crouched on a tree branch, bright eyes narrowed, only a few feet away.

"Oh, no," Amelia whispered, her throat choking, frozen in place. She gripped the paddle.

"La, what be that?" Louise looked up and gasped. She jerked the rack of wicks to her chest. They dangled a dance around her.

"Let's walk slowly, backward, into the cabin," Amelia whispered, watching the large, rusty-coloured cat's ears flatten. Its lips curled and revealed sharp teeth.

A scream—like with the bear—might make the animal angrier. She held the dripping paddle before her, hot drops on her apron, and strained to breathe evenly. Stepping one foot back, she must get inside, to warn her husband.

The cougar growled again, louder. The branch creaked as it crept forward. A huge paw scratched at the air.

Louise didn't move, her face a mask of fright. Amelia quaked with suppressed fear she didn't care to experience, hating her vulnerability. Could she throw hot grease in the animal's face? The cat roared as if it knew her thoughts, and slid low along the branch—which started to crack as the creature prepared to pounce.

Nerves shredding, she shot out a hand to drag Louise beside her and backwards.

The cabin's rear door opened. Gilbert rushed out, his musket in hand. He aimed and fired. The smoky blast made Amelia and Louise flinch. The cougar fell from the branch with a thump.

"Is everyone all right? These beasts usually hunt after dark." He swept his arm around Amelia and pressed her to his side, his gaze intent on hers. Louise moved close to them and whooshed out a shaky breath.

"We're fine, my dear. I assure you." Amelia's body rigid as oak, her stomach doing flips, she still took comfort from his embrace. She must pretend this was an everyday occurrence. "Do I... Must I gut that cat as well?"

* * *

Gilbert inhaled the fresh air, heady with loamy scents. May could be such a beautiful month, even if the journey today might not turn out well. He'd bought a cart and mule and escorted Amelia along the sandy riverbank of the ice-free and flowing Kennebecasis. They'd circle around Grand Bay and pass the town officially incorporated as Saint John. A significant introduction awaited him, and he must remain steadfast.

The noise of chopping drew his attention. Men were clearing land of trees to haul to the many sawmills that had sprouted up as building continued to house the expanding population. Sad, to see so many stumps in what used to be forests. He stared straight ahead again, through the mule's long ears.

"It's disheartening to see all these trees felled," Amelia said, echoing his thoughts. "They should plant new ones to keep the forests lush."

"You have a clever idea, *mon amour*. But the forests replenish quickly here if only given the time." He smiled down at her, the soft curve of her cheek as she surveyed the landscape.

"My Father said the Loyalists import mahogany furniture from England, instead of using the local wood. Which is a small relief for the trees." She turned to him with a laugh.

"These richer men build their manor homes, then neglect them, wasting land." Gilbert steered the cart over a bumpy corduroy bridge, logs shoved together to make crossing the marshlands easier. "They don't know how to survive here."

Scarring his country, too many of the newcomers were incompetent farmers. Some had already fled to England, shocked by the amount of work they confronted.

Gilbert fought a triumphant smile as he drove the cart alongside meadows alive with clover and lousewort flowers with their small, yellow petals that resembled snap-dragons. Birds chirped in the scattering of trees. Spring came late on the Fundy coast, often with wind and rain. Today nature accommodated then, crawling out to bask after the long, freezing winter.

"I must learn to survive the many pests in this colony," Amelia said as they both swatted black flies from their faces—an unfortunate aspect of spring. Before they'd left the cabin, Amelia had rubbed lavender on both of them to deter insect bites.

She pulled her kerchief closer around her neck. "These and the mosquitoes are a plague. I'll have to grow an entire crop of lavender and sweet basil." She leaned into him on the bench. Their fingers touched. "Or I could try mixing the herbs with the bear grease you prefer."

"The natives use that remedy and it's always worked well for me." He tried not to sniff his perfumed self as he caressed her hand.

The smaller bay spread out to their right like a glistening mirror in the rare sunlight. A refreshing breeze wafted over them, ruffling tendrils of her hair that he longed to stroke.

His mood darkened as they rumbled past the trading post he might soon lose.

"When will you speak to Mr. Wilcox about Mr. Jarvis regarding the post?" she asked.

"I must track down the agent. It's been over two weeks." Twisting at the mule's reins, his brow furrowed. He'd demand a resolution, or he was moving to the peninsula. He had a wife to provide for. Gilbert smiled again at Amelia, so satisfied with her resilience and tender ways. He'd given up his solitary life to fit her into his constant consideration. "I believe my maman's land is safe now. The ninety days have come and gone with no word from Bent. I will write the governor for its title."

They reached the river gorge at the south end of Grand Bay, where the city would soon encroach.

"I'm so very relieved. I'd hate to see your mother displaced. And you've both worked hard on that property." She clasped his arm. "I'll pay for a messenger to bring you a copy of the registered deed. Please, let that be my gift to your mother."

"Another gift? Don't worry, I think she's beginning to like you, but she won't dare show it." He chuckled. "You'd impress her more if you grew a vegetable garden and skinned a moose while planting."

"I'll try that…someday. The moose, I mean. I'll have my garden started soon. I'll be ready to establish fresh healing herbs at whichever trading post we end up at." She looked around. "I wonder if Father will show. He is quite stubborn."

"A man has to protect his pride. Sometimes it's all he has, and you defied him." Gilbert shrugged, though he hoped the captain came to please her. They were to finally meet with her father, Gilbert's first introduction, at the reversing falls. A beautiful event he wished to show Amelia that might also ease this awkward gathering.

"Pride? He managed to easily disavow his marriage." She thinned her lips. "I know, I need to forget that and forgive him."

"*Eh bien*, we savage men have needs, as you know." He kissed her cheek, wishing to tug out her smile again. "But I am sorry he disrespected your mother."

He reined in the mule at the jagged-rock gorge, where the Saint John River narrowed below Grand Bay, then emptied into the Bay of Fundy. The immense bay's water already churned in frothy waves. A thick fog rolled over the water in the distance, wiping Partridge Island from view.

"High tide is coming in from the bay and will crash into the river's flow going out. It creates a funnel, which many say resembles a reverse falls." Gilbert drew in a whiff of beached seaweed, then caught his flowery scent, embarrassed to meet the captain fragrant like a woman. Then again, would the captain show him any respect? "The result is more like rapids than a falls."

Fifteen minutes later, a man with a red coat rode up on a grey horse, whose hooves scattered the green carpetweed's white flowers. The captain touched his hat with one finger. Gilbert stiffened even so, leery of his reception. He never thought he'd be in the position to have to impress an English officer.

Gilbert left the cart, all his senses on edge. This meeting needed to go well enough to placate Amelia. He bit back his own pride, along with the distrust ingrained in him since birth. He assisted his wife down beside him.

"Father, I'm glad you're here." Amelia's eyes lit up, although her smile was tentative. "I realize how busy you are with all these trade problems and the immigrants. Are the officers from the rebel states settled yet?"

"Some of the disbanded troops are on plots, but many of the soldiers prefer active duty. They thrive on discipline." The captain dismounted. He wasn't tall, but appeared sturdy in his uniform and neat wig under a black cocked hat. His analysing blue eyes—in a slightly lined, long face—matched Amelia's. "But we'll prevail."

"Captain Latimer, I am Gilbert Arsenault. Amelia's husband." Instead of making a show of being too personal too soon, he pointed to the rising water. "I'm certain you have witnessed nature's magnificence here. Amelia has not."

"And I am in earnest to witness such a marvel," she said. Her gaze darted to her father, her words almost strident, as if she too didn't trust her parent with Gilbert.

"I have seen the reversing falls, yes." The captain nodded, his tone guarded. "It is a beautiful sight." He glanced sidelong at Gilbert as he spread his booted legs, hands clasped behind his back.

The Saint John River thundered through the rock-faced gorge, beneath the pine trees and beech wood that clung to the top. The Bay of Fundy swirled and rose. The river smacked into the bay's higher tide. Water twisted and pushed up in a huge splash of sound. A funnel turned over in the air, tide battling flow. White water gushed, almost like a falls as it roiled upward, throwing back the river. A fine mist sprinkled over them. Water fowl took flight, screeching.

"This is magnificent, as you said, dear husband." Amelia laughed in obvious enjoyment, though it held a brittle underlay. She stepped apart from the men, as if to encourage them to talk.

"I'm pleased to meet you, sir." Gilbert thrust out his hand, intent on catching the captain off-balance.

330

Captain Latimer rocked on his feet, head lowered. Then he turned and took Gilbert's hand in a quick shake. "I trust all is well with—both of you. Out there in the wilderness."

"We are managing, *oui*. Amelia is a brave woman. You would be proud of her." Gilbert kept his tone even.

"I'm practically a frontier wife." Amelia, in her plain blue gown, again approached her father.

Latimer kissed her cheek. "Are you happy, my dear? Do you...require anything?"

The river continued to splash and roil beside them. As it settled, the fog swirled closer, like a great white beast hunting prey.

"Very happy, Father." Her smile looked genuine and Gilbert's heart swelled. "You needn't fear for me. My husband is a wonderful man."

"Does he take good care of you?" The captain squeezed both her shoulders.

"I do, sir." Gilbert's words came out abrupt. He was being defensive, still unsure of his ability *to* take care of her. Amelia had offered part of her inheritance to help him build a new post on Henri's land—but that stubborn male pride! He slipped his arm around her. "And she takes care of me."

The air temperature dropped. A mist crept over them. The biting flies faded away.

"Of course, Father, he takes the best of care." Amelia cuddled a shawl around her shoulders. "Perhaps you could visit, and see how well I prepare dinner."

The captain half-smiled. "Perhaps, when I can make the time."

Gilbert flexed his fingers. Her father didn't sound totally averse to accepting their hospitality. His wife looked hopeful, her smile anxious. He hugged her against his side protectively and changed the subject. "How has the merger of the city gone, Captain Latimer? I know there are warring factions."

"Indeed. The legislature has difficulty agreeing. Former New Yorkers argue with agents who fled Massachusetts. People taking sides, calling themselves Lower Covers and Upper Covers." Latimer spoke quickly, then glanced away.

"We all want control, the upper-elite and the lower-placed of us." Gilbert wished for fairness, but would that ever happen? "I heard that violence has taken place, true?"

The captain gripped his hands behind his back again. "The army is constantly on alert. There have already been fierce fights in the taverns, people injured. We intervened, we've been ready."

Once Gilbert might have encouraged fights, to chase the English from the colony, but now he hoped for a civil peace.

Fog drifted around them, his feet soon covered in the creeping mist. "The fog is rising fast, as is its habit. We can't stay much longer."

"I pray you stay safe if there is violence, Father." Amelia tightened her shawl about her shoulders. She pressed her parent's arm. "Aren't the people insisting on a more...democratic government as in the new United States?"

"Some are, but I serve the king. I'm an officer of the Crown." Her father stiffened to attention like an obedient soldier. "Strict regulations are needed."

Gilbert shoved away his resentment toward a faraway king who seemed to rule with an iron hand. That's why the United States had rebelled in the first place.

"Men of intelligence should favour equal rights." Gilbert strained to sound neutral. Might a revolution start in New Brunswick, and how would that affect him and his people?

Captain Latimer turned and arched a brow. "The upper ranks assure order. That's why we've tried to settle the officers and their men in blocks, to encourage towns with leaders."

Gilbert heard the disbanded soldiers preferred rum to organizing towns. "If the leaders aren't corrupt." He nodded to the captain, a fist behind his back. "The merchants do better than farmers, with not enough fertile land for so many people."

"We all have our opinions. England must encourage more settlement farther north in the Canadas," the captain said, his voice brusque. The fog inched up his black boots.

"I agree with equal rights, justice for decent people," Amelia said, watching them both. "But let's not quarrel, and just enjoy the day."

"The winters north of here are even fiercer. The Loyalist complain now of the cold." Gilbert reeled in his other 'opinions'. All of New Brunswick's people needed to work together to prosper. Was this Amelia's influence? Or his own newly realized determination to be a part of the changes.

"We should go, Monsieur. I trust we'll meet again, over dinner, as Amelia suggested."

Gilbert offered the invitation for his wife's peace of mind. He really didn't care for any more soldiers near his cabin. Nevertheless, he'd treat them with politeness as long as it was returned. They must adapt, though having his say over rights had irritated the captain.

"I'll—look forward to it. Good day, my dear. Mr. Arsenault." Her father tipped his hat, mounted and rode off, disappearing like a ghost into the miasma.

"He'll stay aloof for a while. He isn't an easy man to know." Amelia threw her shawl over her head. "I cannot believe how thick the fogs are on this coast." The shifting white mass snaked up their legs, her skirt.

"The weather is notorious." Gilbert hurried his wife to the cart. "Don't let your papa disappoint you, *ma cherie*. He will do what he will, because of his position."

They quickly boarded, and he urged the mule to plod back around Grand Bay. The mist was about to obliterate them, but only until they rode beyond it. The world was constantly unstable, especially with the needs and greed of men, and he must hold his place—gallop before the storm—with both hands. Best of all, he had Amelia beside him on the journey.

Chapter Twenty-six

"*Voila*! The title to this property." Gilbert held up the paper, signed by Governor Carleton and his registrar, with witnesses. The document's edges rippled in the wind off the Kennebecasis River beside his maman's cabin. His chest filled with warmth at being able to protect her.

Marie-Cateline straightened and wiped sweat from her forehead with her sleeve. "*Bon, mon fils*. This is a grand day for us. You did well." She smiled then bent to her hoeing once more, chopping seaweed and manure into the garden she'd plant with turnips, potatoes and carrots, her arm muscles straining.

Gilbert had already asked if he could perform this duty but had been rebuffed. The earthy smells still pleased him. The title in his hand relieved so much of his apprehension. He glanced toward the road. Wilcox should be here shortly with news about Jarvis. Dare he imagine that all would be settled? Too bad his maman would stink of cow dung—hardly the alluring bait.

Soon, a horse and rider appeared. The bulky form of Wilcox dismounted and the agent joined them. "Ah, Madam Arsenault, do you require help?" He removed his hat.

"The only help I require, *monsieur*, is that you have done your best to convince this Jarvis to leave my son's post as it is." She continued to chop, revealing moist earth, backing up to create rows, not bothering to look at them. Her sabots were covered in mud.

"Have you come to an agreement for me with Monsieur Jarvis?" Gilbert asked, unable to tamp down his impatience.

"He's a contentious man, as you're aware. Now he says he has partners to consult with." Wilcox moved closer to where Marie-Cateline swung the hoe. "I won't give up on him, never fear. I asked him, nicely of course, to let me know by next week."

"I will count on it, *mon ami*. I'm grateful for your efforts. But I would be careful where you wander there. My maman may not be so accurate with her hoe." Gilbert forced a dry chuckle. Still no resolution! Could he relent and use Amelia's money to build a new post on Henri's land, and attract customers to a different location?

His mother stopped and leaned on the implement. She swiped her face again with her arm, smearing dirt on her cheek. Her black hair hung in loose tendrils from under her hat. Her dark eyes sparked. "This Jarvis, he sounds like a selfish *scélérat,* a scoundrel. We Acadians have been in this colony many years. We live humbly, but he expects to come here and live like a prince."

"That is true, Madam." Wilcox replaced his hat after a slight bow. "You both seem to be hard-working, honourable people. I admire your ethic." He smiled, his appreciation of her obvious, even in her dishevelled state. "I will do my best with the young scamp."

Gilbert stifled a real laugh. His respect for Wilcox, who he'd learned had been a widower for over eight years, grew. "Will you come inside for tea, or coffee?"

"And some of your lovely mother's delicious cooking?" His eyes twinkled.

"I've had little time to cook today, Monsieur Wilcox. So you may quiet your silver tongue, *non*." She wagged a finger at him, her plump mouth almost sulky. Her words weren't harsh, they were almost teasing. Was she playing the coquette to keep him on their side?

Gilbert wasn't sure which one he wanted it to be, genuine or a farce.

"Then coffee would be welcome." The agent nodded at Gilbert. Then he looked back at Marie-Cateline. "I must endure and forego your delicacies of the hearth."

"I'm no woman of leisure like you English." She hacked into the earth again with the hoe. Soil overturned and scattered about, further dirtying the hem of her apron over her striped skirt.

"But, my good Madam, I'm American, not English." Wilcox pressed a hand on his breast.

338

"I admit my being a Tory and on England's side has chased me onto your shores…"

"Like I say, English." She shrugged and dug another row with her measured backwards steps.

"I must insist that not all of us Tories are your enemy. Some are traders, and profitably, for *both* sides, engaged in the fish trade with you Acadians." Wilcox gave her an indulgent smile.

Maman's mouth worked, as if she resisted her own smile. She turned to Gilbert. "Take in the basket please, *mon fils*." She pointed with the hoe.

A basket of fiddleheads, bright green in their swirled shape, sat beside the garden. Gilbert picked it up. His maman cooked these plants, gathered on the riverbank every spring, for vegetables.

"Odd things to eat, wouldn't you say?" Wilcox peered in.

"You've much to learn about subsistence in this colony." Gilbert waved Wilcox into the cabin. "I think you've charmed my mother." He chuckled. "She didn't throw the hoe at your head."

He still doubted his stubborn maman would ever consider a non-Acadian as a beau—or any beau at all. He swallowed his groan that he still had to contend with the self-serving Jarvis.

* * *

339

The sun on Amelia's face brightened her spirits. After scanning the tree branches for feral animals, especially cougars, she picked wild celery, good as a diuretic and carminative. "For passing water and relieving gastric ailments," she told Louise as they strolled in the woods near the cabin. Birds chirped in the black spruce and oak tree branches above and squirrels scurried through the leaves, chattering.

Alone, with Gilbert at his mother's, Amelia kept listening for heavy footsteps, a bear—even a moose. She'd stuffed her muff pistol in her apron pocket, though it slapped hard against her left leg when she moved. The tiny gun would hopefully scare off any large beasts with its noise.

The maid held up a fireweed plant with its pretty pink flowers. "Mr. Arsenault says these flowers an' leaves can be eaten raw. Looks too pretty to eat. Don't think I'd like the taste."

"I suppose when you're starving, as his people did, you'll eat most anything." At least he finally had the title to his mother's land. One problem solved. Amelia inhaled the fragrant air. "I know we should be fishing, scrubbing floors, or tanning something, but it's so mild outside, I'd rather gather herbs." Her muscles already ached from the never-ending work. Her hands and nails were in shambles. At first she'd worn gloves, but had finally given up on that affect.

She sighed. She must think of these duties as a challenge and not a burden. Out with the flora was what she preferred, to enjoy the breeze and the sinewy feel of the plants.

Louise laughed. "Aye. I'd rather be outside, too, Miss. That were a long, long winter. But not so much fogs here than at the fort."

"We must be thankful for that." A purple butterfly floated past them on delicate wings. Amelia thought of her husband's warm kisses, his loving arms around her, his kindness—and her reduced circumstances were worth the sacrifice.

"I best take up knitting next winter, to provide us with mittens and scarves." Or would she soon have a babe to keep her occupied? Amelia flushed at the idea. She plucked Speedwell, which had striking white flowers with lavender stripes. "This tastes like pepper, so I'll use it in cooking." She picked ragwort, good for 'female' complaints and placed it in her basket, her fingers dusty with greenery. "My tinctures and syrups are selling at the post, but will we have to abandon the place if the baron's brat of a son has his way?" Her mood sank.

"We might like it on the pig farm." Louise's nose twitched. She didn't sound convinced.

"And his cousin by marriage is being generous to offer us an acre to rent." Amelia glanced toward the pens Gilbert was building near the cabin. "Soon we'll have goats, for cheese and milk, and chickens to care for."

341

"I must learn to milk goats." Louise gave a tentative smile.

The two women pushed through the plants, their tangy scents, searching for more useful herbs, always keeping the cabin in sight.

Something rustled in the bushes. Then again, louder. The birds fell silent. The entire forest seemed to still as if waiting.

Amelia's neck prickled. It had to be a predatory animal. "I…think we've done enough for the day. Let's return inside. I have bread to bake."

In the kitchen, they set their baskets brimming with fragrant herbs on the table. Amelia pulled over the large earthenware bowl full of rising dough. "I know my husband likes his flatbread, but I'm preparing a good, old-fashioned loaf."

Louise checked the Dutch oven on the hearth floor, the large iron pot surrounded by hot orange cinders. She placed more twigs around it. "We'll both be good cooks someday, aye?"

"Then we can work on sewing, actually fashioning sturdier clothes." Amelia punched the soft dough a few times. She sprinkled flour on the table and pulled the stretchy lump from the bowl and plopped it atop the flour. "Your learning from your seamstress mother puts us in good stead." She laughed. "Gilbert threatened to buy me a spinning wheel."

The mule brayed from the stable. Then another sound of moving about, the cart creaking. Amelia wiped her hands and started for the front door to check on the activity. Was Gilbert here?

A loud knock came at the door. Amelia halted. Louise glanced at her. The latch rattled.

Amelia put up her hand to stop her maid from answering. "I'll check to see who it is."

She blew out her breath. Touching the pistol in her pocket she walked over and peered out the wavy lead-glass window. A man in buckskins stood there, his face in shadow. It could be a friend of Gilbert's, or a lost stranger. Yet that uneasy feeling she had in the woods returned.

She hesitated, then lifted the latch and opened the door a crack. "Good day, sir. What can I do for you?"

"I have fresh venison for you and your man," the stranger said. He looked gaunt, half-starved, with a dirty, scraggly beard. His eyes narrowed.

Her hackles rose. "That's very kind, but—"

The door suddenly pushed in on her. She stumbled back with a gasp.

The man, now scowling beneath his ratty beaver hat lunged inside, pointing a musket barrel into her face.

Chapter Twenty-seven

"How dare you!" Amelia felt ripped inside-out with terror. She staggered further back, bumping into Louise who had screeched when the man stormed in. Amelia clutched the trembling maid to her, but had to grip onto bravery. "What do you want?"

"Land was taken from me by that Frenchie bastard. Now I'll take what's his," the stranger snarled. He reeked like a pig that had rooted in rubbish.

"Are you Bent?" Amelia croaked out the words, stomach clenching. "Wh-where have you been? The sale was posted for three months in the local paper."

"In gaol, in Québec." He darted his eyes about the room as if looking for anything of value.

"Lower your musket, before something bad happens." She stiffened to keep herself from trembling along with Louise, resolved to appear in charge.

"Ha, Missy. Somethin' bad *is* gonna happen. You two are comin' with me." He snickered, showing yellowed teeth.

"Mercy, no! It's all over. The land now belongs to my husband. The governor signed the document. It's legally registered." Would this make the man reconsider or become angrier? Staring into his bleary eyes, Amelia shuddered, petrified that he'd fire his musket and extinguish the married life she'd barely started. "Please, think about what you're doing."

Louise whimpered, burying her face against Amelia's throat.

"I have thought, chit. Now get movin', out the door." He waved the musket in that direction, then swung the weapon back on them. "He steals somethin' precious, then so will I."

"Please listen, Mr. Bent. My husband purchased the land fairly, years ago." Amelia didn't budge, though her knees grew weak. She had to stall him. Louise wriggled like a ferret in her arms.

"The name's Oram. Bennett Oram. Your Frenchie tricked my uncle into givin' him the parcel." Bent lurched forward, the musket inches from the women.

Amelia flinched, stifling a scream. Louise cried out and began to sob.

Amelia clutched the maid closer. Could she calm this insane man until Gilbert returned? "Please. There's no need for this. Your uncle wasn't tricked. Let me explain—"

"No more natterin', wench. Out the door!" He rounded behind them and poked the musket into Amelia's back.

She jerked forward and said a prayer. Bile rose in her throat. Tears dampened her eyes, yet she refused to become a hysterical female. It wouldn't help the situation. She kept her voice even. "Please don't hurt us. We're innocent of any wrong. And so is my husband."

"Shut up! Keep movin'!" Bent pushed her with his hand, and the two women staggered toward the open door, their arms still wound around each other.

Amelia's head spun. Outside, she saw that Bent had hitched up the cart to their mule. That's what she'd heard right before the knock. How could she stop whatever he was planning to do? She still had her muff pistol in her apron pocket.

"Is he goin' to kill us, Miss?" Louise whispered as she clung to her.

"I don't think so," she whispered back, though she wasn't certain herself. She chewed on her lip. "He's using us as bait."

"Shut your mouths! Get in the cart bed and lie down." Bent pulled back their canvas cover.

Amelia ached for Gilbert to return, *now*. She and Louise crawled into the bed, the wood rough beneath her hands. "Where are you taking us?"

"None of your bloody business." Bent threw down the canvas, enveloping them in darkness. "Keep quiet. If you try to jump out, I'll shoot you dead."

Amelia clutched Louise to her, their combined fear-sweat engulfed her, the girl's

346

cheek damp against hers. The cart bumped off, the wheels squeaking. They both prayed as Amelia rocked Louise. She must think of a way—*any* way—to escape this madman.

* * *

Gilbert entered the cabin, still elated over the deed success, and amused by Wilcox's flirting with his maman. Would she ever allow a man into her heart?

"Amelia, where's the cart and mule?" He looked about the main chamber, searched the bedroom, the privy, and out back to the edge of the woods. The place was deserted. "Louise?"

Had they gone somewhere in the cart? In the kitchen, he saw the basket of herbs, the blob of dough on the table. No note. Uneasiness crept through him. He stepped back outside and checked the hay-scented stable. No clues.

He left the stable. Vaillant, still saddled, snorted and tossed his head.

Gilbert rubbed his soft, whiskery muzzle. "I wonder where they went, *mon ami*." Amelia wouldn't have left unless something was wrong. It was a long way to any village, except a Mi'kmaq camp near the river.

He studied the ground in front of the cabin. There was an extra set of boot prints. A man had been here. Anger mixed with fear surged through him. He leapt on his horse and followed the wagon tracks, until they faded along the rocky earth.

347

Galloping west, mind in a whirl, he passed the long carved sticks etched with hieroglyphics shoved into the earth that the Mi'kmaq used to mark their hunting ground. The markers were supposed to keep out the Maliseet.

He reached the Kennebecasis River that burbled past on its way to the bay. A blue heron poked stalk-like legs among the water pygmy weed tangled on the shoreline. A small Mi'kmaq settlement was here with their spruce sapling dwellings covered in birch bark, lashed at the top to form a cone. The aboriginals survived by fishing for salmon and eel. Might any of them have seen Amelia?

Gilbert dismounted. His own people had hidden in the Mi'kmaq villages during the Acadian Expulsion. They'd fought together to chase out the British after treaties were broken, but had lost.

His gut churning, he entered the camp. Women in long, moose-hide tunics cooked over iron pots emitting fishy odours. Small ebony-haired children ran about. A man stalked toward him. He wore a tanned deerskin breechcloth and moccasins, his brown chest naked except for a wolf-skin around his muscled shoulders. His long black hair draped down his back.

Gilbert recognized him as Mooin, which meant 'bear'.

"*Pjila'si*. Welcome, trader," Mooin said in Mi'kmaq then French. "What do you need? Do you wish to visit the chief?"

"*Non*. My wife may have been on the trail past here." Gilbert clenched and unclenched his hands. He kept darting his eyes toward the path, the birch and spruce trees. "Have you seen a white woman with a girl go by recently? In a cart or on foot?"

"I have not. I will ask the others." The brave did so then returned. "I'm sorry, no one saw any white women. Can we help find them?"

"*Merde*," Gilbert hissed under his breath. His pulse thundered. "If you've hunters out in the woods, when they return, please ask them about my wife. If you have any unoccupied braves, you could send them to search. I will find a way to pay you back."

He thanked Mooin, re-mounted his horse and galloped off, heading south toward Saint John. Could Amelia have had enough of this primitive life and returned to Fort Howe? He twinged, but couldn't believe that. She loved him, he knew it. Either there was an accident and she'd sought medical help, or she may have been forced from the cabin. He kicked Vaillant to more speed.

* * *

Amelia didn't know how much time had passed as she bumped about in the cart bed holding her shivering maid. Sweat and darkness clung to them in the confining space, the canvas slapping against their heads. Soothing Louise kept Amelia from falling into a dark pit of despair. She whispered to the girl to be brave and stay still, then crawled like a snake as quietly as possible toward the bed's end. Lifting the cover an inch, she peered out. Louise sucked in her breath.

The country was still untamed, the road barely a path, the pine trees thick. Of course, for Amelia, most of this colony was unfamiliar.

"Don't try to jump out! I'm watchin' you," Bent yelled. He slammed what must have been his musket barrel down on the canvas. It just missed Louise's head. She cried out and shrank down.

Amelia flattened herself. Panic bubbled up her throat. She scooted back, scraping her hands on the boards, her knees catching on her long skirt, to compose Louise.

Finally, the cart stopped. The vehicle rocked as Bent left the bench. The covering was swept from the bed.

Amelia blinked in the sudden light, though the sky looked angry, darkening. The man who glared at her matched the weather. She swallowed through a tight throat, her hand gripped on her maid's.

"Get out, now. Hurry!" Bent motioned with his musket.

The two women crept from the bed. They were in a cluster of ramshackle buildings and muddy lanes, near a small river. The air stank of animals and dung.

Amelia used every ounce of courage she had to appear unintimidated. "What are your intentions, Mr. Oram?"

Louise clung to Amelia, her eyes scanning about.

"You'll see." He snickered. "Your Frenchie lout will know he can't get away with theft."

Another man had come out of the nearest cabin. He had a long, filthy beard, and worn, stained buckskin clothing. His creased face showed at least forty years. "What do we have here?"

"You do know that my father is an army captain at Fort Howe." Amelia lifted her shaking chin. How could they escape these rough-looking backwoods rogues? Would Gilbert figure out where she'd gone? "Do you want the entire army down upon you?"

Lightning crackled across the sky, followed by a boom of thunder. Fat raindrops started to fall. Louise dug her fingers into Amelia's side.

"If they don't want you killed, them soldiers will stay away." Bent ordered the women up three rickety steps of that cabin and toward the door.

The man on the porch eyed Louise. He grinned, showing rotten and missing teeth. He had deep crinkles on his leathery face and greasy grey hair. "Can I have this leetle one?"

God help us! Amelia grabbed her maid and rushed her into the stench of the dim cabin.

Chapter Twenty-eight

Gilbert travelled the road toward Saint John, anxious to catch a glimpse of his wife. Every rider he encountered coming the opposite way said they'd seen no women as he described. A drizzle started. Thunder rumbled—matching his pulse.

When Fort Howe up on its grand hill loomed into view, the rain had increased, soaking him and Vaillant. A swifter wind buffeted against them. Would Amelia have gone to the fort to visit her father? But why had no one seen them? Additional worry twisted at his thoughts. She wasn't the type not to leave a note. Had there been an emergency?

In town, he paid a boy to take a verbal message to the fort. Was the captain's daughter there? Now he felt a coward for not riding up himself. He must counter his past loathing for English soldiers, a hate that shouldn't be sustained with his recent marriage. Waiting with Vaillant under an overhanging roof, the rain dripping off the edge, Gilbert rubbed his stiff jaw. He flexed his hands in impatience. Surely there had to be a simple explanation for her to leave with the cart and mule.

The boy returned about twenty minutes later, his feet covered in mud, chubby legs spattered. "She's not there. Hasn't been seen."

Gilbert asked around the city, in the grocers and elsewhere, his voice growing sharper in his desperation. No one had seen her.

"*Ma foi!*" He remounted, his gut in knots. Who had come to his cabin and created that extra set of boot prints?

He galloped his horse out of Saint John, back onto the road, heading north. Windblown rain splashed into his face. Lightening streaked then thunder roared, like an omen of doom. Past the fort, a horseman bolted up beside him, calling to him. An officer.

Gilbert was astonished to see Amelia's father. He reined in. "Monsieur *le capitaine*?"

"Your messenger came to the fort, asking questions. I was alerted." The captain furrowed his brow. "What has happened to Amelia? Where did she go…I don't understand?"

Gilbert explained Amelia's absence, the missing cart. Bent's belligerent face flashed in his mind. Was it possible? His rage heated his soaked body. "I can only think of one more place to search. A village of miscreants on the Black River." He told the captain about his property troubles, and the threats.

His jaw tightened even more. Had this been what that menacing, misspelled note he'd received had meant?

Another soldier joined them. The young *espie* Gilbert had encountered before. They eyed each other with suspicion.

"You need not bother, Captain. I can find my own wife." Gilbert's pride boiled up like the bay's incoming tide.

"Please, allow me to help. She's my daughter. We'll ride to this village at once," Captain Latimer said, his blue eyes alarmed. "Private Roberts, tell the lieutenant on duty to form a search party. Then you follow us."

"Immediately, sir." The private raced off.

"*Laissons-nous presser.* Let us hurry!" Gilbert leaned into his stallion, the moist smell of the animal's familiar coat, grateful in some way yet wary of the help. What would the captain expect from him? The two men galloped on, their horses' hooves spattering through the mud.

He could *not* lose her! He couldn't think it might come to that, never again to hold this woman whom he had nurtured as she'd nurtured him. A bleak hole ripped open inside him.

* * *

Rain pelted the dirty windows, leaking in through cracks. The steady drip pinged in Amelia's brain. Thunder boomed overhead like drumbeats. She and Louise huddled, crouched in a corner of the cabin on the splintered, scuffed floor. Cobwebs matted the rafters, and a rat sniffed along one wall. The place reeked of urine and filthy bodies.

She watched the two men, schemes tripping over one another in her thoughts. What would these rogues do to them? She whispered courage to Louise while she shored up her own. They had to flee from here.

A lantern, the only light in the room, sat on the rickety table where the men slumped on stools. Shadows draped everything else in gloom.

"You're sendin' no message?" the man with rotten teeth she'd heard was named Jack said, again, as he drank from a tankard of rum. "No taunt for the Frenchie?"

"I will, I will, but let him search for a while." Bent slouched across from Jack, his musket near his dirty hand. "You sent my note to make him afeared like I asked?"

"I don't write so well, but I did. He was addin' to his cabin like he's fancy English."

"We should burn it down some night." Bent grimaced. "It's not my fault my uncle was an addlepated fool. Land on the river is worth a fortune now. We old-comers deserve to own it, so we can sell for a good profit."

Amelia filled with anger, which coated her fear. And Gilbert never told her about a threatening note.

"Aye, we do deserve the land. My father was there when the army shipped them vermin

Frenchies away." Jack slurped his rum. "Or killed them off."

"So was mine, a sergeant, wounded, and died after years of sufferin'." Bent swiped a grubby sleeve under his nose and sniffed.

Amelia steadied her breathing and listened for hoof beats—Gilbert arriving to save them. But he wouldn't know where she was.

"My da also fought the rebels from the south who banded with them savages to kill us good Englishmen. But we're mightier." Jack raised his tankard high. "Now we need to chase out the damned Tories. We own this colony."

"Aye, the strongest and most connivin' survive. We'll get others, fire on that 'Loyalist' town, Saint John." Bent drank from his tankard, slopping rum into his beard. He belched. "They're already preachin' dissent at McPherson's Tavern in Lower Cove."

"Another rebellion!" Jack slapped his hand on the table. "While we wait, what should we do with these 'ladies' to amuse ourselves, eh?" He glanced over, his smile a leer. "Shame to waste good tail."

Amelia cringed and squeezed Louise close. "My husband and the army will be here soon. Let us go and no one will get hurt." Inside she trembled at her lie. How would Gilbert find her? She felt the weight of her tiny pistol on her thigh, but it had one shot and there were two men. Was she brave enough to shoot someone?

"I hadn't thought 'bout usin' the women that way." Bent scratched at his head, stirring his stringy brown hair. "Let me think, dammit."

Jack stood, a little unsteady. He picked up the large jug of rum and poured more in his tankard. "*I'm* thinkin' on it, and I'd like a kiss from the sweet young one."

Louise recoiled. "You-you will *not*." She sounded sturdier, more furious than afraid. Her fingers gripped Amelia's arm. Thunder boomed again, the rain pounding the cabin's roof. Water continued to leak in at the windows and corners of the ceiling, adding to the mouldy smell.

"Don't tell me what I'll do, wench." Jack swayed as he laughed. "I take what I want, when I want it."

"You'll regret hurting us. They'll hunt you down and hang you." Amelia forced a haughty authority into her words. She rubbed the aching muscle in her neck, then pressed on the pistol through the cloth of her apron. She darted a glance at the musket near Bent's hand.

"I don't want no damage," Bent said, gulping more rum. "I want to swap the chits for my land, the deed. What's mine."

"Then you need to tell the Frenchie you have them *soon*, don't you? Your plans are a muddle, like always. Stuck in gaol for almost killin' a man." Jack took a step toward the women.

Amelia stared at the broken window. Could they climb out and risk being shot?

"I was soused, that's all." Bent shrugged, then took another gulp of rum. "The arse deserved the drubbin'."

"Well, I'm gettin' busy." Jack weaved closer, a swampy stink swirling around him. "One kiss and tickle won't matter."

"Leave her alone." Amelia scrambled to her feet and dragged Louise with her. She pushed the girl behind her. "Don't touch her, or you'll be sorry."

Bent heaved to his feet and staggered near. "Sorry, eh? Back yourself off, Jack. If anyone has some fun, it'll be me."

Jack punched Bent's shoulder. Bent swung and pushed him back. He then grabbed Louise by her loosened long blonde hair and jerked her toward him. She hollered, resisting.

"Stop!" Amelia's muscles clenched, her entire body shuddered. She snatched the pistol from her pocket and held it tight in her hands, arms thrust forward. "Stop, both of you. Let her go or I'll shoot!"

Bent stared down at the pistol. He laughed. "With that leetle thing?"

"A lead ball in your belly could kill you." Flattened against the cabin's damp wall, Amelia pointed toward his stomach, swallowing hard. If needed, she must pull the trigger.

Bent twisted the girl's hair, then released her, but still smirked. Jack edged toward the table, the musket.

"You won't shoot no one." Bent scoffed, not sounding as sure now. "Give that toy to me."

"Release us, right this minute," Amelia demanded, reluctant to fire. Perspiration gathered at her neckline, under her kerchief. She released the safety. "And no one will get hurt."

Louise jumped to the right, shouted and flailed her hands. Distracted, Jack turned toward her.

Bent lunged for the pistol. With an angry hiss, Amelia pulled the trigger. A bang, then acrid smoke and gunpowder clouded the air, burned in her nostrils. He grabbed his side. Crimson blood seeped between his fingers.

"You bitch!" Bent stumbled back, eyes wide in shock.

Jack sprung toward the table, reaching for the musket. Louise dashed over and picked up the rum jug. Her hands wavered. Jack raised the weapon. Louise smashed the crock over his head. Pottery shattered and the smell of sweet alcohol followed the rum's splash.

Jack dropped the weapon, collapsed to the floor. He held his bleeding head and moaned. Both men blocked access to the musket.

Amelia threw down her now useless pistol, grasped Louise's hand and they fled out the cabin's door, into the pouring rain.

Chapter Twenty-nine

Gilbert bristled with his fears for the women as he swept rainwater from his face and eyelashes. The wind pushed like a wave against him and the captain as they rode on. Private Roberts re-joined them about forty minutes later. A search party of five would scatter into the hills and woods to look for Amelia and her maid.

The storm lashed down like a tidal wave as the three men turned southeast for the Black River.

Gilbert glanced at the captain. The idea the English officer might think him weak and unworthy of respect gnawed at him. Self-recrimination flayed him—what kind of man lost his wife? *Where was she?*

"Perhaps I was wrong in telling my daughter she shouldn't learn to fire a weapon," the captain said, his saddle creaking with the horse's movement as he rode closer.

"She does know, I promise you." Gilbert wrapped the slippery leather reins around his fist, his mount heaving beneath him. Mud splashed up and coated Vaillant's legs as well as his. He could only pray that Amelia had prevailed in whatever happened. His heart lurched.

"She'd have been safer at the fort." The captain's tone grew sharper.

"We have a good life together. She is happy, *beau-père*. This is no time to argue." Gilbert fumed, but couldn't blame her father's ire. Her assailant, if there was one, had to be Bent. Who else was so bizarre? Where had he been all this time? Gilbert vowed to strangle the bastard with his bare hands.

The horses galloped through growing puddles, and worsening mud. They rode up on the grass verge in a place where the road had washed out completely. The pine tree tops swayed in the gale.

He shivered in his soaked clothes and wished he had an oilskin cape. Was Amelia out in this storm—or in more danger than he dared to contemplate? He wooshed out a breath. He must not give in to despair, but it was his duty to protect her.

The captain grunted then cursed. "If this man no longer has a claim on your property, why would he—?"

"He's a drunk who seems half-witted. His actions never made sense." Gilbert prayed Bent wouldn't violate the women. If he hadn't taken them, where could Amelia be? His gut twisted further. Nothing could happen to her. She was one of the best things in his life. If he lost his trading post location, they'd start over, as long as they had one another.

They rode off the track, for the coast, the Bay of Fundy east of Saint John, where the Black River spilled into the surging bay.

The rain lightened, the wind still strong. Galloping through a grassy valley, where jagged rusty-coloured rocks thrust up on the slopes, Gilbert saw a movement to his right.

A Mi'kmaq brave in an elk tunic sprinted across the sward. "Trader! *Naqa'sit.*"

Gilbert reined in with the captain and private. "Have you news, *mon ami*?"

"One of our hunters saw your cart." The brave thrust his hands on his hips, a bow strung over his shoulder, his words mostly French. He flicked a glance at the captain. "A skinny man in torn buckskins drove. No women. But a canvas covered the bed."

"Can you trust this native?" the captain whispered.

"*Mais oui.*" Gilbert turned back to the brave. "Where were they headed?" His mouth went dry, his chest heaving. He removed and shook water from his leather hat. Vaillant danced in edginess beneath him.

"Toward the Black River, south." The native pointed, his long hair whipping in the wind.

"*Bon!* That's where we're headed." Gilbert translated quickly to his companions, anxious to race on.

"The hunter has seen him before," the Mi'kmaq continued. "Looks like the scout that lives in the camp of shacks on the river."

362

Gilbert growled. "I know the scoundrel. Come by my post. I'll reward you and anyone else who helps. *Merci*." Boots jammed in the stirrups, he urged Vaillant into a run, a thread of hope—shaded with dread—invigorating him. Bent!

* * *

The earth soggy, grass slick under their feet, Amelia and Louise ran from the ramshackle settlement into the woods, slogging through and over underbrush. Their hair was soon plastered to their faces, caps drenched, and their skirts and petticoats stuck to their legs.

"I hit him, Miss. I were strong!" Louise sputtered.

"You did, you were. I'm *very* proud." Amelia huffed air into her lungs as they wended their way around tree trunks. Tripping on exposed tree roots, they held each other up and continued to run, their saturated skirts bunched up in one hand to make movement easier.

"An' you shot t'other one."

"Hopefully that keeps them from following." Had Amelia killed Bent? She'd never wanted to kill anyone, but... She stopped, gasping, and looked around at the denser woods. The scent of resin was a relief after the fetid cabin. The canopy of branches above kept some of the rain at bay. "I don't know which way to go."

"Should we head home, or to the fort?" Louise pulled her kerchief close about her neck, then quivered, the garment drenched.

Lightening crackled in a brief flash. Thunder boomed, but sounded farther away as if the storm moved off. The dark, bleak sky brightened a shade.

"No, I meant I'm totally lost." Amelia swiped her wet hair from her face. The effort to run had displaced her fright for the moment, and warmed her body. "I don't know north from south from here. Let's look for some sort of path that could lead to a village."

They hurried on through the white cedar and spruce, hopping over roots, around hemlock plants, careful to avoid sprouting poison ivy. The rain slowed to a mist.

Pausing again to catch their breath, Amelia leaned against a tree trunk.

"We might find them savages, too." Louise glanced behind her, hazel eyes wary. "What if they try to scalp us?"

"You're strong now, remember?" Amelia gripped the girl's shoulder. "We both are. And Gilbert says the tribes are friendlier to the English than they once were."

Footsteps sounded in the distance, heavy and awkward. Friend or foe? Her loving husband whose arms she longed for?

"We need to hide—to see who this might be. It could be help or danger." Amelia rushed her maid behind a choke cherry bush, wide enough to conceal them.

Waiting, nerves prickled, Amelia squinted between the pungent leaves.

Through the trees farthest away a skinny beaver-hatted man appeared. He held his side and limped.

The reprobate Bent! He'd survived. How did he find them? Fear scoured through her. "Hurry, this way," she whispered to Louise.

They turned and scuttled down a small ravine, tripping and sliding in the mud. Amelia's hands were scratched, stockings ripped, everything hurt. The women grasped hands again and ducked into the thickest of the woods.

"I can track you!" Bent shouted from the top of the ravine, his breath wheezing. He howled in anger or pain. "That's what I do! Muddy footprints, I see 'em."

Amelia shuddered, half disgust, half terror. She rushed Louise on. Low branches smacked and scraped at their faces and fingers. They could be lost forever in this wilderness. Or caught and injured by a madman.

* * *

In the cluster of tumbledown cabins, Gilbert saw his mule and cart. Fire in his chest, he jumped from his horse and raced into that cabin.

365

A grizzled man sat at a table, wiping a stained cloth over his grey and reddish hair.

"Where are they?" Gilbert demanded after a desperate look about the cluttered room. "Tell me now, or I'll thrash your rancid hide."

Captain Latimer marched in behind him. "What have you done with my daughter?"

Private Roberts brought up the rear, his pistol pointed at the stranger.

"The whole damn cavalry's here?" The man bared rotten teeth in his creased face. It was obvious now that the red in his hair was blood.

Gilbert thrust his pistol forward. With his other hand he grabbed the man's shirtfront. "Where is my wife?"

"Who are you, blackguard? If you've hurt her, either of them, I'll have you before a firing squad," the captain spewed, his neck crimson.

"Name's Jack Pace." Jack slowly raised his hands in the air, fear flickering in his bleary eyes. "The women's gone. Ran off. That fool Bent went after 'em."

Gilbert noticed blood drops leading out the cabin door. His heart pounded. "Who was wounded?" He jerked the man closer, the gun probing his forehead. Jack's foul breath burst out as the dirty shirt ripped. "The women? Tell us what happened. *Sur l'heure!*"

"Bent was wounded, not the women. Your wife shot him. Bloody wench that's with her crashed a jug over my head." Jack grumbled, leaning his face back from the pistol. "Waste of good rum."

366

Gilbert released him with a shove. Hand fisted, he had to restrain himself from striking Jack. Amelia shot Bent? "Did you see which way they ran?"

"Nay, Frenchie." Jack rubbed at his scalp, glass shards in his hair. "Prob'ly in the woods. To the north most likely."

"Secure this poor excuse of a man, Private," the captain ordered, his mouth in a grimace.

"At once, sir." Roberts scrounged around the cabin, found rope, yanked Jack's arms behind his back and tied his wrists. Jack yelped. A disturbed rat scurried out from a corner.

"If they've come to harm, I will kill you myself," Gilbert threatened, his rage scorching.

Latimer glared at Jack. "You will be punished. You'd better not have laid one finger on my daughter or her maid."

"*Merde*. We ride into the woods! We must find them quickly." Gilbert stomped from the cabin, praying that Bent was dying from his wound and would never reach Amelia and Louise. Two town girls who knew little about roaming in the wild. Misery flooded through him.

* * *

Amelia nearly tripped over a porcupine. A spray of quills pricked into her leg above her muddied half boot. She cried out in pain at the tiny stabs, limped to a rock outcropping, and she and Louise fumbled to pull the little needles out.

Amelia winced with each pluck that left dots of blood on her already shredded stocking. "It's nothing," she assured her maid. "Let's keep going."

Staggering to a shallow brook, they cupped hands and took a quick sip, the water freezing but refreshing. Birds squawked at their intrusion. The brush far behind them rustled.

"He said he's tracking our footprints." Amelia gasped for slower breaths, her chest aching, along with other stings on her flesh, especially where the quills had punctured. "We should walk along the stream. He won't see any then."

"Aye, Miss. Good thinking that be." Her voice unsure, the girl pressed on her own chest, her scratched cheeks flushed. Her hair was tangled about her face. "Do you think that Bent blockhead has his musket?"

"I'd hope he wouldn't fire on us. He needs us for hostages." She didn't say her other fear. He could kill Louise. Amelia was the prize to persuade Gilbert.

They stepped into the brook, single file, balancing on the smooth, slick pebbles in the bed. Lifting skirts and feet higher the two of them waded downstream as fast as they could manage. Frigid water seeped around Amelia's shoes, the leather already dark. Thankfully, the shallow brook only reached over the top of her boots, the current slow. Louise too wore boots, but soon they both shivered as the icy water soaked through the leather.

Trees lined the bank, throwing the area into shadow. The rain had stopped, the storm rumbling away. Amelia focused on her footing, and hid her distress that Bent would find them anyway. She refused to die without seeing her husband again—the man she loved so much. Anxiety clogging her throat, she blinked to clear her eyes of tears.

"I'm sorry I brought you to this, Louise," she whispered, finding it more difficult to lift her soaked boots.

"Please don't say that, Miss." Panic edged the girl's voice.

"I'm…done in with this water. Let's climb the bank." Stumbling in shoes that sloshed, Amelia crawled up the higher bank, using exposed roots to pull herself through slick mud.

At the top, she helped up Louise. The two collapsed on a rock, trying to squish the water from their shoes, futilely brushing muck from their clothes. Amelia dragged her fingers through her matted hair. Her legs ached with exhaustion. The flesh where the quills had poked itched.

"I need-I need to find some comfrey…to rub on my wound." Amelia heaved a breath. Were they safe yet? "But we should keep running."

A shot rang out, echoing around them. Amelia's heart jolted. She ducked, but it seemed to have been fired into the air.

"The sot's still a movin', still after us?" Louise hissed, her voice thick.

"He's the devil's spawn. Let's be off." Amelia and her maid leaned low and scrambled into a thicket of trees. *Was* it Bent, warning them he was on their heels?

The two women rushed deeper into the forest, trying not to fall. Amelia stifled a furious scream—these could be her last moments on earth.

An oddly dressed man stepped from the tree's shadows and they almost slammed into him.

Chapter Thirty

Gilbert stared at the ground from the back of his mount, following two sets of small footprints in mud strewn with pine needles. Further into the spruces, thankful the storm had continued to the east, he saw larger footprints mixed with the small. A lightning bolt of wrath burned through him.

The captain rode behind him. Private Roberts had been detailed to take the rogue Jack to the magistrate in the new capital, Fredericton.

The remnants of strong wind—carrying the tangy, damp scent of the tree leaves and plants—pressed Gilbert's wet clothing to his body. He shivered. Vaillant shook himself like a dog, jerking him in the saddle.

"You do love my daughter. I saw it in your devastation at the cabin," the captain whispered.

"Of *course* I do, Monsieur. She's everything to me." Gilbert bit back his pain, picturing Amelia's face. Her endearing smile. He concentrated on the tracks.

Riding some distance in alert silence, the only sounds were the horses' steps and the occasional bird tweet. They reached a small ravine.

Loud groans came from below. Gilbert's pulse skittered. He directed his horse, slipping down a slope. The captain followed.

A man in a beaver hat was hunched over near a brook. Gilbert drew his pistol.

The man stood slowly. It was Bent. A dirty cloth was wrapped around his middle, drenched in blood on one side. He gripped a musket.

"Don't move. Stay where you are," Latimer ordered. "Where—"

"Where are they?" Gilbert jumped from his saddle and stalked toward Bent, pistol aimed. "Where is my wife, *ma femme*?"

Bent wheezed in his breath. "The bitch shot me. I shot at her—them. Don't know where they went." Obvious pain screwed up his gaunt features. The musket tottered in his hands. "Give me back my property, frog-eater."

"Put down your weapon, now." Captain Latimer dismounted, his face in a scowl. His eyes sharp with worry, he'd also drawn a pistol. "Which way did the women go?"

Bent raised his musket, which wavered violently in his hands. He swayed on his feet. Blood dripped like red paint down his left side. He glared at Gilbert. "You cheated my uncle."

Gilbert, fury suffusing him, leapt forward and kicked the musket from Bent's grip. It landed feet away with a clatter. He snatched the scout by his throat. "I cheated no one. Your own governor signed my deed. Tell me where they are or I'll blow off your face, *imbécile*." He

372

jabbed his pistol barrel into Bent's stubbled cheek.

Bent squirmed, shoving his shoulder into Gilbert's chest. Gilbert touched the trigger, ready to fire. "I'm ending your worthless—"

"Mr. Arsenault. *Stop.* We'll let the law deal with him." Captain Latimer pushed between them, his glower on Bent. "Now, sir, you are under arrest. Where the hell is my daughter?"

The guide coughed, then hunched over again, clutching his side. More blood seeped out. "I ken...they went downstream." He pointed. "Couldn't track them from here." He groaned, his eyes red-rimmed. "My damned uncle was a lackwit who left me with nothin'!"

"*Mon Dieu.* You deserve nothing, and better not have touched either of the women." Gilbert rushed to his horse and mounted. Had Amelia really gotten away? He had so much left to share with her—and be damned if he wouldn't. She had to survive. He loved her more than he thought he could love again.

"Please find her, and the girl," Latimer called out, his voice pleading.

"I *will.* I'll ride down and look for signs." Gilbert galloped off before he might throw Bent into the stream and push his face under the water.

* * *

373

Amelia and Louise lurched backwards from the savage blocking their way.

The man's dark, tilted eyes bored into her. He wore a deerskin tunic decorated with tiny green and yellow beads.

"Let us pass, sir." Amelia's frustration thrummed through her. She was frantic to reach safety. "If you please, which way is it to Fort Howe?" She and her maid backed up further, their wet skirts clinging like extra skin to their legs.

"*Temonu*." He thrust up his hand. "*Voulez-vous attendre?*"

"I heard some French," Amelia whispered to Louise. She strained to remember her schoolgirl French and what she'd picked up from Gilbert. And the Acadian French was different from what she'd learned—so confusing!

"Don't scalp us." Louise touched her hair near her askew cap. "Please, sir."

"Can you help us...*pouvez-vous nous aider?*" Amelia stumbled over her translation.

The muscular man stepped forward. The scent of animal oil wafted off him. He wore a deer hide headband in his long, black hair; and leather leggings and moccasins. A quiver of arrows was strapped to his back, a bow on his shoulder. "*Witsehkehsicik*. My name Atian."

"I suppose he won't kill us since he gives his name." Amelia tried to sound confident, to keep them both from melting into hysterics. "Do you speak English?" she asked in her limited

374

French. Were the unfamiliar words his own language? She repeated, "*pouvez-vous nous aider?*"

"Not good *anglais*. Will try to help. I'm Wolastoqiyik, also called Maliseet." He waved them to follow him. "*Nuhsuphoqalal.*"

"Oh, I don't know if we should go with him," Amelia whispered. Her skin felt rubbed ragged against her sodden clothing. Her stays pinched. She refrained from scratching herself, plus dropping to the ground in exhaustion. "But I'm so weary."

"Aye, Miss. Me, too." Louise moaned, eyes sharp on the native, her hand stroking the back of her head, bunching up her hair as if to protect her scalp.

"*Nuhsuphoqalal.*" Atian gestured them onward again. "We had word, women taken. Go to *forteresse?*"

Amelia glanced over her shoulder. Was anyone trailing them? Where was Bent? Hopefully he was too weakened to keep up the pursuit. The stranger's black eyes now flashed with concern, or was she only fooling herself? She'd caught the word 'fort'.

"*Oui*, fortress. *Merci.*" She stepped forward, arm linked with her maid's—her practically-a-sister in this catastrophe. She had to trust someone. Her stomach growled with hunger and she almost laughed at such an ordinary response after all that had happened. She suppressed the uneasiness that lingered.

*　*　*

Gilbert hurried Vaillant along the brook, the horse slogging through the mud. No sign of Amelia and Louise. His mind buzzed with alarming thoughts. Had they the foresight to walk in the water to hide their footprints? He prayed they had. His admiration flared. Amelia had shown her daring, her propensity, in shooting Bent.

The tree-covered banks rose higher, leaving the brook in a narrow ravine. His horse barely had footing. Kicked aside pebbles tumbled into the stream in small splashes. Then on the bank to his right, the mud was disturbed with long, fresh gouges, as if someone climbed it.

He surged with hope. The women or a large animal? Rushing Vaillant forward, he rode to where the bank lowered again, and jumped his horse up a two-foot rise. They rustled through ivy and fleabane, back along the bank's crest to the climbed site. On the other side of a large, flat rock, were more small, muddy footprints.

Weaving through the trees, Gilbert ducked under branches.

An arrow hit a tree trunk with a loud thwack. Vaillant reared up, Gilbert clinging to the saddle. He cursed.

A native ran along the track from behind him. "Trader!"

"Are you trying to kill me?" Gilbert demanded as he settled his horse.

The Mi'kmaq stopped a few feet away. He was Mooin, the brave from the camp not far from Gilbert's cabin. "I only wished to halt you. My aim is good."

He'd changed his skimpy breechcloth to an elk-skin tunic belted at the waist, his bow clutched in one fist.

"Have you any information for me?" Gilbert gripped his saddle's pommel and swallowed his affront, anxious for Amelia.

"A boy says he saw a Maliseet take the women, walking to the west." Mooin gestured. "I'll keep tracking them." He sprinted off, into the woods like a stag.

Taken by a Maliseet? Willingly or unwillingly? The Acadians had worked with the Maliseet tribe as well, in the fish trade especially since these natives had first settled around the mouth of rivers that spilled into the Bay of Fundy. When the English arrived, they were pushed inland.

Gilbert galloped on and prayed the Maliseet brave meant the women no foul treatment.

* * *

Leg calves straining, feet feeling mushy and growing numb, Amelia lumbered through the damp-smelling forest. Blisters formed on her toes. Louise hobbled beside her. The Maliseet man strode ahead of them, his moccasins like whispers in the mud. Water dripped from the tree leaves.

He plucked gooseberries from a bush and offered them to the women. Amelia ate the tart, red fruit, encouraging Louise to eat as well. They trudged on.

"I pray he's leading us in the correct direction." Amelia shivered with chills, her clothing not yet dried. She pictured the brave dragging them to his camp, imprisoning them.

"The savages here don't eat people, do they, Miss?" Louise asked in a small voice.

"Oh, no. They would never do that." Amelia pressed the girl's cold hand on her arm. At least she was fairly certain there were no cannibals in New Brunswick, but her mind was so fogged with fatigue. These indigenous people *would* resent the whites who conquered their lands.

An arrow flew past them, striking a tree in front of Atian. The women muffled their cries and jumped to one side.

Atian sprung about, jerked out an arrow and readied his bow.

Amelia pushed Louise behind a grove of oaks. The sound of hoof beats to the right, the way they'd come, raised Amelia's pulse in fear and yearning. She stared in that direction.

A familiar buckskin stallion appeared in the distance, a man riding.

"It's Gilbert. It has to be." She fisted a hand on the tree's rough bark.

"La, Miss, I do pray we be safe."

Another native stepped from the woods on the other side of the track. He spoke to Atian in a language she couldn't fathom. Both men glared at one another, arrows pointed.

"*Arrête tous les deux!*" Gilbert shouted. He reined in his horse before the natives, who lowered their bows.

Amelia nearly collapsed against the tree in relief. Louise sniffed loudly, pressing into Amelia's shoulder blades. French flew back and forth among the three men, too quickly for her to decipher.

"Gilbert, oh, Gilbert! Thank goodness you've found us." Tears in her eyes, she limped from behind the tree and headed for him, Louise following. His and his horse's legs were coated in mud—what a divine sight.

"*Mon amour!*" Gilbert leapt from his stallion and pulled her into his arms. "Are you all right? *Mon Dieu*, how I've worried." His eyes glistened with unshed tears. He reached over and drew Louise closer. "And for you, too, *ma petite*."

"We're fine, mostly." Amelia panted with release, trying not to give in to the qualms that had drummed through her. She drank in every inch of his handsome face. "Only filthy, wet, and very tired."

"You were both courageous." Gilbert kissed her mouth, squeezing her to his chest, his hand stroking through her hair. His touch was like a tonic.

She revelled in his embrace for a moment, then pulled back. "Did you find that horrid Bent person?"

"Bent's on his way to Fredericton. Your father has him under arrest. The rascal may not survive the journey after you shot him." He told her the details, which mangled in her weary brain. Her father was involved?

Atian stepped forward and spoke in French to Gilbert.

"He says he was taking you to the fort." Her husband looked to her for confirmation.

"Yes, he was. Please thank him. Wait, I can thank him." Amelia turned and bowed her head to the Maliseet. "*Merci beaucoup.*"

"I thank him the same, I do." Louise bobbed a curtsy, her tangled hair swinging.

He nodded, then tipped his chin to Gilbert. He spoke more of his own language, then Atian left them, running down the path.

The other native moved into view. He and Gilbert exchanged a few words.

"This is Mooin. He helped to track you down." Gilbert put his fist to his chest. "I'm in his debt."

Amelia and Louise thanked him with another bow of their heads. Mooin nodded, waved to Gilbert then dashed off through the trees and disappeared.

"I must learn some of these tribal languages—and more French." Amelia spun to

Gilbert and buried her face in his dank coat, inhaling his comforting scent of leather and man. Her breath hitched in the firm arms of her beloved husband. "Take us home before I fly into a fit of screaming. And we've seen no bears."

Chapter Thirty-one

Gilbert scrutinized the chocolate-brown martin pelts he'd just received from a Maliseet trapper at the trading post. The fur was used for mittens. The lanky Mr. Jarvis—who'd entered a minute earlier—sauntered into his peripheral view and stood on the other side of the counter. The shorter, stockier Wilcox, face impassive, was beside him.

Fougère, his expression vexed, immediately joined them.

"Have you decided to accept my terms? I warn you, I won't change my mind." Jarvis's eyes gleamed, brows arched, in his pointy, pitted face. "A twenty percent rent increase is what I need."

"Twelve is as high as we can go," Gilbert replied, though he resented it. He knew these Loyalists were receiving money from their government, along with the free land. Gilbert understood more of their plight now, but this man left no room for sympathy.

"That seems more than fair, Mr. Jarvis," Wilcox said with his cajoling smile. "We can seal the agreement at once for a number of years."

Fougère grunted, arms crossed. "If we must...twelve. But I'm not happy about it."

"No, twenty as I first said." The young man, his neck wreathed in a silk cravat, glanced around at the post, the customers. "You can afford it. I need something to show for my exile in this uncivilized country. I plan to marry. I need the coin."

Gilbert's insides burned at his arrogance. "That leaves us little profit. We too must survive, *non*?"

"With twelve percent, you'll do quite well, Mr. Jarvis." Wilcox nodded to Jarvis, hands clasped behind his back. "You can still build your fine house."

"Whose side are you on? It's supposed to be mine." Jarvis stiffened, lips pursed. A spoiled aristocrat who demanded to have his way. "I daresay I might find another agent."

"It's good business to keep your tenants happy and not overreach, Monsieur." Gilbert wearied of this debate. He wanted peace, and the ability to support his wife. Also, to help her set up a permanent herb shop. Jubilant to be done with Bent—who was sentenced to several years in a military jail in the capital—he desired the happiness he thought he'd lost when Amelia was kidnapped.

Now, without her knowledge, he had a brave watching the cabin when he worked.

"No. Twenty percent or nothing. I'll give you one more week to agree, or you'll have to take your trade elsewhere." Jarvis glared down at Wilcox. "Don't bother with your persuasion, sir. You are dismissed." He turned in his blue velvet frock coat and tight white breeches and left the post.

"As you wish, sir." Wilcox gave a quick bow in the young man's general direction.

"Should we move from here?" Fougère asked, grimacing. "Never mind, we'll talk of it later." He walked across the room to help a customer.

"I think Jarvis wants to tear the building down and erect his 'castle' on this bank." Wilcox sighed and glanced out the windows that overlooked Grand Bay.

"I'm sorry for your loss of income." Gilbert folded up the soft furs. He'd grown to like this merchant from Massachusetts. "A bad deal for us both."

"To tell the truth, I'm glad to be rid of the prissy fellow. The lad rarely followed my advice. He should never have confronted you on his own." Wilcox shrugged broad shoulders. "I have my own money. Since coming to this colony, I've had some ideas on trade where the profits are lean but it would be beneficial to the population."

"I've asked my cousin's husband about renting part of his farm on the peninsula north of here for a new trading post. He owns many acres. He has agreed." Gilbert had an in-depth discussion with Henri, aware of Jarvis's egotistic nature. Lisette's husband was an amiable man. The rent would be half of what he paid here even before the disputed raise.

Henri's pig farm was on the Saint John River, not far south from the growing Loyalist settlement of Kingston. He'd managed to hold on to this valuable property because his sister had married into an influential English family.

"Every boat or ship sailing upriver to Fredericton will also pass any new enterprise." Gilbert opened a chest and smoothed in the furs. He glanced about at the log post he'd built. The display of weapons and knives. The iron pots and pans. Native baskets and blankets. Every item could be relocated. This building was, after all, only a structure. "My wife agrees with me, about making the change."

"That does sound like a wise decision. The new surveyor-general, Georg Sproule, has finally arrived and land dealings and battles over ownership are even more contentious. People are fighting over where cows are allowed to graze," Wilcox said with an ironic chuckle. "What will your partner do?"

"We've spoken of it. He doesn't like change, but hates being pushed around more. I hope he comes with me." Gilbert half-smiled, his decision made. A great weight shifted. The hell with Jarvis and other so-called entitled people. "So what is your trading scheme, *mon ami*?"

"Grain. Enlarging a grist mill, ovens. And improving my life, if a certain woman will take my interest seriously." Wilcox winked. "Cheaper bread for the masses. And, hopefully, the joys of a lovely wife."

Gilbert laughed. "Good luck with that 'certain' woman. *Ma foi*, you will need it. Your hands will be beyond full with a wildcat, but you have my permission to try."

Once he would have scorned an Englishman paying court to his maman, but now he wished her a share of happiness, if she'd bend to agree.

* * *

Amelia opened a window, but the August heat was just as humid outside as inside the new trading post. A slight breeze wafted off the Saint John River several yards away.

"This heat is oppressive." She fanned herself and inhaled the pleasing scent of freshly cut and honed wood.

"Aye, Miss. The air's much thicker than in England." Louise opened a rear window to draw the breeze through. Pigs snorted from the pens beyond a field. On certain days, the smell wasn't very pleasant. So Amelia put lavender-filled sachets on the window sills that faced the farm.

"And I suppose we shouldn't complain about the piggy inhabitants who were here first." Amelia laughed.

"No one else seems to mind much. But if I raised one of them cute piglets, I could never eat it." Louise shook a sachet, the air now redolent with lavender. "I do like this place."

"After all our travails, we're fortunate to be here."

Gilbert with his cousins and friends had cleared trees to build the post, and by July the log building was finished on this section of Henri Bouchard's land south of Kingston. The dandy Jarvis had already begun to tear down the other post to build his 'castle' on Grand Bay.

Amelia picked up a can and watered her herbs in their earthenware pots. The lavender-flowered Mandrake, an anesthetic. The thin-leafed Cleavers-Bedstraw for high blood-pressure and skin ailments. Rue with its small yellow flowers, also good for blood circulation and to sharpen one's eyesight. The fuzzy-leafed Burdock for burns and purifying the blood. The earthy scents tickled her nose.

She also had slices of tree barks in baskets. Birch for colds, white willow bark for aches and pains. Hemlock spruce bark was used for an astringent, promoted sweat—hardly needed today—and helped one pass water. Her bottles of other remedies lined a shelf.

"Your herbs are doing well, *non*? People are interested?" Marie-Cateline clipped across the pine-wood floor in her sabots and long striped skirt. "We Acadians always use herbals in our medicines."

"*Mais oui*." Amelia liked to try out her French to impress Gilbert's mother. "The Loyalist women who'd lived in the cities in America appreciate my advice about the local herbs." Amelia was proud to be able to help people with their disorders.

"Loyalists, *peste*, they like to take whatever they can and act helpless." Marie-Cateline studied the plants. "I'll bring you some tansy. It's good for fevers and stomach ailments."

Amelia knew this, but thanked her as if surprised. "How are you today, *belle-mère*?"

"I'm more concerned in how you feel." The woman half-smiled and glanced down at Amelia's abdomen.

"I'm much better in the afternoons." Amelia had realized she was with child the previous month. An exciting prospect, except for her queasy mornings.

"You are drinking the peppermint tea I gave you?" Her mother-in-law touched a yellow flower on the Rue.

"I am, yes." Amelia couldn't wait to cuddle her first child—no matter her suffering.

The front door opened. Gilbert and another man lugged in a large cabinet. The post was open for business, but still in a little disarray.

Between Kingston and the upriver boat traffic, they were doing very well as word got around.

Gilbert set down his end of the cabinet. The other man did too, and left. "Do you approve of the changes, Maman?" He'd built new shelves since the last time she'd visited. All the items from his previous post were displayed.

"*Bien sûr*. You'll be successful here." Marie-Cateline smiled, the warmest smile Amelia had seen from her. "It is convenient, since I'm right across the river. Easy for me to catch a boat over, to see how your wife fares."

This finger of land, called the Kingston Peninsula, separated the Saint John and Kennebecasis Rivers that then flowed into Grand Bay. Amelia and Gilbert travelled by cart to his mother's, then took a boat across the Kennebecasis. Met by one of Henri's sons in another cart, they journeyed overland to the post.

Amelia didn't come every day, but she insisted on bringing Louise with them after their ordeal with Bent two months before. She wouldn't leave her alone at the cabin. At least now, Gilbert's mother respected her after learning she'd shot the scoundrel. Amelia was relieved Bent hadn't died—she didn't want that on her conscience, no matter the low character of the 'victim'.

Gilbert tugged out a handkerchief and wiped sweat from his brow. His mouth twitched as he watched his mother. "I heard the loquacious Mr. Wilcox has been by to discuss enlarging the grist mill."

"He's speaking with the owner. He also wants to build large brick ovens to bake bread. Then he comes to the house and expects to dine with me." His mother's cheeks flushed ever so slightly. She averted her gaze. "Hiram—what sort of name is that? He's a tenacious man, this English. Or as he says, American." She shrugged. "I'm getting used to him, *peut-être.*"

"I'm so pleased by your tolerance and good will." Gilbert slipped his arm around Amelia and winked. He kissed her cheek. "You aren't tiring yourself, *mon amour*?"

"I'm fine, don't worry," she whispered. "I think your mother is more intrigued with Hiram Wilcox than she lets on."

Louise hid a grin behind her hand. She then arranged a display of cotton cloth on a table. Gilbert's mother joined her.

Three customers entered, chattering women dressed in finery, silks and feathers and other frippery—Loyalists who resisted adapting to the rustic frontier. They resembled wilted flowers as well as drooping birds in the heat. The fresh petal scent of Attar of Roses perfume drifted from them.

Mr. Fougère lumbered in right after. He lived in a wigwam with his wife behind the post. He paid Mr. Bouchard rent for the spot. The couple seemed content.

"Sorry I'm late after my dinner. *Mon Dieu,* my rheumatism is flaring." He bowed to the fancy ladies, then winced at the motion. "May I assist you, my lovely demoiselles?"

"I'll make you some willow bark tea. I should trade herbs for ginger root in the city," Amelia told the older man. "It's also good for pain."

Two red-coated officers entered, and inspected the 'Brown Bess' muskets on the wall pegs.

She turned to Gilbert. "Have you heard the rumour? The infamous American traitor Benedict Arnold is supposed to be settling in Saint John with his family."

"Arnold's treachery didn't help the war's outcome. Now he's on the English side, your side, *mon amour*." Gilbert winked with his tease. Then his mouth thinned. "The general's presence here may cause conflicts."

"I've told you, I don't *have* a side. Father will have to deal with the man." Amelia thought of the already volatile relationship between their colony and the United States. Peace seemed always just out of reach. "And remember, Father expects us to join him for dinner this Saturday at Mrs. Sutton's."

"I have not forgotten." Gilbert stroked her cheek. "Will it trouble you to be with Mrs. Sutton again?"

She tingled at his touch. "I'll have to…endure the woman. Father hinted that he might marry her." She'd dismissed his transgression, and wouldn't allow resentment to fester inside her. A strong bond between her and

391

Father was important. She enjoyed her life and was thankful for all she had. The colony of New Brunswick was growing, new roads built, more towns created with churches and schools. New Brunswick's motto was, *spem reduxit*—a restoration of hope.

Amelia would be a part of it, beside this man she adored.

"What a feast we'll have." He chuckled. "Your father doesn't quite approve of me, and you won't totally approve of his future wife."

"I'll try to get to know her better." That's all she could promise. She ran a finger down the soft leather of his buckskin jacket. "At least we approve and love each other."

"To the deepest recesses of my heart, *ma cherie*. And our soon to be child." His back to the customers, Gilbert caressed her belly. He gave her a quick kiss on the lips. "A child to insist on his, or her, place in this evolving country."

The End

Bibliography

BELL, David. *Loyalist Rebellion in New Brunswick*, Formac Publishing Company, Ltd. Halifax, Nova Scotia, 2013

FACEY-CROWTHER, David. *The New Brunswick Militia 1787-1867*, New Brunswick, Canada, New Brunswick Historical Society and New Ireland Press, 1990

GAIR, Reavley (general editor). *A Literary and Linguistic History of New Brunswick*, Fredericton, New Brunswick, Canada, Goose Lane Editions, Ltd, 1985

REES, Ronald. *Land of the Loyalists*, Halifax, NS, Nimbus Publishing Ltd., 2000

MACNUTT, W. S., *New Brunswick, A History 1784-1867*, Toronto, Canada, Macmillan of Canada, 1963

SOUCOUP, Dan. *Know New Brunswick-the Essential History*, Published by Canada, no date listed

WRIGHT, Esther Clark, *The Loyalists of New Brunswick*, New Brunswick Branch of the United Empire Loyalists' Association of Canada, 2003

Documents

THE LOYALISTS AND LAND SETTLEMENT IN NEW BRUNSWICK, 1783 - 1790

A Study in Colonial Administration
Robert Fellows
Provincial Archives of New Brunswick, 1971

New Brunswick Fort Howe History-sources: (PDF no dates listed)
Reflections of the Past by Horace Macauley
History of the Church of Ascension by Wm. M. Jones
The History of Apohaqui by Mrs. Harley S. Jones
Friends and Family of Apohaqui Elementary School

NEW BRUNSWICK LOYALISTS (PDF no date listed)
based on an article by Linda Hansen Squires

Websites

Acadia Lifestyles
http://www.virtualmuseum.ca/edu/ViewLoitLo.do?method=preview&lang=EN&id=15527

Acadian Eighteenth Century Names and Origins

http://www.acadian-home.org/names-acadian.html

Acadian Recipes
https://www.acadian.org/culture/popular-acadian-recipies/

Fort Howe
https://en.wikipedia.org/wiki/Fort_Howe

Fort Howe National Historic Site of Canada
http://www.historicplaces.ca/en/rep-reg/place-lieu.aspx?id=13001

Geography and Governance: The Problem of Saint John (New Brunswick) 1785 - 1927
http://www.gedmartin.net/martinalia-mainmenu-3/237-geography-and-governance-the-problem-of-saint-john-new-brunswick-1785-1927

Historic Sites from the English Period on the Saint John River
https://johnwood1946.wordpress.com/2016/03/02/historic-sites-from-the-english-period-on-the-saint-john-river/

Information on the Loyalists
http://www.uelac.org/Loyalist-Info/Loyalist-Info.php

Loyalist Documents : 1755-1880

https://loyalist.lib.unb.ca/node/4202

Loyalist Land Grants
http://archives.gnb.ca/associates/Newsletter
s/2012-35-Fall-e.pdf

Loyalist Women of New Brunswick
http://preserve.lib.unb.ca/wayback/2014120
5153705/http://atlanticportal.hil.unb.ca/acva/loy
alistwomen/en/documents/

Mi'kmaq Dictionary
http://www.20000-
names.com/dictionary_micmac.htm

Mi'kmaq Online
https://www.mikmaqonline.org/

New Brunswick History: Government of
New Brunswick
http://www2.gnb.ca/content/gnb/en/gatewa
ys/about_nb/history.html

New Brunswick Map
http://new-brunswick.net/new-
brunswick/maps/nb/gl12.jpg

Old New Brunswick: the Loyalists
http://davidsullivan.ca/oldstandrews/scrapb
ook/oldstandrews/loyalists.1907.html

Saint John, New Brunswick

https://en.wikipedia.org/wiki/Saint_John,_
New_Brunswick

Saint John New Brunswick
http://new-
brunswick.net/Saint_John/loyalist/pg3.html

Settlement, Revolution and War
http://www.blupete.com/Hist/NovaScotiaB
k2/Part3/Ch04.htm

Diane Scott Lewis books

Also from Books We Love

Escape the Revolution
Ladies and Their Lovers (Miss Grey's Shady
Lover/ The Defiant Lady Pencavel)
Rose's Precarious Quest
The Apothecary's Widow
A Savage Exile – Vampires with Napoleon on
St. Helena
Hostage to the Revolution

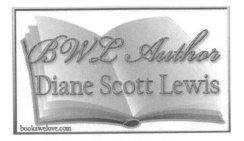

Diane Parkinson (Diane Scott Lewis) writes book reviews for the *Historical Novel Reviews* magazine and worked at The Wild Rose Press from 2007 to 2010 as a historical editor. She is a member of the *Historical Novel Society* and the *Napoleonic Historical Society*. Most of her novels are set in late eighteenth-century England. She lives is western Pennsylvania with her husband.

For further information about the author, visit her

Website—http://www.dianescottlewis.org

BWL Author
Nancy M Bell
bookswelove.com

Nancy M Bell has publishing credits in poetry, fiction and non-fiction. Nancy has presented at the Surrey International Writers Conference and the Writers Guild of Alberta Conference. She loves writing fiction and poetry and following wherever her muse takes her.

*Ple*ase visit her webpage

http://www.nancymbell.ca

She posts on the Books We Love Blog on the 18th of every month

http://bwlauthors.blogspot.ca/

You can find her on Facebook at

http://facebook.com/NancyMBell

Follow on twitter: @emilypikkasso

Nancy M. Bell books also published by Books We Love

Canadian Historical Brides Collection

His Brother's Bride ~ Ontario

Young Adult

The Cornwall Adventures

Laurel's Quest ~ Book One

A Step Beyond ~ Book Two

Go Gently ~ Book Three

Romance
Storm's Refuge
A Longview Romance Book One
Come Hell or High Water A Longview
Romance Book Two
A Longview Wedding
A Longview Christmas Seasonal Novella
Arabella's Secret Series
The Selkie's Song ~ Book One
Arabella Dreams ~ Book Two

Co-Authored with Pat Dale
The Last Cowboy
Henrietta's Heart
The Teddy Dialogues
Historical Horror

By N.M. Bell
No Absolution

bookswelove.com

38227599R00223

Made in the USA
Middletown, DE
06 March 2019